Terrier Town
Summer of '49

Terrier Town
Summer of '49

David Menary

Wilfrid Laurier University Press

We acknowledge the support of the Canada Council for the Arts for our publishing program. We acknowledge the financial support of the Government of Canada through the Book Publishing Industry Development Program for our publishing activities. We acknowledge the Government of Ontario through the Ontario Media Development Corporation's Ontario Book Initiative. We acknowledge the financial support of the Waterloo Regional Heritage Foundation. heritage

National Library of Canada Cataloguing in Publication Data

Menary, David, 1959-

Terrier town : summer of '49 / David Menary.

ISBN 0-88920-427-6

1. Galt Terriers (Baseball team)—Fiction. 2. Baseball stories, Canadian (English). I. Title.

PS8576.E536T47 2003   C813'.6   C2003-905606-6

© 2003 David Menary

Cover design by David Menary and P. J. Woodland
Interior design by Ampersand Studios

Every reasonable effort has been made to acquire permission for copyright material used in this text, and to acknowledge all such indebtedness accurately. Any errors and omissions called to the publisher's attention will be corrected in future printings.

www.wlupress.wlu.ca

∞
Printed in Canada

No part of this publication may be reproduced, stored in a retrieval system or transmitted, in any form or by any means, without the prior written consent of the publisher or a licence from The Canadian Licensing Agency (Access Copyright). For an Access Copyright licence, visit www.accesscopyright.ca or call toll free to 1-800-893-5777.

For my father, Reid, and my son, Erik.

Terrier Town—Summer of '49

Acknowledgements ix

Introduction 1

Game Seven 9

A Time and a Place 13

Beginnings 23

Twinkletoes 31

Winter and Spring 39

Waiting for Warren 51

Tom Padden 55

Friends 67

The Red Sox 75

Pennell and the
Prime Minister 85

Rivalry and Legends 101

Born of the Spring 105

May Day 111

Summer Day at Mill Creek . . . 119

The Dog Days 125

More Dog Days 133

Summer Days,
Summer Nights 141

Lefty Comes to Town 145

Honus and the Boys 157

The Glovebox 165

Hustlin' Gus 169

The Race 177

Tex 179

Only the Ball Was White 187

Young Blood 197

Murderer's Row 201

The Hodge Boys 209
Downfall 211
Billy Gibbs 213
Across the River 217
Hitting the Fence 221
Back Door into the Playoffs .. 225
The Prelude 231
The Playoffs 239
The Last Game 247
Old Leaves and Autumn 259
The Last Game: Aftermath ... 265
Old Man 269
Afterword 275

Final Innings

Johnny Lockington 283
Billy Gibbs 289
Stan Lipka 291
Tex Kaiser 297

Don Gallinger 301
Ernie Goman 307
Frank Udvari 311
Lefty Perkins
(Harry Sollenburger) 317
Johnny Kumornik 321
Wes Lillie 325
Tulsa Tommy Warren 333
Johnny Clark 341
Jeff Shelton 345
Connie Waite 351
Laurie Brain 353
Connie Creedon 361
Goody Rosen 365
Bert McCrudden 369
Tom Padden 371
Larry Pennell 377
Gus Murray 389
Charlie Hodge 405

Acknowledgements

I BEGAN RESEARCH FOR THIS BOOK WHEN I SPOKE WITH GUS Murray many years ago and am deeply indebted to him for being so generous with his time. I recall fondly the many meetings we had at his house on Lowry Avenue, and above his old store on Main Street. Sometimes Walter Reid was there, and the decades seemed to roll back to that magical season. Gus gave me a real sense of what it was like that summer.

Larry Pennell and I met countless times in the last decade and he, too, was most generous with his time. I am grateful to Justice Pennell for the gift of friendship he has given me, and I came to look forward to our meetings. Initially we spoke about baseball, but as the years came and went, we expanded our discussions to books and literature, politics, and virtually everything else under the sun that caught our imaginations. His encouragement has been an inspiration, and a blessing.

There have been too many others who have helped make this book a reality to properly thank them here. Thank you to all the players and others who willingly submitted to interviews and phone calls and follow-up interviews. Many of them are now gone, including: Stan Lipka, Bert McCrudden, Jeff Shelton, Johnny Kumornik, Don Gallinger, Ernie Goman, John Lockington, Jack Murray, Mickey Owen, Dennis Smedley, Watty Reid, and George Gibson.

Those who remain, and who were exceptionally helpful include: Harry Sollenburger, John Rosen, Wes Lillie, Bill Gibbs, Tex Kaiser, John Clark, Ed Heather, Fred Worton, Theresa Padden, Jack Scott, Richard Mirco, Terry Clark, and Keith Murray. A special debt of gratitude is extended to John Cheyne, for reading an early draft and offering suggestions. My heartfelt thanks to all for their insights, their time, and their interest.

Some offered encouragement through their friendship, and by listening to what I had to say. They include Herb Payerl, Al Findlay, Cam Allan, and Garry Bell, cherished and valued friends all.

Carroll Klein, managing editor at WLU Press, went above and beyond the call of duty in accommodating my schedule, and her enthusiasm was greatly appreciated, as was the encouragement of Brian Henderson, director of WLU Press.

One of my first coaches, John Riddell, nurtured my early love for the game. And Michael Farber, senior writer for *Sports Illustrated*, offered kind words of encouragement about my writing along the way.

My father did not live to see the published book, but he read an early draft and always believed in me. His unwavering faith and pride in me has given guidance and inspiration when inspiration was needed. Without my father – the childhood he gave, the home he provided, the family we shared, the values he espoused, and the stories he told—this book would never have been possible.

Thank you.

Family

Introduction

There are legends born of the Canadian spring…

LONG YEARS AND MANY SEASONS AGO I GREW UP IN A GOD-FEARING Presbyterian baseball family, in the small southern Ontario town of Galt, a picturesque valley town which had been hewn out of the bush a century earlier. We lived beside an old Mohawk river called the Grand, in the southern part of Waterloo County. I was a churchgoer back then, as were a lot of kids, and I learned early on that of my father's two great passions in life—religion and baseball—baseball was the more important and that if I wanted to please him I would strive to be a better-than-average player. My dad was an elder at our church, served on city council, and, as more than one person told me when I was growing up, had been a natural ballplayer in his day. But dad gave up on a promising ball career to run the family haberdashery on Main Street, and although he was a good provider and we lived in a large house, he confided in me once that he often wondered just how far he might have gone had he stuck with the game. On our bookshelf was the collected Ring Lardner, right beside the Holy Bible. Both were used often—the Bible by the women, Lardner by the men.

The war had just ended four years earlier, and my older brother, whom I emulated and idolized, had been caught up in the maelstrom.

He left town one bright, fresh Saturday in the spring of 1942 as the magnolia trees and trilliums were blooming, parading in his uniform, lanky and confident of himself and his country, full of the invincibility of youth. It was a coming-of-age morning. Mom kissed him and embraced him a little too tightly, if Jimmy's face was any indication, but mothers know no other way. Besides, that hug would have to last him across the Atlantic and see him into war. She cried at his leaving. Dad shook his hand solidly, gripping it longer than was usual. The touching of their hands was really a coming together of leather baseball mitts, one man's weathered old hand reaching out to another, more supple one; a father communing with his first-born son who had been a boy only yesterday and was now somehow a man, the pride of his family. That image has haunted me all these years. It was the last time I saw him.

I never cried over his death because it wasn't until the war was finished that I realized he was gone from me forever and that he would never come loping over the hill into the town valley, or play another inning of ball on the river flats at Dickson Park. I have spoken to him many times since those years just after the war, in prayer, in silence, and sometimes aloud when I hear myself sighing, "Oh Jimmy, if only you were here…." But I catch myself in midstream, fearful of I don't know what, so that I don't talk to him long. I am haunted by his departure.

He never knew the summer of '49. That it was the summer Tom Padden came to town. Over the years, as my children grew up, I would tell them about their uncle, about how he was awarded a Victoria Cross by Montgomery for acts of bravery in the field, and about that summer of '49 when Padden came to play for Gus Murray's Terriers. The stories became family legend, and several times I was encouraged to write a book about that baseball season, that summer just four years after my brother died. But each time something else came up and the project was put on the back burner. Living in a university town, and being an academic, I was asked by our local newspaper to write on a topic other than what I would normally publish. They were interested in the Terrier stories and requested several over the span of two years, and each of these had been so well received that they tried to encourage me to write a full-length book. But my life was busy and there were other writing projects. And then, one spring day when my children were grown and had families of their own, a carbon copy of the day, so many years earlier, when I had waved goodbye to my brother as he set out for Europe, I could wait no longer. I read with sadness that Goody Rosen, one of the key players on our Galt team of 1949, had died in Toronto, and I realized that others would be dying soon and that any book would have to be written while as many of them were still alive as possible.

When I returned to my birthplace after a lifetime away, I had been retired three years, my hair was grey, and I was the proud papa of four grandchildren. I stared long and hard at the brooding town, the quiet town square, the century-old stone churches with their needlepoint spires on top of massive bell towers, the library and curling club, and the immovable cannon facing up Main Street through the fountain, all of which had seen so many sun-ups and sundowns as to make the days of my life seem minuscule. And I saw, too, the streetlights illuminating what by day was not visible; I saw the people on Main Street, where all that had changed in half a century was that the faces were different, and yet, they were the same faces of every man's generation. On the three bridges and at the place I remembered as the four corners, life went on, people came and went, and a town breathed and moaned a rich ancestry speaking of not only blood but stone, and how without the one there wouldn't be the other.

The stone and brick buildings, the archways and sidewalks, alleys and town hall, pillars and fountain, hadn't changed a lick. I could see the Grand River where, each morning, early, the mist of an autumn day would slowly burn off as the sun grew warm and high and where, at night, when daylight fed properly into darkness, when the water was glass-black and smooth, the great blue heron stood silhouetted in moonlight, its long spindly legs a thing of beauty, wading in the shallows as the townspeople slept. And always the water flowed, a stone's throw from the aged curling club, and the parade ground square, the war memorial, the YMCA, the swaying maples near the thick-walled nineteenth-century stone churches whose spires reached heavenward to God Almighty. This was the social and spiritual soul of the town. On the river flats at Dickson Park, five minutes to the northwest, was the heart.

Nowhere could I see my old teammates, and though I hated the realization, neither, by then, could I see my brother when he was young. I could only see old men, standing or sitting, pawing for an elusive moment that was possible only for one summer—one summer long ago when there were no old men. It was then, and only then, that I realized the universality of death, the inescapability of it, and the coming of the end of the century and how both were stalking me and my generation all at once.

What would that long-ago summer, that season, mean when there was no one left to remember it? The whole sum of our lives was fading into oblivion. The paper trail we each leave in our life's wake—letters, clippings, and certificates from decades of striving and doing—would last only as long as some descendant valued them. Then, without an afterthought by the custodians who follow us, they would be discarded back to the earth from whence they had come, buried like the living person had been returned to dust and ash. The cycle of life and death had repeated itself generation upon generation, but I had believed my generation was different. In the end, there would be no immortality; just a few years gone by too quickly. A brother I never got to grow old with. Ball seasons we never knew together. An empty space, a vacuum, which never filled.

The town square, Main Street, the ballpark and fairgrounds, even the trees on which we had climbed and harvested chestnuts in youth, would outlive us, and the next generation, and the next. How very small was the town, this patch of earth where we once lived and played out our lives; where we celebrated the mileposts of each year—the birthdays and anniversaries, weddings and baptisms, all the snow-white Christmases of childhood. And the Easters, the Halloweens, the Thanksgivings. We suffered and sang through the winters; we breathed in the earthy smell of autumn and saw the oaks and maples change with the years. And through all the seasons of our youth was the ballpark: how fleeting its memories. All the hopes and fears come and gone; all the years.

And off in the distance, as I walked this hill-girt town that was the centre of my old universe, remembering all that was and will continue to be, my eyes looked up past one Presbyterian steeple and then the other, and then slowly off into the blue sky with its clouds and its warmth of Indian summer and the russet leaves of autumn, and I wondered, still, even though I am old and thought I had acquired some answers, if there is a Heaven, if there is a hell. What small lives we all live.

My early memories are of baseball, of Jimmy, and of my mother and father. They're all mixed up together, and even though Jimmy was not there to see the Terriers of 1949, he is as much a part of the story in my mind as anyone is. I was eighteen that winter, still in school, and as spring came and the afternoons grew warmer, I became conscious that my days at the collegiate were numbered. On opening day that season our course work was done, though we all had to go to school on Saturdays because Frank Ferguson, our English teacher, had taught everything about the world we lived in except the course outline. We had to go in for extra tutoring to see us through the departmental exams, though none of us minded. Frank was everyone's favourite teacher and I count as a great blessing that I had him for a guide at all.

In the fall I planned to go to university, though what I would take and where I would go were as unknown to me then as why Karey Mannion lifted her skirt and called my name when we both stayed inside the school one recess back in Grade 2. But that had been many years before. I never forgot Karey, nor did I forget that brotherless summer of my eighteenth year. That summer was the last summer I spent with my dog, and it was the summer when baseball games at Dickson Park got in my blood. Never did a summer mean as much. At the end of September I would leave town, as it turned out, for good. My childhood years were over. But no matter where I was, or how many years came and went, the baseball team I had played on—the Galt Terriers—never left me, even though I had been a young rookie and rode the bench.

Charlie Hodge

There was no shame riding the bench then. Indeed, I thought it a great honour just to watch four former major-leaguers perform their magic. I have seen many a major-league team since that blood-moon summer when I came of age in southern Ontario, and I now know, if I didn't then, that those days were the simplest, the purest, the most profound of my life, and that no baseball team ever meant more to a town, or a native son, than those Terriers in '49.

I remember that there were three former big-leaguers in camp on opening day and that a fourth would come soon afterward. No semi-pro team in Canadian history had ever boasted more. And heading the list was Tom Padden, an Irish-descended New Englander who had spent eight seasons as a catcher in the big-leagues, mostly with the Pittsburgh Pirates. He had played with and against Babe Ruth and reminded me a lot of my brother Jimmy. He took me under his wing that summer, as did a lot of the older players, but he was also our coach and taught me about so much more than baseball. I could see, even then, that he had a flawed character, but that only made him human. Perfect humans don't make good coaches, and good coaches don't make perfect human beings.

Even more flawed was Tulsa Tommy Warren, a half-blood Indian from Oklahoma, who was the second former major-leaguer. He had been up with the Brooklyn Dodgers for a year after an impressive season with the Triple-A Montreal Royals of the International League. When he was on, there wasn't much he couldn't do, including pitch, play the outfield, and hit. Though it was five years since he had gone 1-4 with the Dodgers—he would be thirty-two that July—and his powers were waning, he was still enough of a ballplayer that summer to shine in the Intercounty.

And then there was the barrel-chested Connie Creedon. He'd been up for a short stint with the Boston Braves in 1943 as a right fielder, but by the summer of '49, the six-foot, one-inch two-hundred-pounder was hanging on to a baseball career long past its prime. He turned thirty-four that July, just days after we all saw him wrestle on a pro card at the local arena, beating a guy he was supposed to lose to, and though he'd never done much in the majors, he had been an exceptional minor-leaguer.

Rosen, a Canadian from Toronto, hadn't joined our club for opening day, but the one-time Brooklyn Dodger and New York Giant star had agreed to play for Galt. Just four years earlier, when Ted Williams was becoming a highly decorated fighter pilot and Hoyt Wilhelm and Warren Spahn were winning Purple Hearts in the Battle of the Bulge, the entire Dodger outfield of Dixie Walker, Rosen, and Luis Olmo hit over .300. He was a bona fide big-league star before the war and, as such, his services weren't cheap, but he was worth every penny Gus Murray paid him.

Those were the four big guns, the imports, I came to admire and who taught me that even boyhood idols are human. They formed the nucleus of our team, but three other imports, Connie Waite, a first baseman, Jeff Shelton, a pitcher, both from Buffalo, and pitcher Lefty Perkins, were also destined to play pivotal roles that season, as were a handful of homebrews, especially one by the name of Tex Kaiser. I can tell you with conviction that every one of them had the talent to play in the majors, and though my words now might not carry any weight, I remember talking to Padden one night after a game in Brantford and he told me—as he would tell me again later—the only team he had ever played on with as much talent had been the 1928 New York Yankees and the Pirate teams of the early 1930s. I never forgot that. I think people in Galt and around the league that summer generally knew that Galt had an all-star team, but I don't believe anyone truly knew just how remarkable were the Galt Terriers.

Introduction

I had mixed feelings about the arrival of spring that last year of high school. It had been a good winter, and our basketball team had made it to the county finals. Spring was a time to start playing baseball again, a time when I began to think daily about my lost brother and the good times we had shared while growing up. But this spring would be different. In June I would be finished high school forever, and we would all go our separate ways. I believed there would come another global war before I was much older, and I was scared to death of such a prospect. Not for myself, but for my generation, all our hopes and dreams. Jimmy had wanted a family. He was good with kids at the ballpark, and he had a sensitivity that most people would find surprising, given that he was, like our dad, a natural. I always knew he would make a good father. He never got the chance. The war took the boys of his generation, and I didn't want people like my parents to suffer again the same anguish they suffered when Jimmy didn't return home.

I was genuinely looking forward to trying to make the Terriers ball club that spring. And I remember, early one morning, taking my trusted Siberian husky out for a run. I could see her exaltation on that crisp day—the white warm mist blowing from her long snout with each breath, her tail wagging furiously, her big brown eyes afire with the pure joy of our friendship and the possibilities of another day. She ran playfully by me, barked, and made several passes. That was the morning of our first practice at Dickson Park. Damned if that dog didn't somehow remind me of, and look like, Jimmy that morning.

A treasured reminder of the summer of '49

Game Seven

In the valley of the Grand ...

SEPTEMBER, 1949. GAME 7. SUMMER WAS DYING. YOU COULD SEE it on the land, taste it in the air, and feel it on your skin. There were the small signs, like the first falling leaves already crisp and brown on the ground. The days were growing shorter. And the baseball season was coming to a close.

Late in the afternoon, under a clear blue sky that held all the promise of youth, the crowd began filtering into Dickson Park. I noticed the old green Ford sedan first, because it reminded me of a car my grandfather used to own. A family of four emerged—I didn't recognize them—and then I saw the licence plate and I knew they were from Brantford.

We were all licence experts in those days. If a car came to town from Toronto we could usually tell just by a glimpse of the plate. We knew our cars, too. And this car was one I'd seen before, though I couldn't tell whether I'd seen it at another game in Brantford, or in Galt. But I'd seen it.

I was early for the game, the seventh game of our semifinal series with the Brantford Red Sox. As I walked to the park, glove in hand and ball cap on, I was stopped three or four times by friends and acquaintances, all wishing me well that night. Not one of them was going to miss the game. All of Galt, and Brantford, too, would be there.

My day at P.W. Gardner's lumberyard on upper Main was over and the foreman had let me out early so I could get to the park. He was going to the game too. As I made my way toward the park, I noticed the clear azure sky, the freshness of the day, the shadows growing longer. I was not yet nervous.

It was summer, but already there were some dead leaves on the sidewalk, and as I looked across the street, I saw leaves against the curb. I remember thinking it was too early for the leaves to fall, but I reckoned they had fallen off sick trees and that their time had come.

The warmth of summer was still with us, and that afternoon, in the heat of the lumberyard, with the smell of sun-drenched maple, oak, and hickory filling my nostrils, I had sweated with the others, and put in an honest day's work. Forever more, the sweet smells of a lumberyard would remind me of my youth, and those prescient days during the summer of '49. But now, after a long day at work, I was tired, and I knew the chances of me playing that night were slim.

My senses were heightened as I made my way to the park. If I were to tell you everything, I would tell you of the striking young woman who smiled at me as I passed the library, and how her perfume scent stayed with me until I crossed the bridge. And I would also describe her appearance, for she had lovely features. Her reddish-brown hair was parted to one side, and flowed freely down her back to her shoulder blades. It caught the sun, and shone in the light. Her smile revealed soft red lips, reserved but inviting, and the skirt she wore was short enough to display gazelle-like legs, which seemed in keeping with her long, swan-like neck.

And I would tell you of the other people I saw, going about their everyday business, and how two well-dressed men nearly walked into me as I passed Gus Murray's store on Water Street.

I would somehow portray the aroma of the river as I crossed the north bridge and got nearer the park, and admit to you that the sound and feel of the water always brought my thoughts back to boyhood and my older brother Jimmy. Many were the times we had fished those waters below the dam. So now, as I crossed the bridge and looked upriver, I inhaled those memories and it was good to inhale them.

I would tell you, if I were to be honest, that I shed a tear on that bridge as I looked west to the dam, for these were Jimmy's stomping grounds. He was long gone and I missed him. And I would try to explain how so many emotions—I was at once happy and sad, wary of the future and eager to embrace it—could be felt in such a short walk.

Connie Creedon, my teammate, was already at the park, as were Tommy Warren and our playing coach, Tom Padden. It was Padden I saw first. He was sitting in the stands, shaded under the roof from the hot sun, and had the team list in his hands and was marking it with his pencil. He looked up, as if in contemplation, as I strode over the grass, and he called out my name and gave a subdued wave. I flung my arm up in reply, as I said, "Coach."

It was still early. The game wouldn't begin for another two hours, and by then the sun would be lower to the west, above the grandstand, blinding the pitcher and the infielders. I exchanged some small talk with Creedon and Warren, and I could see that Creedon was ready to play, but I was puzzled by Warren. He didn't seem like he was occupied by baseball that night, though I figured the game was still a long way off and he had time to take stock of the most important game of the year.

Soon other players arrived, and fans were beginning to fill up the grandstand. By then Padden had left the stands and was in the dugout. Cars crowded the lot an hour before the opening pitch, and other vehicles were parked on all the neighbouring streets and laneways. Women wearing hats, children, and men wearing fedoras were standing, or staking claim to their seats in the stands, or on the hill along the third baseline. Chairs were set up there, and though it was years before the term "tailgate party" would be coined, barbecues were burning and the smell of the ballpark was everywhere.

We took to the field an hour before game time. The stands were almost full by then, and so was the western hill. The Red Sox had arrived about ten minutes earlier and were greeted by our team president, Gus Murray.

The stakes had never been higher for both teams. After six hard-fought games, it had come down to a seventh and deciding game, with the winner advancing to the Intercounty finals. There was a lot at stake, but there was no doubt in my mind, or in the minds of our fans, that we had the better team, the better players.

I have tried to set it all down here, but I could not possibly say everything. I could not tell you, for instance, of my gut, just before the game, and how it was churning so much I thought my teammates could hear it. Nor could I adequately describe all that happened in the game, or the exact way it happened, and the way fans reacted. Neither could I describe properly the way the game progressed as the afternoon transformed into a steel-blue evening, and how the lights changed the complexion of the game. It made me feel quite good to look down our bench and see Padden, and know he had played with Ruth and Gehrig, and yet when the lights came on and the night grew dark, I did not feel good.

I had never seen a game as big as this. It is no exaggeration when I tell you we had more Brantford fans alone in our ballpark that night than most Intercounty teams had fans.

That was the way it was as Warren ran out to centre field, and Lefty Perkins took to the mound. The noise was deafening, then all was quiet. Seven thousand of us were waiting to exhale after Perkins's first pitch.

Dickson Park

A Time and a Place

Dickson Park was a playground for boys and men. In summer there was baseball and football, and a game we all called Tibby. We knew the trains, the trees, the bridges, the river. But most of all we knew the park. In winter we played hockey on the outdoor rink. "We were truly blessed," said Peter Gzowski. "Galt was really a wonderful place to be a boy."

SPRING, 1949. WHEN I WAS A BOY, I KNEW LITTLE OF OUR town's history. But over the years it gradually seeped into my pores and bathed my soul. My world centred on Galt, and on baseball. Living through the war years, and losing my brother when we were both young, shaped my view of everything that I knew then and all that was to come. I knew that those years had been hard on baseball players as they had been hard on everybody. Careers were ended in midstream, or delayed several years. In 1948 the Galt Terriers baseball club, a semi-pro organization composed almost completely of local Canadian players, had been a lacklustre team, both on and off the field. Despite the fact that the Terriers had a long and prestigious history in amateur ball, in 1948 they played before some of the smallest crowds to ever see Senior Intercounty baseball games at Dickson Park. The Terriers were an elemental part of summer in Galt; summer came, and you knew they would be there. But people did not flock to the ballpark in droves during those summer months of 1948. No one wanted to see a losing team.

Still, a special relationship existed between Galt citizens and their sports teams. Galt had produced many championship baseball squads in the past, and was also known for its Junior A hockey team, the Galt Red Wings, whose most famous alumnus was Gordie Howe. Plenty of future hockey stars spent time in Galt including Terry Sawchuk, whom some people regard as the greatest goaltender of all time. Sports had always been the lifeblood of the community. On any Saturday night through the winter Galt Arena was filled to capacity. And most summers on the river flats, which were both ball field and fairground, Dickson Park was overflowing with people. This was the way of all summers in the small town beside the Grand River, and this was the way of the winters.

No one had the foresight to know what was on the horizon; to know what would happen in a decade or two, when fans would become busy with other things, and become even too busy to go to the ballpark. A decade later the Intercounty Baseball Association, born and bred in the heartland of Canada, had seen its best years and was in decline. By then, of course, our way of life had changed, the clock had become a tyranny no one could escape, and the rush was on to beat it. The days and weeks were never the same after that.

Galt was a medium-sized city of about 15,000 in 1948. Brantford, which was virtually Galt's twin, was situated eighteen miles downriver. Anything that could be said of Galt could also describe Brantford. The Grand River and its verdant valley cut through Galt, running downriver to Lake Erie, flowing quietly all year round except in spring when it scathed through its channel like a torrent, first through Galt and Paris and then Brantford, where Alexander Graham Bell developed the telephone and where, in the late 1700s, in the aftermath of the American Revolution, Mohawk Chief Joseph Brant settled his followers after fleeing the Mohawk Valley in central New York. We always knew, as kids, that Indians had played a big part in our past, but it wasn't until the old Indian village and its many longhouses were unearthed during construction of a subdivision off Myer's Road that we came to fully understand it. Today the Grand River is a Canadian heritage river, carrying the old sediments of millennia, and through it flows all that has been and will be; diluted in its waters are all the seasons of my childhood. I see my brother reflected in its pools; I see men and boys and baseball.

In Galt, tree-lined streets shaded old houses, including the stately homes on the west-side hill above the ballpark. On the street overlooking the park, a boy by the name of Peter Brown (Gzowski) had grown up; Gzowski came to know players with names like Moth Miller and Friendy Graham. But he left town in 1948, never to see the fabled Terriers of '49. On both the east and west hills overlooking the river valley were houses where people slept and ate, and tended their gardens and chatted with neighbours. In the valley below was the downtown proper, vibrant, mercantile, alive with market and banks, with taverns and hotels. Galt residents slept on the hills but worked and played in the valley. In that valley were all the town meeting places, including the arena in winter, and Dickson Park in summer. It was the valley of life, of events that shaped the town into the city. In Dickson Park was the very essence of summer. There was, in truth, more to summer than Dickson Park, but there was nothing more to Dickson Park than summer and the Intercounty Terriers.

The park itself got its name from the town founder. A Scot out of Niagara named William Dickson, and a carpenter from Buffalo, Absalom Shade, founded the town in 1816. Throughout the 1800s the voices heard on the sidewalks and in the stores were the accents of Scotland. Less than a century later, an association football (soccer) team from Galt, comprising mostly graduates of Galt Collegiate, went to the 1904 St. Louis World's Fair and Olympic Games and brought home the gold medal. When they returned to town by train via Chicago, they were met by a horde of well-wishers, more than 2,500 strong. The local boys had beaten the world's best. It was the biggest celebration in Galt's history.

I remember a newspaper writer once writing that Galt was like a cemetery with lights. You could see it, but nothing went on there. Still, in 1949 there were three movie theatres in town, several dance clubs, a huge castle-like collegiate that went back seemingly to the beginning of time, and a baseball team. People didn't need much more than that. In this town that grew up along the Grand, losers weren't appreciated, and nowhere was this more in evidence than with the 1948 Terriers. The junior Galt Pups outdrew the Terriers at the gate that summer. As far as the Galt Terriers were concerned, 1948 was a season to forget. The Galt Terriers of 1949 were an entirely different ball club. A man by the name of Gus Murray, president of the club in '49, was poised to make people forget the year before. Indeed, he did in Galt what no one in the history of the Senior Intercounty has done since: he brought fans out in droves.

In Brantford two men, Larry Pennell and Mike King, were doing likewise, as was a man by the name of Ernie Goman in Waterloo. They were, each of them, products of their times. It is doubtful that any of them would have been as successful at promoting the Intercounty as well as they did without the others. Murray, for all his promotional genius, needed Pennell and King in Brantford, and Goman in Waterloo. And certainly, the others needed him. Together, they brought the Intercounty to the pinnacle of its glory. Crowds had only once been as great, and that had been in the 1920s. With Murray's Midas touch in Galt, and with the promotional work of Pennell and King in Brantford, and that of Goman in Waterloo, it quickly became apparent that the summer of '49 would be unlike any previous summer. No one knew it then, and it probably wouldn't have changed anything if they did, but there would not be another season like 1949. And never again would there be the crowds at Dickson Park to rival those that followed the Terriers that season. People lived baseball that summer. They ate it, breathed it, and loved it. God, how they loved it.

By the time 1950 came you sensed 1949 had been the twilight of something good. You just knew it, and it left a bad taste in your mouth when you realized it was gone and that there was nothing you could do about it. Murray had brought excitement back to a people who desperately needed it in the years immediately following the war. Nineteen-forty-nine was, said Brantford's Larry Pennell many years later, the signal season of the Intercounty's halcyon years—what was good, even great, and what will be no more.

Pennell, who helped run the rival Brantford club for several years, later became a high-ranking cabinet minister in the Lester Pearson government of the 1960s. He would grow animated, like Murray and Goman, when he spoke of that year. A season like that you just don't forget. It stays with you, as anything does if it is lived intensely enough, and it is always there. So it was with 1949.

Where do I start? It was the year the Soviet Union tested its first atomic bomb; the year Newfoundland came into Confederation; the final year of the Nuremberg Trials; the year Hugh MacLennan, who had already written the Canadian classic *Two Solitudes*, won a Governor General's Award for non-fiction. But literature, like baseball, was soon to suffer as it fought a losing battle with technology. In only a few years it became obvious that people were reading less, and going to ball games less. Critics said television was to blame.

True enough, television and radio were gaining an increasing audience. Though CBC Television would not come into existence until 1952, American television had been growing quickly. Even movie theatres were seeing record crowds in 1949, the same year Ginger

Rogers and Fred Astaire danced together for the last time on the silver screen. When, in June of that year, popular entertainers Lucille Ball and Desi Arnaz wed for the second time, television was in its infancy. Few people in all of Canada owned a set. Sam Collard over in Preston had one; Gus Murray had another in Galt. When the *I Love Lucy* show premiered on October 15, 1951—a Monday night at nine—the writing was on the wall for baseball. People were buying televisions in ever-increasing numbers, and ballpark crowds were starting to decline.

So in 1949, with television not yet a dominant force in people's lives, people in Galt followed the Terriers. They were Gus Murray's Galt Terriers in '49; navy blue felt pennants, which were hustled to local fans for a buck apiece, proclaimed as much. Fans in Galt would have to wait to see Lucy on television. People still got their news from the newspaper and the radio. No one knew that within a generation, television would begin to dominate almost every household, and society would become more mobile and fast paced. Or that soon there would be regular hockey broadcasts on Saturday nights during the winter, and Tiger baseball feeds from Detroit. In just a few years a wide range of distractions would keep people away from ballparks. Individuals were on the move; society was on the move. Roads were being built, travel was easier. People were flying and driving. Cottages beckoned.

But all that would come in the years after 1949. In 1949 the war was in everyone's recent memory. It was the final year of the first half of the century. The last half of the century called, and with it so did progress. Technology promised to make our lives easier, safer, more enjoyable. Cars were becoming streamlined, and movies were being made in colour. A slower, more community-based way of life was ending. Cities and their suburbs were growing. No longer did old-timers know everyone they passed on Main Street. The Great Depression was not that distant, yet the boom times were beginning. In January that year a United Nations body told builders in all industrialized nations that "backward handicraft" methods of building should be scrapped in favour of quick mass production methods by prefabrication. This was the modern way, it was argued. Only by mass production could the world's acute housing crisis be eased. That very month another headline noted that idleness in the general population was rising. New technologies seemed to fuel the fire of progress, but many felt the social changes were taking away our collective sense of community and replacing it with a more self-indulgent and isolated, even softer, existence.

In 1949 Dr. Albert Einstein was still doing work on his theory of gravitation, which reduced the basic physical laws of the universe to series of equations. It was the year cortisone came into use; the year a B-50 bomber circled the globe non-stop. China was in a state of civil war; the proliferation of automobiles made suburbia a household word; traffic jams became commonplace; Israel won a seat at the UN; the nipped waist with lower hemlines, along with higher heels, crossed the Atlantic from Paris; Ingrid Bergman was ostracized by the American film industry for her affair with Italian film director Roberto Rossellini; golfer Ben Hogan was involved in a near-fatal auto accident; thirty-four-year-old Oklahoma Sooner coach Bud Wilkinson, who would later become well-known in the Canadian Football League, was named U.S. college coach of the year after guiding his Sooners through a second undefeated season; Sugar Ray Robinson was at the height of his career. It was the year they filmed *Sunset Boulevard*; of gadgets and gizmos; of time and leisure; the beginning of the baby boom. The year the New York Yankees signed a young kid from Commerce, Oklahoma, by the name of Mickey Mantle.

Yet despite the panoply of events and the whirlwind of changing times, Galt was still small enough that a policeman who happened to have a few drinks on the job one Saturday night found himself mysteriously handcuffed to a maple tree in Soper Park. Churchgoers the following morning saw the spectacle as they walked off to Sunday service.

But more than anything else, 1949 was a baseball summer. Years later Milt Dunnell, considered the dean of Canadian sportswriters, could still picture those large crowds when he thought of the Intercounty and the Galt Terriers.

It is an old league. The Senior Intercounty dates back to 1919 and four original teams—Galt, Guelph, Stratford, and Kitchener. Galt went to the finals twelve of the first thirteen years and won eight of them. In 1949 coach Tom Padden, and other American professionals, were impressed with what they saw on Intercounty fields, but they knew nothing of the history of baseball in Galt. To know about the Galts, or what baseball meant in this industrial southern Ontario city back then, you have to know something about the origins of baseball in Canada. The game had not been new to Canada, or southern Ontario, even in 1919. It had a home on Canadian soil long before the Intercounty was born. Indeed, the first record of a baseball game being played in Canada predates the year Abner Doubleday supposedly invented the modern game at Cooperstown, New York. The first documented Canadian game was played at Beachville (near Woodstock), just twenty miles from Galt, in June of 1838, a full 130 years before the National League Montreal Expos were granted a franchise. The game has been played across the country, first in Ontario and then, gradually, the other provinces, every summer since.

By the late 1920s and early 1930s the Intercounty was regarded as the nation's premiere amateur league. Then the Second World War came, and many of the best players joined the armed forces. Several players who would play with the Galt Terriers that summer of '49, like Warren, Perkins, Shelton, and Clark, had their best baseball years taken from them by the war. When those who survived came back, the league was poised on the threshold of its glory years. On a good day the Intercounty was regarded as Triple-A in calibre. Professional players were brought in. Bidding wars were waged for players, some of whom were signed under assumed names. The calibre of ball had never been better. "It was really great baseball," said Pennell. "You could go two or three games without seeing an error."

The seasons passed, stories were told, legends born. And through it all, countless players came and went, all leaving their mark, to a greater or lesser degree, on the town they played in. They still talk of Jesse Orosco's no-hitter of June 16, 1977, when the Terriers beat Guelph 15-0, and how Orosco was pictured in *Sports Illustrated* after his '86 Mets won the World Series just a few years later. Or of the summer that Ferguson Jenkins came home to Canada to play in the Intercounty following his retirement from the majors. It was Jenkins's way of saying thank you to his country. They talk of Rob Ducey from the 1980s, and of the season Bradshaw hit .698, and they talk of Goody Rosen's grand slam that was hit into the Grand River. If any one play symbolized that summer of '49, Rosen's grand slam would be it.

The Terriers were the class of the Senior Intercounty that year. Indeed, if a more talented team ever came down the pike, we never knew of it. Homebrews, American imports, former big-leaguers—the Terriers had it all. We had our criminals, our kids, our Murderer's Row, our hockey player who would, in two short seasons, play alongside the Rocket in Montreal. We also had our pitching aces Lefty Perkins and Jeff Shelton, the latter one of only two blacks in the league that year and only the third (Guelph had signed the first black player in the 1930s) to play in the Intercounty. And, of course, we had the inimitable Gus Murray, a character if there ever was one. No one would ever forget him.

So it was not surprising that crowds came to see us play at home like they hadn't come to see any other Galt team since the glory days of the 1920s. Throughout the league that summer the Galts drew record crowds wherever we went. We were even written up in the *Globe and Mail*. Everybody wanted to see our brand of baseball. But not everyone liked the controversial new head of the Terriers. Some fans ridiculed Murray for the way he would order all the foul balls retrieved; many of his own players denigrated him, though it was Murray who ultimately signed their paycheques. He was undaunted by it all, being more concerned with fielding a winner that would bring fans out to the ballpark. Murray, who would try anything and everything to achieve his goals, prided himself on his baseball knowledge, but the players, especially the Americans, knew his baseball knowledge was limited. Murray, after all, had never played in the big leagues, nor, for that matter, had he ever played at any high level of amateur ball. If he had, he might have garnered more respect. Still, Larry Pennell in Brantford had never played high-level organized ball, and his players universally respected and admired him for his fairness and honesty.

Nearly half a century later almost everyone once connected with the Senior Intercounty league would probably agree that Murray was one of the greatest ball promoters the league has ever seen. He could bore people with endless statistics about who hit how many home runs, or which pitcher ended DiMaggio's fifty-six-game hitting streak—he loved trivia questions just like these—but his skill wasn't that he could teach a player to throw, or hit, or run. What he did do was bring thousands of fans through the gates at Dickson Park. He was a promoter. With Murray, promotion was an art. No one ever did it better. But even after he brought in George Selkirk, the man who replaced Ruth in the Yankee outfield, to talk about an affiliation with the Yankees, some people were skeptical. Later, when he tried to hire Mickey Owen, a big-league star who had played in the outlawed Mexican league, his critics began to smell a rat. But then Padden came and soon Murray's credibility rose.

That's not to say everything was smooth sailing for the embattled Murray. Which is why today, some people look back on those Galt Terriers of 1949 and say they were a squad of first-class ballplayers and second-class citizens. Others, like long-time *Brantford Expositor* sportswriter Ted Beare, say even that description is too charitable. As good as they were on the field, some of them could be awfully bad away from it.

A Time and a Place

That season Murray modelled the Terriers on the New York Yankees—everything from player contracts to pre-game warm-ups. Even their uniforms, which bore the distinctive Yankee pinstripe, were big league. Moreover, he had a working agreement with the Yankees. In fact, it was Selkirk who suggested Padden for the managerial post. Padden had managed the Yankee farm club, the Manchester Yankees, in New Hampshire the season before. He knew his baseball, said Selkirk.

Soon it was spring. There was excitement in the air, carried in like a fresh scent from the southern Ontario countryside. It was the same in Brantford. Exhibition games were arranged. In the fresh new light of spring, on opening day in May, there was the stage of Dickson Park, and the cast of players who would form the foundation for one unforgettable summer in Terrier Town. On that stage, through the next few months, would pass the players and the other teams. And by September, after the crises that seemed to come daily, one upon another, the fans of Galt knew team president Gus Murray, and his wife Grace, and his son Keith, and playing manager Tommy Padden, and the rest of the imports and the homebrews, and the ball boy, and Jack Spencer the groundskeeper, and Johnny Kumornik the umpire, and Waterloo's talented Don Gallinger, and Larry Pennell's Brantford Red Sox with Big Billy Gibbs, and speedy John Lockington and steady Stan Lipka. Galt fans would come to know the team, like they invariably did for any and all seasons, and they would come to know Terrier Town. They were a part of it. The seasons would come and go in Galt with the usual fanfare. They had always done that. Over time, player upon player would enter the grass stage at Dickson Park in the spring and then leave at season's end. But the Galts that summer, the stories of where they had come from and where they would go, were different. They were not time-honoured and traditional. That they were even assembled together in one place at one time was the result of Murray's hard work and vision. He was to be given the credit. Or the blame. Murray was the heart and soul of the Galts that final summer, that twilight summer of the 1940s.

Gus Murray

21

The stories are many in this Terrier Town. The ballpark has known more than any one person can tell. The summer of '49 has its own story to tell, for in all seasons before or since, there has not been another like it. There have been many great seasons, many great teams at Dickson Park, but none were as extraordinary, nor as mercurial, as the Galts were that spring and summer in the last year of the 1940s. The lights were only two years old at Dickson Park and it seemed like baseball would continue to grow and prosper. The crowds had never been bigger, nor had the games been of a higher calibre. And so, for a season, and for a couple more summers, the people came.

This is the story of that team and those players. A story of that time when the war had just ended. A story of the greatest semi-pro league in the world, and of a place known as Terrier Town.

Lefty Perkins

Beginnings

You thirst for a baseball season like that one. You are always thirsting. Walking down Main and Water, even in winter, when the snow is deep and the roads are wet from the cars passing by, seeing the ancient stone buildings that have stood their ground for nearly two centuries, you are still thirsting for the spring and the baseball it will bring, and, if you are lucky, and if there is a god in heaven, you hope, desire, for a return to all that was great and good one summer when you were young and the world, so wide and varied, was inviting you to explore its four corners and its seas, and yet for the moment you knew you could not leave this small patch of ground you would come to call your native land. You have seen that season once, and it has spoiled you because it is not possible to live through another like it, and the truth of this you are not willing to see. And still you search, even though you know that one red-letter season was all you can rightfully expect in a single lifetime. You wait, and the summers come and go, and always you are disappointed. Once, in a very long time, comes a season ...

SUMMER, 1987. BASEBALL WAS IN LEFTY'S BLOOD. PHYSICALLY IN his blood. If there was a test for a baseball molecule, he was sure they would find it among the red and white corpuscles coursing through his body—especially in the spring and summer. Now, as an old man, and with summer yawning, those molecules brought him north. He was returning to the city of his youth. The scent was there. The closer he got, the stronger he could taste it. He embraced this feeling—the way driving down a road can make you think things you thought were gone forever. It was impossible to reconcile the feeling, and thinking about it would destroy all that was good about it. So the old pitcher didn't think. He just let the intoxication take over and he felt twenty-eight again. Younger, virile, reckless, even carefree, the way a young man feels invincible in the years before he marries. The way he used to feel when he stepped on the mound, rubbed his cleats in the dirt, worked the ball with his hands, and believed he was unbeatable. But he was nearly seventy now, and the change to his mood was so infecting that even he wondered how such a thing could happen so suddenly and without warning.

Why did he want to feel all these things? He knew no answer. Or rather, he could speak no answer. But the feeling of vigour and youth was unmistakable; it was pounding in his chest and coursing out to his limbs, like an explosion from the inside out; every capillary was working and the drumbeat of life was palpable.

The morning heat was stifling, but it was midsummer, and midsummer meant baseball. Southern Ontario in July can be hot, as Lefty Perkins and his wife Patricia knew only too well, though other American visitors might be surprised at the burning heat of a Canadian summer. But not Perkins. He had known this land in the summer. And once he had known its ballparks and its people. Summer now hung in the air, hot, breathy, the scent of green foliage everywhere; the sweet smell of strawberry fields in places. The country was beautiful, Perkins thought. Even though he had always remembered it with fondness, the American had forgotten just how striking the scenery was. As they drove north into Waterloo County on the road that followed the Grand River, they could see the water, and occasionally a bright blue sky would emerge from the treed canopy above them. All of this made them not sorry they were returning.

Galt was small when he had last left it—it had a population of 15,000 people in 1950—and though there was a wealth of industry and commerce, making it unmistakably a city, there had been a rural feel about it. The countryside seemed to encroach into the city; fields and farmland were everywhere. As new subdivisions were built out into the country, backyards would look out onto cow pastures. Holstein and Jersey cows would come grazing up to front doors. The ties to the country could be seen every Saturday morning at the farmers' market in the city hall parking lot where the fat of the land, the produce from some of the finest soil-rich farmland in Canada, was bought and sold.

Beginnings

Perkins, a gifted pitcher earmarked by professional scouts for a career in the majors before the Second World War intervened, had come north out of Fayetteville, Pennsylvania—just a few miles from Gettysburg—to visit relatives of Patricia's in nearby Paris. A bonus this day, their stay with the relatives now over, was that they were seeing the extreme northern limit of the Carolinian region of North America with its teeming flora and fauna. The Carolinian region abounds with life—both plant and animal—and reaches up into southern Canada along the Grand River valley as far north as Galt. It is here where the natural range of the once great but now blight-stricken and nearly extinct American chestnut tree extends to its northernmost limit.

He had not been this way in a very long time, so his head was fresh to take it all in. There were even butterflies in his stomach. He was remembering a time so remote that only his wife really understood; only she knew what Galt and the Terriers had once meant to him.

Galt was only eight miles upriver from Paris. During the drive, which was very pleasant, he had time to think many things. It was a good feeling to be near Terrier Town. Though he had only pitched with the semi-pro Galt Terriers baseball club for two seasons—1949 and 1950—he remembered the city and

Tom Padden

the Senior Intercounty ballparks of southern Ontario well. Those two years had left their mark on him as a man. They were two of the best summers of his life. Especially 1949. He had thought often about that year, about his teammates and the small town beside the Grand River.

"That was the best team I ever played on," he said, turning to his wife.

"Better than Newark?" she asked.

"Better than Newark," he said. "Better than Newark."

There was a pause.

"I've forgotten that catcher's name," she said.

"Ah, you mean Tom Padden. Tommy was a good man. Best catcher I ever played with."

"Didn't he have a scrapbook with pictures of Ruth in it?" she asked.

"Yup," he said. "And remember me telling you 'bout that ball signed by Ruth, the one I saw when Padden took me to his home in Manchester?"

"No, I'd forgotten that," she said.

Padden and Ruth were good friends. As a Yankee, Padden had known Ruth and Gehrig. His scrapbook, which Perkins had seen, showed newspaper clippings from spring training in Florida with the Yankees in the late 1920s. Padden was pictured alongside Ruth and Gehrig, among others. Perkins had plenty of fond memories of Padden.

"Remember Tex?" he asked.

"Yes," she said. "Of course. It's been years...."

"Christ, could he hit that ball."

Tex Kaiser was an outfielder and home run king who, within two years, would play hockey on a line with Rocket Richard in Montreal. Of all the guys Perkins came to know that summer, Kaiser was the one he knew best.

"And that black pitcher. What was his name?" He hadn't spoken it in years, but it was on the tip of his tongue. "Jeff," he said. "Jeff, Jeff ... Jeff Shelton. That's it. Jeff Shelton."

Now the names and faces came flooding back. Connie Waite, the first baseman. Infielder Wes Lillie and the other kid, Charlie Hodge. Catcher Johnny Clark. Pitcher Bert McCrudden. Former big-leaguers Goody Rosen and Tommy Warren. Jim Bagby. Bill Hornsby. Sportswriter Laurie Brain. Names never forgotten over a lifetime.

"Where are they all?" he asked.

"Most of 'em are probably dead now," she answered. "Maybe even Gus."

In Paris that morning he had seen a man wearing a T-shirt saying "Canada is Hockey. Period." The man, thought Perkins, knew nothing about the Intercounty Association or the Terriers and the Red Sox. Of course, none of his friends back home in Fayetteville knew much about his two years playing ball in Canada either. Or if they did, they dismissed it. But the ball had been good in southern Ontario. Lefty Perkins had come to that conclusion soon after he arrived at Galt in July of '49. Americans had a tendency to think of baseball as an American game, and though they had embraced it, developed it, and built it up into mythical proportions, the game was as much Canada's as hockey. Baseball was not foreign to Canada, as the

American imports in the Intercounty league all came to realize in those post-war years.

It was the last great age of amateur ball in Canada. Now, years later, Perkins had no trouble remembering, but had Galt forgotten him? Hard as it was to imagine, he was having difficulty even finding the place. The road should have taken him directly into town, but nearly forty years had passed since Perkins had stood on the mound at Dickson Park wearing a Terrier uniform, and he had only a vague sense of his bearings. It was ironic that the Perkinses had had no difficulty finding Paris, a small town with 8,500 residents—that was almost the same number of people who had watched him pitch the last game of the '49 season—and the site Alexander Graham Bell selected as the destination for the first telephone transmission in 1875.

There was no roadway sign for Galt, no indication that Terrier Town even existed or had ever existed. For a moment he thought maybe he should have played for Larry Pennell in Brantford in '49. At least Brantford was still on the map. Galt was not even listed. It had just disappeared. Either the rest of southern Ontario had grown and eclipsed this once prosperous city, long known as the Manchester of Canada for its manufacturing, or Galt had simply died out as towns do from time to time. But he didn't want Galt to die. Or fade away. If it did, it would diminish that summer of '49 and all that had happened. The town should be preserved, if only to give hard evidence that it was there, one summer long ago, that the Terriers assembled one of the most talented and powerful teams ever to take to the field in Canada. On a good night, mused Perkins, those small-town Terriers could have taken on a major-league club and held their own.

When he thought of those days and those men, he wasn't unmindful of Dickson Park with its short right-field fence, and its hill in left field; or the endless centre field that was always, and still is, unbounded by any fence. He wanted to see the park again. He wanted to see the people, like Kaiser, the hockey player who spent his summers playing baseball. Kaiser stood up for Perkins at his wedding and was his best friend in town those years. Perkins had to see Kaiser. And he had to see Gus Murray.

We all yearn to see the places we knew when we were young; to see if our memory has distorted anything; to see if what we left is still as we left it; to see the landmarks of ballpark and building, of town square and Main Street, and, if life has allowed it, those people still living whom we knew so many seasons ago. Perkins was coming to Galt for all these reasons. Looking at the map, they found nearby places like Kitchener, Waterloo, Guelph, and Brantford. Patricia remembered Brantford from '49. And wasn't that where the hockey player, Gretzky, hailed from? They could see Stratford, and London; they saw every other city that fielded an Intercounty ball club in 1949, but Galt, the place he remembered as Terrier Town, had vanished into thin air. Galt had not been so small as to just disappear, he reasoned. But what had happened? It is one thing when a ballpark disappears through the wrecker's ball, or when people die, as everyone eventually does given the passage of enough years, or when other landmarks such as buildings come down and new ones go up—but an entire community?

When he saw the sign for the city of Cambridge, Perkins was genuinely confused. Galt was around here, he thought. But where had this Cambridge come from? There had been no Cambridge in his recollections. What he didn't know was that Galt, in name only, really had disappeared. In 1973 the former communities of Galt, Preston, and Hespeler amalgamated into Cambridge so that the erstwhile Galt existed only in the minds of old Galtonians. Not surprisingly, as Perkins drove into this new city, he was caught off guard. Enough of the place had changed so as to look unfamiliar, yet there were landmarks that gave him a sense of déjà vu. Then, finally, when he spotted Gus Murray's paint and wallpaper store near the four corners of Main and Water Streets, he knew he had arrived.

Now, after all those years, he walked into Murray's store tentatively. Patricia was behind him. No one recognized him and he recognized no one. The midday sun streamed through the plate-glass windows at the front of the store, washing faces and floor. He strode slowly past the sunwash, going blindly into the shadows.

"Can I help you?" came a voice from the rear of the store.

His eyes were still adjusting to the light.

"Maybe," said Perkins. "Maybe you can."

"You look familiar," said the voice, which was approaching. Now the unseen speaker came into view. Perkins saw the brushcut, then the face, which hadn't changed, then...

"Gus Murray?" he said loudly.

At that very moment Murray was running a hundred names and faces through his mind. "Lefty?" he asked. "Lefty Perkins?"

"That's me," said Perkins. "I'm the one. But what's my real name?"

"Harry Sollenburger," answered Murray without hesitation. "Well, am I sure glad to see you. How are you?"

Perkins remembered the 1949 version of the Galt Terriers as the single best team ever to take to an Intercounty field. At least, people had said that at the time. Without a doubt they were the best slugging team Galt, and the league, had ever seen. Six of their players batted .300 or better that season. Where they had come from, who they were, and where they would eventually go was Gus Murray's business that year. He brought them in, paid them their worth, sometimes more, and, at season's end, would ask them back or release them. They were a bunch of characters on that team, thought Perkins, but the biggest character of them all, without a doubt, was Murray himself. Perkins, unlike some other players, always got along with Murray. Now, so many years later, he had found Galt, or Cambridge as it was now called, and there he had found Murray. He had also found part of himself, of his youth, when baseball had coursed through his veins. So he and Murray talked. They found that the years had changed them, each in different ways, but not so much that Perkins wasn't warmed by Murray's hospitality, and by knowing that their shared history—two summers, really—would always be there and could always be drawn upon.

Murray, too, was delighted that another of his old players had looked him up on his way through town. Others had kept in touch over the years, and most of the local players, like Lillie, who had grown up on the same street as Murray, would stop by his store from time to time to shoot the breeze. Baseball talk. Hockey talk. Always something to talk about. There was a kind of general-store atmosphere in there with Murray as the colourful ringleader, never at a loss for words. A person might not agree, or more likely, might not believe what he was saying, but Murray made life interesting.

Just as he made life colourful that summer. As the seasons progressed and the century closed out, Perkins came to realize what an essential role Gus had played in all their lives and how he had made the summer of '49 the summer it was. For sports fans across North America, it was the summer Joe DiMaggio returned from the injury list to once again grace the Yankee lineup. His injury had shown us our heroes were mortal after all. And it was the summer Ted Williams and the Boston Red Sox went down to the wire for the American League pennant with the Yankees. But in Galt, 1949 was so much more. Some years are forgotten, solely because there was no Gus Murray to enter life's stage and make them unforgettable. And that is what 1949 was: a season in the sun, one that would stand through the years and last through all of time.

Gus Murray

Twinkletoes

Gus was always running around, going a mile a minute, like a fart in a windstorm.

U NLIKELY AS IT SOUNDS, A GUY NAMED TWINKLETOES HELPED turn baseball around in Galt. Former New York Yankee outfielder George "Twinkletoes" Selkirk came to town in the fall of '48 and changed the face of Galt baseball forever. And the man who brought in Twinkletoes was none other than Gus Murray.

People in Galt could never quite get a handle on Murray. In later years Perkins would come to the conclusion that the term which best described Murray was helter-skelter, because the harried Galt boss was always in a state of disorderly haste. In a characteristic frenzy he had brought together an all-star team, just like he said he would, and yet there were plenty of critics around town; people who wanted to see him fall flat on his face. There was something about him, some quality in his character, which antagonized certain people. Maybe it was the way he bragged about his virtues of staying away from drink and profanity. Or maybe it was the way he dropped names. Or the way he exaggerated, as all good promoters do with impunity.

Milt Dunnell, a St. Mary's native then writing for the *Toronto Star*, once wrote a column about the beleaguered Galt president that showed just how little respect some of the Terriers had for their boss. I remember the story because Dunnell wrote it almost exactly as it had happened, and that had somehow surprised me because I didn't think they wrote the truth in newspapers. Gus was sitting at his lunch counter reading a newspaper one day when Connie Creedon strode stealthily in and lit the paper on fire. For a big man, Creedon moved quietly. Gus sat there, his legs crossed, the paper to his face. When the flames shot up he jumped off the stool and started waving the paper wildly, thereby unwittingly fanning the flames. Finally he threw it to the ground and stomped on it. I saw the whole thing from the back room with Wes Lillie. Creedon, of course, was long gone. The incident was indicative of what Murray had to contend with that summer. Many of his players held him in contempt. But it was also true that many of his own players underestimated him.

He was not an imposing man; indeed, he was far from it. He was below average in height, trim, with a classical nervousness that people never forgot. He was the kind of guy who would jump when someone sneezed. But it was his ever-present crewcut, shaved almost stubble-flat on top, the way the short grass is on a putting green, his hair standing straight up about a half-inch from his scalp, that distinguished him from most others. Years later people could still picture the crewcut Gus jumping around the stands to retrieve foul balls, or hurrying through the stands to reach the field. You would never guess he was the team president. He redefined a club president's role and did it in a way that few club presidents ever did before, or since. Murray always liked to say he didn't lie, but truth be known, he was never averse to exaggeration. "Don't let Gus tell you he did all the work for that '49 Terrier team," someone once told a reporter. "It wasn't all Gus, though he might take all the credit." But many people sang his praises, even while recognizing his faults. One time Gus was approached by some people trying to start a league of some sort, and he reached into his pocket and pulled out thirty-five dollars and handed it over without saying anything. He could be generous at times.

Murray was born optimistic. He always kept a list of motivational sayings handy and was constantly adding to them, refining them, using them in his daily intercourse. "Never give up. I don't have to be Number One. If I place second or third I can IMPROVE. A goal and aspiration will come. HAVE A GOAL AND GO FOR IT." His list went on to include "Only cowards lose their temper," "When the going gets rough, the tough come through," and "When plan A is not working, switch to plan B promptly." There were others: "Luck is not the answer. Hard work and long hours make a champion. Opportunity comes to those who are prepared. The best win; they are always ready. Never quit. We have respect for a good, clean athlete. It's not what you have, it's what you do with what you have. Baseball, the perfect game, play it hard." And then there was the old logic that came from hockey's Conn Smythe: "If you can't beat them in the alley you can't beat them on the ice."

Murray took great delight in telling people: "I don't drink, I don't smoke, I don't swear, and I will not lose my temper." In his opinion, anyone who smoked—and many ballplayers of the era did—"was a sucker." To hear Murray explain it he had none of the vices common to mortal man, but some who had dealt with him on a business level, or in baseball, thought him shady. He was considered tight, always overly concerned with the bottom line. What Murray lacked, many people thought, was compassion or sympathy. So what if he said he didn't swear, or smoke, or drink. Maybe if he had, like other people, he would have been more human.

But he had a deft touch with customers down at his paint and wallpaper store. He was always saying complimentary things about children to their parents, or about parents to their children. On the ad for his store was the saying "We do everything right, and we do it quite well." It was one of his favourites and he put it on his business card and in newspaper ads. Forty-five years later he could rattle off each of the sayings at the drop of a hat.

There was another saying Gus had memorized: "The person who takes the greatest risk is the winner." Murray was a man full of sayings. And, in 1949, he was the biggest risk taker of anyone in Galt. He could have lost not only a lot of money, but the respect of ball fans young and old had his grand experiment with bringing in so many name imports been a failure. He had high hopes to go with those soaring risks he was taking, which meant the chance for failure was very real. But Murray was optimistic; he didn't plan on losing any of his own money. As a businessman he never went into debt, a practice he had learned from his parents as a youngster, and lived by as an adult, just as he followed his parents' advice of never having a mortgage or buying things on credit or "time." The strategy seemed to work; by the time he was fifty he was wealthy. He always seemed to have his hand in one thing or another, anything that could make him an extra buck.

In the winter of 1948 I dropped into Murray's wallpaper store to talk about playing ball that summer. I had played for the juniors the year before and knew Murray from that team. "So you want to play for the Terriers?" he said. I felt uncomfortable saying yes. I would

33

have preferred to just show up at practice and do my talking on the field. "Well, he said, "you know, in all likelihood Mickey Owen is going to coach the team." I had read that. "And it looks like we're going to have a few other major-leaguers," added Murray. "You've still got another year of junior left, don't you?"

"Yes sir," I answered, "but Wes and I are both wanting to give senior ball a shot."

"As you know, we play forty-two games," said Murray. "And it's a good league." He paused and I didn't say anything.

Then, "I'm going to do what I did for Wes a couple of weeks ago. I'll set up a ball on a string in your garage so you can practise batting. When spring comes you'll already have a head start."

From time to time that winter I would drop in on Gus and he'd ask how the hitting was going and I'd tell him just fine. I think I swung at the ball two or three times one day. The rest of the time I was busy playing hockey or at school playing basketball. It was on one of my visits to Murray that I caught sight of a letter he had written to a Robert Latshaw in Baltimore. "I was talking to George Twinkletoes Selkirk this morning," began Murray's letter, "and he said that he thought you should be able to help our ball club a whole lot.... We have only a short schedule plus the playoffs and a few exhibition games, so the most we could guarantee you would be $2,500 for the season. We would however put a clause in your agreement that if we won the pennant we would give you a bonus of $500. Another thing we would do would be to hold a Special Nite for you. We did this last year for our coach and he got a radio, washing machine, and a hundred and one other things." Murray also promised the player a rent-free apartment and said the club would do "everything to make sure your visit is a happy one." The letter was pure hype, which was just as well, for Robert Latshaw never did come to Galt. The coach Murray referred to from the previous year never got a "Special Nite," and if he did, he wouldn't have been given a washing machine and radio and "a hundred and one other things." But that was Gus; he would promise the moon if he really wanted a player.

Murray had an exceptionally good memory and for every acquaintance or friend he would remember something unique about the way they were or what they liked to do. "Lou Gehrig never liked wearing an overcoat," he told me one day. "Neither do I." Gehrig was Murray's idol. Murray could often be seen in the dead of winter wearing just his jacket or sweater. Even when he and his wife, Grace, went curling, he never wore a coat. And rarely would he wear a hat. Later in life he would relax his dress code, but back then he was young and believed if it was good enough for Gehrig, it was good enough for him too. Today he has softened up enough that he wears a cap the odd time.

The newspapers called Gus Murray "Hustlin' Gus" and "Gustin' Gus" that spring and summer. A couple of times he was even referred to as Gorgeous Gus. In glue-like fashion they followed him, always wanting a quote; Murray always had "news" to report. Much of it was anything but concrete, but Murray had only to open his mouth and his words would be in print on the sports pages of several area papers the next day. Even Toronto's Dunnell would often write about him.

The owner of a paint and wallpaper store and an adjoining restaurant in downtown Galt on Water Street, Murray was on the younger side of being middle aged, and he was shrewd and nervous. "You had to wake up pretty early in the morning to fool Gus," someone once said.

"What would you say about a man who wears lifts in his shoes?" Wes asked me that summer.

"Is this one of them tall tales?" I asked him.

"Yes, sole what?" he replied in an instant.

"Lifts? What're you talkin' about. And who?"

"I saw his shoes, Gus's, down at the restaurant the other day, and they had lifts in 'em. Gus wears 'em."

"Gus?" I said, surprised.

"Gus," he replied.

"You're kiddin' me," I said.

"Nah, I ain't kiddin."

Gus was always busy, "like a fart in a windstorm," said neighbour Archie Stewart. Murray had that type of personality. "He was running around in circles that year," said Stewart, himself a former Terrier player from the 1930s. One night Murray and Stewart met outside their homes and started chatting. Murray looked preoccupied. "Oh, I'm in trouble," Murray told Stewart. "Goody Rosen won't play tonight unless I buy his boy a bicycle."

That night, when Stewart went to the game he saw Rosen's boy riding around the track on a new bicycle. "The players were holding him up left, right, and centre," Stewart said. Another night Murray told him how Waite and Shelton were planning on sitting out if he didn't come up with more money. Murray ran a precarious tightrope that summer, always wanting to keep his players happy, but also trying to stick to his budget. It was a busy time. Too busy, thought Dunnell, for Murray's own good. "They didn't have any free time," said

Stewart of the Murrays, who lived just around the corner. "They both ran the store and Gus ran the ball team," he said. Grace, Murray's wife, like Gus, was always in a frantic hurry. "They'd run everywhere," Stewart said. "She would come flying home and she'd be out of the car before it stopped along the curb and three minutes later she'd be hanging towels outside on the line. This went on all the time. Between her and Gus it was a whirlwind." Gus seemed to have a hand in everything. In the late 1930s and early '40s he had even taken some pictures of the local hockey team at Galt Arena Gardens for the *Galt Evening Reporter*. "I got along well with all the people at the *Reporter*," he said. He had learned early that it paid to get along with sports writers and editors.

The *Reporter*, in those days, was one of Roy Thomson's—he was later Lord Thomson of Fleet—first newspaper acquisitions and stood almost next door to Murray's paint store. Like a lot of my friends, I delivered the rag for several years. Thomson, who hailed from North Bay, a community that became famous as the Dionne Quintuplets' home (it was in nearby Callander) bought the *Galt Evening Reporter* and the *Woodstock Sentinel* at roughly the same time. I remember when his son Ken came to town to learn the business. He curled a lot, sold ads, and lived on the east side in an apartment across the road from a corner store where, each morning, he would walk in and ask for two eggs. The clerk always obliged, but word got out and Thomson soon got a reputation for being a little different. As I write this I hear that Thomson is the wealthiest man in Canada.

Murray was friendly with sports editor Bert Steele at the time. The two were talking in the *Reporter* office one day not long after Thomson bought the paper. Steele was a neighbour of Murray. Murray used to take a few pictures for the paper and hang around there. Naturally, they were all customers, and Bert was not only a good friend but a good customer, so he was always up in the *Reporter* office. One day Roy Thomson came in and Bert Steele was there and Bert said, "Mr. Thomson, could I have a few words with you." And Mr. Thomson said, "Sure."

"Well, you know," started a hesitant Steele, "I've been a sports reporter here now for several years and I've got a wife and two kids and I'm still getting twelve dollars a week." At that time there was a woman by the name of Sue Wright working at the *Reporter* who was earning only six dollars a week. Virtually all Thomson employees were earning low wages and continued to earn low wages while Thomson's power and wealth grew by leaps and bounds. Employees at some papers were even charged for the pencils they used. "I would like to get more money," said Steele.

"You said you work in the sports department?" asked Thomson.

"Yes, sir," answered Steele.

"Well, you know, sports reporters are necessary evils. You want to make any money in this business, you've got to go out and sell advertising."

The following Monday Steele was selling ads. He was later promoted to Windsor.

A young sports buff by the name of Laurie Brain replaced him at the paper.

Water Street, outside of Gus Murray's store, during a flood in the 1940s. Murray is standing in the doorway with his arm out.

Winter and Spring

When I was a kid, and the world was simpler, Waterloo County was the centre of the universe.... At the epicentre was Dickson Park.... In spring, as soon as the creeks in the surrounding countryside had begun to run with their cheerful rivulets of icy water, we took to the park for the first sessions of what we called Tibby.

— Peter Gzowski

IT SHOULDN'T HAVE BEEN SURPRISING THAT MURRAY USED HEEL lifts. Some players Murray considered bringing to Galt that spring were older than he was, and in an effort to gain the appearance of authority, Murray improved his height. The lifts made him about five-foot-nine. He would typically lie about both his height and his age, always adding several years to his real chronological age. No one then, or even nearly half a century later, knew how old Gus actually was. Later in life he would underestimate his age. Long-time friends and former players figured he must have been at least eighty in 1994. But in 1949 Murray, who looked young, would tell players he was ten years older than he really was. He would say almost anything to get an edge.

As for knowing baseball, Murray was learning. Throughout the 1949 season he would sometimes sit on the bench beside Padden, where he listened and learned from a master. "The experience I had in baseball, prior to 1949, was all with the juniors," he said. "I was very young at the time. To step out of junior and take on the chore of running a senior club, that was an awful big jump." He'd never had any problems with the juniors, but now, running the star-studded senior club, he wasn't prepared for the problems he would be called on to solve. Still, he was always an optimist, and moreover, he was prepared to do what it took to have a successful season, to do what Dunnell had called "working his ass off." "The team comes first," he said. "I was prepared to take a certain amount of abuse because the team comes first."

Though one paper called him Mr. Baseball, he was probably more of a self-described Mr. Baseball than a real one. He knew a lot of facts thanks to a book he had picked up that winter called *Big League Baseball*. The book had articles written by some of the best sportswriters in America: guys like Damon Runyon, John Kieran, Bill Slocum, James Cannon, Bill Corum, and Bugs Baer. There were all-time batting, pitching, and fielding averages, records, trivia questions and player profiles, and photos galore. Murray and his book were never far apart. Gus liked to stump people by asking them a question that only he could answer. But pure baseball knowledge, like how to hit, or throw, or field, and positional strategy, was all relatively new. He knew more than most lay people, having been in charge of the Pups the year before. But when compared to his players, he knew very little. Still, like a sponge soaking up water, he was learning. He picked up baseball know-how that summer—he already had the parlance—but more importantly, he was becoming a master of the art of promotion. And he knew what he wanted on the field. In a word, it was quality.

He eventually got quality in Padden, though he had not been his first choice. That honour had gone to Mickey Owen, another former major-leaguer, one who had bolted from the St. Louis Cardinals to play in the high-paying but outlawed Mexican league. Several underpaid American League and National League stars opted to do likewise, despite a threat of being blackballed from the majors. In 1949 the Mexican League, led by the wealthy Pasquel brothers, was dealt a bitter blow by the baseball commissioner, who suspended those players who jumped for five years. One such player was Danny Gardella, who sued baseball for conspiracy to deprive him of the opportunity to make a living. The case, based on interstate commerce and antitrust violations, was settled out of court.

Despite the fact that Owen had played in Mexico—he'd left the Dodgers with Luis Olmo for Mexico in 1946—Murray, fresh to seize upon a playing manager with big-league experience, went after him.

Owen, predictably, had never heard of Galt. He'd gone to Mexico for money and he would come to Galt, Murray reasoned, if the offer was attractive enough. Besides, Murray thought Owen was finished in the big leagues.

So he wrote to the star on October 14, 1948. The season was almost seven months away, but no time was too soon for Murray. The plan had been simple, really. Bring in big names, improve the product, and then promote the club like it had never been promoted before. Give away stockings to the women who came to the games; or roses, or instant cake mixes. Give the kids balloons and pennants saying "Gus Murray's 1949 Galt Terriers." Then charge the highest admission price of any ballpark in the Intercounty. That would help pay the big salaries. It was a sure-fire formula, thought Murray. But to make it work, he knew he needed some names. So Owen was the first big name he sought. And for a time, he appeared to be "in the bag." But after showing an initial interest, Owen declined, answering Murray's letter on November 1, 1948: "Thank you for writing regarding me playing baseball in Canada. I can't come because I must settle down and make a home for my wife and family and it can't be done traveling around."

Even as late as January 29, 1949, Murray was still hoping Owen would change his mind. He sent a telegram to Owen in Springfield, Missouri, stating, "Affairs of our ball club have reached a point where we can not proceed without your presence. Can you arrange to come to Galt next week for a short stay at club's expense so that affairs now awaiting decision may be finalized. Wire or phone me collect." But Owen wouldn't change his mind.

He still had aspirations of returning to the big leagues as a player, which he did in the summer of 1949, hitting .273 in 198 at-bats for Chicago of the National League. Owen went on to play three more seasons in the majors, his last being 1953, when he saw action in thirty-two games for the Boston Red Sox.

At the same time that Murray was trying to convince Owen to come to Galt, in late October of 1948, George Selkirk, a Canadian from Huntsville and the man who replaced Ruth in the Yankee outfield, paid Murray a visit. Selkirk, who now headed the Yankee farm system, had been a star with the Yankees through nine seasons beginning in 1934. His visit that fall was duly noted by the local paper, the *Galt Evening Reporter*: "The baseball wheels started to turn in Galt yesterday when George (Twinkletoes) Selkirk, former New York Yankee outfield star, arrived in the city to discuss with local baseball bigwigs the possibility of a connection with the American League club."

Selkirk had come at Murray's invitation. His arrival was big news in the little city. He was pictured in the next day's paper flanked by a dapper, crewcut Murray—they were all wearing suits and ties for the evening reception at the Iroquois Hotel on Main Street—and outgoing Galt Baseball Association president Frank Currie as well as Murray's right-hand man on the Galt executive, Walter Reid. The story went on: "The meeting was considered a huge success and Selkirk got the ball rolling when he announced that the Yankees would conduct a baseball school in Galt next summer. The New York club may be able to give Terriers some aid in the way of playing material but nothing definite along those lines will be known until after Mickey Owen, former Brooklyn Dodger star, and prospective playing-manager of the 1949 Galt team, arrives here next week."

The meeting with Selkirk had indeed been a success. It gave Galt, or more properly Murray, an in with the Yankees, even if only unofficially. The town's baseball community had come out to see and hear Selkirk. Murray had come through in his first real duty as president of the 1949 Terriers. If he could bring in a man of Selkirk's stature, maybe all his other plans were legitimate. Selkirk's visit had certainly given Gus some credibility. Galt residents saw the picture in the next night's edition of the *Reporter*. Maybe Mickey Owen would sign on. And others. The papers would keep a keen eye on what Murray said next, and on who he said he was trying to bring to Galt.

Gus and Twinkletoes

Years later I had the opportunity to talk to Owen. He told me how he'd spent his early years in Nixa, Missouri, where even as a youngster he was known for his throwing arm. At school he was the only kid who could throw a stone over the roof of the building. Another time he and a friend of his mother were walking down a nearby country road when his mother's friend saw a rabbit running through a field. "Oh, I love young rabbit," said Gussie Harris, a schoolteacher. "Do you think you can hit him?" she asked young Mickey. The rabbit was about forty feet off and running. Owen, who had been walking with a handful of stones in his hand and throwing them at fenceposts, threw and hit him clean between the ears. The rabbit somersaulted and Owen ran to retrieve him. "Anyone who can throw like that is going to be in the major leagues some day," said Gussie. Owen just smiled. He didn't know what that term, major leagues, meant.

By 1949 Owen, remembered for one of the most famous passed balls in history, was a big name in the majors. Newspapers throughout North America carried a small story that the job in Galt was Owen's if he wanted it. He had been Brooklyn's catcher in 1941 when the Dodgers were beating their cross-town rivals, the Yankees, 4-3 in Game Four of the World Series. In the bottom of the ninth inning Brooklyn was one out away from tying the series at two games apiece. I was a young kid at the time, but I remember my father talking about that play for years.

Owen received more than five thousand letters in the off-season, most offering encouragement. "The missed third strike, instead of ruining my career, will make me a better catcher ... until the day I hang up my glove and mask forever," Owen wrote in a 1942 *Collier's* magazine article. And true enough, in thirteen major-league seasons Owen played in 1,209 games and hit .255 with a fielding average of .981. He hit just fourteen home runs in his career, but one of his major-league records is a slugging one. He hit the first pinch-hit home run in an all-star game—a record that can't be broken—at the Polo Grounds in 1942. And for years he was also one of only three players to hit a game-ending grand slam.

By the fall of 1948, when Murray had first approached Owen, the news that some minor-league team in Canada had offered Owen a job to manage and play didn't escape Ben Gould, a sportswriter with the *Brooklyn Eagle*. On February 28 Gould wrote to Murray in Galt. "A few days ago I read that your team had been offering the job of manager to Mickey Owen. Inasmuch as I'd like to write an article on Mickey, I wonder if anything new has come up on the subject? Will you please advise? I'd also appreciate it if you would send me Mickey's home address."

Murray didn't mind obliging Gould. But he would have preferred to announce that Owen had decided on Galt. "We thought if we got Owen and imported one or two other players we could put Galt back on the baseball map," explained Murray. "Mickey had told us he would want to catch every game and that would have suited us." Nevertheless, Murray knew he could count on Selkirk if need be. But before seeking Selkirk's assistance, Murray would pursue several former professional players. With only a few months to go before the home opener, Murray was starting to get antsy. He needed a manager. His next choice, after Owen, was a local man by the name of George Brown. Brown had no major-league experience, but he did know baseball from his years as a player with the Terriers of the 1930s. He played on a couple of Intercounty championship teams during those years.

"He offered me the job," said Brown, "and, to be frank, I thought he was out of his mind." Brown questioned Murray's often-reported attempts to lure Owen. "I thought he was crazy going after Owen," Brown said. Whoever heard of bringing in someone of Owen's stature to play and manage the Terriers? The idea was too far-fetched. As far as he was concerned, the new live-wire Terrier president lacked credibility. "Besides," added Brown, "I was newly married and we had a child and I didn't want to get mixed up with all that."

Brown's opinion of Murray was shared by a number of people that winter. "There was a lot of jealousy when I took over the ball club in 1949," Murray believed. "A lot of people said I was a sucker." Murray clearly had his detractors, but he also had his supporters.

"George Brown later told me he was sorry he turned me down," said Murray. But with Brown refusing the offer, time was running out and Murray was growing more anxious by the week. Finally, as a last resort, Murray called Selkirk. "He had given me permission to phone him any time I wanted to," said Murray. Tom Padden's name came up. Selkirk had played against Padden when Padden caught for the Pirates, and the year before, Padden had managed the Yankees' minor-league team, the Manchester Yankees, in the New England League at Manchester, New Hampshire. But the team and the league had folded, and Padden was looking for another team to manage.

Like Owen, he had never heard of Galt, but that didn't stop him from accepting Murray's offer. The house on Ainslie Street was a plus, situated downtown only a stone's throw from Dickson Park, and the salary of $750 a month was good pay in 1949. Padden, wanting to stay in baseball, took it. Money was tight. He arrived at the end of March, a day or two behind schedule, because his little boy was ailing. The closest I got to him then was to see his picture in the *Reporter*. Then he returned home before finally arriving back in Galt in mid-April.

As Padden was making his way to Galt early that spring, Murray was firming up his roster. Padden said he knew of a pitcher who had played with him the previous summer, Harry Sollenburger, a southpaw, who might be available. Murray and Padden had already discussed the fact that former Brooklyn Dodger star Goody Rosen was playing centre field just down the road for the Toronto Maple Leafs of the International League. And Murray had signed Creedon, a former Boston Brave, who had been staying in New York.

Cornelius Stephen Creedon, born July 21, 1915 in Danvers, Massachusetts, was big, strong and fast. He was twenty-eight years old in 1943, the summer he got called up to play with the Braves. Old for a rookie, but the majors had lost many top players, along with many of their rank and file, to the war. So Creedon went up to Boston, as they say, for a cup of coffee, playing in five games for the Braves, and batting just four times (with one hit). But as the spring of 1949 approached, he was available, and the fact that he had been called up to Boston only six summers earlier was good enough for Murray. So Murray fired off a Canadian Pacific telegram to the Hotel Bristol in New York City, agreeing to pay Creedon two hundred dollars a month until the season started, and then four hundred dollars a month until season's end. On March 22 Creedon replied: "Very interested playing with your club. Will play under following conditions. To report immediately and receive $250 monthly until season opens, then $450 month. You to pay room and board throughout. Check my records in Guide, Atlanta Southern (Association) 1945, Port Chester Colonial 1947. Bat left throw right. Twenty-nine years old. Perfect shape. Phone me Hotel Bristol New York City tomorrow noon. Your decision. Hope we get together."

Creedon was no sooner in town than he demanded $500 a month. "He was a big man," Murray said, "but he could run fast." He would have been an asset to any team, even if it was obvious he had lied about his age. Creedon was no twenty-nine-year-old. Probably closer to being in his late thirties, guessed Murray. One day at practice Murray agreed to a footrace with Creedon. Murray had run track at Guelph Collegiate and was still in good shape. "I thought I could beat him," explained Murray. The ballplayers stood watching from the sidelines as the pair got ready to race around the long oval dirt track that encircled the ball field. Horses had raced there late in the 1800s. "The players egged us on," recalled Murray. "They were all watching. It was fairly close, but Creedon won."

In the days before the season began Creedon was the object of much discussion in several area newspapers. Guelph's Rex McLeod, who wore a fedora like that worn by Connie Mack, had questioned the pitching quality in the Quebec League, where Creedon had played in 1948. "We are quite familiar that Mr. Creedon is rated quite highly as a slugger," wrote McLeod. "There isn't any doubt that Galt scored a ten strike when they signed him. At the same time, we don't believe for an instant that he will compile any .430 batting average in the Intercounty, not even if he adds Gus Murray's weight. And unless the Provincial League in Quebec has progressed by leaps and bounds, its pitching isn't up to Intercounty standards." Of course, he was right when he said the Quebec League played poorer-calibre ball than was played in the Intercounty. The Intercounty was the best semi-pro league in the country. But Galt's Laurie Brain took exception to his remarks, and reprinted McLeod's column word for word in his own column. Wrote McLeod in his next column, "It cluttered up at least half a column, and, we blush modestly, for it saved him many tortuous minutes of concentration. But was he grateful? Did he say thank you? Nah, the disrespectful schlemiel!"

Brain disputed McLeod's contention that the Quebec League was inferior and that Creedon's .430 batting average of 1948 was inflated. Said Brain, "McLeod's column caused the boys in the know to double over with belly-laughs." Countered McLeod in his next column, "It's okay fellas, always glad to give the Galt sporting public a chuckle or two. They haven't had much to gloat over these past few seasons." Creedon, in fact, would go on to hit .309 that summer in Galt.

In April Murray contacted former major-league star left-hander Carl Fischer. But so had Guelph and Waterloo. Later that month Fischer would visit all three cities, though he was favouring Galt. On April 12 he wrote a one-page note to Murray from his Medina, New York, home. "I expect will run over the nineteenth or twentieth and see if we can get straightened out on salary. I don't see how I can afford to come under what I told you, as I have a couple other good offers banging fire. I am contacting Dave Haley, [the] infielder I spoke to you about from Lockport today to see if he is interested. I wrote Mullia in Buffalo and expect to hear if he is interested or not shortly. Would appreciate you calling me if Padden isn't going to be there on the nineteenth or twentieth, as will save me trip over until he arrives."

Just two years out of Triple-A ball, where he closed out his career, Fischer was in his late thirties that spring. Few doubted he still had the goods. A baseball man from Medina, when told Fischer might suit up for an Ontario team, said he had watched Fischer in an exhibition game the previous summer against some well-known semi-pros. He fanned seventeen batters and allowed one hit. The former American Leaguer once played for Detroit, Washington, Chicago, and Cleveland and worked under managers like Mickey Cochrane, Bucky Harris, Jimmy Dykes, and Steve O'Neill. Like Warren, he didn't have the stuff of old, though he was expected to be a star in the Intercounty. But he never did sign with Galt.

Homebrew Tex Kaiser, who actually hailed from nearby Preston, would return from his pro hockey team in Springfield to play left field and third base for us that summer. I always considered him one of the top players in the Intercounty. He could run, hit, and throw with the best of them, and he was young. The only thing he couldn't do was slide. At least, he couldn't do it well. Perhaps with Padden at the helm he would learn. Kaiser was the best of the local players, but there were others, like Johnny Clark, a Galt native, who would try out for the catcher's position.

Then there was Wes Lillie, a relative youngster like myself, who had played for the Galt Pups the season before, and who Murray thought was as good as any infielder around. Lillie, a shortstop, lived just down the street from Murray on Lowry Avenue. There were a bunch of kids on that street, including Lillie, the oldest, and Dennis Smedley, and Keith Murray, Gus's son, who, at four, was the youngest. Murray frequently went outside and tossed a ball with the kids. "Sometimes I'd take a load of kids to Woodstock, Brantford, and Kitchener to see the games," said Murray. Lillie and I were usually in that group, though the difference between us was that once we got to the ballpark, Lillie and I donned our uniforms and took to the field. Other members of the Lowry Avenue gang would watch from the stands.

It was no certainty that Lillie, who was a better player than I, would make the team, but he would try out. He was, at the very least, regarded as a good shortstop, though his hitting was suspect. In Lillie's mind, if he failed to make the Terriers he would go play elsewhere, perhaps in Guelph or Kitchener. Besides, he was still of junior age. He could simply play out the season with the Galt Pups and get an extra summer of seasoning.

We joked even then about Lillie's poor hitting, as did everyone, but I could remember the previous summer when he and Wig Wylie and myself were called up for a game with the Terriers. Manager Turow recalled years later: "I brought you guys up to sit on the bench, but we went twelve or thirteen innings with Brantford so I put Wes in and he got the winning hit." Over the years Lillie would get enough clutch hits to convince me he was a good hitter when it counted. He was a skilled player.

Murray once told me he preferred that his players use skill rather than brawn to win games. "I always tried to be careful,"

Wes Lillie

he said. "I never went for too much rough stuff." But there were times when you had to play tough, and Murray knew this. "At second base you've got to protect your base and there are a few dirty tricks you have to know. I was always small—I never weighed more than 155 pounds when I was playing—but I'd tell the players I knew how to slow a runner down at second base. When he slides in you throw it straight at him, not around him."

Murray believed he could lure Rosen away from the Triple-A Toronto Maple Leafs, and he was also looking forward to the arrival of Warren, Rosen's old Dodger teammate. Warren, born Thomas Gentry Warren in Tulsa, Oklahoma, on July 5, 1917, was a pitcher with the Dodgers in 1944 after being wounded during the war in North Africa. That year he posted one win against four losses, the only losing season he would have in his life. Murray knew that, as a pitcher, Warren could probably do well against the Intercounty's batters. But he could also play the outfield and hit with power. Warren made a trip to Galt early in the spring and signed a contract for five hundred dollars a month. He returned to Tulsa briefly before arriving back in Galt in late April.

A couple of other local players, veteran pitcher Bert McCrudden and junior Gord England, had also confirmed with Murray that they would be trying out for the team. And Gus had asked Kitchener's Frank Udvari to come down and play for the Terriers. Udvari, a Yugoslavian native, had spent his formative years in Guelph, where his love of sports became deeply rooted. What was interesting about Udvari, thought Murray years later, was that he hadn't learned to skate until age twelve, yet he would go on to be inducted into the Hockey Hall of Fame as a referee. Part of the reason he'd started skating so late was the Depression, when skates were almost impossible to come by for a poor family. And his baseball experience was equally limited. Murray could see he had an awkward style about him, but he would usually get the job done. Udvari had always played softball, and indeed, that is where he was, with the Electrohome team during the war, when Father David Bauer of Waterloo asked him out for the Waterloo juniors. That was in 1943–44. He was eighteen and had never played hardball. Incredibly, two seasons later he had graduated to the Kitchener seniors. "I sat on the bench a lot, but I enjoyed it," he always claimed. "My weakness?" he would say, pausing for effect: "A pitched ball." Officiating hockey games was his top priority, even back then. Two years after playing with the Terriers in '49 he was signed by Carl Voss, the NHLs referee-in-chief, to work NHL games, a position he would keep until 1966 when he was named first supervisor of NHL officials. In 1973 he was inducted into the Hall of Fame along with Doug Harvey, who failed to show, Charlie Raynor, and Senator Molson.

I always believed Wes would make the team, but I was worried I might not.

The pride of a town

Waiting for Warren

The Terriers had always been there, at Dickson Park. Championship seasons came and went—all the summers and winters—and as the years progressed, even the legendary Terriers succumbed. No man, no matter how heroic, could outlast time. But each spring, when the land was wet and fragrant, and the *Reporter* began doing stories on the ball team, there was hope reborn.

WARREN SEEMED TO FIT PERFECTLY INTO OUR EXPERIENCED lineup, but who was this guy the papers liked to call Tulsa Tommy? We new little of him, other than he had played in the majors. By the time his father came up from Oklahoma in midsummer, rumours were circulating that he had been in trouble with the law. Murray had been one of the first to hear about it in the spring. But such reports, troubling though they were to Murray, were hard to reconcile against the backdrop of his playing ability. Warren, who had applied for the Terrier coaching job earlier in the spring, had, at times, performed exceptionally well. Some days he would be cold, but on the whole he had hit, played outfield, and pitched in fine style. He had lived up to his reputation as a former major-leaguer and he was a valuable asset to our team.

Yet umpire Johnny Kumornik didn't like him. It was just an intuition, an instinct, call it what you will. Kumornik had been around and had a knack for being able to judge a person with a fair degree of accuracy. "I knew he was a bad character from the first time I saw him," he said years later. Kumornik, a former player, had lived life enough to be able to tell a good apple from a bad. This new pitcher Galt had brought up from Oklahoma was bad news, he thought. But what business was it of Kumornik's anyway? Warren was a baseball player. He wasn't brought into town to do good civic deeds.

Early in the summer Warren had failed to show when we gathered at Dickson Park for a trip to Windsor to play an exhibition game. Years later the story emerged that the Terriers were barred entry into the United States because there was an all-points bulletin out for Warren's arrest. In any case, on this day Warren was late, and since time was of the essence—it took five or six hours to make the trip to Windsor in those days whereas today the drive takes under three hours—a car and several players were dispatched to the Sulfur Springs Hotel in the adjoining town of Preston where Warren was living at the time.

We were mortified when we got there. We found Warren all right, but he was plastered. He could barely walk. He'd been down at the Hamilton Jockey Club the night before—Tex Kaiser and a few others had gone along—and he'd lost thousands. Where he got that kind of money, no one knew, but it was becoming clear that some of the stories about him might be true.

Warren's life had been dominated by ball and the navy. That's all he had known. So when he was approached by Murray about the prospect of his managing the Terriers in '49, Warren was interested, if only because the money was good and he could spend another summer playing the game he loved. But there was a problem that spring, one that he failed to mention to Murray in his correspondence to Galt. He had been arrested that spring in Oklahoma, prompting him to write a letter to Murray.

> Dear Gus,
>
> Well, just a few lines today along with my release. The weather here has sure been fine but I turned my ankle pretty badly during a workout Sunday before the game and haven't been able to work out since then. The doctor told me to stay off of it for at least ten days. I hope to be able to work out three or four days before I start back up there.
>
> Most of the boys here have already signed to play ball for the season and I will have to look around for some new ones to sign up.

Gus I sure did enjoy my trip up there and liked the people and the town. You couldn't have picked a better baseball man or a finer fellow to manage your ball club. Tom Padden will give you a winner.

Well Gus, will close and mail this. Tell all hello for me.

As ever, Tommy

Warren, entangled in a legal web after months of bilking unsuspecting "investors," was trying to buy time. He had already declined the offer to manage the Terriers but was enthusiastic about Padden leading the team. There was a postscript to his letter. He had ordered his own Tommy Warren signature bats and Murray had agreed to pay for them. He wrote, "Those bats should be in any day now so be sure and get that money order down to me." He hadn't set foot in Galt and already he was asking Murray to send money.

Still, Murray was eagerly awaiting the arrival of this former major-leaguer. He was counting on him.

Tommy Padden in his prime

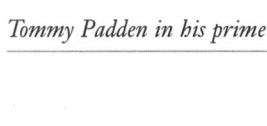

Tom Padden

Padden? Say, he's a darn good catcher. He is a good hitter and has a good arm. A great prospect and bound to make good. Don't worry, the Yankees are going to keep him within easy reach.

— *Joe McCarthy, New York Yankees manager*

Alf Turley's barbershop faced south, toward the river, though there was a row of townhouses just opposite, which blocked out the view of the Grand. Not that it mattered. People didn't go into the barbershop for the view. But Saturday mornings the place was always sunwashed and bright, and the sun would glisten off the hair on the floor, making it look auburn.

Turley, whose own hair was rather unkempt, had been a barber all his life. His hair was longer than that of most other men, and though he was of an age that his hair should have been white or grey, Alf's hair was jet black.

None of this mattered a lick, of course. What did matter was that Turley knew everybody, and that his barbershop was the centre of the universe. The way he cut hair was an art I have never seen repeated, and though every subject under the sun was discussed, the main topic of conversation seemed always to be baseball. Seasons were played out in their entirety, legends were born and repeated, and hair was combed and cut. Day after day, week after week, year after year, men came and went, and all the while they communed and shared, analyzed and laughed, told and listened. Years later I would hear of people who paid good money to do with a therapist what came naturally in Turley's barbershop.

Getting a haircut took a back seat to the informal chatter and gossip that was always going on there. I grew up in that barbershop, listening to Alf Turley direct the flow of customers. He was the ringleader, a master of the art of conversation. It was what we called small talk, but when you emerged from the barbershop, with your hair short and trim, you felt better for the people you chanced upon in Turley's shop, and for all the banter you came to enjoy and expect.

We learned all about the town and its people in there. I remember early on when my dad would take Jimmy and I in for our monthly cuts. Jimmy was brave, I always thought, because he never flinched when his hair was being cut. But I can still remember one of the first times I entered Turley's as a youngster, dead set against having anyone with scissors cut my beloved hair. I was young then, and had heard the story of Sampson, so I fussed and argued and made Turley's job all but impossible. My father, who was a friend of Turley's, wasn't happy, but I soon grew out of that stage, and began to accept haircuts as a normal part of life.

I came to enjoy walking down to Turley's as I grew up, sometimes with Jimmy, sometimes without. The street was alive with people, and my father's store was not too far away. As I came to the chrome-capped and twirling barber pole, with its red, white, and blue carnival stripes, I would look into the big front window to see who was in there. Alf had three large swivel chairs, each with a shaving strap down one side. I marvelled at those men, seemingly oblivious to Turley with his sharp razor, as he shaved their faces and necks. I didn't think I could ever trust someone enough to shave me. I never had a shave there, for I was too young, and by the time I was old enough, it was common practice to shave at home and let the barber just cut your hair.

That summer Alf's barbershop was, even more than usual, a hotbed for gossip and a meeting place for the men and boys of Galt. Thursday nights he would stay open late, and many a time people would drop in on their way by to simply take part in what we jokingly referred to as our town hall meetings. Decisions were made there, opinions expressed, and all the while Turley was in charge, cutting hair and occasionally mopping up the cut hair—white, grey, black, brown, and sometimes blonde—on the hardwood floor.

In 1949 memories of my brother and I going to Turley's barbershop were distant. But the place reminded me of my brother. I could see him sitting in the chair as Turley cut. Early that summer, with school all but done, and my spot on the Terriers assured, I wandered down after supper, past the huge steeple at Knox Presbyterian Church, past Ritchie's Red and White store, for a fresh cut. I wanted to look like a big-leaguer, even if I was only destined to ride the bench. As I approached the pole, I looked in and saw Padden in the chair. Until then, I had never pictured him as a normal human being, as someone who needed to eat and sleep, or go to the market, or get a haircut. It struck me as odd that he would be in Turley's barbershop.

Tom Padden as a young man

Alf and a few others were quite intrigued by his background, and his days with the Pirates and the Yankees. The way they talked to him, casually, and the way he responded, it looked as if they had all known each other for years. They wanted to hear about Ruth and Gehrig, and about Forbes Field. Who was the best pitcher he ever faced? Or caught? Who was the best hitter he had ever seen? Who did this, or that?

"There's the best young player I've ever seen," Padden said, pointing to me as I walked in the front door.

"Charlie, they've been asking me who was the best player I ever saw, and you walked in." I laughed when he mentioned me, and though I took my baseball seriously, and aspired to become a good player, I knew my limitations. Still, Padden was kind enough to say to the men in Turley's shop that I had loads of potential, and that I was undoubtedly one of the top juniors in the county. Trouble was that the Terriers had an all-star lineup that season, which was good for the team and the town, but bad for developing players like me. He got me to play a number of games with the juniors that summer.

"Who is the best you've ever seen?" I asked, curious for his answer. Padden was a reluctant hero, though others liked placing him on a pedestal. He was modest, and you could tell from his body language that he didn't like bragging, or the appearance of bragging, and he had developed a self-effacing manner so as not to appear to be better than anyone else.

Of all the people in Galt that summer, perhaps the most interesting was Padden. He was a quiet man, yet sure. Lean, tall, solid, with thighs like oak trunks even though he was middle aged, Padden spoke matter-of-factly, with no sign of boastfulness or pride, nor any hint that he had known some of the giants in baseball. At first, in the spring, I admired him, but as the summer wore on, I came to respect him. None of the hundreds of men who came to know Dickson Park had more of a God-given right to grace that field, as player or manager, than Padden.

He first arrived in Galt in early April for a brief visit with Murray, before heading back to Manchester to wind up some last-minute business affairs. Then he returned to Galt on April 15. His wife and three children followed as soon as school was done.

I met him on a wet Saturday morning in late April. I had gone to the early practices held by Gord Bradshaw, and by the time Padden arrived, we were all in pretty good shape. Still, on the day Padden was to take over, I was more than a little intimidated by the plethora of talented imports and by the presence of Padden, a man who had played, I was told, with Ruth and Gehrig.

Then this likable fellow with huge thighs and a friendly smile approached and offered his hand. "I'm Tom Padden," he said. "I'm Charlie Hodge," I replied. I respected him from that day on. We exchanged a few pleasantries, and then he asked all the juniors to take to the field. It was obvious he knew what he was doing. For the next two hours he put us through various drills.

It was much later in the season, when I had dropped by Padden's home on Ainslie Street, that we sat around for an hour or so on the front porch and he told me over a Coke how he had seen Ruth's last three home runs. But that day at the barbershop, many weeks earlier, he had told Turley and the other men some of the story that I now repeat.

Everyone was spellbound as Padden explained that only fourteen years earlier he had the great good fortune to witness baseball history. The Boston Braves and their aging star Babe Ruth—he was forty and newly acquired from the Yankees—were playing an afternoon game at Pittsburgh's Forbes Field on May 25, 1935. Forbes Field had been in existence for twenty-six years, which was, coincidentally, Pittsburgh catcher Tom Padden's age at that time.

Padden played ninety-seven games for the Pirates that season, though teammate Earl Grace started behind the plate for the Pirates that day. For an aging Ruth, the most celebrated player of his generation, the day would merely add to his already formidable legend. It was also a singular moment in the history of Forbes Field, and in the life of Padden.

Waite Hoyt, Ruth's friend and former teammate, was by then playing with the Pirates, but on that day he was not scheduled to see any action. He was more than a little amused listening to all the concern about Ruth expressed in the Pirate dugout. Pirate manager Pie Traynor had held a powwow on how to pitch to Ruth, even though it was mentioned more than once that Ruth's legs and eyes were failing and everyone considered his career over. "Traynor held the score card in hand, running down the Braves lineup to analyze batting weaknesses," recalled Hoyt.

Red Lucas was scheduled to pitch that afternoon and he had one question. "How do we pitch to Ruth?"

"Aw, he's through," said another Pirate player. "He's not hitting. Nothing to worry about."

"Never mind about him being through," said Lucas. "I'm the guy pitching to him, and he might start again."

Then the players turned to Hoyt, who was sitting on the end of the bench in the corner. Hoyt had played with, and against, the Babe for fifteen years. So they asked him how Lucas, known as the Nashville Narcissus, should pitch to him. Though Lucas had been up in the majors since 1923, he had spent all his time in the National League, mostly with Cincinnati. He'd heard about Ruth, of course, but he'd never faced him in a game.

"The best way to pitch to Ruth," began Hoyt, "is to pitch behind him. He has no weaknesses except deliberate walks. You have your choice—one base on four balls, or four bases on one ball." Hoyt was serious, but his teammates were unconvinced. This was no time for frivolity. But Hoyt told them he wasn't kidding.

Then pitcher Guy Bush, the former Cub great, spoke up. "I pitched against him in the '32 series," he said, "and I got him out throwing sinkers."

"So did Charlie Root," said Hoyt. "Charlie threw the Babe a sinker that the Babe dropped into the centre-field bleachers." Padden, who was also sitting out the game, had known a younger Ruth from the days at spring training with the Yankees in St. Petersburg, Florida, when Padden had gone to his first camp. Indeed, Padden had caught behind Ruth at spring training two consecutive years, so his opinions regarding Ruth were more than just passing knowledge. He agreed with Hoyt. Even if a pitcher was throwing his best stuff, Ruth had the ability to put the ball over the fence. This was Babe Ruth they were talking about, after all, and though it had been a few years since he'd seen Ruth in a game, Padden said anybody who didn't respect his hitting would come to regret it.

Lucas, by this time, still had not decided how he would pitch to Ruth, but it was time. He walked purposefully to the mound. Ruth came to the plate, taking his familiar pigeon-toed stance. "Lucas scratched, pawed the ground with his spikes, took a long windup, and pitched," said Hoyt. Then Ruth hit his 712th home run. Nudging Pirate teammate Cy Blanton on the bench, Hoyt said, "What did I tell you, Cy? He should have pitched behind him."

Bush, who relieved Lucas, served up Ruth's second home run of the day. So when he had to face Ruth once again, and with Ruth already having hit two home runs that day, Bush was more than a little unnerved. By this time Padden had come in for a shaken-up Earl Grace. "I told my catcher, Tom Padden, he [Ruth] was not good enough to hit my fastball," recalled Bush years later. "I came through with a fastball for strike one. I missed with the second. The next pitch I nodded to Tommy. I was going to throw the ball past Mr. Ruth. It was on the outside corner." Hoyt, sitting in the dugout, said Bush put on a big show "whipping two balls past the big fellow."

"Bush was hot," recalled Hoyt. "He bounced up and down as if his knees were all springs—sort of a freewheeling effect. His third pitch came after a fancy, exaggerated windup to throw Ruth off balance." There was a crack. The ball left Ruth's bat and sailed out over the right-field roof. At the very moment the ball left the stadium, Hoyt nudged Cy Blanton again. Blanton winked. There was no need for either of them to say, "I told you so."

Bush, for his part, didn't mind his role in Ruth's day. Long after his seventeen-year career—he posted 176 wins against 136 losses—closed, and indeed, right up to the end of his life (he died in Shannon, Mississippi, in 1986), Bush would remember Ruth's final home run with fondness. "I don't recall the first home run he hit off me that day," said Bush years later, "but I'll never forget the second one [Ruth's third of the game]. He got hold of that ball and hit it clear out of the ballpark. It was the longest cockeyed ball I ever saw in my life." Added Hoyt, who'd been around long enough to be choosy with his compliments, "It was tremendous."

The Associated Press reported it was the longest drive ever hit at Forbes Field. The stadium had been built in 1909; the roof in 1925. No one had ever hit a ball over that roof before Ruth. The *Sporting News* story chronicled the historic event. "Babe Ruth rose to the heights and poled out three home runs and a single in four times up before he departed in the seventh inning amid an ovation from the 10,000 fans in attendance; But his Herculean efforts were not enough and Pittsburgh defeated Boston Braves 11-7."

Padden and the rest of the Pirates didn't cheer outwardly as Ruth circled the bases slowly for the third time. But they were cheering with admiration on the inside. In the clubhouse after the game someone made the observation that Ruth didn't look like a hero; indeed, he looked more mortal than many onlookers in the stands. Padden and Hoyt said nothing, but shook their heads. The newspaper reported Ruth's 714th home run had gone 600 feet before being stopped by the roof of a nearby house. It was the longest drive ever seen at Forbes Field and perhaps the longest ever socked by Ruth. Several fans offered rewards for the ball, but observers said it bounced off the roof into the street and a boy made off with it. Ruth, a week from retirement, had given one final show for the ages. And though he was not the Ruth of old, the sight of him labouring around the bases one last time was an enduring image.

"That poor fellow," thought Bush. "He'd gotten to where he could hardly hobble along. When he rounded third base, I looked over there at him and he kind of looked at me. I tipped my cap, sort of to say, "I've seen everything now, Babe." He looked at me and kind of saluted and smiled. We got in that gesture of good friendship. And that's the last home run he ever hit."

Padden had never seen anything like it, and neither had his wife, Theresa, who was sitting in the stands. "I was there with all the other player's wives," she recalled. "We were all there. The Babe hopped around the bases like he used to do and the place went wild."

It was Ruth's last stand, though he didn't call it quits for another week. He played his last game May 30 and retired June 2. People would somehow always believe that it was Ruth's last game, and that after his third home run, he circled the bases slowly and went into the dugout, through the tunnel to the clubhouse, and called it a career. It was Ted Williams, a generation later, who hit his last home run in his final at-bat in the ninth inning.

Only days after Ruth's swan song Pirate owner Bill Benswanger took another of his many steps designed to create some interest among Forbes Field patrons during ball games. He had the yardage from home plate to various points in the outfield painted on the walls, a practice soon to be copied elsewhere. When a ball would smash against the barrier, onlookers would know exactly how far it had travelled.

It was not surprising that following the game Padden walked over to Ruth and shook his hand. Ruth thanked him.

Twice Padden had gone south to spring training with the Yankees; at first, he was sent down to the Kansas City Blues for seasoning. He was only a kid in those days, fresh from Holy Cross College in New England. Clippings that survive from Kansas City are telling; sportswriters, even Joe McCarthy, manager of the Yankees, said the young Padden had all the tools to play in the majors. His was a future loaded with promise.

At St. Joseph's High School in Manchester, New Hampshire, Padden lettered in football, baseball, and basketball. He captained the basketball team and, after graduation, played basketball and baseball at Holy Cross College in Worcester, Massachusetts. It was there, at Holy Cross, that Padden first caught the eye of Yankee scouts.

"They told him to just play baseball," recalled Theresa. She was Theresa Farmer back then, still a few years away from marrying her high-school sweetheart. "They didn't want him to play anything else. They told him not to play the other sports because he might get hurt."

Padden had dreamed of going to the majors ever since playing for coach Barney McLaughlin on Barry's Field at St. Joseph's. McLaughlin, who'd been, in his day, one of Manchester's best baseball products, had a lasting influence on the impressionable Padden. It was through McLaughlin that Padden honed his baseball skills, gaining the confidence he would need to pursue his dream of making it to the pros. McLaughlin had been one of the top players in the New England League, and earned a tryout with the Boston National League club. Later, even when he was serving four terms in the New Hampshire Legislature and the House of Representatives, he would be remembered as Tom Padden's coach.

Padden was so small when he first reported to McLaughlin for a catching position that he wasn't allowed to go behind the plate for fear he would get killed. He weighed in at only ninety pounds soaking wet. So the coach placated the young Padden by letting him try out for second base. He liked Padden and could not see to quash his dreams of being a catcher. A couple of years later, after Padden had grown, McLaughlin finally let him catch. Wrote a Manchester sportswriter at the time of McLaughlin's death: "As Tom became huskier he went behind the bat and everyone knows that under McLaughlin's tutelage Padden was a real catcher by the time he was out of high school."

Padden's first trip south for spring training after signing with the Yankees was in 1928. The *Manchester Union-Leader* chronicled his progress that spring. "Tom Padden, Manchester's best bet in years to become a major league baseball player, is off on the big quest. He left here yesterday en route to St. Petersburg, Fla., with the first batch of Yankee players, veterans and rookies, and next week, while we are swashing around in slush and drifts, he will be in uniform showing his stuff to Joe McCarthy, new Yankee manager. Tom is primed to give his best in the training camp in a great effort to climb to the top."

Padden's biggest handicap was his lack of speed. But after a couple of seasons in the New England League, he corrected that. One reporter had once said he "lumbered along rather than ran." But he got plenty of experience running bases on such Yankee farm teams as Hartford, New Haven, and, finally, Baltimore. Padden had been playing basketball too that winter before going south with the Yankees, and by all accounts, it helped. Playing for the Knights of Columbus team, he looked as smooth on the floor as any other player. He was as fast as Joe Bozek and Jimmy Horan, both of whom were known for their speed. Gone were any signs of the clumsiness that had characterized his base-running in previous years. Besides, catchers didn't have to have blazing speed. Padden knew that. They did have to have strong legs; legs that could bear the weight and strain of kneeling game in and game out. Padden always had massive, strong legs. And he had a strong arm.

His third year with the Yankees—he'd been called up for several games only to sit on the bench while future Hall of Famer Dickey caught—he went south to spring training believing he would make the team. His first two seasons in the Yankee organization he had hoped to make the team, but didn't expect to. Now he had matured, both on and off the field, and he really thought he'd stick with the club. He was game, cool under fire, patient, and a hitter. Though he batted just under .300 at Baltimore in the International League, when night games were subtracted from that total his average climbed to .330 or better. As soon as Baltimore put in the lights, his average dropped. So his overall average of under .300 was not considered a fair sign of what he could do. Even Yankee owner Colonel Ruppert didn't put much stock in such averages when night games were figured in. Night baseball, said Ruppert, "cut down the keenness of the eye in locating the pill." Today scores of baseball players would agree. Baseball lost something when it went to night games.

There were some terrific battles in those early years at spring training. Bill Dickey was the top catcher, and Cy Perkins had the number two spot locked up. It was between Padden and Jorgens for the third-string job. When Padden won out, it was a heady time, for among his teammates were Ruth, Gehrig, Pennock, Johnson, Reese, and Lazzeri. Those training camps were formative ones for Padden as he spent his days with some of the best ballplayers who ever lived. There was Ruth, bigger than life to most people, but he was there in the flesh, taking batting practice, doing catching drills, and, perhaps, off the field, playing as hard or harder than he did on it. Then there was Gehrig, the polar opposite to Ruth. Clean living all the way. In many respects, Gehrig was a good role model for Padden, who was, himself, a churchgoing Catholic. But, like many ballplayers then and now, Padden was becoming friendly with the drink.

Spring training wasn't all work in those days. A picture in the *New York Times*, about 1930, shows he and his Yankee teammates, along with Connie Mack and Judge Kenesaw Mountain Landis, at the unveiling of a stone tablet inscribed in the memory of manager Miller F. Huggins at the Yankee training camp in St. Petersburg. Padden is standing just to the right of Miss Myrtle Huggins, Miller's sister. His friends back in Manchester got a big kick out of seeing him in such illustrious company.

Padden was a ballplayer, wrote sportswriter Fred Lieb at that time, because he would rather play ball than do anything else. "He belongs to the type of Mack, McGraw and Jennings, other boys of Irish ancestry. I think this love of the game will make a hit with [Joe] McCarthy, who also played ball as soon as he got out of his rompers." There were catchers, said Lieb, and then there were catchers. Of the seven in camp, only Dickey, Perkins, Jergens, and Padden could rightfully be called catchers in the sense that Lieb had meant it. They were the best. "Padden has been throwing well," wrote Lieb that spring, "and meets the ball well in practice ... he is only twenty-two and looks like a boy who will improve steadily. Then his ambition, his love of the game and his close study of its fine points should put him over. Sometimes I marvel at the baseball ignorance of young ball players who have decided to make their livelihood in the national game. The name of a player who starred two or three years is meaningless to them. Not so with the Irish kid from Manchester. He has read and studied the batting averages since he could decipher a column of figures."

By the time Padden got to Galt in '49, what he lacked in youth and strength he made up for in experience and knowledge. He had, years earlier, achieved his biggest dream: he had played eight seasons in the majors. He had reached the pinnacle and now he had a gold card, a perk supplied to veteran retired major-leaguers entitling them entry into any professional ball field in North America. No matter what else happened, he had been a success. But, like major-leaguers before and since, once his playing days were up, he was left with only what he knew best to fall back on: baseball. If becoming a player had been a difficult task, becoming a coach or manager was even more difficult.

Padden had been called up into the big leagues when the league consisted of only sixteen teams. Players who made it then were good. Moreover, he'd been scouted and signed by baseball's most celebrated team, the New York Yankees. "Rooting for the Yankees is like rooting for U.S. Steel," wrote Red Smith.

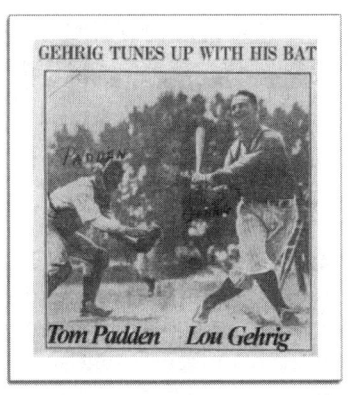

Lou Gehrig and Tom Padden

The Yankees had signed him in his sophomore year at college, and he'd never finished Holy Cross. Baseball had been his life. In Manchester, where he was a celebrity, he could always count on some work. If a career in baseball's managerial ranks wasn't in the offing, there were friends and admirers at home who would see he got something. Padden had a lot at stake that summer. Do well in Galt, and perhaps bigger and better things would be around the corner. But fail at Galt, and the writing would be on the wall.

Few people, if any, can be found who disliked Tom Padden. And to a one, they say he knew his baseball. Murray, who sat on the bench with Padden most games in the summer of '49, had never known anyone as knowledgeable about the game as Padden. It was an opinion shared by most of the Canadians, like Kaiser, who said he learned what it meant to play baseball that summer thanks to Tom Padden. Kaiser, who had a career-long feud with former Boston Bruin star Eddie Shore, when Shore was the minor-league owner who had his hockey rights, had always played baseball. As a youth in Preston, he had been coached by Tim Turow, a man widely respected in amateur baseball circles. Turow, like Padden, had grown up around baseball, but unlike Padden he'd done his growing up in Preston. No one had ever shown Turow the proper way to play the game. Turow, whose name is now carried on the city's athlete of the year award, had simply played, and learned by playing. There were no experts around who could show him the way.

"We thought we knew about baseball," laughed Turow, "but when Padden and some of the Americans came here to play, we realized we didn't know anything. They showed us how to play the game properly."

While Turow hadn't received proper coaching, Padden had learned from the best. He had been coached by some of the greatest names in the business. Indeed, Honus Wagner and Tris Speaker, his coaches at Pittsburgh, were among the first four inductees into the Baseball Hall of Fame at Cooperstown in 1939. Pie Traynor and Joe McCarthy, two others who coached him, would enter the Hall of Fame in later years. Moreover, Padden had been to spring training with the Yankees. That spoke for itself. Murray and his Galt Terrier baseball executive, not to mention Galt fans, many of whom had never seen a major-league game, were glad to have him.

And so, in a way, we breathed in stories of life and death and events from afar that day in Turley's barbershop. Our reach extended out into the world, and we could hold and grasp many things that had always been beyond our reach.

Pitching ace Jeff Shelton

Friends

I have forgotten more friends than I can remember, but I can still see their faces, and the haunts we used to frequent. A long time ago we gathered chestnuts, played Tibby, skated on the outdoor rink at Dickson Park, and followed the train tracks out toward Blair. Some friendships lasted a season, or two, and then faded; others were destined to last a lifetime.

TWO OF THE GUYS I GOT TO KNOW BEST THAT SUMMER WERE Jeff Shelton, an import from Buffalo, and Johnny Clark. Both were war veterans and we had talked a few times about my brother Jimmy. I think they wanted to be friendly with me because my brother had not returned and they both had. Lots of war veterans were plagued by feelings of guilt for having survived when many others of their generation had not. I felt a bond with them because of the war.

Shelton came up to me one day after practice that April. "Kid," he said, "they tell me Jimmy was a natural."

"He was a good one," I replied. "They say he played like my father." Shelton hadn't heard of my father, so I said I'd introduce them sometime. "Wes and I are going to Gus's lunch counter for a soda. You and Connie want to join us before heading back to Buffalo?"

"Yes," said Shelton. "I could use a drink. We'll have one in memory of Jimmy."

I was sure Shelton wasn't accustomed to drinking Coke floats with high-schoolers, nor was Connie Waite, our first baseman and the fellow Shelton drove with from Buffalo. Waite was more hard edged than Shelton, less outwardly friendly, though that was just the way he was and I came to accept it.

Wes and I cycled over to Murray's small restaurant in the dark, the air fresh with the scent of spring. Shelton and Waite met us there minutes later. The place was almost empty at that hour, but two people I didn't recognize stared as Shelton and Waite sat on vacant stools beside us at the counter. Shelton, you see, was black, and was probably the first black to ever walk through Murray's front door. He was certainly the first black to ever play ball in Galt, and sitting there, Wes and I, with two veteran ballplayers, we felt pretty worldly. That was the night Shelton told me about the Negro Leagues.

Just days earlier it appeared Wes would not make the team. It was the Saturday of our final cuts and Padden gathered all the players round on the infield at Dickson Park. We all knew he had made the final decisions on who would stay and who would go. Both Wes and I expected to make the team, though Wes was thinking he would be a regular player and I was thinking I would probably ride the bench much of the time. But we were young and full of ourselves. It didn't seem possible that we would not make the cut. We got along well with the veteran players, including the imports, and we took this as a sign of acceptance of our abilities. We both, I think, figured they wouldn't invest any time in us if they didn't believe we were going to be around for the season.

Like me, Wes was impressed with the way Padden conducted practices. "Tom had a lot of guys trying out from the area," recalled Lillie years later. Padden represented the old guard, and Lillie looked up to him. "I'd heard about him before, as a kid, but that was the first time, at spring training, that I'd met him." What impressed Lillie was Padden's knowledge of the game. In two weeks he learned more about the game than he had in the previous ten. Lillie really wanted to make the team. He wanted to play for Tom Padden.

"He got all thirty or forty of us who were left in camp, behind the mound," recalled Lillie. "Then he called out names of players who had made the team." We both heard 'Charlie Hodge,' and I winked and gave a thumbs-up sign to Lillie. In my mind I was thinking that I would be joining Wes for a summer of ball with the Terriers. But in my excitement I didn't even think to listen for Wes's name. That he would make the team was a given. So I was more than a little surprised when, after all the names had been read, Lillie came over looking like he'd just lost his best friend, and said, "I didn't make the team."

"What?" I protested. "How could you not have made the team?"

"I didn't make it. Did you hear my name?"

"No, but ..."

"That's because he didn't say it."

"Wes, there's got to be some mistake. Ask him."

"Charlie, it's the first time I've ever been cut from anything." He stood there, his head down, his pride hurt, his dream of playing for the Terriers ended.

"Go ask him, Wes," I urged.

While Padden had read off the names, Lillie had been waiting to hear his name. The seconds seemed to take an eternity. Finally Padden had said, "That's it. I want to thank all of you for coming out this year. For those of you who didn't make it, don't take it personally. There's a lot of good talent here and we happen to have what I consider to be an extremely strong team this year. I'd encourage you to keep in shape and try again next spring."

"My name wasn't on the list," said Lillie. It was a bitter disappointment. His worst fear had been realized. There were things he had to work on, to be sure, but he was young. His weaknesses would improve with time. At eighteen, he still harboured the dream that one day he would make it to the majors. He was young enough to want to improve, but more importantly, he was young enough to still be able to improve. As he thought about this unexpected turn of events, he remembered hearing Padden call out a funny name. "There was a Lewis named to the team," Lillie said. "But I couldn't remember any Lewis at camp. So finally I went up to Padden and asked him about it."

Padden looked at him, his face showing surprise. "Oh no!" he said. "You stay. You're going to play." He had meant Lillie all along, but he had thought his name was Lewis. So Lillie rode his bike home that afternoon feeling older than his eighteen years, and bigger than a kid from Lowry Avenue usually had a right to feel.

Murray was pleased Lillie had made the team, though he had little say, if any, in who made or didn't make the team. Not that he didn't want more control. He was club president and he would have liked nothing better than to run the whole show. But Padden had been picked to handle the field duties, and when it came to judging players, no one had more experience than Padden did. And Padden liked what he saw in Wes Lillie.

Lillie, only a few years earlier, had been responsible for one of the most memorable plays at Dickson Park. It had happened in 1943 when he was playing third base for the juveniles. A good friend of ours, Wiggie Wylie, was at short. The opposing team had the bases loaded when Lillie and Wylie went to the mound to talk to the pitcher. There was a pause as they talked strategy, and Lillie secretly took the ball from his pitcher and deftly slipped it into his pant pocket. A few seconds later he and Wylie returned to their respective positions. The old hide-the-ball trick was on and Lillie had apparently carried it off perfectly. All that remained was to make the play. Which is what Lillie then tried to do. The runners were off their bases, oblivious to Lillie's trickery, when Lillie slipped his hand into his pocket for the ball. But there was a problem. The Galt juveniles were wearing old hand-me-down uniforms from the Terriers. They were one class up from rags, really. I know. I was playing centre field on that team. To Lillie's horror, the ball wasn't there. He reached down, and then he could feel it, but he couldn't get his hand on it. The ball had fallen through the seam in his pants and was inside the lining. The runners soon realized what had happened and started advancing, while Lillie was desperately struggling, almost comically, to retrieve the ball. Wylie even ran over to help him, tugging at the ball lost in Lillie's leg, from the outside. But as they struggled, all three runners scored. Lillie never tried the trick again. Whenever I picture Lillie and Wylie frantically reaching for that ball I break out laughing.

Gus liked Wes Lillie, not only because he had grown up in Murray's neighbourhood and had, from time to time, played with his young son, Keith, but because Wes was a good kid. He had played for the Pups the previous summer, when Gus had been the general manager of the juniors, and Wes had been one of their stars. He could play the game; Gus knew that. Now he would have a chance to show his stuff against the big boys. And with Padden as the manager, Wes stood to learn a lot more about the game than young kids on other Intercounty teams. It would be a learning season for Lillie, but he would be expected to perform. He would need to play like a seasoned veteran come late August and playoff time. Gus thought enough of young Wes to give him a job in 1949 and part of '50 at his paint and wallpaper store.

Murray had been involved with the junior Pups for a couple of seasons before he became president of the Terriers and he had seen Lillie mature. It was his opinion that Lillie was the best fielding second baseman in the Junior Intercounty ranks. Whenever Pups coach Dode Hoffman—he and Boyd "Red" Shewan had been brought to town to play for the Terriers in the late '20s with secure teaching jobs as the incentive—was away on a teaching course, Murray would take over the Pups. Occasionally Murray would take Lillie in Rouse's loudspeaker car to talk up the game throughout the downtown core. He would hand Lillie the script and Galtonians would hear: "C'mon out and see this team of hitters!" In truth, the Junior Pups probably had the lowest hitting average of any team in the league at that time, but their attendance grew to outstrip that enjoyed by the Terriers.

So Wes and I were in. Jimmy would have been proud. I know my dad was. He would often come down to the ballpark after supper to see us practise. Occasionally he and Padden would chat afterwards. My dad liked Tom Padden and even invited the Paddens over to our house for dinner a few times that summer.

The week after Padden had named Wes and I to the team, I happened to be at the Galt Spring Horse Show, where I saw Murray and Watty Reid working the bleachers taking tickets. Earlier that week Reid had advised Gus not to give players like Connie Creedon more money every time they asked for it. Creedon, since arriving from New York a couple of months earlier, had his hands out for money every time he saw Murray. The baseball season hadn't even begun and he was already asking for a raise. Creedon was being paid $250 a month prior to season's start, then would get four hundred and fifty dollars once the season started. He also got a meal ticket at Murray's place, and took all his meals there. But, like many of the imports, he was constantly seeking advances on his pay. Ten dollars here. Twenty dollars there. Finally Reid and the directors told Murray enough was enough. "No more," they said.

At the horse show Creedon, being trailed by several young boys, approached Murray in the bleachers. "Give me ten bucks, Gus," he said.

"Connie," answered Murray, "I can't give you any more money."

"C'mon, Gus, I need ten dollars."

"The directors have told me not to give you any more," Murray explained. "I'm just following their directions."

"I need ten dollars," repeated Creedon, still surrounded by kids.

Finally, Reid said, "Why don't you give him a few bucks?" So Murray, who had just been advised not to give in to Creedon, took out a two-dollar bill and handed it to Creedon. "Here," he said. "Take this." Creedon took the two dollars and turned around, handing it to the boys.

"Go buy yourselves some ice cream," he told them. The boys were appreciative.

"Thanks Connie!" they each said, before leaving to spend the loot. Then Creedon turned back to Gus.

"Now Gus, I need ten dollars," he said. "That was chicken feed. That's not going to do me any good. I need ten dollars."

Murray was becoming annoyed. Then Reid, who had been emphatic earlier when he told Murray to discontinue the practice of giving advances, now said: "Well, Gus, why don't you give him ten dollars?"

There were two players on our team that spring who I never really got to know; two guys who kept a distance. One was Creedon. The other was Tommy Warren. We all knew that both had major-league experience. But beyond that, they were as mysterious as the dark of night.

⚾ ⚾ ⚾

On Saturday, May 2, a full two weeks before our home opener, we played an exhibition game at Dickson Park against the Toronto Earlscourt West Yorks. Padden still hadn't chosen his starters. The game served as an opportunity to see all players in game conditions. Eighteen of us played.

"It started out like a sad Saturday afternoon for manager Tommy Padden and some of his 1949 Galt Terriers," wrote Laurie Brain in the paper. Brain would follow us all season, and come to know us better than anyone. He continued: "But before the long drawn-out session was over, Terriers had come back fast and were a little unfortunate to have dropped the verdict 11-10."

The West Yorks were a smart-looking outfit. Wrote Brain: "A clever bunch of young ballhawks pounced on starting pitcher Bert McCrudden for seven runs and ten hits in the first three innings." We finally started hitting in the fourth and Creedon, a fan favourite who was written up as "the people's choice," hit a mammoth grand slam to deep left centre.

The tobacco-chewing Creedon, who Murray always thought of as Ruthian in his physical appearance, was a popular player with fans that spring. Along with Padden and Warren, his contract had been guaranteed by Murray. And like the contracts for Padden and Warren, it was one of the highest on the club. Fans expected a lot from players like Creedon and he didn't disappoint. When he hit in another run in the sixth, the park was abuzz with talk of the former major-leaguer.

But later, he hit a double, and then took his time getting to second and was thrown out. Padden didn't like what he saw. He wouldn't take anything but all-out effort. He went right up to Creedon and said, "You were loafing. You can run a lot faster than that."

"No I wasn't," came Creedon's reply.

"Like shit!" said Padden. He kicked the water bucket at him, sending water splattering everywhere. Creedon was white with anger, but didn't say anything. Padden had set the ground rules, and no one would challenge his authority after that.

Then first baseman Connie Waite, a new face, got a hit in the eighth inning. Padden went to bat for young Fred Worton in the eighth, but he was robbed of a home run when left fielder Doug Smart made a sensational one-handed catch of his liner to left centre.

We still had a good chance to win it in the ninth, but failed to make good after Waite connected with a long smash to deep left—a certain home run—but missed second base and had to settle for a double. If not for that miscue, the game would have been tied. Then Padden, who in his best year with Pittsburgh had hit .334, was intentionally walked and we couldn't bring him in. But we had played well against a strong opponent. The Yorks had won the Earlscourt senior league the previous season and seven of their number had played with the Ontario Baseball Association finalist junior club in 1948. Padden didn't care if we won or lost that day. He told us as much in the locker room. He wanted to see us in action. The game had accomplished that. In total, we had produced fourteen singles, but had left sixteen men on base. This was fun, thought Padden; what baseball was supposed to be all about.

That night Creedon and a couple of others went to the neighbouring town of Preston to see a wrestling match. Creedon had done a little wrestling himself in the off-season, and he hoped to make a few contacts. Tuffy Trusdale, a professional wrestler out of Jackson, Mississippi, had a bout lined up at the Preston Arena with a 388-pound alligator in a steel cage. There weren't any professional ball clubs in southern Ontario competing with the Terriers for fans that summer, but at times there were wrestling cards, and movies.

Everything appeared set for opening day, even if Creedon was contemplating a wrestling match to earn a few extra bucks. But just days before the home opener, two more American imports came into camp. They were so good that Padden planned to use them on opening day. A few weeks earlier George Selkirk had given Murray a lead on a shortstop by the name of Pepper Kalpinski—"He was a real pepper pie," said Murray—and a left fielder named Pezeulo. Both were from Rochester, New York, and they were good, solid players. Murray gave them each twenty-five dollars for the game and fifty-dollars for travelling up to Galt. As well as they performed on the opening Saturday, they never played another game in a Terrier uniform after the league clamped down on commuting players and they became ineligible.

The last snow hadn't melted too many weeks earlier. After all, it was only May 2 and spring in Galt could be cold that early in May. I was a Kentucky Derby fan back then, and I remember hearing that first Saturday in May about Calumet Farms' Ponder winning the Derby in Louisville. In Galt, fans had been treated to a show by Padden's men. And Padden himself, though he was forty years old that summer, had looked like the former major-leaguer he was. He wore the uniform well: dark socks almost to his knees, baggy trousers, and the number twenty-four on the back of his jersey, which covered a dark, long-sleeved T-shirt.

Justice Larry Pennell

The Red Sox

"We drank some of that water down there in Brantford," he said. "It was awful. Our water in Galt was clean and clear. It all came from artesian wells. But Brantford took their drinking water from the Grand River. The big saying in those days was, 'Galt flushes the toilets and Brantford drinks the water.'"

EIGHTEEN MILES DOWNRIVER, BRANTFORD RED SOX PRESIDENT Larry Pennell and the team's general manager, Mike King, were also getting ready for the 1949 season. They were confident they had a fair team; certainly not as strong as London, or Galt, but as solid a team as Brantford had had in several years. For the most part, the players were all homebrews, something that could be considered a potential weakness, or might possibly turn out to be a great boon. Pitchers Alf Gavey and Billy Gibbs were two of the reasons for Pennell's optimism. Gibbs, one of the youngest members of the Red Sox at twenty-two, had returned from a stint in the Cardinal chain in the U.S. He was more than ready, and capable, of handling the best hitters the Intercounty could put up against him in 1949. In addition to Gavey and Gibbs, Brantford also boasted another quality hurler by the name of Nig Parker. And in the outfield, young John Lockington, who ran a sports store with his older brother, patrolled centre field the way few others in the Intercounty could. Lockington's trademark was his speed. Only a couple of years before, he had been a track star at the

University of Western Ontario. But he left school when the opportunity to open a sports store in Brantford availed itself, though he lost none of his speed. His ability to chase balls down was probably the best of any centre fielder in the league that summer. He could fly.

Gavey's arrival had come about almost by accident. Pennell had known about Gavey, and about how the Cardinals had signed him after seeing him play softball in Hamilton as a teenager. "They moved him up the organization pretty quickly," recalled Pennell. Pennell called Gavey in Savannah, Georgia, that winter to get a lead on some prospects. But Gavey said he was interested in coming to Brantford. The Cardinals had sent him to St. Louis for surgery on his throwing arm, but then had released him. Pennell was overjoyed at the thought of getting someone of his calibre to play for the Red Sox, so he sent down terms of the proposed contract via telegram, and Gavey wired back that they were acceptable.

Pennell and King were to meet him upon his arrival in Brantford that spring at the YMCA. As Gavey entered the room, Pennell nearly fell out of his chair.

"He came in wearing a cast on his pitching arm," said Pennell. "I almost died when I saw him. Holy Toledo!"

Gavey held up his contract as proof he was who he said he was. King, too, was stunned, and for one of the few times in his life, almost speechless.

"Oh God," he gasped.

There was Gavey, the pitcher they were pinning all their hopes on, wearing a cast on his left arm. He was a southpaw, and the season-opener was just a few weeks off.

"We signed this guy to a contract?" he asked Pennell.

Pennell shook his head. "Yes, we did. And it's guaranteed, even if he can't pitch."

"It's [the cast] coming off in two or three days," reassured Gavey.

Gavey was a strapping young man, built to pitch, but there he was in the flesh and he was obviously in no condition to pitch. Why, they wondered, hadn't he told them of his arm?

It was a good question, one that Gavey answered without blinking. "I'll be ready for the season opener," he promised. "The cast is coming off in two or three days."

Sure enough, the next week he threw twelve strikeouts against Stratford to earn his first win in a Brantford uniform.

Later Pennell would count that story among his favourites. Gavey was responsible for another. When he agreed to come to Brantford he asked Pennell if he could find a "publican notary" to sign his car insurance form.

"He had spent so much time in Georgia that he assumed the term public notary was 'publican notary,'" explained Pennell.

"I don't know if I can find a Republican notary, but I'll be able to find a public notary for you," he reassured Gavey.

Brantford also had an extremely talented third baseman by the name of Stan Lipka. Mickey Page, the manager of the Niagara District Bright's Wine team, had steered Pennell in Lipka's direction. Years later Pennell would say that if he was starting a team from scratch, the first fellow he would want would be Stan Lipka. Born in 1919 in Toronto, Lipka signed his first pro contract with the Class C Grand Rapids, Michigan, team, a Dodgers farm club, in 1941. By the spring of 1943 he was playing third base for the Class Triple-A Montreal Royals, and had a promising future, scouts thought, in the majors. The talk was how he and a couple other Royals infielders would go up to the majors the following season. Lipka was hitting .325 that June before he went into the service. The actor Chuck Connors, who went on to *Rifleman* fame on television a few years later, was at first.

Alf Gavey and Stan Lipka

But Lipka's season came to an abrupt halt that year when he heard a knock at his door. Decades later Lipka still remembered clearly how his season ended. "The Royal Canadian Mounted Police came up to the house and said I'd have to go. That kiboshed my ball career." A couple of the other infielders, including shortstop Bob Ramazzotti, went up with the Dodgers the next year when Lipka was overseas. Connors got his call in '49.

Lipka was away three years, and when he came back he found that a whole new group of young players had come up in the intervening years. Older players coming back from the service were at a decided disadvantage. When he returned he signed with Nashua, New Hampshire, in the Class B New England League after attending the Montreal Royals training camp. It was at the Montreal Royals camp that spring where Lipka met a young, exciting, and aggressive black player named Jackie Robinson. Robinson was the first black that

Lipka had ever seen at spring training, yet he was surprised when no one would talk to him. "The only guy to talk to him was me," he remembered. "I thought he was a hell of a fellow. But the southern boys wouldn't have anything to do with him."

Robinson impressed Lipka with more than just his playing ability. He seemed to have an inner fire that allowed him to cope with the rampant prejudice he faced. And he was educated, having attended UCLA, where he had been a star running back on the Bruins football team. Lipka even heard a story that Robinson had been court-martialled in the Army for refusing to sit at the back of a bus but had been acquitted.

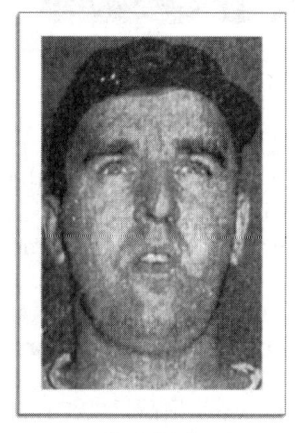

"I was a Canadian," Lipka related, "and I didn't know much about racism." But that changed quickly at spring training when he saw how Robinson was treated. Robinson was forced to eat separately from the other players, to change into his uniform in a coloured section. "He had all sorts of ability," he said. "He could hit, throw, and run. It's remarkable the way they called him names. If it had been me, I would have ended up in jail for murder. But he loved the game." Robinson had promised Branch Rickey he would turn the other cheek at insults, and, indeed, he showed remarkable restraint during the knock-down pitches and the threat of a strike. But it took a toll, and Robinson, who had not broken into the majors until he was twenty-eight, was dead at fifty-three.

Stan Lipka

Had it not been for Lipka's three years overseas, he might have been a teammate of Robinson's at Brooklyn in 1947. But it was not to be. Still, playing at Nashua had plenty of high points. "It was fantastic," he said. "We won everything. What a team we had." His teammates that year included Don Newcombe, Roy Campanella, Billy Demars, and Carl Furillo. He stayed with them for one and a half years before he was assigned to St. Paul. But Lipka refused to go and instead went to St. Hyacinthe, Quebec, to play in an outlaw league in 1948. Connie Creedon was playing there too. The pay wasn't bad, but when Pennell approached him about coming to Brantford, and offered better pay, almost on a par with what he could have expected to get in the majors, Lipka was hard pressed to turn him down. "I could make as much or more in Brantford with the full-time job," he said. Lipka was more than just another player. "He had natural ability," said Pennell. "He was hitting .330 and what's more, he always got the ball from third to first just in time. He would beat the slowest runner by a hair, and he would beat the fastest runner by a hair. But he always beat them."

Creedon, whom Lipka always remembered as being exceptionally strong, was in a similar situation. The fact that he went to Galt, along with the other major-leaguers, made them the team to beat, though Pennell and King were reasonably pleased with the talent they had assembled. "Galt had a Triple-A club, or better," said Pennell, "but we had better pitching in Gavey and Gibbs." What's more, the Red Sox had Lipka at third and Lockington in centre field. No matter which way you looked at it, Pennell and King had done wonders in just four years, building the Red Sox into contenders.

Other people around the league always wondered what drew Pennell and King together. "They were an odd couple," thought Waterloo's Ernie Goman. On the one hand, Pennell exuded class and deportment, while Mike was a little rough around the edges. Pennell, who was seven or eight years older than King, was always regarded as a steadying, rational force within the Intercounty. "He was always a gentleman," Murray said years later. When Murray was trying to get Satchel Paige and Josh Gibson to play in Galt, Pennell and King were going after Hank Aaron and Wilmer Fields.

"Mike was a remarkable person in his own way," said Pennell. "He used to get under Ernie's skin sometimes, but he loved the game and he was the ultimate sportsman. He did all he did for the sheer love of the game. He was just a lovable character and a dear friend of mine."

King was a born salesman, the kind who could never be out of a job long. Someone would snap him up if he was available. And he had the famed Irish sense of humour. One of his favourite expressions was "Never fought and was never defeated." Or "Stand back, let the dog see his hair." He used to go on forever when he was with Pennell or other good friends. If Pennell and King shared a love of the game, they also shared something else: both enjoyed the keen rivalry with Galt. When Galt played Brantford, it was always a particularly strong rivalry.

The two communities shared a lot of similarities: both developed along the banks of the Grand River, and both were almost exactly the same size. From the very beginning of their existence in the early 1800s, the rivalry was a natural one. Galt teams had always played Brantford teams. To be sure, Galt had important rivalries with Kitchener and Waterloo, as well as Guelph, all because of their close proximity, but in Brantford Galt was looking at itself. Neither town was content to lose to the other.

"Geographically the Intercounty was a dream come true," said Pennell. "We didn't have to go more than fifty miles to play any team, so from that perspective it was ideal, and still is." The teams were spread out over southwestern Ontario. "It was great," Pennell said. "A real compact league." But the thing that endeared the Intercounty to legions of fans was more than just the close proximity of all the teams. "It was community," he said. "That's what it was all about. It was a community thing." In Brantford everything centred around the downtown, just as it did in Galt. People would go downtown, mill around, and at times, thought Pennell, it was just like old home week. "You'd drive downtown, circle around, and see all your friends."

Bad blood had existed between Galt and Brantford since at least the late 1920s. Loyal Galt fans would always travel the eighteen miles to Brantford for road games, just as hundreds of Brantford fans would come to Galt for games at Dickson Park. "We used to call it the trolley league," remembered Pennell. "Same with hockey." The cars would be bumper to bumper on the road, but there would always be lots of people who simply hopped on the train to Galt and vice versa for games in Brantford. On such nights there was a steady stream of cars going from one town to the other. All people had to do was follow the road that runs along the Grand River for eighteen miles.

Fights between players on the two teams were not uncommon, nor were fights between Brantford and Galt fans in the stands. No matter which town the game was being played in, there were always plenty of fans from both sides in attendance. Sometimes police had to be called. More often than not, the police, some of whom were off duty and being paid by Murray or Pennell, would already be there. Experience had taught that it was just easier that way.

But perhaps the biggest dispute between the two cities took place in 1929. That was the year the Galt Terriers signed two Brantford boys, Bradshaw and Pickering. Gord Bradshaw, as a teenager, was regarded as the best ballplayer—softball or hardball—in Brantford. His best friend, Stan "Beaner" Pickering, was also highly regarded. The two formed a perfect battery: Bradshaw was the catcher; Pickering the pitcher. They were inseparable. "They were like ham and eggs," said Gord's younger brother Doug. "If you ever saw one you saw the other." Doug later played ball for the Red Sox, and he was a pretty good player, but nothing like his famous brother. "I was fair," he said, "but I wasn't as good as him. He was outstanding."

They were called the boy battery for the Red Sox in 1928. Wrote a Brantford sportswriter of the era: "His [Gord's] work thus far has been the outstanding feature of the local team. Without making Brad's head swell, it must be admitted he has all the earmarks of a big leaguer."

But when Bradshaw signed with Galt in 1929, Brantford fans were furious. To add insult to injury, Pickering went too. The Bell City had lost its gold-dust twins. The Red Sox had lost much more. "They complained like hell," said Doug. "A Brantford sporstwriter wrote that Galt had stolen the best two players from Brantford." Of course, it was true. But hard feelings or not, the fact was that Bradshaw and Pickering now wore Galt Terrier uniforms, and, as it turned out, would wear the Galt uniform the rest of their playing days. Brantford fans felt betrayed, though, curiously, they didn't hold it against the gold-dust twins. They were angry at Galt. Bradshaw and Pickering couldn't help it. Times were tough. Jobs were scarce. It was the start of the Great Depression, and when Galt's Robert Scroggins, owner of a prosperous shoe factory and, coincidentally, a member of the Terrier executive, offered Bradshaw a job, Bradshaw couldn't refuse. Job security meant everything in 1929. One of Bradshaw's colleagues at Scroggins in the mid-1930s was Laurie Brain. Brain, a good athlete in his own right, hadn't yet taken to sportswriting. He played on some company hockey teams with Bradshaw.

Beaner Pickering was also hired onto the Scroggins Shoe payroll. Their impact was immediate. Galt, already a strong team, would go on to win the Intercounty title that season. The husky Bradshaw—five-foot-ten, 210 pounds—caught every game, refusing to wash his uniform because he was going so good. Pickering pitched part of the final game that earned Galt the Intercounty title. And Brantford cursed Galt like they hadn't done in a century. "The thing about Gord," recalled Archie Stewart, the Terrier batboy in those years, "was he was a heavy guy, but he could run and he had a knack for stealing bases."

Galt went into the Ontario finals that year and quickly disposed of the Native Sons, winners of the Greenwood Park (Toronto) loop, before losing the Ontario championship series. Wrote a Toronto sportswriter: "The highly-touted Bradshaw, catcher for the Terriers, who the Leafs are after, made good with a vengeance. In his first appearance at the plate he drove one far over the right field fence for the circuit. He also drove two fouls out of the grounds. And he showed up well behind the plate."

My father had played ball just a few years before Bradshaw, and had passed on the Bradshaw legend to Jimmy and myself. When

Jimmy and I were growing up, Bradshaw was a kind of god, and we payed homage to his legend, in our prayers, by asking the Lord to make us like him.

If it wasn't apparent to Brantford fans in 1929 that Galt had snatched up the best hitter the Intercounty had ever seen, it became only too obvious the next season when Bradshaw hit .698, an Intercounty record that still stands. He won the Arthur Holle Trophy as the league's most valuable player, and the Oscar Hett Memorial Trophy as the league's outstanding hitter. Galt went all the way that year, winning the Intercounty title before taking the Ontario title. In 1932 they again won the coveted all-Ontario crown, beating Toronto's St. George. "We won the final game in Hamilton," Stewart recalled. "We had won here [in Galt] and they won in Toronto so we had to play a third game on a neutral field so we played at Scott Park in Hamilton. Bradshaw practically won the deciding game by himself. "The thing I remember about Gord in that game was we needed a run badly near the end of the game. He got on first, stole second, then stole third, and then stole home. He had them running in circles. He was quite a ballplayer." That autumn, seventeen seasons before Murray and Padden would appear on the baseball scene, there was a dinner at Galt's best and biggest hotel, the Iroquois, on Main Street, followed by a parade. It had been several years since they had won back-to-back Intercounty titles (1922–23), but since the league began operations in 1919, Galt had won the league title nine times and finished runner-up four times. There wasn't a Brantford fan alive who didn't hold Galt responsible for the fact that Galt had stolen the boy battery.

Bradshaw was always superstitious about washing his uniform. "There was no way you could get him to wash it as long as he was going well," said Stewart. "The other guys would clean their uniforms every few days, but Gord, being a catcher, he'd be black from head to toe." There was only one player on the team back then who would show up regularly with a clean uniform. George Weaver's wife would wash his uniform before every game. The kids used to call him Sleaver Weaver and one of them, Bob Hunter, maintained to the end of his life that Sleaver Weaver was responsible for the greatest catch ever made at Dickson Park. Hunter claimed that Weaver popped out of an irrigation ditch at the last moment and caught what appeared to be a sure home run. The catch had ended the game and gave Galt the Intercounty pennant.

Our town longed for baseball. A picture of the Galt Terriers playing St. Thomas in the OBA semi-finals in 1924 at Dickson Park reveals a park filled to the brim with thousands of fans. They packed the grandstand, stood twenty deep down the first base line, lined the outfield beside and behind their cars, and filled the left-field hill for four hundred feet. The picture, one of the most famous in Galt's history, was taken by photographer Elliot Law, on September 13, 1924. Another Law picture taken of the Terriers the summer before shows a similar scene at Riverside Park in Preston. The entire field is surrounded by fans. Years later, Stewart, who was at both games—he was about seven years old—sent his copy of the Dickson Park picture to Toronto Blue Jays play-by-play radio man Tom Cheek. He wanted to show him just how popular the game was in the heart of southern Ontario so many years ago. American observers generally felt that baseball was an American game and that Canadians knew little about it. Canadian fans were quiet during games, they thought, because they didn't know the game. Few people seemed to realize that the game had roots in Canada as deep as those in the United States, nor did they know that the Senior Intercounty Baseball Association was Canada's premiere—and oldest—league. Stewart never heard back from Cheek, even though he asked for the return of the picture (he'd sent a stamped self-addressed envelope).

The Intercounty league has long suffered from a lack of respect. Even the Canadian Baseball Hall of Fame didn't seem to know much about the league. They had information on Ruth when he had begun his professional career in Toronto—they even had the first ball he hit for a home run in Toronto. They had names and statistics on Canadians who had made it to the majors, including Galt's own Rob Ducey, who broke in with the Blue Jays in 1987, but they had virtually nothing about the Intercounty or those strong Terrier teams from the early part of the century. It was a shame, believed the late George Heggie, a former Terrier player and one of Galt's best-known sportsmen. Heggie had visited the Canadian Baseball Hall of Fame and was disappointed at not seeing anything about those vaunted Galt teams of Intercounty fame.

Today only a few old-timers can remember that 1930 season when Bradshaw hit .698. Teammate Clare Hoffman was next in the batting race with a .400 average that season, while Wilbur Kress, another Galt boy, was the league's top pitcher, with Pickering right behind. That year, Bradshaw hit nearly .500 in the playoffs. The pro scouts were watching. Charles Good, in his "Sports Parade" column, wrote that Baltimore of the International League had offered Bradshaw a contract for the 1931 season. But the Toronto Maple Leafs, another

International League club, were also interested, though in the opinion of their chief scout, Bill O'Hara, Bradshaw needed some more schooling before he would be able to play Class AAA ball.

But Oscar Hett, a long-time umpire and a big Bradshaw booster, thought Bradshaw had all the tools, even then. Good reported that Hett thought Bradshaw had "very little to learn and should be ready to break into fast company after one trip around the International circuit." Preston's Tim Turow, later president of the Intercounty, recalled watching Bradshaw play. "It was unbelievable," said Turow. "He was really something. That year he couldn't do anything wrong." And though the Intercounty has long been ignored by Americans, those who knew baseball in Canada regarded it as the best amateur senior league in the country.

Only eleven years before Bradshaw's record-breaking season, a man destined to be prime minister of Canada one day, Lester Pearson, played for the Guelph Maple Leafs. Pearson was a pretty fair ballplayer in his day, though he always said he wasn't as good as his brother, who also played for Guelph back then. The year was 1919 and it was the inaugural summer of the Intercounty. Galt and Guelph were charter members. It is that history of the league, and its high calibre of play, that makes the league so important, said Pennell. He noted that the Intercounty's history is as old as any league's in Canada, and he believes the league is the oldest continuously operated baseball league in Canada.

"Boys," commanded my father one evening as we sat around the radio listening to the Tiger feed in the late 1930s, "there isn't a better league in the country."

"But Dad," answered Jimmy before I could get a word in, "it's not the major leagues."

Dad paused and interminable seconds passed, but we listened, the both of us, for we knew he was about to speak.

"It is Canada's major league, and long years before the Intercounty was around, they were playing ball in Dickson Park and at Woodstock. Long before."

*John Lockington, Wilmer
"The Great" Fields, and
Justice Pennell*

Pennell and the Prime Minister

We should have called ourselves the Nine-and-a-Halfs.

– Larry Pennell

IN THE SPRINGTIME, WITH THE PROMISE OF WARM WEATHER, Pennell and King had come to the conclusion that 1949 would be the best Brantford season since the war. Already they had Clayton Cooper lined up to catch. Cooper had a strong arm, and he could hit. And, in addition to pitcher Alf Gavey, the Hamilton native whom Pennell had recruited after arm trouble forced his release from the Cardinal organization, they hoped to use Gibbs, a junior just back from a stint in the pros. Normie Hann would play second, Art Hillman left field, Lipka, who'd played Triple-A with the Montreal Royals, would play third, and there were two more pitchers, Frank "Nig" Parker and Harrison Fisher, who would complement Gavey and Gibbs. And centre fielder Lockington would anchor the outfield on speed alone, between left fielder Harry Mooradian and George Carruth in right field.

Clearly, the Red Sox of 1949 promised to be a good team, but what was surprising was that they were a bunch of homebrews. Three years earlier, in May of 1946, Brantford had been readmitted into the Senior Intercounty Intermediate Division only a week prior to the start of the season. Galt had a team of veterans in the same division called the Galt Vets, as did Hespeler and several other smaller communities. The war had just ended and Pennell was late in getting things organized. There were no players, no team, no uniforms, but Pennell was born to organize. "It came to me very early," said Pennell, "that I was a manager, not a player."

But in June of 1946 the Intercounty had already drawn up a schedule. Pennell made a late application to the Intercounty—the season was set to open in one week—and it was accepted, probably because of the difficulties immediately following the war, and partly due to the fact that Brantford simply belonged in the Intercounty. "Galt and Brantford games were always the biggest rivalry," Pennell would later recall. "It was like the Boston Red Sox and the New York Yankees," he said. League president Otto Manske said they'd have to revamp the schedule to accommodate Brantford, but they'd do it. Now all Pennell and the Brantford people had to do was sign some players and get some uniforms. Neither would be easy on such late notice, but Pennell was undeterred.

Lockington, who'd played with London while attending the University of Western Ontario during the war, put Pennell and King onto the trail of some uniforms at the London Armoury. Uniforms were in short supply immediately after the war; for years, all materials had been earmarked for military use, and there was a delay in getting things back to normal after the war. They had tried getting uniforms in Toronto and Montreal and elsewhere, but without success. Now Pennell spoke to someone at the London Armoury by phone, and was told they had eleven uniforms that Brantford could buy for $100. But time was running short. On the day of Brantford's season opener, King and Lockington drove to London to pick up the uniforms. Ten tops were found but only nine bottoms. Later they would all joke that they'd started the season with nine and a half uniforms. "We should have called ourselves the Nine-and-a-Halfs," said Pennell. Some players wore old uniforms from other leagues. One wore an Alberta uniform. The important thing was they had enough players to field a team, and each of them was in some uniform, even if it didn't say Brantford across the front.

If uniforms were hard to come by that summer, so too was baseball equipment. When the first few practices were held that spring, there was virtually no equipment. I remember one player had two bats, the only bats we had, and he had to leave practice one time with his bats and that ended the practice. Pennell had bats on order, but it took time for them to arrive. In any case, King and Lockington arrived back at the ballpark on Opening Day just half an hour before game time.

"We opened at home on the 24th of May that year against Galt," recalled Pennell. And perhaps not surprisingly, they lost. That was in the morning. That afternoon they travelled to Hespeler and won their first game of the post-war era, which helped to buoy spirits. During that season opener in 1946 someone in the stands said he could play, so King, a former catcher, took him behind the stands to see what he had. King quickly determined he didn't have what it took, but the mere fact that he was willing to give him a chance to show his talent was an indication of just how desperate Brantford was for players.

Like Pennell, many of the Brantford players had been in the war. Pennell, who was born in Brantford in 1915, enlisted in the air force in his final year of law school at Osgoode Hall. Pennell's father had been superintendent of Brantford Malleable Iron, a U.S. concern owned by a man named Sherman. But Sherman believed the future was in steel and went on to found Dominion Foundry and Steel Company, or Dofasco, in Hamilton, which became the largest steel company in Canada.

Sherman persuaded Mr. Pennell to move to Hamilton and work at Dofasco. Larry was two years old at the time, but not long afterward Mr. Pennell developed silicosis from being around the furnaces for so many years, and had to leave. Seeking fresh air, the family moved to the country near Grimsby. Sherman was kind enough to give him a modest pension.

Larry did most of his growing up on that farm on the Niagara Escarpment, but they had relatives still in Brantford and every summer, when he was old enough, he worked at Brantford Cordage, sponsors of the Intercounty baseball team and the largest maker of binder twine anywhere in the British Empire in the 1930s.

Baseball had always been in his mind. So had hockey. He loved sports, though he had come to the realization early on that he would never make it as a player. He played various sports in his youth, but there was no dream, as exists in the minds of the most talented youngsters, of one day playing in the majors or the NHL. Still, he knew he wanted to be involved in sport. As a youngster he would sometimes skip school in the afternoon during the World Series and head over to the train station where the telegraph office was, and where crowds would gather around to hear the reports. There he would get the latest news from the game hot off the wire.

After graduating from high school he enrolled at Hamilton's McMaster University, taking a B.A. in economics and history. "I had a shallow purse in those days," he said. Times were tough. So he boarded in Hamilton. "Those were the golden years at McMaster." Paris, Ontario, native Syl Apps, one of Canada's greatest all-round athletes and a future Hall of Fame hockey player, was his classmate at McMaster, just a year ahead of him. Pennell remembered how Apps, whose grandfather lived in Galt, would run back punts during football games, or play on one of the greatest hockey lines he ever saw with Carl Liscombe, a Galt native, and Toe Blake with the Hamilton Tigers senior team.

It was during Apps's time at McMaster that Toronto Maple Leaf boss Conn Smythe first heard about him. Smythe went to see him play football one afternoon, and Apps looked unstoppable. Pennell was at the game. Smythe was so impressed with this tough, talented football player, that he went down and spoke to him after the game, asking him to play for the Leafs. But Apps had other plans. He was a gifted pole vaulter, the best in Canada, and wanted to stay with it until the Olympics in 1936. Smythe said he could understand that. They made an agreement that once the Olympics were finished Apps would come play for the Leafs.

Apps, said Pennell, was not only immensely talented as an athlete, but was a gentleman. He never swore and was admired by virtually everyone. Years later Pennell was talking with Hap Day, Apps's former coach with the Leafs, and Day told Pennell that Apps rarely got mad, yet he was a fierce competitor. One game someone had given him a high stick and broken some of his teeth and Apps came back muttering, "Darn, why'd he have to go and do that."

But Smythe related another time when he was flagrantly hit and he retaliated in no uncertain terms by flattening the guy. He was a clean and gifted hockey player, but no one was going to get away with anything against him. When it came to toughness, he was as tough as they come, which was what Smythe had seen, and liked, on the gridiron. Pennell never forgot him either. Many years later, when Apps died, Pennell wrote a glowing tribute to his friend in the McMaster alumni magazine.

And shortly afterward, he visited Apps's grave in Galt's Mountview Cemetery, just a stone's throw from Dickson Park. Apps had known the park as a youngster and once told his daughter Joanne Flint how much of an impact the park and the old Terrier teams had on his boyhood. He and his grandfather would take in games there on a regular basis.

After McMaster Pennell entered law school. It was the fall of 1938, and money was still tight, so he would hitchhike to school in Toronto each Monday, waking up early and heading off for Toronto at 5 A.M. from near Grimsby, suitcase in hand. He would return home each Friday afternoon. In Toronto he paid two dollars for an attic room. It wasn't fancy, but it was all he needed. He bought his own food on a shoestring. Indeed, it cost him just $5.50 a week to attend law school, food and lodging included. Meals were twenty-five cents. He would spend half of each day going to law school, the other half working for a big Bay Street law firm, White, Rule and Bristol, solicitors for, among others, the Imperial Bank of Canada. He had one suit and wore it every weekday of the year, keeping a single dime in his pocket at all times for emergencies. He couldn't even afford law books, so he spent most of his free time in the library.

Friday afternoons, as soon as the last lecture ended, he'd catch the streetcar out on Queen Street in front of Osgoode Hall, and take the Longbranch to the Queen Elizabeth highway, where he would walk and hitchhike, sometimes not arriving home until 2 A.M. "But that didn't bother me," he said. "I was just so happy to be in law school during the Depression when four out of every five people had no jobs."

He wrote his final exams in January of 1941 and then went into the air force, having already enlisted before writing his last exam. He spent the next four and a half years as a navigator, first on the east coast, and then overseas in North Africa, where he was attached to an RAF squadron (he was RCAF). There, in the heat of Africa, he organized a fastball league with three teams including an American one. "I got some of the natives to play to fill out the roster," Pennell said. They had a ball. "They would roll and rock in laughter at the game. They got a lot of fun out of it." His wife had sent him his glove, but most of the other equipment was provided by the Americans. "Our team won and I declared that we were the champions of Africa." From then on he could rightfully say he played on a continental championship team.

The Allies would have won the war without him, he figured, but regardless, he had served his country when he was needed and was discharged in September of 1945, returning to Brantford in late October. Back home he took a refresher course at law school, and then joined his dear old friend from McMaster, Sam Wyatt, to form the law firm of Pennell and Wyatt. "I did all the court work and he did all the administrative work like real estate."

The following spring Pennell and King got the Red Sox back into the Intercounty, though it was in the intermediate, not senior, ranks. Galt, behind the pitching of Cracky Liscombe (a brother of Carl Liscombe), welcomed them back by beating them on that opening day back in 1946. Liscombe pitched shutout ball for eight innings but had to leave after suffering a freak injury while at bat. The ball had hit his bat and hand and he wasn't able to throw.

One season later, in 1947, the summer Galt installed lights at Dickson Park, the Red Sox moved up into the senior league, and by the spring of 1949, Pennell and King were eager to see what kind of a team they had. It might not win any pennants, but it would be competitive. During that time Pennell was also active in hockey, having begun the Big Four league with St. Catharines, London, and Oshawa the year he moved back to Brantford. He and King would devote all their spare time to baseball in the summers and hockey in the winters, much like Waterloo's Ernie Goman was doing.

But, increasingly, Pennell was spending much of his time in the courtroom, and that, coupled with his involvement in Brantford's sporting community, made him the best-known man in town. He was always busy, and he was so well known that his wife, Anne, would tell him he couldn't go shopping with her because it would take them too long. Every minute someone would come up and talk to him. In addition to his law practice and courtroom work—he successfully defended eleven people charged with murder, including getting two death-row convictions overturned on appeal—he was coach of his son's peewee baseball team, president of the Optimist Clubs of Ontario, chairman of the Brantford Suburban Planning Board, and chairman of the Brantford Parks and Recreation Board. All this in addition to his involvement with the Red Sox and Brantford hockey. When someone would inevitably ask how he managed to do it all, he had a simple reply. "It's easy," he would say. "You just work eighteen hours a day and sleep six and it's no problem at all."

Pennell was a well-read, intelligent, and erudite man and was often asked to address various groups. Through it all his wife, Anne (née Andrews), stood by him. She was always there for him. Later, with two children, and Pennell running in three federal elections in four years in the early 1960s, his wife carried the burden of raising the children. Though he was in Ottawa through the week, he'd catch the train back to Brantford every Friday and return on the midnight train to Ottawa each Monday morning. He stayed in government for seven years, once serving as Canada's solicitor general and attorney general at the same time for eighteen months. Through it all he maintained his love for sports.

Ever since his father and uncle took him to see Brantford play a ball game in the old Michigan-Ontario League, Pennell had loved the game. When Toronto Maple Leafs baseball owner Jack Kent Cooke asked him, years later, to come work for him, Pennell seriously considered it. "But I loved my law practice, and with Cooke, I could have been general manager in a couple of years, or fired in two weeks. You never knew." So he and his wife chose stability. The community of Brantford was the better for it.

Throughout all the busy years Anne was, as Pennell would describe her, "God's most precious gift. She's one in a million. Without her I wouldn't have been anything." She encouraged him in anything he wanted to do, which included going to Ottawa in 1962 as the first Liberal Member of Parliament from Brant-Haldimand elected in more than 100 years. He shone in Ottawa under Prime Minister Lester Pearson, just as he had distinguished himself in Brantford and around the Intercounty.

He admired Pearson. The two got along well. They had baseball in common, among other things. Both were avid fans, and Pearson had even played in the Intercounty—third base with Guelph—that inaugural season back in 1919. Pearson had just returned from World War I when the Intercounty began operations.

Years later Milt Dunnell remembered Pearson's love for the game. "When the Expos first came to Montreal they made Lester an honorary president of the team," he said. "We were at Daytona Beach—I used to go to the Expos camp before the Blue Jays came along—and Lester spent a week as their guest." Both Pearson and Seagram's Sam Bronfman (who had 83 on his jersey) were out on the field with ball caps on. "Lester told me that his brother was the better player," Dunnell said, after asking him if he ever thought he could have made it to the majors. "You know," Pearson said, "actually the big baseball player in our family was not me but my brother Fred. He was an excellent player." Fred and Mike both played for Guelph in 1919. Dunnell recalled how Pearson loved those spring days with the Expos. "He was out there enjoying himself. He was a hell of a nice guy and he loved the atmosphere." The description was equally applicable to Pennell, who found a similar excitement in politics.

When Pennell was first elected as a Member of Parliament, he took a sizable wage reduction. As a lawyer he was earning $26,000 a year; as an MP he earned $10,000. But he didn't enter politics to make money. To make matters worse, he had to keep an apartment in Ottawa, where he roomed with Eugene Whelan and Maple Leaf star Red Kelly. "It was hard going," he said. "It was quite a financial setback for me but I don't regret it. It was just a wonderful experience for me."

In 1965 Pearson asked him to become the solicitor general and Pennell accepted without hesitation. He knew he would have to make some tough decisions, but he was up for it. "It was a real honour," he said. Soon after, when the minister of justice became ill, he took on the attorney generalship as well. That lasted eighteen months.

There were plenty of happenings to remember from those years in Ottawa, but he recalled one incident when the Liberals were two votes short and Kelly, still playing hockey with the Leafs, was a key man in the final tally. They couldn't afford to have any absences when votes were taken, so one night Kelly had to stay late for a vote in the House of Commons on the night of a game against the Montreal Canadiens at the Forum in Montreal. A car was waiting outside Parliament Hill to take him to the airport immediately following the vote. But the vote was later than usual, and when it was finally over, Kelly rushed to the car, then to the airport, hopped on a charter plane and arrived in Montreal, where another car was waiting to take him to the arena. When he arrived the game had just started. He was lacing up his skates while the first shifts were out. It was the Stanley Cup finals, and the Leafs went on to win hockey's most coveted prize that night. But Kelly couldn't rest. After the game he had to catch the train back to Ottawa, to be on Parliament Hill the next morning, but the train was delayed several hours because of an FLQ scare. Kelly, exhausted, walked up to their Ottawa apartment just as the fresh-faced Pennell and Whelan were walking out the door to go to the hill. They passed each other saying, "Good morning."

Kelly was in terrific shape, said Pennell. "I would see him do one hundred push-ups before going to the Hill in the morning. I'd be tired just watching him. I don't know how he could do it [juggle two demanding schedules], but we needed him. We needed every vote to survive and he didn't let us down."

It was there, in Ottawa, that Pearson would bring in a television set to the prime minister's office during the World Series. Sometimes Pennell would be there too for a spell. Baseball was in their blood.

It was Pennell's view that Pearson was often misunderstood by the general public, and "the public had the wrong perception of him. The man I knew was just a great fellow, very conscious of the public purse.

But the man I knew disappeared when he got on the platform. It just wasn't in his makeup [to be a great speaker]. He would not be able to rouse emotions, but rather tried to reason. He had an open door to all back benchers, too open, I thought. And he had great sympathy for the underdog, but it didn't show through in public." Besides, said Pennell, "I always thought that if a fellow is a sports fan he can't be too bad." And Pearson was a sports fan, in addition to being a former ballplayer. During the World Series he would have the ball game on. Although he would be working, he would glance at the TV from time to time. As a senior cabinet minister Pennell was often present. "He was a great baseball buff," said Pennell. On one such occasion Pearson looked over to Pennell: "Oh, but Larry, you were a manager. I was a player." Pennell was quick to reply, "Yes, Mr. Prime Minister, but you're the manager now and I'm the player."

"He loved baseball," said Pennell. "He fell in love with it young and he never lost his love for it. I was in his office at times, and he'd be working with the TV on. It wasn't a case of him just sitting down. He'd have a pad in front of him and a pencil and correspondence he'd be dealing with at the time, or he'd be writing a memo. He'd be working but he'd keep an eye on the TV. A few times I happened to go in and he'd break and we'd watch it for probably an inning and then I'd be out." That was about 1964 or 1965, just before Montreal got a major-league franchise, and more than a decade before Toronto got the Blue Jays. Later, when Toronto played Montreal in a special exhibition game each summer, it was called the Pearson Cup, in memory of the former prime minister who had such a keen interest in the game.

Pearson died in 1972, about five years after his retirement from federal politics. "He was a great fellow," said Pennell. "The most democratic man I ever met. He never stood on ceremony. He had a great mind and tremendous wit." The description fits Pennell, too.

Pennell was always easy to get along with. Others found him well versed in many fields, intelligent, warm, and a gentleman. He and John Diefenbaker, though they were from two different political parties, always got along well. "He always treated me with a great deal of respect and I treated him with respect. I really cherished that." Part of Pennell's personal success with others stemmed directly from the influence of his father. "My father taught me not to quarrel," Pennell explained. "I have always refused to quarrel. I've gotten mad, and I've made others angry, but I have always thought that if you can't reason with somebody, you're not going to change his mind. I've believed in that all my life, as a lawyer, in sports, and as a judge." He credited that philosophy, or a large part of it, to his father. "I never once saw my father get in a quarrel." If someone can't agree, in the end, Pennell would simply say sorry, and walk away. "You've got to respect others and treat them with respect." Others sometimes abused him, but they eventually came around if he treated them with respect. They would realize they got angry and blew their cool. "I can't recall arguing with anyone," he said, "I really can't. I've reasoned with people, not always successfully." The same applied at home with his wife, who he had been married to, by 2000, for fifty-eight years. Early on his father taught him to say, "You were right, darling," and mean it. If reason didn't work at first, finally, at least at home, he would concede. "It's worked," he said not long after his eightieth birthday.

But in Parliament, others might go to him and say he was wrong in a decision he made. "You may be right," he would say, "but I have to make the decision and I've made it."

Once, when he was first running for office, he knocked on someone's door and got a surprise. The man said he had never voted Liberal. Indeed, he was a staunch Conservative. "But your father was the finest man I ever knew so I'll vote for you. This isn't a vote for you, but for your father." The man had once worked for the elder Pennell. Those words Larry never forgot. "That gave me a great lift. That was the nicest thing I ever heard in all my campaigning."

But politics was still years away when Pennell and King arranged to field a Red Sox team in '46. By 1949, their second season of senior ball, things were looking up. One reason was the signing of Gavey.

He had played for Hamilton in the PONY League before signing with the Cardinals. A Cardinal scout had gone to see a PONY League game but had noticed a pitcher playing softball on an adjoining diamond. "My God," the scout thought, "a fellow who throws that hard could make it in hardball. Have you ever considered hardball?" He signed him on the spot. Gavey then went into the Cardinal farm system, eventually playing AA in Savannah, before developing arm problems. "He had all the earmarks of a major-leaguer," believed Pennell. But it was not to be. By the time Brantford obtained him he could throw only once a week, but when he threw he invariably struck out ten or twelve batters and pitched exceptionally well. "He could throw hard, but only if he had enough rest," said Pennell. With Gibbs, the two made up one of the most feared one-two pitching combinations in the Intercounty that year. Gibbs, too, was built for pitching. We all called him Big Bill Gibbs; he was six-foot-five and two hundred pounds.

Like Murray and Goman, Pennell wouldn't hesitate to import players. "I always figured I would lose more money on a bad team than I would on a good team," he reasoned. So he would try to get the best players he could get. In the early 1950s that meant bringing in former Homestead Gray star Wilmer Fields. It was Pennell who gave him the epithet "the Great." Said Pennell, "He was very good, so I started building him up in the media as 'Wilmer "the Great" Fields.' And people ate it up."

A couple of seasons after Fields came to Brantford, the Toronto Maple Leafs of the International League showed an interest in acquiring him. "Jack Kent Cooke owned the Leafs in those days and he called me," said Pennell. "He asked if he could take Wilmer Fields." Cooke pressed Pennell awfully hard, but Pennell said Brantford wasn't interested in losing its star. Nevertheless, Pennell agreed to talk to Fields about the offer. Fields wasn't anxious to go to Toronto. "But then we talked some more and decided that if he was going to go anywhere, this was his break into professional baseball." Fields hit .297 that season. "He was a little old to be going then," said Pennell later. "Wilmer, like thousands who'd come before Robinson, never got a fair chance." Pennell thought Fields lacked only one thing. "He lacked speed," said Pennell. "He was a big, towering chap, about six-foot-three. He could hit well and field well, and he also played third base, but he didn't have great lateral movement. But he had a wonderful personality and was very popular with the Brantford people. He was well-spoken and was a real addition, a real plus for the team."

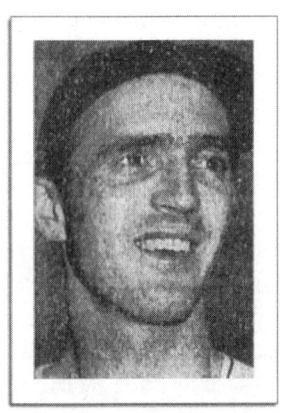

John Lockington

Fields always maintained he didn't get that much more salary in Toronto than he had gotten in Brantford when all was said and done. Many people thought that if Fields had gone to Toronto in his prime, like the year 1946 when he posted sixteen wins against one loss pitching for the Homestead Grays, he could have gone on to the majors. But his prime playing days had come and gone before Robinson broke the colour barrier.

In Galt in 1949 Goody Rosen, said Pennell, always had that prestige of having played in the majors. "Just making it into the majors was awfully tough back then," he noted. "The openings weren't there.

It was a closed system with old-time players always fighting off new players, which made it tough on newcomers trying to break in."

Regardless, Fields was recognized as a great baseball player, one of the best to ever play in the Intercounty. Before Pennell signed him, few other blacks had played in the league. Shelton in Galt had been one. And even before Shelton, Pennell had signed a black player. In 1948 he signed Abbie Scott, a black from Chatham, Ontario, not far from the breeding ground of future Hall of Famer Ferguson Jenkins. Scott, a second baseman, got upset one game when the opposing team put on a double steal and their catcher didn't throw the ball to second. When the inning was over Scott rushed back to the bench. "Why didn't you throw the ball to second?" he asked the catcher. "There was a slow runner and I could have gotten him."

"There was no one covering second," said the catcher.

"No one covering second?" said an incredulous Scott. "Why, I was there. Are you colour blind?"

That story would always bring a tear of laughter to Pennell's eyes.

Another black player had played for Brantford in the early 1930s, and Guelph had a black player by the name of Hap Lawson in the mid-1930s. But the most famous player who almost came to play for Pennell was a young black by the name of Hank Aaron. Pennell and King had gone to Buffalo one night in the early 1950s to see a Negro League game at Offerman Stadium. Indianapolis was playing Kansas City and 10,000 people were on hand to see it. Pennell and King were two of only about half a dozen whites at the game. One of the young players, a well-built kid of about sixteen or seventeen, hit a home run and impressed them enough for them to try to sign him. But when they approached him they got some menacing looks from the others. "What do you want?" someone asked them. "We're just talking to a friend," Pennell said. They tried to convince Aaron to come to Canada. "We'll even give you the money before you leave."

So young Aaron said he'd think on it in the time remaining before the bus was scheduled to leave. The bus was leaving at 6 P.M. "We'll give you two hundred dollars U.S. before you even leave and if you don't like it, you can keep the money."

"I'm inclined to come," he told them, though he was young, hesitant, and had never been to Canada. But Pennell and King had gotten held up dickering with another player, and arrived just as the bus was boarding. By then it was too late. "If you had come a little sooner I'd have left with you," said Aaron. But his teammates and coach had talked him out of it. "Geez, they've been speaking to me. I told them

I was going and they really talked me out of it. I was tempted though." Years later, Brantford's John Lockington spoke to Aaron and Aaron still remembered it.

Perhaps the best player Pennell ever signed was Bob Thurman. "He left us on Friday and by Monday was playing with Cincinnati." Not long afterward he hit four pinch-hit home runs to tie the major-league record. "That was in '53," said Pennell. "Imagine, the major leagues stealing a player from us."

In the summer of 1949, Pennell and King had high hopes for their Red Sox. Normie Hann, a big, rangy player, would be their coach that season. Hann had played with Stratford the previous summer and had some Double A experience in the Southern Association. "We asked him to take on the coaching duties, even though he was brought in as a player," said Pennell. But the team wasn't playing like a team in the early going, and there seemed to be something not quite right. "It was an internal thing with some of the players and as management we had to make a decision," Pennell said. So he had a talk with Hann and told him they were going to relieve him of his coaching duties but they wanted him to continue as a player. "He was a good hard worker," Pennell said. "He was slow of foot but he could hit. The ball would always seem to go long when he was up." Hann had no hard feelings. The Red Sox would continue to pay him what they had agreed to pay him as a playing coach.

By mid-season, Pennell and King made the decision to get Speed Cotter to coach. Cotter was agreeable. "We thought we had a club that could win," said Pennell, "but there were some altercations between some of the players, and we thought, for the good of the club, we needed Cotter to coach." Cotter was relaxed, easygoing, soft-spoken, and never swore. He was a little older than Hann, and well-spoken. "Speed just worked out from the day he came," Pennell said. "We wanted harmony on the club. That was the big thing." They finally got it with Cotter.

Soon after they'd decided on Cotter, Pennell and King called a player's meeting to tell them of the change. "Anyone who is not happy with it, we'll give him his release," Pennell told his players. Big Angelo Torti, a Brantford boy who pitched and played outfield, stood up. "I'll take my release," he said. He looked around the room and saw he was the only one standing. "What," he said, astonished, "no one else?" Torti was standing alone and was thunderstruck that no one else had spoken up. Earlier several other players had said they'd do likewise, but when the moment of truth came, he stood alone. He later told

Pennell, "I knew I had booted it when no one else moved." So he left, but was back wearing a Red Sox uniform the following season.

Pennell always liked to tell the story that the first major-league all-star game in Canada was not played, as commonly believed, in Toronto in 1993—an earlier all-star game took place in Montreal in the summer of 1982—but rather, in Brantford in the autumn of 1950. The game actually took place on October 16 that year at Agricultural Park, and saw a group of American League all-stars play a team of National League all-stars. The game had been scheduled for Toronto, but the field was unplayable. The following day was a travel day when they were going to Buffalo. Pennell got a phone call from the Toronto promoter handling the game. "Larry," he said, "for five thousand dollars we'll bring them in for an afternoon. The players have all agreed."

Pennell welcomed them with open arms. "I said yes on short notice and put it on the radio and we filled the park with five thousand people. At a dollar apiece we broke even." The promoter gave each team $2,500. "They were all there," said Pennell. "All the stars." One player, Jerry Coleman of the New York Yankees, spent some time with a group from the Institute for the Blind in Brantford. "He went up and talked with the blind in the stands," recalled Pennell. "It was a real nice gesture." Also on hand that day were Dom DiMaggio of the Boston Red Sox, Cleveland's Early Wynn, and Brooklyn's Duke Snider and Gil Hodges. "They made those barnstorming trips a number of times," noted Milt Dunnell. "I remember talking to Dom DiMaggio one time when he was up here. They used to get together after the World Series and make extra money playing exhibition games," he said.

"What the hell do you get out of it?" Dunnell asked DiMaggio. "Why do you guys do it?"

"The money," he replied.

It was because of promoters like Pennell, Murray, and Goman that the Intercounty entered into what Pennell called the Halcyon Years. Big stars drew big crowds. "You lose less money with a good club than you would with a poor club," explained Pennell. In other words, if a club paid name players big bucks, they would lose less money than if they tried to hire run-of-the-mill players and pay them skimpy salaries. "It proved to be true," said Pennell. "People responded to the quality. A dollar a game in those days wasn't bad at all, really. It was first-class entertainment. You couldn't get better baseball, and there was no major-league team in Toronto of course. And there was no TV, but there were lots of community rivalries."

Of course, the biggest rivalry was between Galt and Brantford. Nearly a decade after the Terriers snatched Bradshaw and Pickering from Brantford, Gord's younger brother, Doug, began playing second base for the Red Sox. The Bradshaws were a family of ballplayers. One of the brothers, who died early, was reputed to be even better than Gord.

Pennell remembered seeing Doug Bradshaw, in the early 1950s, come cursing back to the Brantford dugout after striking out. He was fuming. "That pitcher's stupid," he would say. "Just stupid. What a stupid pitcher. Stupid."

"Why do you say that?" asked Pennell.

"Because he blew two fastballs by me and then threw a curve. He should have thrown another fastball. I couldn't touch them. I wasn't expecting a curve."

"But Doug," said Pennell, "he still struck you out just the same."

"Yeah, but he's a stupid pitcher," repeated Bradshaw. "He shouldn't have thrown a curve. I couldn't touch his fastball. Why didn't he just throw another fastball? Because he's stupid."

In many ways, Pennell and Murray, of different temperament and style, were accomplishing the same thing. They were each fielding quality teams and they were creating a great deal of interest in the Intercounty league. "Gus was a very enthusiastic promoter," said Pennell. "And he was very good at the meetings. He wasn't in it for any possible monetary returns. But he was like anybody else—he didn't want to lose money. He put a good product on the field and he enhanced the league a great deal." Pennell recalled several hastily called Intercounty meetings at Murray's store. "Those were fiery days back then. There were a lot of heated arguments. Oh, it was wild and hot going with all the owners and operators of the clubs."

It may have been wild that summer. The stakes had never been bigger. But things had not gone well for Brantford early on. All that changed when Speed Cotter came to coach the team in mid-season. Brantford still had an uphill climb, even though they had managed to take the Intercounty lead at one point early on, but Pennell and King were confident that their team, composed predominantly of homebrews that season, would be competitive. Galt looked like the class of the league, but in baseball, as in many other sports, anything could happen. "It's a game where you never know if you're going to win," said Pennell. "You may have the best club but somehow fate would be against you. Sometimes a team will win it when they shouldn't, but it all levels out, I guess." As the summer wore on and Galt's Murderer's

Row began dominating the league hitting statistics, Pennell and King were hoping that somehow Galt would fade. But they had more pressing concerns. They had to make the playoffs. The only time when Pennell wasn't at the ballpark, it seemed, was when he had a case to present in court.

So the summer of 1949 began taking shape for the Red Sox and Pennell after Cotter came on board. It was only mid-June. The dog days of summer were still to come, and with them the last half of the season. Sure Galt looked strong, but then, Brantford didn't look bad. There were still many games to be played before any pennant was won. Brantford players never lost sight of that fact, nor did they come to think of themselves as anything less than the best team in the league. It was necessary for them to have confidence in themselves, even if few others did. And then there was little six-year-old Rich Mirco, already a diehard Brantford fan, sitting up in the stands along the first baseline. He was a believer. He honestly thought he could help his Red Sox by sheer willpower alone. They were the champs in his book. Or, at least, they would be the champs. Just wait till the end of the season, he thought.

The legendary Gord Bradshaw

Rivalry and Legends

Legends of ball games and players were around long before I was born. There had been baseball before the Terriers, though I always found this hard to believe. But I remember old-timers telling me, when I was young, about famous players who worked their magic at Dickson Park in the 1800s. I never wrote a word of it down, for I was young and too busy playing ball myself. Now their stories are forever lost.

EVEN BY THE SPRING OF 1949, BRADSHAW'S LEGEND AT DICKSON Park still haunted the place, and although he never had another season comparable to the .698 season of 1930, he was a consistent .300-plus hitter. With him catching, Galt won three straight Intercounty titles beginning in 1929. "I'm eighty now," said Pennell in the summer of 1994, "but I can remember him well. He would have made professional baseball at the upper levels without a doubt."

Stan Markarian, who moved away from Galt to Detroit as a boy— he later became a sportswriter for the *Galt Evening Reporter*—was sixteen years old in the summer of 1930. He spent part of his summer holidays in town that year, and it was while he was here that he first heard about Bradshaw. "Naturally, as a baseball buff, I was anxious to see him," he wrote. "Along with a boyhood chum I meandered over to Dickson Park for a look-see at the Intercounty's new super catcher-slugger. En route my chum said, 'Better make sure there's a safe place to watch the game. The way that guy Bradshaw hammers the ball around the ball park it would be safer to look through peepholes in a steel fence.'"

Markarian's friend said that "Bradshaw punched holes in the scoreboard at right field, tore bark off the maple trees in centre field, wrecked the cow pens on the left-field embankment, smashed windshields of cars parked around centre field, and even loosened the structure of the grandstand with foul balls." Markarian, the young Tiger fan from Detroit, was spellbound. "As I stood in the old bandstand situated between home plate and first base, I, like some big-time scout, watched every move he made." At the end of the game Markarian turned to his friend: "What the heck is that guy doing in this league? He should be in the majors." Markarian could see him fitting in well with the Tigers.

But Bradshaw never turned pro, something that remains a mystery to this day. Gord's son Bob was only ten when his father died suddenly of a stroke in the early 1950s. He had never really seen his dad play in his heyday, but he grew up hearing a lot about his father's baseball prowess. He has always wondered, too, why his dad never turned pro.

We may never know the answer. Two stories carry some weight. One was that he was offered a contract, or at least a tryout, with Toronto. But, according to his brother, Doug, himself an Intercounty veteran, "I think Gord got screwed around." He heard that Hett, the umpire, arranged for a tryout with Toronto, and Toronto sent a letter to Bradshaw via the Galt Terrier executive. Though Doug was hesitant to name names—"some of them are still alive"—he believes that the letter never reached his brother. "Gord never saw it." The Galt executive, Doug maintains, didn't want their star player to leave, so they withheld the letter.

The next time Hett saw Bradshaw he was incensed. "What the hell kind of a guy are you?" demanded Hett.

"What are you talking about, Oscar?" answered Bradshaw.

"About the Leaf tryout I arranged for you. The least you could have done was answer the letter they [Toronto] sent you."

"I don't know what the hell you're talking about," said Bradshaw. "I never saw a letter."

According to Doug, "someone on the old Galt executive—I don't want to say who, because you don't want to stir old things up now—was to blame. But somebody there, in plain language, just screwed him out of a big-league contract. I have seen guys catching in the majors, even today, who couldn't carry his jockstrap. He was that great."

Another theory, one that Bob heard over the years and one that he gives some credence to, was that Mrs. Bradshaw, his mother, wasn't keen on her husband moving to Baltimore or some other city so Gord could pursue a baseball career. Baseball was a game, and she felt that he should be at home working at a real job to provide for his family. She never gave him the letter.

Bradshaw, the Brantford native who came to be associated with the great Galt Terrier teams of the early 1930s, died suddenly at age forty-two in 1951. When he died the undertaker made quite a fuss over the size of his biceps. He had been an undertaker in northern Ontario and had worked on lumberjacks with large arms, but Bradshaw had the biggest he had ever seen. Bob, who still lives in Cambridge, has possession of the Oscar Hett Memorial Trophy. "He was the king of the hill," said Doug. "He was a natural."

Bad blood, like that arising from the Bradshaw affair, is the genesis for good rivalries, and Galt-Brantford games were always some of the best anywhere. The two communities are only a few miles apart; fans wouldn't hesitate to travel to the other town for road games. "I'd say four to five hundred would make the trip from Brantford to Galt and vice versa," said Pennell. Playoff series between the two teams would often be referred to as the trolley series because the Lake Erie and Northern Railway, part of the Canadian Pacific, ran between the two cities. Begun in 1913, and running along the east side of the river from Brantford, through Paris, to Galt, the line was finished in 1916, just three years before the Intercounty came into existence, after a delay caused by the intervention of the First World War. The terminus of the line was at Port Dover on Lake Erie, a popular resort town about an hour south of Galt. But more people took their own cars than rode the train. "There'd just be a steady stream of cars going up on a Friday or Saturday night between the two towns."

There were other rivalries around the league and other teams also had high hopes as the season approached. In Stratford, the Nationals announced the appointment of a new manager, George "Pappy" Smith of Massena, New York, and eleven players. Like Padden, Smith would also play. Unlike Padden, he could draw on no major-league experience. Of the eleven players who had signed with the Nationals by May 2, a couple were from Montreal, a few were from Brockville (near Kingston), and Ken Hulley was from Galt. The Nats were expected to field the youngest team—Galt had one of the oldest—in the Intercounty, with a sprinkling of experienced players.

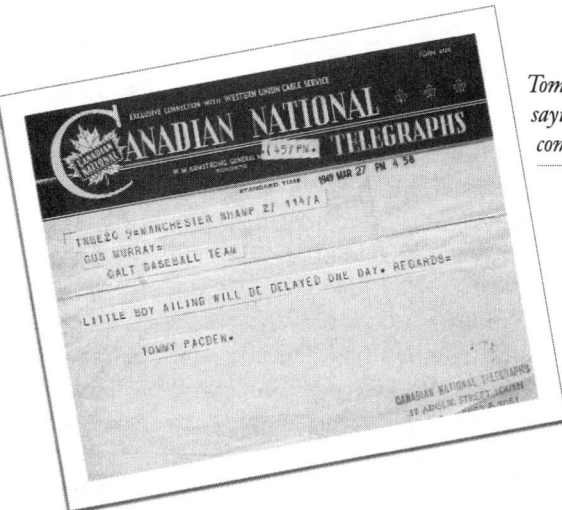

Tommy Padden sent this telegram, saying he would be delayed in coming to Galt.

Born of the Spring

"What are you going to get out of it?" asked Dunnell.
"I'm just trying to build a winner," replied Murray.
Dunnell, who began at the *Star* in 1942 and had just moved over to the sports department in 1948, knew Murray had mortgaged his house to operate the club. "I think you're nuts," he said. "You're working your ass off, and for what?"
That was the way it was that summer.

BORN OF THE CANADIAN SPRING, FRESH-WET AND FULL OF promise, there was a confidence about Galt's Terriers as the home opener approached. Optimism seemed to abound in the small southern Ontario city as the warming sun stretched the days of spring into the scent of summer. Spring always brings confidence, new life, new beginnings. The sun was setting later every day, and the soil in the countryside was ready to be used. Winter shed its blanket of snow and the land began to breathe. Children ran, and old people bounded, where in winter they had conserved and been docile, almost to the point of hibernation. Brantford was taking a whiff of the same tonic, as was Stratford, and Guelph, and the other small communities of the Intercounty.

But in Galt it was different. Much of it had to do with Padden. Now, as the season was to start, it was left to simply see what he could do, to see what kind of a team we would be that summer. Murray was impressed with the former big-leaguer from the beginning. Padden, who had come to town early that spring by train, had left his wife and children in Manchester, New Hampshire, for the time being. They would come later. But Murray wasn't impressed by Padden's financial position. "Tom never had a car while he was here," recalled Murray. "He didn't have much money. In fact, he had no money at all. He was in bad shape financially."

Padden had been a top major-leaguer not that many seasons before, but circumstance had dealt him a bad hand. It could happen to anybody. Soon after Theresa Padden arrived in Galt with her children, Murray and the rest of the Galt Terrier executive held an afternoon tea for her at Murray's home. All the wives were to attend. But Theresa couldn't come, she said, because she had no decent dress to wear. "It was sad to see that," said Murray.

If the Paddens were going through hard times, it was impossible to see at the ballpark. When Padden took to the field he was all class. "Padden was a real picture behind home plate," said Murray. "He could catch the ball easily in one hand. You could tell he was a pro. A catcher has got to be a good showman; he's got to show the pitcher the mark. Padden did that."

Larry Pennell remembered the first time he ever saw Murray. It was at an Intercounty executive meeting one night in Galt. All the team presidents were automatically given the title of vice-president of the league, which meant that Murray, Pennell, and Goman in Waterloo were just three of eight league vice-presidents that year. But Murray was a new guy. When Pennell saw him sitting at the table he wondered who the young kid was, and why was he at the table. It was typical that anyone who met Gus would not soon forget him. The brush cut made him stand out, but so too did his frenetic manner, his enthusiasm, and his promotional plans. Murray had a serious face; his eyes and face somehow looked shrewd, sly. It was not an inviting face, and in the months to come, more than one of his players would look at Murray and figure he was cheating them of their money.

Murray was only on the senior Intercounty scene for five years, a time so short in comparison to others that one would think he would have soon been forgotten. That wasn't the case, and one who never forgot Murray was Dunnell, who began his newspaper career at the *Stratford Beacon Herald* in December of 1923, but had left Stratford in 1942 for Toronto, destined to become one of the nation's most widely read sportswriters in the ensuing decades. "Murray was a nut who just worked his ass off for baseball in Galt," said Dunnell years later. "He was quite a promoter, there's no doubt about that, but the main beneficiaries of all his work were the imports he brought in."

The imports got big salaries, bonuses, and the goodwill of local townspeople, while the local kids had to work full time during the day and then play ball at night for a paltry sum. Nearly fifty years later Dunnell remembered how Murray would hold giveaways at the ballpark, much like small-town theatres and movie houses used to do. "The theatres would have a time before the show when they would say anyone in the audience with a Swiss Army knife would win a prize, or anybody with some other article would win cash. It got to the point where people would take ten dollars worth of articles in a bag in the hope that they would win a two-dollar prize. Murray adopted that type of giveaway. He was a promoter. No question about it. He did things no one else had ever done in the Intercounty."

Dunnell, who began at the *Star* in '42 and was national news editor and assistant city editor before moving over to the sports department in 1948, thought he even recalled hearing that Murray had mortgaged his house to help the team. "I remember telling him what a nut he was, working his ass off, and for what?"

But Murray could not tolerate mediocrity, and as president of the club he was going to do all he could to make the team a success. Murray had a list of words at home that he would try to use as often as he could. "Sacrifice" was on that list. So was "persevere" and "determination." "There is no such thing as luck," he would say. "There is skill, knowledge, education, and hard work." So he took his own advice, much to the continual amusement of Dunnell.

"What are you going to get out of it?" Dunnell would ask Murray. To which Murray would say he was trying to build a winner. Gus wasn't in it for any personal gain, though if business picked up at the paint and wallpaper store, so much the better.

Dunnell came to Galt and visited other Intercounty teams frequently that season, and while he was impressed with the enthusiasm in the city toward the Terriers, and the big crowds of five and six thousand people, he could see Murray was burning the candle at both ends and would, in fact, be burned out in short order if he kept up that pace. Murray, as a subject, proved irresistible for Dunnell's column, and he wrote several on the beleaguered Galt boss. "Murray told me about some of the players and how they abused privileges," Dunnell said. Some of the import players, like Connie Creedon, had meals provided free at Gus's lunch counter on Water Street. Dunnell recalled hearing about how players would order more food than they could possibly eat, and even invite friends along so that they could get free food.

Creedon was a special case. "Everybody was scared of Creedon," recalled Dennis Smedley, a good friend of Lillie and a member of the Lowry Street gang, an informal group of kids who hung around together. Creedon and Tommy Warren went into Murray's restaurant one afternoon that summer when Gus and Padden had gone to Toronto to see the Triple-A Maple Leafs play the Newark Bears— Murray and Padden were going to pick up uniforms that Padden had arranged to come north with the Bears—and they grabbed a large ham that was sitting on the counter. The girl who worked for Murray protested. "Gus'll give you hell," she said. "He'll fine you."

"We don't care," they said as they beat a quick retreat out the front door. They walked up Water Street to the dam, a favourite fishing hole, and put pieces of ham onto hooks as bait for carp. As a kid, and even then, when time permitted, I would take my rod and reel to that very spot, along with a jug of orange juice and a few sandwiches, and I never went home empty handed. Usually, my father made me bury the fish in the garden, to be used as fertilizer.

Murray couldn't believe the audacity of Creedon and Warren. It was inconceivable to think of Larry Pennell's players doing something like that down in Brantford. But Pennell had his players' respect. Murray didn't. And though he thought he was treating them fairly—"Consider others first" was a philosophy he learned from his father, who ingrained the "customer is always right" credo—he was learning to be strict when it came to team rules and money. If a player had agreed to a certain salary and then proceeded to have a banner year, Murray was not going to renegotiate his contract. A deal was a deal. And besides, many of these import players were quickly proving they didn't deserve any respect. Their actions spoke volumes. "Murray had all kinds of reasons to treat them with disrespect after all the demands they made," said Dunnell. "So maybe he was right." And the players? They were just being typical ballplayers. If they could get a better deal, they would go for it. There was no limit on greed, or bad manners, even in the Intercounty. The best-behaved, generally, were the local boys who had to live and work in the town after the season ended. They had roots in the community, with family and friends always there, even at games. Murray was finding out that running the 1949 Galt Terriers was a difficult job, and the imports were the cause of most of his troubles.

Like Murray, Dunnell, over the years, was learning to have very little respect for ballplayers himself. Especially after the 1994 strike-shortened major-league season. "Here were true ballplayers in 1994, earning an average salary of $1.2 million per year, and Toronto players were doing even better than that, and they were drawing [in Toronto] a record four million fans a year, and on August 12 they walked out." After seemingly a lifetime of fraternizing with, and writing about, ballplayers and the game of baseball, the 1994 strike left a bad taste in his mouth.

Murray had almost as many bad memories of 1949 as he had good ones. Whenever Dunnell thinks about that summer and Murray's Terriers, he can't help but picture a frantic Gus Murray working twenty-four hours a day on behalf of the Terriers and the various promotions he was planning. "He was a victim," Dunnell believed. "No doubt about it. They were drawing an awful lot of people by old Intercounty standards, but actually, it's like a guy at a racetrack betting fifty dollars or $100 across the board to get a third-place payout."

For Murray, there were plenty of sleepless nights that year; nights when he would be up until three or four o'clock in the morning dealing with baseball business. "He'd tell me about practically working around the clock," Dunnell said. "I'd tell him that even if you sold out the park it wasn't worth the expenditure of time and money."

He was always on the go, from early spring until late fall. More than once that season Murray would laugh at how he was spending so much time in Buffalo bars meeting prospects and making contacts. The funny thing was that Murray didn't drink. Murray had also gone to Florida during spring training to scout for prospects and to solidify his working agreement with Selkirk and the Yankees. And he already knew he would be going to Florida the next spring to do more of the same. And there would be trips to the World Series as well as to Detroit and Buffalo, where Tony Pascoe would give him the latest tips on players in that area. It was the busiest year of Gus Murray's life. If he'd had a regular nine-to-five job he would never have been able to manage it all, but he was his own boss. "And I had a good man to manage the store," he explained. His name was Bill Cartwright, and he gave Gus the peace of mind necessary for him to devote as much time as necessary to baseball business.

In Brantford, Pennell could try to schedule his appointments and courtroom work around baseball, though it was not always possible to do so. Still, had he worked a steady nine-to-five job, he would have been unable to do all that he was doing with the Red Sox in 1949. Murray, Pennell, and King, and Goman in Waterloo, each had one thing in common: they worked tirelessly for their ball clubs. They were busy men, and each seemed to thrive on the extra work they were doing with their particular clubs.

Murray respected Pennell, as, indeed, most of his Intercounty associates did, but Murray harboured a lifelong dislike for lawyers in general. "I've had my problems with lawyers over the years," he said. "Lawyers are not honest." Yet even he conceded there was one notable exception—Pennell. Murray would take great delight in telling lawyer jokes whenever the opportunity arose. "You know what you call a lawyer with an IQ of seventy-five?" he would ask. "You call him 'Your Honour.'" It was a characterization of lawyers, and judges, that Murray would never use to describe Pennell, who, several years later, after serving as Canada's solicitor general in the Lester Pearson cabinet, was appointed justice of the Supreme Court of Ontario.

In early May Padden, Murray, and Watty Reid went to see the Toronto Maple Leafs' Triple-A club open their International League season. It was at the old park down near the lake. "We went with the idea of talking to Goody Rosen," said Murray. Rosen, hitting a little over .200 through the first two or three games, was definitely interested. Neither Murray or Padden was worried about his .200 average. "The older fellows come through at the end," said Murray. He knew that rookie wonders who hit .400 at season's start invariably fall off as the season progresses and that it is the seasoned veterans, guys like Rosen, who come on strong as the season winds down. Rosen had hit .312 in twenty-two games his first year in the majors as a Brooklyn Dodger in 1937. His big year came in 1945 when he hit .325 in 145 games. His lifetime major-league batting average was an impressive .291 through six seasons. That spoke volumes, so Murray and Padden offered him a better salary than the Leafs, knowing that the addition of Rosen would bolster an already strong Galt lineup the likes of which had never been seen on an Intercounty diamond before.

Tom Padden, left, shakes hands with Cracky Liscombe during the season opener.

May Day

Galt, May 15 (CP).—Before a crowd of 4,500 fans—the largest in many years—the Galt Terriers raised the curtain Saturday afternoon on the 1949 Intercounty Senior Baseball League season with a cleancut 9-1 victory over the Guelph Maple Leafs.

The weather was ideal and there were the customary opening ceremonies with a parade of bands, Indians, cowboys and decorated vehicles of all kinds. Mayor Mel Moffatt fouled out on a pitch by Ald. Art White.

Tommy Warren, ex-big leaguer, went the route for Galt with manager Tommy Padden catching for six frames.

Features of the game were a home run in the eighth by Verne Kaiser, three sensational catches in deep centre by Ab Conick for the Leafs, and the general all-round performance at first base for the Terriers by Connie Waite, who engineered two double plays, the second unassisted

I HAD SEEN MANY OPENING DAYS AT DICKSON PARK, BUT NONE quite like that Saturday in '49. I couldn't believe the crowd. Even my father commented that the great Terrier teams of the 1920s and '30s rarely played before crowds that size. Canadian Press carried the story of that first game across the country, but they got the crowd size wrong. There were closer to 7,100 fans in attendance, considerably more than the 4,500 they had reported. The discrepancy came from the thousands of free tickets Murray had given away in the week prior to the game.

Dickson Park was a great place to play ball, but it was a terrible place if you were a fan who had to go to the washroom. The women had it much worse than the men, though in both cases the facilities were wholly inadequate for the thousands of fans at every game. Ladies lined up patiently at the top of the stands for their one designated washroom, while the men lined up at the side. I never saw inside the women's washroom, but in the men's there was grand total of one rather short trough that could accommodate perhaps six men at one time, and two stalls. It would have been bad enough with one thousand fans, let alone seven thousand. Everywhere you looked there were people. I'd never seen anything like it. And throughout the game, any game, young boys and grown men would relieve themselves under the bleachers along the first base line, or up in the cow barns atop the western hill. The trouble was, if you left your seat, it would be gone by the time you got back. As for the women, they didn't have the luxury of going underneath the bleachers, though more than one story emerged that season, and other seasons, that certain young women were seeing more of the cow barns with eager men than they saw of the game.

Although we won easily, I saw only an inning of action. Warren got the win, but he didn't look particularly sharp for a former major-leaguer. Still, he got the job done. I think it was a month or so later, with the season well underway, that my dad pulled me aside after supper one night to ask what I knew about Warren. "Not much," I said, though in seeing him operate at the ballpark, there was something about him that struck me as different. He always had wads of money, and more than anyone I ever met, he had a way of attracting pretty young women to him. Money and women, and the fact that he was a married man, could only end in trouble, and though I was no paragon of virtue, I told him so one night after a game when he had accepted a ride home from two young women. For a long time I would attribute it all to the fact that he was an Oklahoman and was playing beneath himself in the Intercounty. My father had heard rumours about him, though they were unsubstantiated.

The thirty-year-old Warren had hoped to hide his recent troubles with the law from all of us, and for most of the season he did a good job, even after the *Sunday News* of March 6, 1949, broke a story about his gambling problem. The headline said it all: "Ex-Dodger accused of gambling friends' money." And above a picture of the former major-leaguer, taken just after he joined the Brooklyn Dodgers following a stint in the navy, was the header, "Got Gambling Fever."

But oblivious as we all were to the problems our Tulsan pitcher was going through, we revelled in the parade, the people, the new life of spring with all its hope and optimism. The parade that day made its way from Soper Park, past Galt Arena Gardens, downtown through Main Street, and then on to Dickson Park. Warren led in his cowboy outfit, riding a beautiful white mare—later he said he rode a lot of pretty white fillies from Galt that summer. When the parade reached the ballpark he rode to the pitcher's mound, dismounted, and took off his cowboy clothes to reveal his Terrier uniform. Then, without missing a beat, he started warming up. People left work early to see the parade; some businesses let their workers out so they could not only go to the parade, but see the game. In the Galt of 1949, on that Saturday afternoon, nothing was as important, or as pressing, as the Terrier home opener. People had been waiting all winter for it. Years earlier, at the start of the century, the Reverend R.E. Knowles of Galt's Knox Presbyterian Church took a wedding party to see the Galts play a game at Dickson Park. The bride, Jean McKilligan, and several guests had arrived early, so Knowles took them the few blocks to the park. When the groom, Allan McPhail, arrived at the church for the big event, he found it empty. The famous minister, who doubled as a best-selling novelist and would later become a feature writer for the *Toronto Star*, had left a message explaining the circumstances to McPhail. There was a big game, after all. They wouldn't be long. If young McPhail grew impatient, he could find them at the ballpark.

It was Knowles who was responsible for the team name, Terriers. For a long time it was thought that the name arose because of a small Terrier dog which used to frequent the ballpark in the early 1920s. The dog belonged to young Wylie Wilkinson, who played second base for the Terriers in those years and who also starred on the Galt hockey team of that era. "My dog wasn't the club mascot," said Wylie, "although he was always at the park." The correct story dated to the hockey season of 1921, when the Galt Amateur Athletic Association hockey club was playing the Sault Ste. Marie Greyhounds in Toronto. Knowles, by then a writer with the *Star*—he still lived in Galt and commuted by train to Toronto—was at the game. The Galt club had no name so Knowles, drawing a canine comparison with the Greyhound opposition, called the Galt club the Terriers.

"When we were getting ready for the 1921 baseball season," noted Wilkinson, "we started a movement to have the name Terriers officially recognized here. Earl Werstine of the *Reporter* and Hugh "Tiny" McFadyen were the two Galt men most instrumental in the establishment of the new name." McFadyen obtained papier mâché dogs, which were used at the time to advertise the RCA Victor company. They were stationed upright at ground level prior to Terrier home games and soon became the focal point of the cheering. By the time Gus Murray took over the Terriers in the fall of 1948, the name had become associated throughout southern Ontario with Galt.

Now, on this early Saturday in May of 1949, Galt's Terriers were about to embark on a season full of promise. Lefty Perkins would have enjoyed everything about that day, from the fine weather right down to the new green grass that was still wet with winter. He would have liked seeing the hope on people's faces and in the way they talked. There is always hope in the spring, and on opening day, after a long winter lacking colour and life, there is never more hope than on a ball diamond.

That spring, as Wes and I were desperately trying to impress Padden at the Terrier camp, Perkins had made a trip to Amsterdam. But he was back in Chambersburg, Pennsylvania, when the Galts took to the field in early May. He hoped that he had not played his last season. Perkins knew what only old ballplayers know: that the seasons of a man's life are few, and that to stop playing before one's time is up is unbearable. So he called up his manager from the year before when he had pitched for the Manchester Yankees. He called Tom Padden in Galt.

It was a timely call. Galt had one weakness, and it was a shortage of left-handed pitchers. Michigan's Don Perkins had failed to show, but the Terriers had kept a position for him on their roster. In early April Padden had communicated this weakness to Murray. It was no surprise; they had known they were going to be short of left-handers. Murray was still looking. On April 21 a CN cable was wired to Murray from Bert Pankratz in Detroit. Murray had asked Pankratz about prospective southpaws in the Detroit area and had even paid a visit to the Motor City the week before. Pankratz had said he'd get back to Murray. When a telegram arrived, it said: "Have a good lefthander. Plenty fast. 200 pounds, six feet. Good control. Wants $240 a month. Wire your telephone number. Will call you. Left-hander can report within a week. Will bring down myself."

When a fellow named Ross came up for a tryout, he failed to impress Padden. He was never signed.

Despite that opening-day win, Murray and the rest of the Terrier executive went back to Murray's Water Street store following the game to make further plans for a successful season. One win was no guarantee that the Terriers would contend for the Intercounty title. Besides, there were other players to be discussed. Padden was still talking about a weakness in his pitching rotation. He desperately needed another left hander. Murray and Watty Reid stayed on in Murray's office at the back of the store after the others left that night. And after Reid left, Murray was still there, on the big black phone, looking up contacts and writing letters to prospective players. He had been spending more and more time at his Water Street store of late, and had even set up a bed so he could get some shut-eye after working well into the morning.

Water Street, running downtown along the east bank of the Grand, was a hub of the city in those days, with the Carnegie Library, the Grand and Capital Theatres, Murray's paint and wallpaper store and his lunch counter, the local newspaper, as well as various other business establishments all in close proximity. The street was probably the first roadway in the fledgling village back in 1816, for it was along the southern part of this route that the town founders first came in search of a suitable place to start a mill settlement. Murray's store, in fact, was only a block or two from the confluence of Mill Creek and the Grand River, the place where town founders agreed to begin their settlement.

Much of the ensuing history of Galt took place on or near Water Street. The last bear hunt started when a black bear sauntered down Water Street (and past the spot that would house Gus Murray's paint and wallpaper store a century later) in the late 1830s and created such excitement that a posse of would-be hunters grabbed their guns and gave chase. The bear fled, entering the river across from Dickson Park. It was last seen on the island in the middle of the river behind Galt Collegiate.

Around the time word reached us of my brother's death, I saw Terry Sawchuk standing at the Four Corners, where Water meets Main, in the rain, waiting for a ride. I had seen him there before, in the evening, wearing a zoot suit. But now his goal pads were draped over his shoulders and it was getting dark. One side of his face, which was very pale, was lit up by the street light; the other side was dark gray and brooding, like the night.

Murray's store had a history along Water Street, as did all the businesses lining that roadway. In any given decade the river would overflow its banks at least once and flood the entire street. There had been a severe flood in 1948, and Water Street was entirely submerged. An enterprising photographer with the *Reporter* next door hopped in a boat and paddled across the street one day that spring and managed to get a picture of Murray standing on the front steps of his establishment watching a canoe carry a man and a dog down the street. Later floods would cause untold damage along this street, as when Hurricane Hazel hit a few years later. If there could be another Main Street, Water Street would be it. Murray's store was only one hundred feet from the Four Corners. People would meet at the Four Corners, or use it as a landmark when giving directions. Everyone knew where the Four Corners was. And everyone knew where Murray's stores were. Sawchuk and several other junior hockey players used to stop in for a snack or milkshake a year or two earlier, and even the late Reverend R.E. Knowles, the man who had dreamt up the Terrier name some twenty-eight years earlier, had regularly stopped in for a coffee every night after his train arrived back in town from Toronto.

As we left the ballpark that afternoon we were all feeling pretty good. Young kids were asking Kaiser, Padden, Creedon, and Warren for their autographs, while I merely watched, looking for a couple of my friends from high school. It was still hard to believe that I was playing on the same team as Padden and the others. There were a couple of hours of daylight left, and in the next week, we were told, Rosen would be joining us. That would bring to four the number of former major-leaguers in Galt. And when you threw in the likes of Kaiser, Waite, and Shelton, all of whom had major-league ability, we had seven top-flight players. No wonder there were seven thousand fans in the park that day.

And so we waited for the arrival of Rosen.

Soon, with Rosen on board, and all our big guns hitting their stride, we were winning far more than we were losing. After one game—I believe it was in Waterloo—we returned home via a little hamlet known as Blair. There we stopped off at Nicholson's Tavern, an old hotel and watering hole that had seen its prime some time in the last century. It had long been a favourite of high-school seniors and drinkers.

Kaiser, Padden, Rosen, Lillie, Clark, and I were in Dennis Smedley's car so the seven of us got a table near the back wall. It was, we said, our team table as we were all wearing our uniforms. We talked of the game, and of the memorable plays, and it was then that I heard Lillie speak of the Waterloo shortstop, a married man, someone whose reputation with women had spread far and wide, perhaps even rivalling Tommy Warren's. He had made a hand-grab to initiate a double play in the second inning, and now Lillie thought the time was right to comment on it.

"That two-timing son of a bitch one-timed it," Lillie said, in mock outrage.

We all laughed, and I saw Rosen and Padden look at each other and smile. Much later, with the passage of the 1960s and 1970s, the phrase to describe our gathering and drinking was "male bonding." I could see something in that look Padden gave Rosen. I could see they were going to enjoy the summer in Galt.

"The two-timing son of a bitch!" confirmed Rosen, shaking his head. "The two-timer one-timed it."

I was having the time of my life with these guys, though I was, at times, angry at not playing more.

The next day we were read the riot act by Murray at practice. Someone had complained to a member of the Terrier executive that we had been hoisting a few pints at a bar the previous night, and we had not represented our city well.

"Never again," said Murray, "are players allowed to wear their team uniforms into a bar. If anyone disregards this rule, they will be dealt with severely."

Apparently Padden had taken most of the heat over this.

Goody Rosen when he played for the Dodgers

Summer Day at Mill Creek

The father explained to his son: "As a general rule, you put your worst player in right. That's because most of the hitters are right-handed and they'll usually hit the ball to left field, if they hit it. Right field is the position where the worst ballplayer has the least opportunity to do damage.

"But at Ebbets Field I've seen some terrific right fielders," said the son, "like Leroy Watkins and Goody Rosen. Besides, you told me Babe Ruth played right."

"The major leagues," said the father, "are a different kettle of fish. First, there are no bad ballplayers in the major leagues."

— Roger Kahn, *Good Enough to Dream*

GOODY ROSEN HAD GROWN UP IN TORONTO, JUST SIXTY MILES from Galt. I had read somewhere that he was the little man with the big cigar, an apt description, for he carried his 155 pounds on a five-foot-nine frame. On physical appearance alone, he was an unlikely baseball star.

Just days after Rosen arrived in town he asked me to take him to a good fishing hole I knew out near Killean, on Mill Creek, beside my father's boyhood farm. I was always glad to go fishing in those days and, still being in awe of Rosen and his major-league credentials, I readily agreed.

It was early in the morning when Rosen pulled into our driveway on Barrie Street. There was a heavy mist in the air, the grass was wet, and the street was calm, although there were a few lights breaking the silence. It was Thursday and we had a game that night on the river flats.

"Hi, Charlie," he said in a voice that was too loud for early morning. I was sitting in the wicker chair on our front porch, enjoying the calmness and mist. Galt was always quiet in the mornings. It was the first time Rosen had called me by my name. Mostly he called me "Kid," a name I didn't mind because I had paid no dues yet as a ballplayer.

I packed my fishing tackle, net, and the sandwiches my mother made for us—she was glad to make lunch for a major-leaguer—and then put the bait in his trunk, and off we drove down the grey street shrouded in the mist of a cool, wet summer morning. Soon we were in the country and nearing the creek. The mist burned off slowly in the sun and the air grew hot. I took him to a fishing hole that few people knew, in an out-of-the-way section of the river, far from the road. A snapping turtle the size of a terrier announced our arrival, apparently objecting to our intrusion. But he let us pass through safely.

We had waders and we put them on to get in the creek, and soon the sun was so hot we sought shelter in the cool waters under the shade of a row of willows.

Rosen loved fishing. He asked me about my life, my late brother Jimmy, my father and mother, and about my plans for the fall. None of my answers were long.

"Got a girlfriend?" he inquired, casting his line out into the water where the shade met the sun.

"She's in my class at school," I said. "But we're not really seeing each other any more."

"How long have you known her?"

"Five years, though we've ..."

"You've dated five years already, and you're only ... how old?"

"Nah, it's only been two years," I said. "And I'm in my nineteenth year."

"What're you gonna do come September?" he asked. "Where'd you say you were going?"

"I'm off to university, and so is she. Different ones, so who knows. We're going to stay in touch."

"They got a ball team?"

"No schools in Canada have ball teams."

We spent the morning fishing and talking. I had been worried, when we left, that I wouldn't have anything to say to Rosen, but it wasn't like that at all. When he told me about his life, I was all ears. A few weeks earlier I was a high-school student; now I was chewing the fat with the famed Goody Rosen, and I was feeling pretty good about myself.

"First thing I can remember," Rosen told me, "was throwin' a ball against our house and my two brothers comin' along and takin' the ball away from me. I ran in the house and raised hell. We had what was called Playground Baseball that we played as kids. It's about the same as American Legion baseball in America."

There, as we ate lunch in the tall grass at water's edge, Rosen told me a Babe Ruth story I was to hear often that summer. We had three trout spread out on the ground beside us, to compare, before putting them back in the water bucket. Ruth, said Rosen, was a first-base coach the year he joined Brooklyn, and occupied an adjacent locker in the Dodger dressing room. They were both cigar smokers and had their boxes of cigars side by side on the shelf above. "Babe accused me once of stealing his cigars but I pointed out that my brand was different," said Rosen. "So we set a trap for the thief. We changed the top row in his shelf to exploding cigars. That night we were on the train to Boston. After dinner I see the trainer preparing to light up a cigar. I wave at Babe to hurry into the club car. He arrived in time for the biggest explosion you ever saw. Well, Babe had vowed to murder the guy but he looked so funny, with his face all covered with soot, we couldn't do anything for laughing."

"What was Ruth like?" I asked, before realizing it was a stupid question.

"What was Ruth like?" he repeated. "He was as big as they say he was, and I don't mean just physically. He had a presence that no one else I ever saw had. In some ways, he was bigger than life. But we got along well."

"Did you ever play against Satchel Paige?" I asked him, after he mentioned Paige in passing.

"We played most of the coloured teams," Rosen said of his semi-pro days before Louisville. "Satchel Paige was as great as they say he was. When he was young he was very fast. He struck me out once before I even got the bat off my shoulders. That's how fast he was. He'd go into his kick, throw up that foot of his in the air, and his fastball was by you. Those black players were excellent ballplayers. It's unfortunate that they didn't get a chance to play in the majors until years later."

Rosen was from the old school, one that dictated he be critical of soft modern-day players who complained about one injury or another. I made a mental note never to complain.

"When I was young we just wanted to keep playing," he said. Such was the case early in his major-league career. Rosen was leading the league in hitting in 1939. It was going to be a banner year for the small man with the big cigar. Then came an injury. Rosen was sliding back into first base with a bad strawberry (a raw wound on his leg from sliding) as big as a pie, so to avoid aggravating it he tried a fancy slide. But it failed miserably, and he injured his left ankle. "I was carried off the field and the trainer told Durocher that I couldn't play for a couple of weeks. Durocher started screaming, 'He can play. He has to. He's my leader!"

Soon afterward he told Leo Durocher where to go and was quickly relegated to the minors, a situation that his wife tried to rectify by writing to baseball commissioner Judge Kenesaw Mountain Landis, asking him to give her husband advice:

Dear Mr. Landis:

I know that you are a very busy person, but if you could give me a little of your time, it would mean a great deal to us.

My husband is "Goody" Rosen and is owned by the Brooklyn Baseball Club. Brooklyn bought him in the later part of the 1937 season from Louisville. He joined Brooklyn at the end of the American Association season and did very well, hitting over .300.

In 1938 he had a fair season, hitting .281. leading off ... Why I have written all this is because Goody can play major-league baseball ... But now Durocher won't give him a fair chance.

... he's stumped and doesn't know what to do about his contract because he doesn't want to go back to the minor leagues.

Thank you for your attention and I shall be very grateful for your advice.

But her letter went unanswered by Landis. So the years in the minors passed, Rosen told me. "I don't know where all the years have gone."

He returned to the big time with a vengeance in 1945, leading the league in hitting for most of the season, finally finishing third with a .325 average in 145 games. Said Rosen: "I think I could have put up even better numbers if I wasn't hurt near the end of the year. I played all out for keeps."

"Why come to Galt?" I asked him.

Summer Day at Mill Creek

"Listen, kid, I'm washed up and I know I'm washed up, but I still have some good days and I figured I could help Gus's team."

"From what I've seen, you're a long ways from being washed up," I told him.

"Like I said, I have some good days. But I'm not the player who played for the Dodgers."

Later in life, when Rosen was being inducted into the Canadian Baseball Hall of Fame, Duke Snider told him what Durocher had written in his book: "Rosen couldn't run, couldn't hit, couldn't throw, couldn't field, but if I had nine guys like him I'd win the pennant every year."

When Padden and Murray persuaded Rosen to leave Toronto to play in Galt, it was understood that he would be given a new car to commute from Toronto for the games. Initially that had worked. But soon reports started circulating that Rosen, against Murray's orders, was also playing softball for a team in Toronto. It was all true. One night after practice my father showed me a CP story naming Rosen as one of the stars in a Toronto softball game. Murray fined him fifty dollars, which didn't hurt Rosen's pocketbook considering the contract and fringe benefits Murray had negotiated with him. Benny Bennett was on the team executive and he owned the town's biggest car dealership. But the car deal was supposed to be hushed up. And it was, for a time. Then the local newspaper got wind of Rosen's demand and duly reported it. "One of the former pros Galt Terriers have imported has already placed his order for a new car in the medium-priced field, which means, if true, that he didn't come to Galt for peanuts." The story went on to speculate that Murray must have George Selkirk and the New York Yankees backing him.

There was more than a little truth to that.

I first met Rosen at practice on a Wednesday night. I always respected older people, and though Rosen didn't look like he would tear up the league, I thought he would be able to give some of us a few good tips over the course of the season. I was wrong on the first count. I never saw a better money player. When the pressure was on, Rosen always came through.

"Kid," he said. "Baseball's a great game. Play it as long as you can, but get a good education. You've got some smarts and you're at an age when all your options are open."

"But you've led a remarkable life," I replied, thinking of his travels through the bush leagues and then finally arriving at Ebbett's Field.

"Yeah, bright lights, big city. I'd trade it all for a good education."

"Maybe," I said. "Maybe. But you've had some great years."

"Kid," he said, "the years—they come and they go. They come and they go."

I said nothing, letting his words stare at me for a time. They didn't really sink in that afternoon, nor would they for many years.

Soon we packed our trout in a cooler. The sun was hot and though the water was cool and the shade covered us so that we could observe the heat of a pristine summer day all the while being unscathed by the sun, we had been hours on the creek and it was time to go. That night we had fresh trout on the skillet. Nothing ever tasted so good.

There was only one other player who spent more time with me on the field than Rosen. That was Padden, a man my father respected and admired, and someone I came to regard as almost a second father.

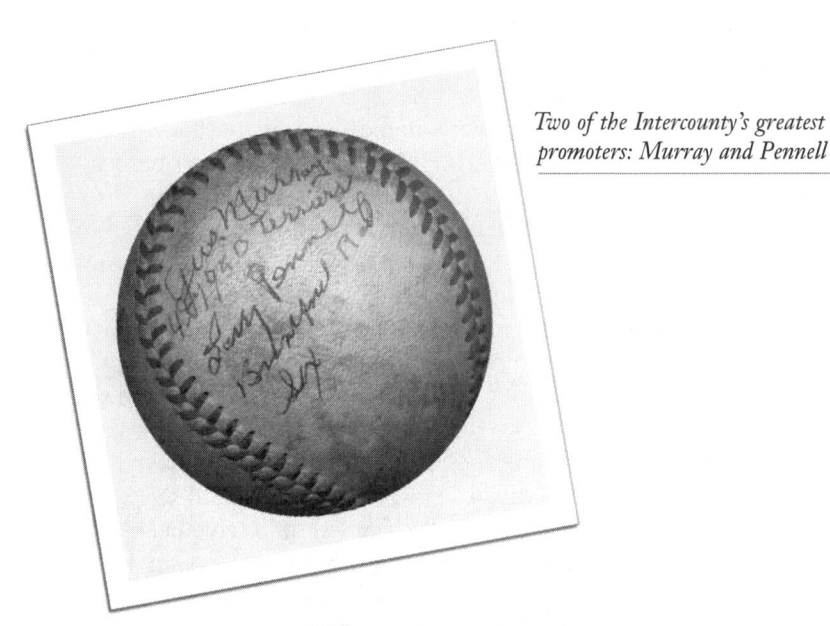

Two of the Intercounty's greatest promoters: Murray and Pennell

The Dog Days

The dog days of summer were upon us, and the heat was stifling. Cigarettes were eighteen cents a pack, Brantford's Jay Silverheels was starring in a new Hollywood flick with Glenn Ford—*Lust for Gold*—and NBC Radio launched a new radio program called *Dragnet*, starring Jack Webb as Sergeant Joe Friday. Wimbledon came and went, Brooklyn was leading St. Louis by two games in the NL, and Tokyo Rose went on trial in San Francisco for treason. I was a kid. I followed the news back then.

GUNMETAL GREY AND OLD LIKE THE CEILING OF ETERNITY, THE sky didn't look promising one night in late June as we took to the field against London. There was no rain yet, though beyond the CPR bridge to the west the sky was dark and the winds were blowing the smell of rain our way. Rosen was out of the lineup that night—later we would learn he had been playing softball—and I was called to start in right field.

Padden told me just minutes before the game, and even at that, we all looked for Goody to show at the last minute.

My first Intercounty start was inauspicious. I had butterflies as I took to the field, even though I had played on this field since I was a toddler. I thought of Jimmy, and how he had looked so effortless running down long balls in centre field not too many years earlier, and then I remembered how we would play catch here. Those thoughts always gave me inspiration.

Early in the game I chased down a line drive, missing the ball as I dove for it with my outstretched arm. The ball bounced just before I got to it, and I knocked the wind out of myself with the dive. Someone yelled from the stands, "You ain't Jimmy!" and I wanted to kill him for invoking the name of my brother. I got up quickly, not wanting to show I was hurt, and Warren, playing left, recovered the ball. He came over after making the play, keeping the runner on first, and asked how I was. I told him okay, though I was still hurting. I remember Jimmy telling me more than once, "Don't ever let 'em see you're hurting."

I finished out the inning, and the next, before Padden removed me from the game. He took me out, I knew, because he could see I was hurt, and that I couldn't stretch out the way I should have been able to. And I knew, deep down, that it was best for the club, but I was angry too, and I showed my displeasure at being removed from the game by muttering something as I left the field, and then throwing my glove hard against the dugout floor.

I wasn't proud of that display, yet at the time my anger boiled over because I knew I had blown a golden opportunity to prove myself. It was a selfish motive on my part. I wanted to stay in the game to show my worth, even though I was hurt.

Padden's eyes cut through me as I picked up my glove seconds later. He was obviously displeased with my ill-tempered performance. For a moment, I felt like a high-schooler, and not the grown-up I was striving to be. I knew Padden wouldn't have done what I did. Yet I was a competitor, and I wanted to play. It was right that he took me out, I later realized, but at the time I was furious with him.

After the game, which we lost, he asked me to walk with him over the bridge to his home so we could talk. As we crossed the bridge in the darkness, with the threat of rain still present, we heard voices coming from the middle of the river, and so we stopped and looked over the concrete rail. It was difficult to see anything, but the voices were loud and we adjusted our eyes to the night and soon made out two figures. One was Kaiser. He and a London player, Russ Evon, were sitting atop the dam—the water was low, though still flowing over the dam—drinking beer. They had a case of beer beside them. It was one of the damnedest things I had seen.

"Ahoy, Tex!" shouted Padden. We both waved.

"Who goes there?" replied Kaiser.

"Florence Nightingale, who do you think," said Padden.

"They wouldn't let you in at the Albion?" I said.

"The turtle soup's better when you get it at its source," answered Kaiser. "It has a snap to it here."

"You're all wet," said Padden.

"Care to join us for a brew," asked Kaiser, holding a bottle aloft.

"Naw boys, not tonight, thanks," said Padden. "The kid and I are talking baseball. Have one for us."

"We'll do that, Tommy," Kaiser said. "And for the kid too."

We walked on, past the Albion and up to Ainslie Street. Padden turned and stopped, looking me in the eye. "You know, Charlie, what you did tonight was wrong."

"I…"

"Just wait," he said. "I'm not finished. Wanting to stay in the game, wanting to play hurt, that's not what I'm talking about. That's good. Can't fault you for that. I was the same. Anybody worth his salt is. You've gotta be that way. If you're not, then I'd question your right to call yourself a ballplayer."

"I know I was hurt, but I wanted to prove…"

"Kid," he said. "Let me finish. You're still a young pup, and I suspect you've grown up a lot this summer. I like you, and I can see some real potential in you, both on and off the field. Playing for the Terriers, with the talent we have, ain't easy. You would be starting for almost any other club in the Intercounty this summer. Fact is, you're an important part of this team. You gotta believe that. Don't let the fact that you don't play much get you down. I know it must, but just remember this: we need you, like we need the others, to win. When you walked into the dugout, you were mad. I understand that. But then you threw your glove, and said a few things. Even that was understandable. But you held on to that anger far longer than is appropriate. You have to let it go. A professional controls his anger and does nothing that will bring the team down. Get angry. Throw your glove down. Kick it. But let it go. There will always be another chance. Always. The game works that way."

"I was sorry I did that almost as soon as I did it," I said. "But I wanted to play to show what I could do. I want to help this team when called on, and I want to play. I feel I can contribute on the field."

"I know you can," said Padden. "And you have. When we've called on you, you've always come through. But remember, we have four major-leaguers on this club. Four. And we've got four more who could play in the majors in Kaiser, Waite, Shelton, and Sollenburger. That's a lot of talent. I'm going to tell you something, Charlie, something I think I've told you before, and you might not believe it, but we have almost as much talent on this team as we had on the Pirate teams of the early 1930s."

"I know," I answered, "but sitting in the dugout is hard game after game."

"I realize this," said Padden. "But you've got to look at this summer as a life experience that might only come once. I chose you on this team because of your talent, and the way I saw the others respect you. They all do. That's not always the case, especially with a rookie. But they like you, they can see your talent, and they want you here. And so do I. You're young. You got all your years ahead of you, and you'll have to take all the good with the bad. You can't go through life with all victories, and no defeats. No one can. We all have them. But playing with this group, this year, is an opportunity for you to learn from some of the best, to get to know some real characters who've lived life. So take this and use it. Maybe you'll write a book about it someday."

We strode up to Padden's home and Theresa followed two of her children out onto the porch to greet Tom. They'd been at the game.

"Evening, Mrs. Padden," I nodded.

"Hi, Charlie," she said. "Can I get you a soda."

"Naw, thanks," I replied, "I gotta be gettin' home. I can feel the rain starting. Can I take you up on that some other time?"

"Any time," she said.

"Good night, Charlie," said the kids.

"Night, kids."

After I left Padden the rain started. I returned over the bridge, but Kaiser and his drinking buddy were gone, having either fallen over the dam to a watery death, or having left to go home and get dry. My guess was the latter. I wasn't worried. Had they been there I might have taken them up on their offer.

☙ ☙ ☙

With the onset of June came the Canadian summer in all its southern Ontario glory. Real summer, when the land around Galt comes alive; when the grass has had time to take root and grow healthy and has been cut several times. Leaf shade dancing across the left-field hill on the late-afternoon breeze when the sun was falling big in the western sky. In May there had been only a hint of green on the trees; by June the trees were fully green, the foliage smothering. There was no chance of cool days and nights now, only heat. And it would get much hotter as the emerald parlance of June started burning auburn by July. In early June we played Stratford at Dickson Park and pounded out sixteen hits, cruising to a 13-6 win. Tulsa Tommy had figured prominently in the win.

"It is becoming more apparent with every passing game," wrote Laurie Brain in his newspaper column, "that the Galt Terriers knew what they were doing when they pried Long Tom Warren from the Texas league. The tall Tulsan citizen, who doubles on the mound and in the outfield, provided most of the fireworks last night [Friday] as the Terriers won their fourth straight game and moved into sole possession of third place by humbling the Nationals."

Warren hit two of the longest home runs—his fourth and fifth of the season—ever seen at Dickson Park and now led the league in both home runs and RBIs (16).

By early summer Padden had seen most of the other Intercounty ball clubs and the other towns of southern Ontario. It had been an eye-opener. He rather fancied our town, a town not unlike his native Manchester, New Hampshire. "I love the city and I love the people here," he told Brain. "They've really been nice to me."

But he had underestimated the calibre of play in the Intercounty. Indeed, it wasn't until midsummer before he was convinced of the strength of the league. "London was my yardstick," he said. "When I saw the London team perform and realized that it had dominated the league for the past few years, I figured we'd be good enough to win. But most of the clubs surprised me ... they really had strength." It was easy to underestimate the league. Until Padden had been approached by George Selkirk, and then by Murray, he'd never heard of Ontario's Major Intercounty League. When he arrived here he found, to his surprise, that Murray had signed Creedon and Warren. That alone was enough, thought Padden, to almost guarantee a pennant. But now it was midsummer, and we were trailing a couple of teams in the standings. Still, Padden had been around ball diamonds long enough to know that there was no need to panic. We weren't on top, but we weren't far off. With a half-season remaining, and the dog days just beginning, he knew that experience would be a factor. And Padden was as experienced as they come.

The heat was causing problems all over the eastern face of North America that summer. By July 6 there seemed to come a respite, after forty-one long days. I remember reading the *Reporter* that day, seeing news of Lisbon, Portugal, and the heat wave they faced, when the thermometer registered a world record 158 degrees Farenheit.

It was around this time that my girlfriend, Jennifer, and I—our relationship had, in fact, wound down and was almost over—rode our bicycles out of town for an afternoon picnic. That day in the meadow on the river flats north of town, with the sun beating down upon our faces and backs and the wind blowing softly, we came close to making love for the first time. It was a magical experience. I remember Warren always using the expression that close only counts in horseshoes and making love.

We were gone all afternoon, and when we returned home, we were both sunburnt in places where the skin was unusually sensitive to the sun. Until then we had been pretty reserved as far as sex went. I had seen and kissed her breasts, and she had used her hand to please me, but we had never been fully naked together at the same time. Now, as we placed our mouths and hands on each other, we were uninhibited in our explorations, and the afternoon passed by almost without notice. Although we were preparing to go off into the wider world that September, and sever our two-year-old relationship for good, we were still good friends and would remain so. Both of us felt, although we didn't articulate it, that it was right that we make love to each other, for we were both each other's first true love. That day, as our relationship was coming to an end, we finally consummated our love, or at least, came close. The heat of our bodies, the sweat, made us wet in the grass, and it was good to feel this. We continued this flowering passion for hours, and it was only later, as we rode back into town, that we remembered having forgotten to eat our lunch, and we stopped and ate, and we looked at each other and felt a closeness, a bond, that seemed odd because soon we would be parting company and going to different universities, perhaps never to feel that kinship again.

I wasn't one to brag, or talk to others about my exploits, nor would I ever be one to do this. No one would know about that afternoon in the meadow except she and I. Perhaps she would tell her friends. I cared not. I was beyond that.

Coming off the first weekend in July, with the heat wave still oppressive, we found ourselves in third place behind only the first-place Waterloo Tigers and the second-place Kitchener Legionnaires. Our 14-7 won-loss record was no great shakes, but I got the sense that if our team needed to, we could win at will. Goman's Waterloo club, led by former NHLer Don Gallinger, now the Tiger playing coach, owned a 13-5 record, while Kitchener was at 14-6. And the surprising Brantford club, which Larry Pennell and Mike King thought was as good as any they'd fielded in several years, was still in the thick of things with a 15-8 mark, ahead of the talented Londoners, who were in fifth place at 11-7. But the season was still young. The fact that four teams were all within easy striking distance of the first-place Tigers was an indication of how close everything was. The level of ball had, by everyone's estimation, risen, but there was no walkaway among the league's top five clubs. We had the best hitting lineup, but London was full of talent, and Waterloo had a strong club too.

I had admired Waterloo's Gallinger for a long time. He was one of the best hockey players I had ever seen in person. A couple of years earlier I had seen him play an exhibition game with the Bruins in Kitchener, and he was the outstanding player on the ice that night. I still couldn't understand why he had been banned for life from the NHL. A season-long suspension would hurt, I reasoned, and yet still allow him to return to the game. But life?

I would watch him closely on the ball diamond, for he possessed all sorts of talent there, too. And I would watch for any hint that his lifetime banishment from the game he loved was getting to him. He was loud, big, fast, and had a good arm. But he smiled a lot, too, and there was nothing I ever saw to indicate the way his life had been destroyed by the ban. Later I would learn the truth. I remember thinking that surely the NHL would lift the ban in a year or two. But that never happened.

At the time, Gallinger seemed to be running the show in Waterloo, even though Goman was really in charge. If I had been older, I would have seen the writing on the wall, for the following season Gallinger would be wearing Terrier pinstripes.

Don Gallinger

Reporter *sports editor Laurie Brain*

More Dog Days

We looked each afternoon to the *Reporter* sports pages, to see what Laurie Brain had to say. His column was a mainstay of my youth.

IN JULY WHEN WE PLAYED THE KITCHENER PANTHERS, LAURIE Brain wrote in the Saturday paper—which hit the newsstands only hours before game time—"This is one of the feature attractions of the season to date." Both teams would be going all out. Shelton, the Buffalo pitcher who was earning the respect of Galt fans as one of our best pitchers, would get the start. His opponent? Former major-leaguer Carl Fisher, who had been courted by Murray that spring.

The previous day, at Kitchener, young Bob Hoffman got the start for us, but after giving up three early runs, including one when Creedon, playing right field, couldn't hang on to a long Howie Meeker hit to right, Hoffman was sent to the showers. It was only the third inning. In came Connie Waite, who found the bases full. Kitchener catcher Bob Mullen promptly singled home a run before the lanky left-hander retired the side. But even Waite couldn't stop the Panthers that afternoon. Waite, whose real name was Waitkoviak, was proving to be more than a surprise for Murray and Padden. Padden thought he had all the tools to make it in the majors, and, in fact, believed the Buffalo first baseman was easily the smoothest in the entire league. When he first showed up in Galt with Shelton in the late spring, Bill Gregg, manager of the Canadian Imperial Bank of Commerce and a member of the Terrier executive, said to Murray, "Gus, don't you have any good Scotch names like Jones, or Ross, or Johnson on this team? Whatever happened to those people? This town was founded by a Scotsman." So the next day Waitkoviak became Waite, which Gus always explained was the Scottish derivative of the Polish Waitkoviak. But there was another reason Murray changed his name. Waitkoviak had been banished from organized ball.

Later that summer a Buffalo daily reported the exploits of a thirty-seven-year-old Buffalo player by the name of Waitkoviak. "He's been playing in the MUNY League for a score of years or more, but he showed one of the largest crowds in history Sunday that he still is one of the best 'clutch' players ever developed locally." Waitkoviak, a first baseman for the Puchalski team of the Jefferson-Collins Division, pitched for the first time that season in Buffalo and defeated the Simons 3-1 in the opener of the Class AA playoffs. "What's more," stated the report, "Connie drove in the winning run himself in the thirteenth inning with a triple, one of his three hits for the day."

An Ontario sportswriter by the name of Lloyd Johnston first made the connection that Galt's Waite was Buffalo's Waitkoviak. Both were thirty-seven, both had connections to Buffalo, and both could play first base and pitch. Wrote Johnston, "Not long after he had established himself as a good fielding first baseman for Galt, it came to light that he could also take his turn effectively on the mound. Connie also came to be feared as one of the heavy stickers on the Galt club." Because we had a day off in the schedule the day after Waitkoviak's supposed brilliant effort on the mound in the Buffalo MUNY League, the story carried some weight. And a pitcher for Gallinger's Waterloo Tigers by the name of Stan Kaczmarek, who also hailed from Buffalo, often claimed that Shelton and Waite were commuting between Buffalo and Galt. Soon we all knew the truth, but it was our job to keep it quiet. We needed Waite, and we needed Shelton.

Earlier that season, when we were facing Kitchener, Waite got three of our six hits, including a two-bagger into the crowd deep down the left-field hill. But he'd also been ejected from the game in the ninth inning by umpire Russ Tyne after a called third strike. Waite was livid and began a tirade that saw almost every known foul word thrust Tyne's way. I cringed when I heard some of the words, though I would hear worse before the season was over. Murray thought the language was going to reveal Waite to be a Buffalo native for sure. Tyne had no choice but to eject him. And all the while league president Otto Manske, sitting in the press box, was within easy earshot. Wrote Brain: "It'll be a good thing for the fans and the league in general if Otto moves to curb the foul tongues of some of the players. Profanity to the degree used by some of the players has no part in sport, especially a sport where so many women and children are in close attendance to the dugouts."

Back home in Dickson Park for a twilight game with the Guelph Maple Leafs, Warren would pick up his third win of the season. He had a 3-1 lead and only three men to go in the bottom of the ninth, but then a strange thing happened. Cam Pickard, who had been missing a couple of fingers for several years after an industrial accident, had dropped an easy pop fly before we finally won it in extra innings. But the win was not without controversy. The Maple Leafs made umpire Jerry Schmidt aware of their dissatisfaction in no uncertain terms. In the seventh inning, with the game tied 1-1, Schmidt had called a balk on pitcher Martin Cooper. It was a crucial point in the game, and Guelph couldn't believe Schmidt would call a balk then. Cooper had stopped in his delivery to the plate as Kaiser broke for home from third. When Kaiser was on base, there wasn't a pitcher in the Intercounty who wasn't worried. He was one of the fastest guys in the league.

So Schmidt made the call, Kaiser scored the go-ahead run, and all Guelph could do was lay into Schmidt verbally. But their anger would grow even stronger in the eighth inning when Cooper was called out after Walsh started to bat out of order. One strike was called on Walsh before Guelph realized the mistake. Veteran umpire Johnny Kumornik then made a miscue, calling Cooper out. It was the wrong call and Guelph knew it. So did Galt, but we weren't arguing. In fact, Cooper should have been permitted to take his turn at bat with one strike against him. The error almost sent the Guelph coaching staff and players over the edge. The Leafs argued with everybody, including the official scorer and the PA announcer. Warren, in improving his record to three wins against two losses, had allowed only two hits until the ninth inning. A new player, shortstop Billy Adams, in his Terrier debut, didn't help Warren's cause, making four errors. But other players, especially Kaiser, had made up for any lack on Adams's part. Kaiser, playing third, had made a diving stab of a scorching Crowley line drive in the sixth frame. As for Adams, whom the press was already referring to as Billy the Kid, he redeemed himself somewhat in the tenth inning when he speared Crowley's line smash over short and tossed to Pickard in time to make a double play at first.

I didn't exactly jump with joy when it was announced that Adams would be joining the club. Wes and I were the youngest guys on the team, and Wes had been getting a lot of playing time to that point. And me, although I was happy to just be on Padden's team, I wanted to play more. Sitting on the bench and not getting in was better than not being there at all, but like any player, I hungered to be a regular. The addition of Adams, who was from Padden's home town, meant my already limited playing time would be even more restricted.

Rosen, who hadn't played in the afternoon game in Kitchener, got our first run in the night game against Guelph when he homered. It was a hard liner that passed between the left and centre fielders. As good as Rosen was, Murray was more than a little concerned with rumours that had begun to circulate, suggesting Rosen was also playing for a Toronto softball team. It was only one more in a long list of worries that Gus had to contend with. Rosen's contract expressly forbade him from playing for any other team. Following the Guelph game, which Guelph promised to protest to the league's governing body, Laurie Brain wrote a column that criticized league president Manske for not issuing an order to all teams to ignore the public address system during games. The PA announcer's words weren't supposed to be taken as official. Teams should continue on with the game the same as it was before PA systems were introduced into baseball parks, wrote Brain. As president of the league, it was Manske's responsibility to send an order out to all teams to this effect. The PA system, which was introduced to Galt, as elsewhere, for the benefit of the fans, helped to keep fans informed, but there had been problems when teams started believing everything the announcer said. Announcers made mistakes. In the Guelph game the announcer became involved in a rhubarb over Walsh going to bat out of turn. But in this case the announcer was blameless because he had stopped announcing the batting order after the first rotation. The system of announcing the batting order the first time around, a system used in professional parks, was adopted in Galt only a week earlier after a similar incident. "If the announcer in all Intercounty ballparks adopted this system it would save them a lot of wind and gray hairs," wrote Brain, "and would place the onus of discovering discrepancies in the batting order strictly up to the opposing teams."

As for Kumornik, he too was taking a lot of flak over calling Cooper out after Walsh had batted out of turn. But Guelph players placed most of the blame on the PA announcer. He had failed to announce the batter, they claimed. Led by Guelph business manager

Johnny Mitchell, the Maple Leafs raised quite a fuss in the press box about everything, from the "terrible" umpiring of Kumornik and Tyne, to the way Guelph was being "robbed" of base hits. Kumornik got the message. He heard from several players, the Guelph coaches, and a fair number of visiting Guelph fans that Schmidt's poor call on the balk was criminal. He got it again when the Guelph player batted out of turn. Even the official scorer was unable to dodge the blame. He was yelled at for not being overly generous on infield errors. More than one observer could see that Guelph was a fighting team. Brain thought that if they saved their venom for the game, rather than the officials, they might improve their 5-14 record.

Injuries were a constant problem. Padden had broken a couple of ribs in June, and Wilf Dippel, a leftfielder who saw spot duty with the team, had bowled over the second baseman headfirst in the Kitchener game. It was a nasty collision. Everyone expected Dippel to come up injured. Instead, it was the second baseman, Bain, who came up hurting. After he limped off the field favouring his left knee, he was taken to the Galt hospital. Baseball was, after all, a contact sport. Each game presented risks. Just a day earlier, in nearby St. Mary's, Ontario, Donald Bradley, a young player with the St. Mary's intermediate OBA team, was struck on the head by a pitched baseball during practice. He died in the ambulance on the way to London.

Shelton soon got his sixth win of the season, and though he had been in difficulty several times during the game, he pitched flawlessly toward the end, retiring the last eight batters he faced. But the play of the game had come when Billy the Kid laid down a picture-perfect sacrifice bunt toward first base. Kaiser and Warren were on third and second. Adams bunted, then stood to one side of the plate, making no attempt to run the play out. Kaiser scored easily, and as Warren was rounding third base, Adams broke for first, taking the play from Warren. By the time pitcher Roy Tredgett had thrown Adams out at first, Warren beat the relay at home. Another highlight came early in the game when a foul tip had completely knocked the mask from the head of umpire Schmidt. Later, in the ninth inning, Schmidt threatened to clear the Kitchener bench after the Kitchener players had been particularly abusive. Kitchener had been without Meeker for the game. Meeker, an NHL hockey player who would become South Waterloo's Member of Parliament a couple of years later, was absent due to the serious illness of his young son. The only other absentee was Dickson Park groundskeeper Jack Spencer. He was unable to assume his regular post due to illness, so his son, Tom, relieved him.

Shelton had pitched well and our team was finally healthy. The only injury during the game came not to a player but to a spectator. Jim McLeod was cut by falling glass from a burst light bulb. More pressing was the problem of swearing. League officials, concerned with the abuse officials were taking and only too aware of the foul language that was becoming commonplace in Intercounty ballparks, issued a warning that the league was concerned over the amount of swearing on the playing field. Manske announced that whenever a player was ejected from a game for swearing the league would impose a fine on the player. Just that day league headquarters had given two players three-game suspensions. One was Galt junior Gord England; the other was Brantford Red Sox third baseman Stan Lipka. Manske was fast losing his patience. Lipka's suspension followed a row with plate umpire Reid Buck, himself a former Terrier star, in a Wednesday-night floodlit game at Waterloo only days earlier. Waterloo had beaten Brantford 4-3 in thirteen innings and Lipka had laid hands on Buck. England, the Galt junior, had done likewise in a junior game at Galt. "If these suspensions do not cut down the rough stuff and disorderly conduct, we intend to get tougher," warned Manske. The suspensions were to act as a warning. "We'll probably follow up with suspensions plus fines," added Manske. The two players were barred from playing or coaching, but they were allowed to sit in the dugout. Brain emphatically supported the suspensions. He wrote: "We, personally, are glad to see the league take action ... There is no excuse for a player pushing an umpire around, and when junior players try to emulate their older 'brothers' in this respect, it's going a little too far. We wonder what would happen if an umpire cast aside the dignity of his position and struck back at his annoyers? Maybe the players wouldn't be so fast with their dukes the next time."

Lipka, Brantford's third baseman, was one reason the Red Sox were among the league's top teams. If he wasn't the best third baseman in the league, he was among the top two. Pennell thought of Lipka as a natural. He made things look easy, especially when he was on defence. It seemed like he always got the ball over to first, but his uncanny way of waiting for the last possible moment had long since failed to unnerve Pennell. Lipka had picked up the habit from a minor-league manager who taught him how to get properly set up before throwing, pointing out that with Lipka's arm, even with a fast runner heading for first, it was better to take a split second to get his footing and get squared before making the throw. "Stan would always get the ball from third to first in time," said Pennell. "He would beat the slowest runner by just a hair, and he would beat the fastest runner by the same margin." Although he had lost a very real chance of going to the majors when he was called into the service in 1943—he had been hitting .326 with the Montreal Royals, Brooklyn's top farm club—he was one of the best Canadian infielders ever. Pennell was just glad Lipka had taken him up on his offer to come to Brantford. And Lipka, for his part, was glad, too, for he settled into Brantford as if it were his hometown. He later became the manager of the government-run liquor store in Brantford.

Galt kids were glad he'd come to Brantford too. They liked making fun of his large hooked nose. "Is that a banana or your nose," they would say when Lipka came to town.

The hub of the city, Galt's YMCA at Queen's Square

Summer Days, Summer Nights

On those summer nights the wind would sail over the field, sometimes gale-force, sometimes just a soft breeze, but always it would be there, fresh, unpredictable, and unexpected, like your first love.

THE LIPKA SUSPENSION WAS A BLOW TO BRANTFORD. They needed each of their everyday players to be competitive with the other Intercounty teams. Pennell knew they could field a top club on any given night, as long as guys like Lipka and centre fielder Lockington were in the lineup, and either Billy Gibbs or Alf Gavey were on the mound. "Galt had an excellent ball club, maybe AA or better," he said, "but we had better pitching with Gibbs and Gavey." Pennell, who always loved getting hold of a tough legal problem and trying to solve it, was the same way with baseball. It was a challenge trying to assemble the right nine on the field. Pennell always liked to speculate, in later years, on who the best Intercounty third baseman of all time was. "I can't make up my mind on that," he would say. Prime Minister Lester B. Pearson, whom Pennell worked for as Brantford's Member of Parliament in the early 1960s, had played third base for the Guelph Maple Leafs in 1919. "Either Stan Lipka or Lester Pearson," Pennell would say. "Pearson [a Liberal] would be better going to his left, but Stan had better range going to his right."

One time in Brantford, Lipka began a tirade against Kaiser that was a show for the fans. He appeared to be yelling—indeed, he was—and was incensed. Judging by his body language, the two were close to blows.

"Want to go out for a beer after the game?" Lipka yelled at Kaiser.

"For Chrissakes," replied Kaiser, "sure I do."

"Okay, I'll meet you at the Overland Hotel," Lipka said. "And bring the others along."

"You got it," shouted Kaiser, and the two parted, appearing to swear at each other.

"Screw you," said Lipka.

"Screw yourself," said Kaiser.

The whole thing was a show, though fans believed the two hated each other.

Lipka's manhandling of umpire Buck was uncharacteristic. Normally he was more subdued than that, though he was known to put on a big show—for the fans—yelling at an umpire who would also be acting, when in fact they were friends. But there were plenty of stories about umpires taking real abuse from players and managers over the years. A few years earlier Galt umpire Gord Bradshaw, who still held the all-time Intercounty batting record from his playing days in the early 1930s, was taken to task by Kitchener's Jack Couch one night in Kitchener. Kumornik, himself a former Intercounty player, was working the game with Bradshaw. Bradshaw was behind the plate, and Kumornik was working the bases. "Gord was tough," said Kumornik. "And Couch liked to think he was tough too." They got into an argument. Couch, the Kitchener coach, didn't like the way Bradshaw was calling the game. "Jack Couch himself was pretty rough," recalled Kumornik. "So stupid Couch comes along and he challenged Gord to a fight."

"As soon as the game is over I'll see you under the stands," said Couch.

"You got it," answered Bradshaw. He never backed down from anyone, though he wouldn't go looking for trouble.

Kumornik witnessed the altercation after the game. He figured Couch lasted about three seconds. "One punch and down he went," Kumornik said. Then Bradshaw walked out from under the stands. Bradshaw, not known to be a violent person, or even an occasional fighter, was not only the greatest hitter the Intercounty ever saw; he was one tough son of a bitch, said Kumornik. Kumornik never forgot it. Neither did Jack Couch.

As a rule, Kumornik believed, it was the non-playing umpires who created most of the problems. One umpire who always seemed to be mired in controversy was St. Thomas native Frank Slota. "He umpired like he refereed hockey games," said Kumornik. "Everybody was thrown out." Kumornik, on the other hand, almost went out of his way to keep players in the game.

If the umpiring to that point in the Intercounty season had been inferior, the calibre of play had improved. But, as Brain pointed out, 39 errors in the previous five Galt Terrier games showed that the umpires weren't the only people making mistakes.

That Monday night we missed a golden opportunity to take over possession of first place when we dropped a 13-4 game to the Tigers. Veteran right-handed pitcher Bert McCrudden, now nearing the end of his career and going after his fifth win against two losses, was the victim of a savage Waterloo attack in the second inning when the Tigers mauled him for eight runs on seven hits. Hoffman relieved McCrudden with two out in the third. The Tigers got early home runs from Gallinger, who blasted a shot over the right-field fence in the first inning. Jada Dahmer, the league's leading batter, padded his average with four hits in five trips to the plate.

It was early July, and the dog days had started. We were in need of more pitching. There was Warren and Shelton, and Waite could pitch as well, but we needed more depth. Around this time a published report had characterized Murray as being like the old woman in the shoe. "He has so many players he doesn't know what to do." The out-of-town press had even stated once that Gus had two teams—one coming and one going. One writer suggested that maybe Hustlin' Gus was trying to start a league of his own. Several pitchers were said to be on their way to Galt.

Dennis Smedley, Wes Lillie's good friend, and mine too, hung around the team a lot that summer, often driving us to away games. He figured Murray's phone bill must have been enormous that summer. Lillie would often comment to Smedley, "I don't know where he's getting all these players." Murray was a wheeler-dealer who would do anything to bring in players and put people into the stands. Murray was always recruiting. He had a seemingly endless supply of names and phone numbers. Earlier in the season he got the green light to bring in nine U.S. college players for the season, but only one, Don "Lefty" Perkins out of Michigan, or Penn State, depending on which version or newspaper report you believed, would come, and he wouldn't make a spectacular first impression. Indeed, early that July he was still trying to work himself into condition. Wrote Brain, "It may be a little too early to pass judgment." It was. Perkins, after working himself into shape, would prove to be one of the best pitchers in the league. But with our loss to Waterloo it was apparent to everybody in the park that what we needed was more pitching. The Intercounty pennant was still anybody's race. And in our last three games we had made fifteen errors. "Hardly the pace of a pennant-winner," wrote Brain. To make matters worse, word had it that the Guelph Maple Leafs would protest their 4-3 Friday-night loss. Rex MacLeod, in the *Guelph Mercury*, said that umpire-in-chief Bill Almas had assured Guelph that they had legitimate grounds for a protest. "Mitchell," wrote MacLeod, "had not decided definitely if he would protest. All that was holding him back was the fact that he doesn't wish to settle all his games in the committee rooms."

The league held a meeting at eight o'clock on the evening of Thursday, July 7, at the Galt YMCA. On the agenda were the OBA play-offs as well as disciplinary matters. Waite's tirade was one issue up for discussion. Swearing was another. Officials felt that with fans so close to the field, such swearing would have a negative impact on the league. The popularity and reputation of the league, the teams, even the game of baseball itself, was at stake. Padden had other things on his mind. He gave word to the media that week that the Terriers were attempting to shore up their pitching staff. He reported that Ralph "Lefty" Hammond, recently released by Guelph, was coming to Galt for a trial. Hammond had been one of the best pitchers in the province at one time. He even had a crack at the pros. He hadn't been a ball of fire the past couple of seasons with Guelph, and his back had been giving him trouble, but perhaps a change of scenery would help. Hammond could also hit and play outfield.

Padden and the Pirates, 1933

Lefty Comes to Town

Perry Como topped the music charts that July with his hit song "Some Enchanted Evening," and Kool-Aid packages (all six flavours) could be had for five cents apiece. The Sunset Drive-In was showing movies to large crowds; life was very good.

B Y THE MORNING OF MONDAY, JULY 11, GUS MURRAY COULD finally inform the press that he'd signed two new pitchers. Only one of them stuck with the team. Lefty Perkins was listed as a Michigan State southpaw. Murray and Padden were relieved. Pitching had been our only weakness, and even at that, it wasn't so much a weakness as a missing piece in a puzzle. Our pitchers were good. We just needed more of them. Padden knew Perkins, but to the rest of us he was a mystery man. Little was known about this new college boy. By looks alone he was obviously no spring chicken. Word was that he'd been in the service during the war, and was only now resuming his college career. Both Padden and Murray knew that Perkins was no Michigan State player. About the closest Perkins had ever been to East Lansing, Michigan, was Galt. Perkins wasn't even his real name. If there ever was a Don Perkins out of MSU, this wasn't him. His real name was Harry Sollenburger, and he was a Second World War veteran out of Pennsylvania. Like Lipka in Brantford, and several others, his best baseball years were spent in the service. He had played for Padden's Manchester Yankees team in the New England League the year before. The real Don Perkins, after agreeing to come to Galt, had failed to show.

Padden first told Murray about Sollenburger early in the spring, but several weeks had passed before Sollenburger contacted him. By that time Padden, thinking the Terriers had missed a league deadline for signing new players, told Murray he knew of a left-hander from Chambersburg, Pennsylvania, who was interested in coming to Canada, but he would have to come as Perkins. "Is he any good?" asked Murray. "You bet," said Padden. "He'll help our club." That was all Murray needed to hear. He trusted Padden. So Murray phoned Sollenburger in Chambersburg and told him to come up. Sollenburger, whose options, by the summer of 1949, were limited, wasn't prepared to quit the game yet. He still had some playing left in him. But what nobody bothered to mention was that he would have to play under the alias of Lefty Perkins.

"I didn't get there until early July," Sollenburger recalled years later. "I didn't know it until I got there but they had a ruling that nobody could join a team after July 1. They had some fictitious names so they gave me one." Sollenburger's pride was hurt somewhat, but he was willing to go along with it. The alias would allow him to play another summer. That was the important thing. Besides, as he soon learned, the Terriers lived like kings in the small southern Ontario city. Their names were household words not only in Galt but in other Intercounty cities. And it wasn't as if Murray and the Terriers were the only ones guilty of signing players under fictitious names. Many of the teams did it. In 1950 Murray signed Bill Horne to a Terrier contract. Horne didn't want to coast on his famous father's coattails, nor did he need the pressure that came automatically with his real last name: Hornsby. With his father's permission, he became, that summer in Galt, Bill Horne. The only people who knew that Rogers Hornsby was his father were Gus Murray and a couple of other Terrier executives. Gus enjoyed his weekly chats with Rogers Hornsby, a legend who was regarded as one of the greatest players of all time. The senior Hornsby was interested in the progress of his son, Bill, and was always eager to hear from Murray.

In 1950 the Brantford Red Sox gave a player an alias, signing a young man known as Pedro Juarez, whose real name was Preston Gomez. Brantford president Larry Pennell, a lawyer, said it was all perfectly legal. "He could have called himself Smith and it would have been okay," Pennell said. "We had his outright release.

Everything was in order." But Gomez, who'd been up with Washington in the majors several years earlier, was concerned that by playing in Canada— he thought the Intercounty was an outlaw league similar to the Mexican league—he would jeopardize the possibility of his ever returning to the majors. That's why he wanted the alias. The practice of giving players an alias was kept up for several more years in the Intercounty. Waite's real name was obscured because he had been banned from organized ball after accusations about him pilfering wallets and valuables. Terrier executive member Bill Gregg, the bank manager, thought Murray had changed Waitkoviak's name simply because he had commented on the lack of good Scottish names on the roster. Murray never told Gregg the real reason he changed the Buffalo player's name to Waite was because Waitkoviak had a less than auspicious past. So there was a certain amount of subterfuge going on. When one team got wind of any impropriety by another team they were quick to bring the matter before Intercounty boss Otto Manske.

Sollenburger's rights, that spring, were owned by the New York Yankees. "But I decided at my age I wasn't going to get too far, and so I asked for my release and called Padden." In some ways it signalled the end of his baseball-playing days, the end of a dream. Under Padden at Manchester in 1947 Sollenburger had gone 6-5, a won-lost record that was nothing to write home about. Still, it was one of the best on the team. "There were a couple of guys who didn't have as near as good a record as me and they were called up and I stayed where I was." He went back to the Manchester Yankees in 1948. But the sad fact was that, at twenty-nine, he was on the way down. Had the war not taken the best baseball years of his life, he could have expected a call-up. But his age worked against him. Sure, he was one of the aces on the team, but he had to do better than that if he wanted to get a shot at the big leagues at age twenty-nine.

"I could see the handwriting on the wall," he said. He knew he was too old. He could still play, but he would never get the chance he had yearned for. There are some people who, when faced with that sobering reality, call it quits when that happens. But Sollenburger couldn't. Baseball was still in his blood. He had always dreamed of making it to the majors. That, and his love for the game, his love for playing the game, had always motivated him. Now, as he realized that his dream was dead, he was surprised to find that he still wanted to play the game. The game was no longer a means to an end. It was an end in itself. That was all that mattered. It would be easy to blame the war years for his failure to realize his childhood dream. Others would use that excuse. Some would go to the grave feeling cheated. Not Sollenburger. He was in the infantry nearly thirty-six months before going to Germany three weeks before the war ended. When he returned to Pennsylvania he resumed his playing career at Sunberry, where he posted a 6-7 won-lost mark before his demotion to Manchester.

Born in Chambersburg, Pennsylvania, on Christmas Day, 1920, Sollenburger grew up around baseball the way Kaiser grew up around hockey. Baseball was his life as much as hockey had been Kaiser's life. "When I was a youngster," said Sollenburger, "that's all I thought about. My dad played a little sandlot ball but he was a farmboy and I guess he didn't have much of a chance."

In the summer of 1935, when Sollenburger was fourteen, his father, along with some of his cousins, took him to see a big-league game in Washington. The Yankees were playing Washington that day, and Lou Gehrig, his idol, was there. "The only thing I can really remember was he went one-for-five and they had a big high scoreboard in right field and he hit a line smash up on that board."

Sollenburger started in the outfield as a kid, but made the switch to pitching when a former St. Louis Cardinal player named Mike Mowery, who also lived in Chambersburg, suggested he give it a try. "I was about twenty then," he said. Evidently Mowery, who had played with the Cardinals in the 1910s, knew what he was talking about. "He wanted me to go as a pitcher, so he wrote the Baltimore Orioles of the International League and they signed me. But about the middle of the year I passed my army physical and had to go in the service and then Baltimore released me."

It was a story to which many ballplayers from Sollenburger's era could also relate. Baltimore was Cleveland's top farm team. If the war hadn't come along when it did, he could have expected a shot at making the Indians. But Sollenburger didn't complain. Stationed at Fort St. Louis, Washington, early in 1946, he was scouted by a New York Yankee representative who owned a sporting goods store in Tacoma. "When I got discharged there was a letter from the New York Yankees asking me to call their head scout, Paul Kritchell." He called. They signed him to a contract and sent him to Sunberry, Pennsylvania, in the Interstate League. "There were quite a few in that league who went up to the majors," said Sollenburger, though he wasn't one of them. By then he was past his prime and, like so many talented players of the time, had been robbed of the best baseball years of his life by the war. Sollenburger was not bitter for he knew it could have been worse.

In Sunberry he posted a 6-7 won-lost record, yet two other pitchers, one with a 2-12 mark, the other with a 4-13 record, went up to Newark for spring training. Sollenburger was sent down to Manchester. The Yankees by then knew it would not pay to stick with him. Although he was undoubtedly one of the aces on the staff, how many years could they get out of him? Not enough, they decided.

He took a trip to Amsterdam that spring, but still yearned to play baseball. Knowing that Padden had gone to Canada, Sollenburger gave him a call. It would only be for a summer, he thought. What the hell. Why not?

On the Monday that Murray announced Perkins had signed a Terrier certificate, Sugar Ray Robinson was preparing to meet Cuban Kid Galivan for the world welterweight title. Galt residents, like sports fans everywhere, were following this story, just as they were eager to see this new college southpaw, Lefty Perkins, in action. Perkins had arrived in town a few days earlier and was now ready to play, said Murray. His certificate had been approved and returned by Intercounty headquarters. Word had it that Perkins might even get the starting assignment for our game that night, a makeup game—our weekend game had been rained out—with the Waterloo Tigers at Dickson Park. Padden was noncommittal when asked by Brain who would get the start. "Either Perkins or Jeff Shelton," said Padden. In truth, he was set to use Shelton, believing Perkins needed a few more workouts before he'd be ready.

We had an exhibition game scheduled for the next night, Tuesday—we had five games that week, beginning with Waterloo on Monday night—against the bewhiskered House of David club, a team that had once counted an aging Grover Cleveland Alexander among its players. Games followed one after the other each night that week against Waterloo, Stratford, and, on Saturday afternoon, the London Majors.

It was a crucial week. A good week would put us on top in the standings, but a bad week could mean dropping out of contention. With just over a month remaining in the season, we had to make our stand soon. I knew we had the talent, and the coaching. Now, when it counted, could we use it? Everyone seemed to take it in stride when, a week earlier, we got news that Guelph had officially disputed our recent win and the league's protest board rendered a decision in Guelph's favour and threw out the game. That dropped us back into a two-way tie for second place with the London Majors; we both had fourteen wins and eight losses.

Game time that Monday on the river flats was eight o'clock, but many people started heading to the ballpark at 7 P.M. Some even got

149

there before six to set up their barbecues and slanted chairs on the third-base hill, beginning what would become known as a tailgate party. Everyone was eager to see the new Terrier college boy named Perkins after Padden had announced that Perkins was to make his first start. Murray, who was busy with another one of his promotions prior to the game, this time giving away free dresses to lucky ladies, was now certain that Galt had the talent to go all the way. But he, too, was curious to see this new guy, the fellow he had asked to go by the name of Perkins instead of his given name of Sollenburger. If he was all that Padden said he was, then we should have a decided advantage, even if Waterloo still held on to first place in the standings.

It would be a tough game. Both teams expected that. Waterloo entered the contest a half-game up on the second-place Kitchener Legionnaires. Perkins was briefed on all this before the game. If we won Monday and Wednesday against Waterloo, we would move into first place. The race was so tight that a couple of Galt wins at the expense of the Tigers would drop Waterloo into fifth spot. Until that Monday night, Waterloo had held the upper hand. They had defeated Warren easily in our first meeting of the season back in mid-May at Galt, and, more recently, they had pounced on McCrudden for eight runs in the second inning and coasted to a 13-4 win in Waterloo. Wrote Brain in that evening's edition of the *Reporter*, which hit the newsstands just hours before the big game: "The answer to the question, just how long can Waterloo moundsmen continue to weave their magic spell over Terrier hitters lies in the bats of the Galt players. Maybe the answer will be forthcoming tonight."

The team feared for its hitting around the league, the same team Lockington said had as good a Murderer's Row as any team ever had, hadn't yet consistently shown their hitting prowess. Everyone knew it was there. As game time neared, Padden, after talking to Perkins and Shelton, had a change of heart. He scratched Perkins from the game sheet and pencilled in our ace, Shelton. Perkins wasn't yet in one hundred percent playing shape. He needed a few more days. Shelton, by contrast, was in mid-season form. He responded by throwing a five-hitter and blanking the Tigers 6-0 for his seventh win of the season. It was our first win over Waterloo in more than two seasons and moved us into a first-place tie with the Tigers. Moreover, it was a convincing win. We not only won a key game, but we had humbled Don Gallinger's Tigers. During the game Intercounty president Otto Manske sat in the front row of the press box near the field. Most of us weren't pleased with the umpiring of Hamilton's controversial Russ

Tyne, nor were we pleased that the league had upheld Guelph's protest, and we blasted Manske all night long. Tyne wasn't popular with Waterloo either, and their players roasted the league president too. The newspapers wrote it up as one of the best ball games of the season.

"It had just about everything one could expect from two top teams," wrote Brain. "Good pitching, some timely and long-distance clouting, daring base running, sensational fielding and a couple of good old-fashioned rhubarbs with the umpires." Rosen was the most vocal of the Terriers. He made it clear what he thought of the cocky little Tyne. Tyne called a second strike on him in the first inning, and Rosen, believing the ball was nowhere close, was livid and argued the call. Nose to nose, Rosen started swearing at Tyne. Tyne was quick to give him the thumb. Manske had recently given a directive that swearing was getting out of hand and he wanted umpires to crack down. In Tyne's estimation, Rosen had gone too far. Brain wrote that Rosen said Tyne was full of "meatballs, or words to that effect." Tyne then pointed to the bench. Rosen was finished. Worse, another new league ruling stipulated that any player ejected from a game be given an automatic five-dollar fine, though that wouldn't cause Rosen to lose any sleep.

Later in the game two Waterloo players also questioned Tyne's judgment on the calling of balls and strikes, but, after seeing what happened to Rosen, they saved their tongue tirades for Manske, in the press box, and the Galt fans in the grandstand. One of the players, Ike Koslowski, wasn't satisfied with merely blasting Manske after he had been made to look foolish while striking out in the ninth. He looked up into the stands and told fans what they could do with their boos and catcalls. Manske, who just a week earlier threatened to impose a fine on any player he heard using foul language, took note. Batting leader Jada Dahmer, who was destined to finish third in the batting race behind Waite and London's Bechard, had also given Manske an earful. What Rosen called Tyne was mild compared to the language used by Dahmer and Koslowski. The difference was that Rosen had mouthed off to Tyne; the two Waterloo players had taken out their frustration on Manske and the fans. That made Rosen all the more furious. How many times had he yelled in similar fashion to umpires in the majors? Hundreds. It was part of baseball, the sort of thing that happened all the time. Smart umpires are well aware of the fact that, in the heat of the moment, players sometimes lose their heads. Most umpires learn to walk away, letting the heated player blow off steam. If cuss words are used, they usually aren't heard the first time. But when the player is insistent in telling the umpire what he thinks of him and his family back to the third or fourth generation, an umpire will fire back with the only weapon at his disposal: banishment. All umpires have a tolerance for a certain amount of abuse. It comes with the job. But in Rosen's case, Tyne had stood his ground. What was more disconcerting to local fans was the behaviour of the Waterloo players. "When a player deliberately walks to the stands and screams profanity at the fans who are keeping him and the game of baseball going," wrote Brain, "the league should take quick action."

Shelton had performed magnificently for his seventh win, even contributing at the plate. Led by Kaiser, Creedon, and Waite, each of whom hit a triple, and two-base hits by Pickard, Warren, and Shelton, we produced nine hits, six of them for extra bases, as we dismissed diminutive starter Al Dumouchelle, chunky Gord Ariss, and, finally, Lefty John Barbeau. The highlight came with Warren at the plate and swinging as both Creedon and Kaiser pulled a double steal, with Creedon making a clean steal to home plate.

The only sour note came in the middle innings when young Patsy Smith of Waterloo Avenue, was struck on the shoulder by a batted ball and received a painful bruise. Bill Martin, our trainer, treated the young girl by applying ice packs to the injury. Patsy was sitting in the bleachers when struck, unlike several dozen other youngsters who regularly gamboled around the ballpark and grandstand, frequently not paying attention to foul balls. There were calls to do something about such nuisance kids before somebody got hurt. "There have been many narrow escapes, but how long is their luck going to hold out?" asked Brain.

Psychologically, beating Waterloo for the first time in two years had broken us of the Waterloo jinx. Mrs. Domianczuk, of 68 Birch Street, won one of the dresses Murray gave away that night. Billy Reynolds, a noted long-distance runner who had competed for Canada at the 1928 Olympics, Dom McMaster, and Mrs. Hunt also won prizes. For Murray, it was just another night of promotions, but he knew the biggest promotion of all were the nine starters Padden put on the field.

It was mid-season. Murray's scheme to put a top-quality club on the field, and to draw fans down to the ballpark, was working. Now all we had to do was win the pennant, followed by the Intercounty title. Then the all-Ontario title.

Next up, the House of David exhibition game Tuesday night. It promised to be a fun game. The team, which represented the House of David religious cult, was one of the most famous team names in semi-pro baseball and was drawing immense crowds throughout North America in those years. Fans liked to see these men play baseball, for they looked like no baseball players they had ever seen. All of them had beards—cutting hair was against their religious beliefs—and none of them, supposedly, ate meat, fowl, fish, or lard. They were the strangest sight in baseball.

Quipped Brain in his "Sifting the Sports" column of July 12, "The idea of wearing a beard on the baseball diamond as the House of David players do, might revolutionize baseball if generally adopted in all parts of the country. Equipment dealers are not in favor of it as it might cramp their style in the matter of selling masks, chest protectors, etc. If a catcher could grow an extra long and heavy beard it would enable him to dispense with a heavy chest protector and if the whiskers were long enough he might also discard his shin guards. Then, too, a number of passed balls would be averted by becoming entangled in the brush. Whiskers also would serve to screen signals from opposing teams."

Second-stringers like me would be given enough playing time to keep our game skills sharp. Nothing was on the line, unlike the game we would play Wednesday night in Waterloo. Of more pressing concern for Galt fans was the hope that the traffic chaos of a night earlier could be averted. At Monday night's game there was a traffic jam, something almost unheard of in Galt, at the park. Only one gate was open to traffic, which meant some motorists were forced to wait more than forty minutes before they could exit from the ballpark. A better method must be found to disperse traffic, otherwise fans wouldn't bother coming out to the games. But it seemed to take several more weeks before traffic was dispersed quickly. The last time Galt drew huge crowds, in the 1920s, most people had walked to the game. Traffic problems caused by so many automobiles were a new phenomenon in the summer of 1949.

Murray, who believed that the Galt Parks Board should be taking a hand in helping to control traffic, had been feuding with the board all summer. He thought the parks board was asking for too much money from the Terriers, and he felt they didn't groom the diamond well enough. The parks board had come under criticism from the Terriers after the Terriers complained that parks board employees forced postponement of their July 6 game against Stratford. Fans had shown up for the game only to find that it was off due to poor weather. But Galt groundskeeper Jack Spencer, who had been looking after the baseball diamond at Dickson Park since 1919, the inaugural season for the Intercounty, claimed he marked out the diamond that day. Superintendent Percy Hill backed up his employee. Contrary to what Murray and Padden were saying, they claimed they were not responsible for calling off the game. Padden and Murray said they had no part in the postponement. Earlier it was reported that Murray and Padden had taken a look at the diamond about 3 o'clock that afternoon, and the condition of the field was so bad they had to call the game off. But a number of local fans were already in Dickson Park before they heard the game was called off. Conditions at game time were much better than they had been earlier in the day. A stiff breeze and intermittent sunshine was drying the grass nicely, and, the fans felt, with a little work on the diamond, the park would have been ready by game time. But since it was considered mannerly to let the visiting team know of the cancellation, in addition to it being league policy, Stratford officials had to be contacted with plenty of advance warning. Some Stratford players would leave their jobs early, grab a quick bite to eat, and then gather their equipment and travel the thirty-five miles to be at the park in plenty of time for batting practice and infield practice. The skies over Galt were still threatening as late as 4:30 P.M., even though they looked considerably better by game time. Now, with neither Murray nor the park attendant taking responsibility for calling the game off, people weren't sure who to blame. It was obvious that Stratford didn't have anything to do with it. Another "whodunit" mystery, wrote Brain with a chuckle, one of many that season.

Meantime, Kitchener beat the Guelph Maple Leafs to move into sole possession of first place. In that game too, a player was ejected for swearing at the umpire. Second baseman Howie Meeker was given the boot by plate umpire Thompson in the seventh inning for arguing a called third strike too vigorously. It was reported next day that Meeker was the first player to be tagged with the five-dollar fine Manske had imposed for ejection from a game. In fact, that distinction had gone to Rosen. Rosen's ejection and fine had come in his first at-bat; Meeker's came later, in the seventh inning of Kitchener's game. It was close, but Rosen beat Meeker by an hour.

The weather was fine Tuesday afternoon, and despite the fact that the game had been heavily promoted—Newlove's Radio Service, a station wagon with two powerful loudspeakers mounted to the roof, announced the game all day around town—only one thousand fans turned up. Nearly six hundred of them had already bought their tickets in advance. Murray had an agreement with the House of David team to be at the park no later than 7 o'clock. Game time was 8 P.M.

When they failed to show by 8:15 P.M., Murray had no choice but to call the game off and refund all the tickets. Fans queued up at the box office for their refunds. Murray, who was apologetic on the outside but seething inside, said he would lodge a complaint with the Ontario Baseball Association, which sanctioned exhibition games with barnstorming teams.

Murray didn't have to wait long to hear what action the OBA would take. The next day it was announced that the House of David and Zulu Giants baseball teams would be barred from playing with any OBA teams until further notice. Some of the proceeds from the Galt game were to have gone to a charitable organization. "We cannot have teams promising bookings and then failing to appear like this," said Snyder. "The agent who handles bookings for the House of David team also handles the Zulu Giants." The ban was to stay in effect permanently, or until a suitable explanation was provided to the OBA. The suspension of all House of David games—the coloured Zulu Giants too—did little to help Murray. He was upset because almost one thousand Galt fans, told their money would be refunded over the park loudspeaker, had to line up and wait an hour or more for their refund. Every one of them had wasted a perfectly good summer evening.

There was speculation that the incident might put an end to such exhibition games in Galt. Barnstorming teams usually got the best of such agreements by not having to put up any guarantee. And oftentimes they showed up late, usually getting off the hook by giving some flimsy excuse if they failed to arrive on time. On the other hand, such teams were always given a rain guarantee, with a straight guarantee of so much money for playing the game, and, in some cases, a percentage of the gate above the minimum. The House of David and the Zulu Giants had hooked the Galt management for $175 on two previous deals and they had yet to play their first game in Galt.

I was deeply disappointed when they didn't show. I had lost out on an opportunity to play a full game. That night I met up with Jennifer and we walked down to the Capitol Theatre to watch *The Great Gatsby*, with Alan Ladd. We kissed under cover of the darkness and the maple trees when I took her home, though there was little of the passion we had known in the meadow. I returned home late that night under starlight, angry with the House of David, and unsure about the impending breakup with Jennifer. In a few weeks, after a game, I would do something stupid, and lose the respect that Jennifer held for me.

Honus and the boys

Honus and the Boys

In all of baseball's lore, there remain just a handful of players who are up among the gods. Honus Wagner was one of them.

WHEN PADDEN HEARD THAT WES AND I WERE GOING TO Detroit to see the Tigers play the Yankees, he pulled me aside. "Bill Dickey is the manager," Padden said. "He's an old friend. Go to his hotel and ask to see him. Tell him Tom Padden sent you. He'll get you guys tickets to the game."

We boarded the night train to Detroit at the CPR station across from the collegiate, and as we crossed the Grand in the dark, I looked out the window and could see the town lights shimmering on the water in the moonlight. Dickson Park was in darkness, and soon we had climbed the grade at Barrie's Cut, the biggest rise between Chicago and Montreal, and were travelling through the southern Ontario countryside at what seemed like a great speed.

Train rides were still somewhat of a novelty, even though we averaged about two trips to Toronto a year by steam train. This was my first trip in the other direction, and the big city of Detroit beckoned.

I still remember it like it was yesterday. After wishing I hadn't found his hotel, or his room, I finally summoned up enough courage to follow through. I knocked tentatively on Dickey's door and this big monster of a guy appeared.

"Hi, Mr. Dickey," I said reverently. "I play ball for the Galt Terriers in Ontario, and Tom Padden is our manager. When I told him I was coming down here, he told me to look you up, that you might have some tickets."

"Kid, I'd love to help you out. Tommy is an old friend, but I just gave away my last tickets. If you had come by a couple hours earlier..."

We exchanged pleasantries, and he inquired about Tom, and then we were off.

Eventually we found some tickets, though we paid top dollar for them. From the stands, Dickey didn't loom as large as he had appeared close up. That night, after the game, we slept on a park bench before returning by train in the morning. Later, Padden asked about Dickey and how we had made out. I told him we were late in getting to Dickey and he had already given away all his tickets.

Padden swore up and down. "All those years I've known him," said Padden, still dumbfounded. He was quite upset. "Dickey could have gotten you tickets."

Seeing him get angry, genuinely angry over a perceived slight against us, made me feel important. I never hid my admiration for Padden, and when I saw him yell at umpires that summer over disputed calls, I could sense the intimidation in his voice, and, I'm sure, so could the umpires. But I knew that was not the real Padden. It was simply his game face. Beneath that hard baseball exterior was a good man with an impressive background.

One morning during the early days of July, Padden confided in me. I'm not sure why he confided in me, of all people, other than he knew I was going off to university, and he knew I would listen. I always figured he believed his story and experiences would somehow add to my education.

In essence, he told me he had woken up and fully realized he was in a new town, in a different country, and with a family—Tommy Jr. was thirteen, Janice eleven, and Robert seven—to support on precious little income. Theresa and the children had come up after the school year ended, and that meant Padden had five mouths to feed on only his income. His managerial career, so far, had amounted to very little. In his mind raced questions about where he had come from, where he was, and where he was going. Galt, he believed, was merely a stepping stone to further his career in baseball. He had been to the majors as a player, and had had a relatively successful go of it; now he wanted to return to the majors as a manager, whether it took five years, ten years, or perhaps longer. I thought he would be a cinch.

Such periods of contemplation were always private with Padden. On the outside he presented an exterior that hid such questions, and self-doubts, looking every bit the major-league manager he aspired to become. Other managers in the Intercounty could see this, as did umpires. A lot of people that summer would remark how he looked like a pro. He knew his baseball, they would say.

Padden might have had doubts about how his life was unfolding, but he never felt uncertain when it came to baseball. As a player he was as sure-footed as they came. If he felt at home anywhere, it was on the ball diamond. All he had to do was think back to his days with the Pirates, when he had listened to Pirate coach Honus Wagner recount one of his many tales, or when he had been at spring training in Florida with Gehrig and Ruth. Anybody who had those types of experiences had a right to feel confident on a ball diamond.

To know Padden you should know something of his past, for he had a remarkable past.

In the early years when he had first gone to the Pirates from the Yankees, he got to know Wagner well. Wagner's first spring with the Pirates as a coach was a memorable one, he said. Wagner was regarded as one of the best players in the history of the game. That spring Padden had left Manchester for Pittsburgh on a typical Wednesday in February, bound for training camp at Paso Robles, California. It was to be the most exciting trip of Padden's life.

Only a small number of players mobilized at Pittsburgh that day. Pitcher Waite Hoyt, a former teammate of Babe Ruth's, was coming in from his home in Scarsdale, New York. Former Pirate great and current manager George Gibson, a Canadian who had played minor pro ball in London, Ontario, his wife, Pirate president W.E. Benswanger, and Wagner were to meet at the train station. The previous two springs he was with the Yankees in St. Petersburg, Florida, and now Gibson believed Padden was finally coming into his own. Here was a potential .300 hitter, he thought. Padden had been selected to the freshman major-league all-star team with a fielding percentage of .987. He had made only two errors out of 132 chances in thirty-two games, and he had batted .262. Those were big-league numbers. Pirate president Benswanger made sure that Padden's 1933 salary offer was substantially increased before they left for California. It was his way of showing the young Manchester native how much he thought of his work.

Actually, it was Gibson who had first proposed the raise. Gibson considered Padden the ideal build for a catcher. He liked the way Padden took the game so seriously. Indeed, it was Gibson, the former star catcher, who had wanted Benswanger to make a deal with the Yankees for the youngster. Benswanger readily agreed. Though they had a star, Earl Grace, behind the plate, the Pirates liked Padden. They had grabbed him the previous season, eleven days after Padden had been let out to Newark, the Yankees Triple-A farm team.

Padden was one of fourteen people who began the Pirates' annual pilgrimage to Paso Robles from Pittsburgh's Pennsylvania Station that winter Sunday. Among the others were players, newspapermen, coach Gibson, a one-time iron-man catcher with the Pirates, and Wagner. Most of the players, with the exception of Padden, were pitchers. Another group was scheduled to leave the following Sunday. There were pictures taken, goodbyes said, and then, for the fourteen, a long train journey west.

In Chicago on a stopover, Wagner, the veteran Pirate star—his baseball card fetched nearly half a million dollars in the early 1990s (Brantford native Wayne Gretzky and L.A. Kings president Bruce McNall bought it)—would help to while away the time by telling youngsters like Padden a few stories out of his huge fund of diamond lore. In Chicago, an International News Photo Service photographer snapped a picture of Wagner telling his tales to Padden and a few others. The picture appeared in the *Pittsburgh Sun-Telegraph*. Padden, holding a newspaper in one hand and with another folded in his coat pocket, was wearing a smart, double-breasted overcoat—he had a suit and tie underneath—and a wide-brimmed fedora with a dark band that mirrored the one worn by Wagner and the others. Padden was smiling, with Wagner looking directly at him. There were plenty of stories; it was a long trip. The newspaper caption back home in Pittsburgh said: "Honus tells the boys a few stories en route."

It had taken almost five years but Padden was finally in the majors to stay. Spending so much time with the legendary Wagner during the trip was not only exciting for Padden, but it gave him even more confidence as his thoughts turned to spring training in Paso Robles and to vying for the starting catcher's job with Earl Grace. When he had gone south with the Yankees the previous two springs he had to battle Bill Dickey for the catcher's post. Dickey was a mainstay in the Yankee nest for years. Now, with Pittsburgh, Padden was facing a similar challenge of having to unseat the star catcher.

He liked Grace and thought him one of the nicest Pirates, though he told reporter Charles J. Doyle that when it came time to battle for the job, friendly feelings were put aside. Padden was twenty-four, and had been involved in baseball long enough to find it difficult to remember how many years he'd been playing the game. He told Doyle: "I'm a bit hazy about my first association with baseball. They tell me I was working on a bottle which held a nipple when somebody dropped a ball into my cradle." His first association with baseball had been early. "I tried to eat the ball," continued Padden, "and I got enough of the cover in my tummy to give me a fever that breaks out in a rash every February."

Padden was ready to make his presence felt at his first spring training with the Bucs. He had high hopes after several months of road and gym work left him in what he told a few others "is better shape than when I went south with the Yankees last year." That winter Padden had varied his daily exercise sessions to relieve monotony; some mornings he would jog through the streets of Manchester to keep his leg muscles supple, ready to respond to the demands that would surely come in spring training. Some afternoons he would work out at the Knights of Columbus gymnasium playing basketball and handball. He would vary the gym work by turning to weightlifting exercises, tossing the medicine ball, and exercising on a horse.

By February 19, when the Pirates left Pittsburgh, the conditioning program seemed to have paid off. He looked to be in good shape; his weight was up six pounds, to 174, from his 1932 playing weight. He was a modest and unassuming young man, someone people back home in Manchester were proud of and felt certain would make a name for himself in 1933. Always smiling, Padden was one of the best-liked athletes Manchester had ever turned out. He had the whole town rooting for him as he left for California.

They had followed the progress of his career in the Yankee organization from the time he was first signed as a sophomore at Holy Cross, through his first pro stint with the Manchester Yankees in the New England League in 1928, then when the Yankees farmed him out to Hartford of the Eastern League the same year. They followed him when he was switched to New Haven in 1929, and then when he started the 1930 season with New Haven. They didn't lose track of him when he was farmed out to Baltimore early in the 1930 season. There he hit .300 and caught nearly one hundred games before being farmed to Kansas City in 1931. Kansas City was his first setback. Until then his arm had been considered one of his biggest attributes, but that year, in September, he developed severe arm pains. It got so bad he could hardly throw. Doctors diagnosed his problem as a case of infected tonsils and teeth. So Padden had the tonsils and two infected molars removed.

"The doctor said I would not be able to throw for eight or nine months," recalled Padden, "and this saddened me because I was slated to go to St. Petersburg with the Yanks. I tried to hide my trouble, but collapsed in a practice game."

Yankee manager Joe McCarthy treated him fairly, Padden thought, after he learned of his troubles. McCarthy, who had always given him words of encouragement and had taken him south twice with the Yankees, sent him to Newark, and he was beginning to return to normal when the Pirates bought him in May for $7,500 from the New York Americans of the American Association. A winter of conditioning helped his arm get back the strength he formerly had—the arm had hurt most of 1932 with the Pirates, but had almost completely recovered by season's end—so that as he made his way to Paso Robles he was confident of both his arm strength and his catching ability. "Any catcher who beats me out this year is in for a fight," he said to a reporter on the train.

The competition, though, would be stiff in Paso Robles. Four catchers in all, but Padden, Grace, and Hal Finney were expected to be the top three. Almost from the beginning things went Padden's way. In an 8-6 win at Seal's Stadium over the San Francisco Seals Padden got three hits in four plate appearances. In another game against the Seals he got three hits again, including a two-run triple, to lift the Bucs to another 8-6 win. It was a lacklustre game under a dull sky; Padden's effort at the plate stole most of the glory. He was robbed of a fourth hit when outfielder Ernie Sulik braced himself against the left-field fence to pull down another big smash.

Grace was still considered the first-string catcher by most people, but Padden was turning a lot of heads. Gibson didn't have to worry about the Pirate's catching ranks for the upcoming season. With Grace and Padden, he had two good ones. Grace, who had watched Padden's performance from the bench in San Francisco—he was sitting out due to a sore arm—was concerned that he might lose his starting job, however. In fact, he did lose it to Padden only a season later.

That season both Grace and Padden saw plenty of action. One time, when Grace was forced to sit out due to a split finger, Padden was there to make the most of it. He went two-for-four at the plate and scored two runs. Eventually he was named Pittsburgh's first-string catcher.

Now, in Canada, there wasn't a day that passed when he didn't think of, or draw on, those experiences. Ruth, Gehrig, Wagner, Arky Vaughan, and Dizzy Dean: he had mixed with some of the game's luminaries. Dean, who was named to the all-rookie team with Padden, was the best pitcher Padden ever handled in the majors.

When asked what his biggest thrill was in baseball, he would always recall Ruth's 714th home run, which sailed over the roof at Forbes Field, though he would also mention one other. He often thought about a game in the early 1930s when the Pirates were playing a doubleheader against the Cardinals. In the first game he hit Dean with two runners aboard to drive home the tying and winning runs. In the second game he made what was described as the most sensational catch of a pop fly ever witnessed at Forbes Field to make the third out and save the game. The catch had involved Padden sprinting fifty feet to the grandstand, where he leaped over the barrier to make the catch. Theresa, his young bride, had been there and had seen the catch and it had made her proud. That was Tom, her high-school sweetheart, the man she was going to build a life with. Some of the other Pirate wives, sitting beside her, spoke their praise of her husband when they saw that catch. He had been instrumental in winning both games.

In Galt, Padden was making what he thought was just another stop on the road back to the major-leagues. He was used to train travel, to new places and new food, to adapting as the situation changed. In short, he had lived the transitory life of a big-league ballplayer for years, so coming to Galt was something he could handle for a summer, even if he did have his wife and three children to support. Murray tried to make his stay here enjoyable, and to that end helped facilitate connections for Padden with various people around the city, all of whom enjoyed having a former major-leaguer in town.

Padden liked to be thought of as a winner. He was here to help the Terriers win. He credited Gene Martin, his manager back at New Haven in 1930, with not only correcting his batting stance, but teaching him "how to be a good loser and an even better winner." Padden had responded to Martin in 1930 and was named the team MVP at season's end.

Galt was a long way from those days with the Babe and Honus Wagner, but he knew that if he did well in Galt, if he managed the Terriers to a pennant and then an Intercounty title, it would be one more feather in his cap. The process was simple: work your way up, and hopefully get a few breaks along the way. There was no direct road from Galt back to the majors, but Galt was a step along the way, and each step was important. Theresa was behind him all the way. Life had been tough since he exited the majors, and certainly less exciting, but she stuck with him, believed in him. Galt may be a little backwards, she thought, but the family was together. Through thick and thin, they would be there for him.

After eight seasons with the Pirates, Padden closed out his major-league career with the Philadelphia Phillies and New York Giants, spending half a season with each. The Giants purchased his contract in a three-way deal with the Senators and Cardinals, following which he was sent to the Giants' top farm team, the Jersey City squad. With Padden in the lineup, Jersey City Giants won their first pennant in thirty-seven years. He spent one season with St. Paul and Milwaukee, and then his Triple-A career was finished. Following that he took an American Legion team to the national finals in California in 1947.

I once asked him who was the best pitcher he ever faced in the majors, and there was no hesitation. "Dizzy Dean," he said. "I caught Diz during a barnstorming trip and he had 'it.'" The two best Pirate moundsmen he ever caught were Cy Blanton and Larry French. "They didn't have very much at Philadelphia and Washington, but the best of the lot were Sid Johnson, Schoolboy Rowe, and Early Wynn, and the latter is still serving them up in the big leagues."

Tex Kaiser

The Glovebox

Years after that summer of '49, the RCMP Musical Ride came to Dickson Park. Thousands of spectators lined the ball diamond. They filled the grandstand and stretched out along the left-field hill. The newspaper said it was the biggest crowd at the park in the town's history. They had never seen the Terriers play in '49.

A WEEK OR TWO AFTER PERKINS ARRIVED, TEX KAISER ASKED TO borrow his car. That night there had been some sort of a problem—"The battery died," said Kaiser—and he opened the glovebox looking for the car registration and the owner's manual.

Out came the ownership, revealing that Perkins was really Harry Sollenburger, from Chambersburg, Pennsylvania. Kaiser was surprised, even though he knew there were a lot of players playing under fictitious names.

His secret was out, though Kaiser held it from us for some weeks. But gradually word got around the league and Manske had no alternative but to investigate.

I admired Perkins, as I did Kaiser. Perkins got along well with Padden, having played for him the previous year in Manchester. So it was not difficult to understand when, at the end of July, Padden caught Perkins against London.

Though he didn't realize it at the time, it was the last game he would have the honour of throwing into Padden's mitt.

165

"We were to play London," recalled Sollenburger, "and Tom said he wanted to catch me. So he caught the whole game."

Sollenburger never forgot it. London had a player by the name of Russ Evon who had won the league batting title in 1946 with a .383 average—he would win it again in 1952 when he hit .361—and he was one of the best power hitters in the league. Pitchers feared him, and with good reason, for he had a habit of making them look bad. "He was a good hitter," said Sollenburger, "but he stood a long way from the plate. I would throw the ball and it would be inside and he'd move back. I'd throw another ball and he'd move back a little more. So I thought, hey, I'm going to get smart here. He can't possibly reach an outside pitch."

Padden called for the next pitch and Sollenburger delivered it on the inside corner. Padden came charging out to the mound. "You're just playing into this guy's hands," he said. Sollenburger didn't understand. Padden explained: "You're throwing inside and he's moving away each time. So you throw outside, but that's just what he hits, outside pitches. So keep coming inside."

Padden had seen Evon exactly four times prior to that night and had taken note of his strengths and weaknesses. It was remarkable. "He wanted me to keep going after it inside instead of going outside because outside was where Evon's strength was and Padden knew it," said Sollenburger. "I've often thought about that, about how he hopped all over me." Padden, of course, was right. He knew his baseball. "There really isn't any doubt in my mind that as a manager, Padden would have gone up to the majors, except for one thing: alcohol." There had been rumours he liked the drink, but to that point in the season he had given little indication that alcohol was a problem for him.

Sollenburger was perhaps the only other person who knew of Padden's history with the bottle. "Oh, he would get plastered," he said. He had seen and heard about Padden's booze problems the year before in Manchester, and it was hard for Sollenburger to take, because Padden had so much talent as a catcher and a manager. The Manchester team had taken a trip to the west coast at the end of the 1948 season, but Sollenburger had stayed behind due to an injury. He'd heard about it though. It was while out on the Pacific Coast that Padden had gone out on the town and gotten so drunk that he didn't even make it to the ballpark for the game the next day. Murray, who had heard only in passing from George Selkirk about his drinking problem, had at first thought there was probably not much to it. A lot of athletes, especially pro athletes who had come up through the roaring twenties and the dirty thirties, were heavy drinkers. Padden had been up in the majors with the Pirates for eight seasons. And no less than Selkirk himself had suggested him for the Galt job. If the New England League and the Manchester club hadn't folded that very year, Murray believed that Padden would probably still be coaching there. Later he learned that Padden's days as Manchester coach were numbered due to his drinking. But until this latest episode at Dickson Park, Padden had been everything Murray had hoped he would be, though some of the players, Frank Udvari among them, thought otherwise.

Udvari had smelled alcohol on Padden's breath more than once that summer, and he didn't like it. How many times was the Terrier executive going to let the manager come to the park with booze on his breath, he wondered. Their tacit approval of his drinking by failing to act was not right, he believed. Udvari could look around the clubhouse and see that most of the other players, especially the former major-leaguers, like Rosen, Creedon, and Warren, didn't pay Padden much attention. It was Udvari's belief that the Terriers should have brought in someone younger, someone with experience but who could still play. In his opinion, Padden was washed up as a player. He could see that Padden's arm was shot. It may have been good when he was with the Pirates, but the years had taken their toll. He would look at Padden and see a man who actually looked years older than he was. "Padden was only in his early forties," Udvari said, "but he looked sixty." Hard living, he speculated, was to blame. "He knew his baseball," admitted Udvari, "but the Terriers could have brought in someone else who could have done more for baseball in Galt, and for the Terriers." His was an opinion I didn't share.

Frank Udvari

That same afternoon, while Padden was preparing for the night game by drinking himself into a stupor at the Albion Hotel, a young woman tried to flag down a Galt bus during the 5 o'clock rush. Passengers were growing impatient as the driver kept waiting for first one hurrying latecomer and then another. Finally shutting the door and starting off, he reached the corner when another straggler tried to flag him down. A sympathetic passenger already on the bus cried out: "There's another woman who wants to get on." But the bus driver serenely continued on his course without stopping.

"Why didn't you stop for that woman?" asked the indignant passenger.

"Because I'm the meanest driver on the route," he grinned. Small-town Galt was becoming bigger. Times were changing. "If I wait overtime," said the driver, "the passengers who are on time complain. If I leave on time, those who are late complain. You can't win in this game."

There were times that summer when Gus Murray was saying the same thing.

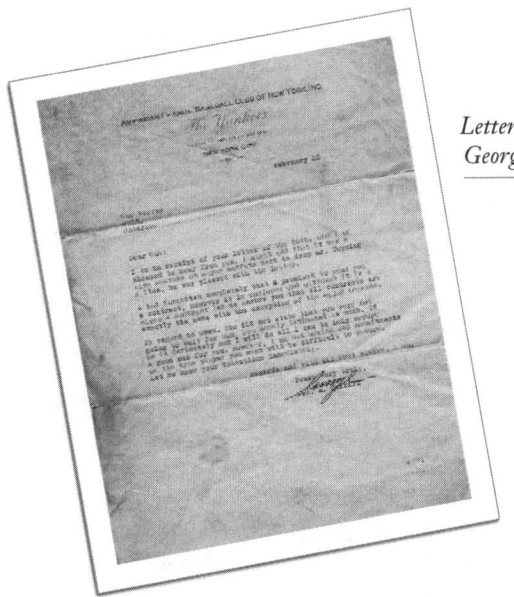

Letter from New York Yankee official George Selkirk

Hustlin' Gus

I remember going to see a game in Detroit one year with Gus and Wes Lillie. It was the World Series and the lineup for tickets stretched on for a mile. Wes and I were in line all night, it seemed, before Wes returned to the car to have Gus spell him off. But Gus was sleeping in the back seat. Wes opened the door and dragged him out by the feet. "Take your turn in line, Gus," he said.

M URRAY WAS AGING A GREAT DEAL THAT SUMMER, AND I could see it better than most, because I had known him, and seen him around town, for years. It couldn't have been easy to deal with the things he had to deal with: player's demands, high salaries, trying to keep his former major-leaguers happy, conniving to bring the fans out game after game. And seeing to it that the Galts of 1949 were contenders. Increasingly, running a competitive team in the Intercounty was taking more and more time. When Murray and others throughout the league had brought in a hoard of imports, salaries rose considerably, and although Murray had been one of the instigators of this change, Goman and Pennell followed suit. "Gus was a promoter all the time," recalled Goman. "And the same thing with me."

But Murray got the ball rolling and the feeling was that the Intercounty would never be the same. Worse still, some observers felt that bringing in American imports and their skyrocketing salaries would cause the eventual demise of the league. They had a point. How long could amateur teams afford to pay such extravagant salaries? And how could the poorer teams compete with the richer teams? Goman eventually believed that though the league, and the individual team, gained tangibly in the short term, they would lose in the long run. But Pennell always maintained that he would lose less money with a star-studded team than he would with a poor team.

"We felt Gus was offering more money than we could afford," said Goman, echoing the feeling among many team operators back then. They would try to tell Murray as much at the Intercounty executive meetings, but Murray wouldn't listen, or, if he did, he didn't buy it. "It was tough dealing with Gus at times," said Goman. "He had his own ideas on how to operate." And so did the powers that be in Brantford.

Brantford's Pennell and King reminded Goman of Siamese twins. They were always together, serving the Red Sox interests with a savvy that made other teams envious. "A lot of people couldn't understand that relationship," Goman said. Mike was a bit of a rounder. And Pennell, a lawyer, was all class. "He was always a good speaker," recalled Goman. "I think one of the last times I saw him I had him come in to address a joint Rotary-Lions Club meeting. He flew in to Waterloo-Wellington Airport from Ottawa and I drove him home."

Pennell would arrive at meetings with his briefcase in hand, as would Waterloo's Goman and Farquharson from London. Turow managed the Galt Terriers in 1948, but had been around for years prior to that. By 1949 he sat on the Intercounty executive as vice-president to Manske. He could see the changes taking place in the Intercounty and maintained it had all started—Goman and Turow agreed on this point—with London. London had a big army base and they would bring in some top-notch ballplayers to the base. After the war many of them made London their home. Two such players were Tommy White and Hank Biasetti. The other teams, in an effort to remain competitive, followed suit; there was no other choice. If they didn't, they would continue to finish in the bottom half of the standings and, as a result, lose fan support. People in Waterloo were no different from people in Brantford or Galt. They wanted their club to be contending for the pennant in late August. One bad year could be forgotten, and forgiven, but not several.

Murray was one of the first to recognize the necessity of signing American imports. In 1948 he went to George Heggie and Ernie Reeves, who ran the Terriers, and outlined his plan. Heggie, a former player and an instrumental figure in the sporting life of the community, knew Murray was right, as did Reeves, and they handed over the reigns. In 1949 it was Murray who would sign the players, pay their salaries, and handle the business transactions. It was a big responsibility, and though he didn't know what he was getting into at the time, he was, at least, eager. He had ideas. Plenty of them. And, if nothing else, he promised to inject some enthusiasm back into the ball club. It would be an interesting season, observers thought, if not a great one.

"Some Intercounty meetings that year," said Goman, "lasted until two or three in the morning. There were always battles about player eligibility. It was quite an era." Pennell agreed. "The meetings were often stormy," he said. "You could write a book just about those meetings." Many of the league meetings took place at the Galt YMCA, a central location for most teams. Manske was always in control. Turow, Manske's second-in-command, whom veteran umpire Kumornik liked to describe as "the only umpire I ever saw who wore glasses," was seen as an honest man, as was Manske. "Otto was a good man," said Turow. "They couldn't push him around." Indeed, with Manske at its head, the Intercounty had a good leader; not necessarily a great baseball man, but someone who could run the league well. Still, that didn't deter teams and players from trying to bend the rules.

One time Goman hired a couple of private detectives to show how London was breaking the rules. Goman got the evidence and then brought a sheriff to the Intercounty meeting one night, much to the surprise of those in the room. "They actually brought in the sheriff," said Turow, "to stop London from using a couple of players from the States. Goman charged they weren't bona fide residents [of London]." Though the private detectives had proof that London did indeed have a couple of players commuting from Detroit, the owners, noted Turow, also had their own proof that the players were, in fact, paying for room and board in London. "They had the receipts to show they had paid money."

"Yes," said Turow many seasons later, "there were some great goings-on." When Murray took over the Terriers in 1949, he had permission to sweep the board clean. "It was quite a change," said Turow. Except for Clark, Pickard, McCrudden, and Kaiser, and Lillie and myself—Turow believed we were both lucky just to make an Intercounty club—the rest were hired guns. Goman and Pennell did the same thing a year later. They had to. They had seen the direction the league was taking and they had thrown up their hands. "To hell with that," thought Goman. "We'll do it too. We have to do it."

Before Murray came along the league had been separated into two distinct parts. There were the teams that had resources to pay high salaries, like Kitchener and London, and then there were smaller teams, like Galt, Brantford, Stratford, and Guelph, who had limited resources. "They just couldn't afford the players," said Turow. But Murray had other ideas. Turow, the former Terrier manager who had only homebrews to carry the team in 1948, was not to be a part of Murray's plans for 1949. It didn't bother him to the extent it would have if the team had comprised local players. "In '49 I knew I wasn't capable of running a bunch of big-leaguers. I wouldn't even have tried to if they had offered me the job. I knew my limitations. I was just a local boy from Preston and I didn't know that much about baseball, not the way some of these Americans knew it. In '48 we had a good contending B team of local players. Whoever Goman didn't want he'd send to us. The same with Kitchener." But that all changed in 1949. Galt didn't need or desire many local players, except for Kaiser, who could have played on any team, McCrudden, Lillie, and Clark, who they would need to catch most games, to be spelled off by Padden from time to time. I agreed with Turow: I was just lucky to make the team.

"It worked out great in the short term," said Turow. "For a while it was very good baseball." But, as Goman and others had predicted, though were helpless to stop, it couldn't and didn't last. "In the long term they priced themselves out of the market," explained Turow. Eventually, in the mid-1950s, a few of the bigger clubs, like London and Kitchener, left the Intercounty for a couple of seasons and joined a league with some Niagara clubs. John Gillis, a lawyer who had been in attendance at the Intercounty meetings when Goman had brought in the sheriff—he was there to protect London against Goman's accusations—became the new league's commissioner. But the Intercounty, with teams like Galt, Brantford, Guelph, and Listowel, survived and carried on like it had done every year since 1919.

Murray was not the top dog at the Intercounty meetings, though he was one of the big players. The meetings would be held once a month, but more frequently if events necessitated. Manske, who Kumornik said had little baseball knowledge but was a good organizer—"he liked banquets"—ran the show. But Murray, Pennell and King, Goman and Farquharson were all big players in the meetings. "I can remember one meeting," said Turow, "with Murray there for Galt. There was a motion on the floor. Gus seconded it and it passed. Then later, when we were discussing the issue further, Gus spoke out.

'I'm violently against that,' he said."

But, as someone pointed out to Murray, "You just voted in support of that."

"I did?" replied a confused Murray.

"He was laying on the bed half-asleep," said Turow. But that was Murray. He was nothing if not sure of himself.

I remember during a game in Kitchener that summer when Gus claimed he lost our team's payroll during a ninth-inning fracas between the two clubs. Murray reported to police that he had lost a roll of bills totalling $150. "It apparently popped out of Gus's hip pocket in the excitement," said the newspaper.

The only other place in town offering that kind of excitement was one of the movie houses. The number of theatres a town had was a good indicator of the size of the town, and Galt had three. Movies were an increasingly popular form of recreation for most Galt residents in 1949. But the theatres suffered on game nights when the Terriers were playing at Dickson Park. Murray knew that the theatres would be a good place to promote his ball club, so early in the summer he came to an agreement with the manager of the Grand Theatre, which sat on the corner of Dickson and Water Streets and was even closer to his store than the Capital. He and a couple of players, like Creedon and Warren, would appear onstage prior to the show and speak to the young people in the audience. Sometimes they'd do it Saturday afternoon at the matinee, to boost interest in the night game at 8 P.M. Kids would ask the former big-leaguers what it was like to play in the majors. Murray made sure everyone knew when and where the game was being played, and who the opponents would be. The theatre benefited because they could advertise their special guests and that would draw more patrons. Many kids came to see the matinee knowing they were going to be there. And Murray's Terriers benefited too, gaining young fans who often brought along mom and dad.

For the older crowd, Murray, when he had a chance, would set up his camera at the Galt Highlands, a local nightspot that catered to dancers, and snap candid shots of groups or couples for a dollar or two. He would always manage to get in a few plugs about his Terriers. Where he got his energy from, one could only guess. But he seemed to have plenty, and in 1949 the Terriers were his baby. He was always promoting them. If it wasn't the Terriers it was his wallpaper business. But more often, it was both. He sold tickets to the games at his store. He was also known to drive out to Ayr, a small village about seven miles out of town, on the pretense of getting a haircut, but with the real intention of selling tickets to Terrier games. He was a natural promoter. No one could deny that. Players might have had their money differences with him, as did the Galt Parks Board, but more than anyone, he was responsible for fielding the most exciting nine in the league.

By the middle of June people were already comparing him with some of the great promoters around the league, like Waterloo's Goman. Eventually other comparisons would be made with Cleveland owner Bill Veeck, perhaps the greatest promoter the majors ever knew. Veeck, who at different times in his career owned the St. Louis Browns, Cleveland Indians, and Chicago White Sox, would come to define the word. He was flamboyant and famous. Later Murray would describe himself as a poor man's Bill Veeck. Veeck's most famous stunt was to use three-foot seven-inch midget Eddie Gaedel to pinch-hit in a 1951 game.

Perhaps Murray's most interesting promotion came in 1950 when he set up a small stove at home plate. He had given away free instant cake mixes to the first five hundred women and the stove was intended to demonstrate how instant the mixes were. From the stove he had a long extension cord that went under the grandstand. What no one knew, except for Murray and Margaret Alderson, the *Reporter's* Women's Editor, who was present to bake the cake, was that the cord was not plugged into any outlet. Murray's wife, Grace, had baked a chocolate cake that afternoon and Murray had placed it inside the oven. No sooner had Miss Alderson whipped up the mix and put it into the oven than she was pulling out a fully baked cake.

Gus Murray orchestrated a "cake baking" demonstration at home plate.

Another time in 1949 Murray had a busload full of jars of cooking oil for a special promotion. But Brantford players managed to get to the bus before the game—they had arrived early—and completely emptied it. Murray was beside himself when he discovered the bus was empty. John Lockington and the rest of the Red Sox players who had been in on the practical joke were looking on from a distance, and loving it. Murray was frantic. "He even called in the police," said Lockington. Finally, someone told Murray where all the loot was stashed.

Kumornik didn't mind most of the promotions Murray was behind—he knew they would help sell the game—but he took offence to one of them. He recalled how Murray would have someone scatter sawdust behind him at home plate, then pour kerosene on it and light it. The crowd loved it.

"Gus was good for the game," he said, "but some of his schemes came at my expense." Kumornik felt like he was a witch being burned at the stake.

Married, with two young children at home, he was behind the plate five or six games a week that season, but he had no regrets about spending so much time away from home. He also ran a confectionary business, going from store to store around Waterloo County. He had to make a living. In addition to his daytime job he was making seventy-five to $100 extra a week as an Intercounty umpire behind the plate. "I enjoyed every minute of it," he said. Baseball had always been his favourite sport. When he quit playing—he had played third base for the 1939 Intercounty champion Waterloo Tigers—he started umpiring. That was in 1945, just after the war. He continued to umpire for thirteen years before taking over first the Waterloo Tigers from Goman, and subsequently the Kitchener Panthers from Gallinger.

Kumornik also took offence to Kaiser on occasion. It was mostly Kaiser's fault. "I used to drive him crazy," he said. "I'd get him so mad." The scene would typically go like this: someone would throw a strike, Kaiser would let it go without swinging, and Kumornik would call it as he saw it. Kaiser would turn around and look at Kumornik, doing his best to look shocked and incredulous. There would be a loud chorus of boos from the crowd. Then Kaiser would have a few words with Kumornik. The crowd believed he was arguing the call, but in reality, he would say to Kumornik: "John, that pitch was right down the centre." Meanwhile, the hometown crowd was getting downright nasty, with the umpire the object of its distaste. And Kaiser would just laugh. Still, it didn't hurt their friendship, even though some fans would come down to the field after the game and call Kumornik names. It was all part of the game.

Kumornik liked Murray. Years later he would ask how that little guy who ran the restaurant on Water Street was doing. "The only thing," said Kumornik, "was that he didn't buy too much stuff from me back then." Kumornik would make the rounds and stop in at Murray's lunch counter, but Murray rarely bought any of the confectionary items or odds and ends for his store. If he liked Murray, he got along even better with Kaiser. "We were good buddies," he said.

Following Kitchener games they would go to Gallinger's hotel, the Grand Union (his father-in-law had brought him into the business), and after Galt games at Dickson Park they might drop into the Iroquois Hotel on upper Main Street, or go over to the Overland Hotel at the edge of town on the way to Brantford. One time, a few years later when Brantford's Stan Lipka was managing the Red Sox, he bolted out of the dugout and headed for Kumornik. "He was talking Polish," recalled Kumornik. "I couldn't understand any of it. It was all a show for the hometown fans. Lipka made it look like he was arguing the call with his body language, but as he was ranting and raving and proffering Polish-language lessons, he said to Kumornik: "I'll see you after the game at the Iroquois."

As for Murray, like Rogers Hornsby, he never drank or smoked. When he and his best friend, Walter Reid, and some others, like Doc Catherwood, took trips to the World Series in Cleveland or New York, it was Murray who was the designated driver. He didn't mind. It was all part of the fun of those times. He could have his fun without booze.

So could the players. Years earlier, about 1930, during a Terrier game against Guelph in Galt, little Jimmie Stewart of Galt was guarding second base. "He was pretty small," said his younger brother Archie. "I was bat boy at the time. There was a great big guy playing for Guelph, I've forgotten his name now, and he was on second base. There was a delay in the game for something." The hulking Guelph player turned to the diminutive Stewart and said: "C'mon over and start a fight." Stewart obliged. "Throw me," instructed the Guelph giant. So Stewart picked him up and, with the Guelph player's help, threw him over his shoulder. Then they started fighting, with the Guelph player lying flat on his back and Stewart on top of him. The crowd loved it. The two were good friends. It was all a put-on. But the way the crowd saw it, this big guy from Guelph was picking on the little guy from Galt.

Galt Collegiate: Charlie Hodge was finishing his final year that spring.

The Race

Glee club faces, in front of the school's main entrance, tell the story. They are young and, like the autumn leaves, they too are vibrant. See fire in them, laugh with them, hurt with them, come of age with them. They are all energy, life, enthusiasm. The world awaited them.

EARLY ONE EVENING GUS ASKED ME TO GO TO PRESTON TO PICK up some baseballs at the Preston sports store run by Tim Turow, so he threw in an old Gladstone bag for the balls and we were off, rocketing up Water Street, past the collegiate, through the Delta, and down Coronation Boulevard

"We'll get a couple of milkshakes on the way back," he said.

"Sounds good."

The sun was low in the west, and as we drove down the Preston highway heading directly into the sun, a car pulled alongside. My hair, short as it was after Turley's handiwork at the barbershop days earlier, blew in the summer wind, and all was right with the world. On the radio there was music playing, and I remember hearing Glen Miller's popular hit of a decade earlier. My fingers were drumming along the outside of the car door to the big band sound. The carefree complexion of youth.

Traffic was very light in those days and Gus stepped on the gas, not wanting to let the other fellow pass. That was the first time I saw Gus go truly wild.

I was stunned at how easily he was pulled into the fray, and as I tensed up and grabbed the armrest with my right hand, I looked at Gus's face, which was seized by a demon, and at his eyes, which were hungry and full of fire. He was in race mode, and I thought then, as I think now, that had my father known what Gus was doing with me at that moment, he would have taken Gus into his hands and broken him.

Past the country club Gus sped up and so did the other driver. He was younger than Gus, and I realized that although it only takes one person to be stupid, it always takes two to make a conversation out of it.

The other car sped past Gus's station wagon, but Gus responded by trying to overtake him. As we flew past the country club, where Tex Kaiser was spending a lot of time hobnobbing with the well-to-do—there were stories about he and a local doctor's wife—Gus jerked the steering wheel hard to the left, climbed the grassy median over the mound, and sped down the highway going against traffic.

Many years later, when I saw the film *American Graffiti*, I would think of Gus during the car race scene. He was wild, and there was a smile on his thin lips as he glanced my way to say, "We got him, kid."

I was still holding tight to the armrest and many things crossed my mind including the thought that Jimmy had died a hero's death, and when they untangled our bodies from the wreckage, they would say I had died a fool's death.

Only the grace of God prevented any cars from hitting us that evening. The air seemed stale after that, although my blood was coursing a mile a minute through my body and I could taste the adrenaline and my back was wet with sweat.

Gus completed his mission a few minutes later. He had gone to Preston to get balls, but it seemed like he was trying to prove he already had some.

Tex Kaiser

Tex

He was big, strong, could run, had a rocket arm, and could hit; he had all the earmarks of a major-leaguer except for one thing. I never once saw him slide.
— *Harry Sollenburger*

Art Wilson was a young man of twenty-five that summer and though he didn't play baseball, he had been a fair runner, having trained with Scotty Rankine, one of Canada's premiere runners—he was Canada's athlete of the year in 1935—of the first half-century. Rankine and another Galt runner, Ab Morton, had both reached the upper levels of their sport, and Wilson seemed the heir apparent. But he gave it up and was out of the sport by 1950. Still, he used to go down to Dickson Park, where he had run some memorable races on the track that skirted the ball diamond, to see the Terriers play ball. Like most Galtonians that summer, he found baseball at Dickson Park to be a nice diversion. Say what you want about the Terriers of 1948, the Galts of '49 were exciting.

Wilson wasn't one to refuse a drink in those days. He had formed a band and was always drinking before, during, and after the show. Following one night game that summer Wilson left the ball game just before it ended, and headed directly over to the hotel in Preston. When he walked in he couldn't believe his eyes. Tex Kaiser, still wearing his Terrier pinstripes, was already there. He'd beaten him to the bar. Wilson just shook his head.

"How did you beat me here?" he asked Kaiser. "I was at the game and left before it was over."

"I left when the game ended and took the shortcut through Blair," said Kaiser.

"That's no shortcut," said Wilson.

"It is the way I drive," Kaiser replied.

Players often stopped off at the bar following a game. Years later Johnny Clark, who went on to play with a Preston team sponsored by the Preston Baptist Church, went to Nicholson's Tavern. They kept their uniforms on but turned them inside out.

Kaiser, the hard-playing minor-league hockey player trying to make it to the NHL, was an inveterate drinker. When, for example, the London Majors came to town, Kaiser would have a cooler of beer ready for his good friend, Russ Evon. Evon would take the cooler back to London after the game and have it stocked full of beer when Kaiser and the Galts next went to London.

I remember one evening, after a win over London, when the bus was heading back to Galt. Kaiser instructed the driver to pull over at a point that seemed to be out in the middle of nowhere.

"Boys, we've got to stop here," Kaiser boomed.

"What for?" I naively asked.

"For a while," he said.

We were stopped alongside an orchard about four or five miles out of London.

Kaiser got off the bus, and I figured he was going to relieve himself at the side of the road. But he didn't. He wandered off into the field, ducked behind a tree, and emerged with a cooler full of beer. It was vintage Tex Kaiser.

He had great potential and observers say he could have made it big in either sport, but he was his own worst enemy. He walked to the beat of his own drummer. "He was wild," said George Brown, the guy who was offered the Terrier managerial post before Padden. Brown had started out with the Terriers as a bat boy in 1932–33, before playing on some memorable Terrier teams in the late '30s and early '40s. He had seen countless players come and go, and by 1949 he'd been around long enough to sum up a player with an economy of words. The dope on Kaiser? "He had a 'I don't give a damn' attitude. He had all the talent in the world, but no discipline."

Clark, with a wife and small child at home, wasn't one to party with Kaiser that summer. He'd have a few beers on the way back from road games, but he wouldn't stay out all night like some of our teammates.

"Besides," said Clark, "I used to pick up Helen's dad and my dad and park the car up above the hill under the trees so they could all watch the game. I couldn't go out afterwards. I had to drive them home."

Others could go out after the games without anyone looking over their shoulders. Warren and Creedon were known to do so. And Kaiser, of course. "Warren used to try to hit players up for money," said Clark, "and he never paid them back." When Clark and his teammates would see Warren in a quiet mood, when he looked like he was in slow motion, they would know he had been out the night before. "They were up here for a good time," Clark said of the imports. "Just up for a holiday."

In the summer of '48 Kaiser had worked full time at Kralinator Filters, but in '49 he decided to play ball and nothing else. Hockey was his career. Baseball was just a way to earn a little extra money to tide him through the summer, and a way to have a little fun at the same time.

Kaiser was like Warren when it came to drinking and staying out all night. "Kaiser would sometimes drop me off at 2 A.M. after we bused home from an away game," Clark recalled. Oftentimes the bus would stop at a bar on the way home and we would quench our thirst with a couple of beers. One year, coming back from St. Thomas, the bus, carrying players and fans, stopped off at the Empire Hotel in St. Thomas. Then, some time later, returning to Galt, the bus driver stopped at a particular school alongside the roadway, a well-known pit stop. We called it the Outhouse School because we used it as an outdoor washroom. People would go behind the school, then return to the bus. On this night, a fan had been drinking too much and became sick behind the school. "He took his teeth out and put them on the school windowsill," explained Clark. Soon afterwards the bus left, and it was several minutes before the toothless man cried out that he had left his dentures at the school. "Don't worry," someone said in a reassuring tone. "We'll be coming back this weekend for another game. We'll stop off to see if we can find them." So, three nights later, we returned and found the teeth still sitting there on the sill.

After such trips, when we got home, Kaiser would try to persuade Clark and a few others to stay out with him. This was usually after we had stopped off for a couple of hours to have a few drinks. Clark's wife, Helen, would be upset, but she'd wait up. Clark would never stay out with Kaiser, but it wasn't for Kaiser's lack of trying. "Once Kaiser got drinking he didn't want to stop," said Clark. He'd tell Johnny he was going over to so-and-so's house after he dropped Clark off, that he was just going to get another drink or two. Or he'd say, 'So-and-so has some beer. I'm going over there.' But he had the luxury of being able to sleep in the next morning; Clark had to get up to go to work at Butler Metal.

Kaiser always denied he was wild. "Aw, hell," he would say, "I was just having fun." As the Intercounty's home-run champion the year before, he was considered by many to be the most improved player in the league. At six feet and 180 pounds he wasn't big by today's standards, but he was powerfully built. And he had a presence that made him appear big and strong and almost immortal. The kids all loved him.

To a young lad named Tommy Conaway from Preston, Kaiser was not only a fellow Prestonian—"He was my hero." If he liked to hit the bar with the boys after games, so what. A lot of players did that. A good many of the American imports, and many Canadians too, had reputations as womanizers. Kaiser, though he was married and had two small children, had such a reputation.

He was considered quite handsome by women. One later said he had a Paul Newman look. He and Warren were both ladies' men, as were many of the ballplayers. In Waterloo, Joe Yosurak also had a way with the ladies. Kumornik recalled how he would cut the sleeves off his uniform. When asked why he did it he replied: "Women automatically go off in their pants when they see my muscles."

Yosurak, said Kumornik, was another player who seemed to hold his drink pretty well. He drank all the time. "I can't say I ever really saw him drunk," he admitted, but one night Yosurak had been quaffing a few at the Waterloo Hotel. Game time was fast approaching and his teammates were concerned. He hadn't shown up at the park yet. They knew where to look. He was brought back to the park—he'd had at least a dozen beers, Kumornik figures—and promptly ordered to run the perimeter of the ballpark several times. That night he threw a two-hitter.

Another time they found him drunk on the curb in a condition similar to that of Warren in '49 when we dragged him out of a drunken stupor at the Sulfur Springs Hotel—where he boarded—to play in Windsor.

Kaiser might have been a wild man, but on the ball diamond he was as impressive as they come. Kids liked him because it always seemed like he produced. They liked the way he laced into a ball. When Kaiser hit, the ball seemed to fly a mile. He even looked good when he swung and missed.

Kaiser had grown up in small-town Preston where everyone knew everyone else. There were only a few things to do if you were athletically inclined. Hockey in winter; baseball in summer. Turow, the Preston resident who coached the Terriers—and Kaiser—in 1948, saw Kaiser mature into a young man. Turow had coached him as a teenager with the Preston Juniors. "He had a lot of raw talent," said Turow.

Kaiser respected Turow. "Tim taught me all I know," he said. "He got me started." But if it was Turow who had given Kaiser his start, it was Padden and the other American imports who provided the finishing. "Tom was a good coach," Kaiser said. "He was patient and he'd stick with you." Kaiser's success was partly due to people like Turow and Padden. A larger part was Kaiser's own natural ability.

"Back then we thought we knew how to play the game," Kaiser recalled. "But when these Americans came up, Christ, they taught us how to really play." Kaiser wasn't the only one who learned from them that summer. Murray was soaking it all up, as were the rest of us, Udvari excepted. And a baseball school run by Padden at Dickson Park that summer for kids was also a beneficiary of his baseball knowledge. Padden's influence would leave its mark on them as well.

"I can remember," said Kaiser, "I was going to catch batting practice one day. 'Throw me a decker,' I said to someone."

"What's a decker?" asked one of the imports somewhat incredulously.

Kaiser had always called a catcher's mitt a decker. "It's a *catcher's mitt!*" said the American.

They laughed at me all year long because of that one," said Kaiser. "But we learned a lot, both Tim and me. I was impressed with what Padden knew."

Baseball, for Kaiser, was just something he liked doing in the summers to occupy his time. Hockey was his first love. As a kid growing up in Preston, he would often sit on the street curb Saturday mornings and dream about playing in the NHL. The dream hadn't yet come true in 1949, but it would soon, when, at twenty-five, he got a call up to the Montreal Canadiens.

"He was quite a guy," said Harry Psutka, a Kitchener Panther who'd played against Kaiser in the Intercounty. "He was big, strong, and athletic."

Psutka, a catcher, had played in the Detroit Tiger chain for four years. "You're a prospect, a suspect, and then after that, you go home," he said. When he got home he found the Intercounty was as strong as it had ever been. As for Kaiser, Psutka said he was a natural. "He was very entertaining and well liked. You couldn't help but enjoy his company. There were always lots of laughs."

A couple of seasons later Psutka got to know Kaiser better when the Galts were heading off to play in the all-Ontario tournament and bolstered the club with a few players from other Intercounty clubs. Years later he told me that Kaiser was still up to his old tricks. "Bobby Schnurr and myself were able to play with them in the playoffs," recalled Psutka. "So one night, on the way home from St. Thomas after a game—it was about 1 A.M.—Kaiser says to stop the car beside the road. Off he goes into the field." Everyone was wondering what Kaiser was up to. "Then he comes out of the darkness with a case of beer. Said he found it behind a tree. He had it planted. He was full of slapstick. He liked to have a little fun." Kaiser had done the same thing with us the year before.

Psutka remembered Kaiser's swing. "He was a wild swinger. You didn't know where to pitch to him. He hit them high one time, and then hit one out of the dirt another. He had a lot of talent in terms of hitting the ball."

As a teenager Kaiser played Junior B hockey with Preston under coach Turow before moving on to play with the Port Colborne Recreationals in Junior A. He was still known as Verne Kaiser back then. Don Gallinger, who hailed from Port Colborne, had played against Kaiser at Galt Arena when the two were youngsters playing for the all-Ontario title. He liked Kaiser. On the ice, they were about equal; on the ball diamond, Kaiser was king.

Kaiser didn't get the "Tex" moniker until 1947 after he signed on with Eddie Shore's team in Washington, D.C., and Shore loaned him to Seattle in the West Coast League. He ended up playing hockey in, of all places, Fort Worth, Texas, and was given a pair of cowboy boots as part of a promotion. The boots stayed with him a decade. He wore them everywhere. From then on he was called Tex.

Kaiser's hockey career was in the hands of Shore, the famous Boston Bruin defenceman who had nearly killed Toronto's Ace Bailey in an ugly stick swinging incident at Boston Garden years earlier. Shore was a tough customer and one of the NHL's all-time great defencemen. As an executive and team owner, he was ruthless. He could make or break anyone who played for him, and in Kaiser's case, there was no love lost between the two. Which was unusual, because there weren't many hockey or baseball people who couldn't get along with Kaiser.

True, there were times when even Murray didn't get along with him, but those situations usually took care of themselves. With Shore, it was explosive and vindictive. Indeed, it was an all-hate relationship. Except that Shore was the boss and Kaiser the underling. Shore controlled Kaiser's hockey destiny. "Nobody liked Eddie Shore," said Kaiser. "He was nuts. Just absolutely crazy."

Though Kaiser had a wild streak, it was a good-natured one. He wasn't out to intentionally hurt anyone. If he was a little self-destructive, as some people remember, he could be forgiven. He was young.

He grew up at 404 Middle Street, the son of William Kaiser, foreman at Eastern Steel Products. Summers he worked at the steel plant. Kaiser clearly remembered being at home on Middle Street, when he and his dad would turn on the big wooden floor model radio after his father came home from work. "My dad and I used to sit in front of the radio and listen to the Tiger broadcasts. They used to give you the whole game at 6 P.M."

The games we all listened to were recreations, complete with commentary and sound effects like the crack of a bat and cheering. "They'd go through the whole game that way," recalled Kaiser. Radio was a big part of people's lives back then when money was short. But nobody seemed to have money, so it didn't bother them. "I remember it with fondness," said Kaiser. "I don't remember the hard times."

Of course, there was always something better than listening to games on the radio, and that was going to the park and actually playing the game. "I'd come home to do chores and then head out to the park," he said. "That's the advantage of the small town, having Riverside Park virtually next door. I loved that park."

Oftentimes he'd catch a streetcar down King Street a few miles to attend classes at Galt Collegiate. But most of the time he walked. Times were tough and he left home at sixteen to pursue his hockey dream. He was as nervous as any sixteen-year-old kid is when he leaves home, not knowing if, or when, he would ever return to live on Middle Street again. That autumn he collected sixty dollars a week playing for Port Colborne's Junior A team. He also got a job welding. But though the excitement of leaving home to pursue a hockey career was with him all that year, his nerves calmed down in short order. He found other young men his own age in the same boat.

Shore first signed Kaiser to a pro contract with a team he owned in Buffalo. Kaiser was ready to board a train for Buffalo when a couple of RCMP officers stopped him and refused to let him go, saying his welding job on boats was important for the war effort. "I actually got on the train after Shore told me to come," said Kaiser, "and they took me off." He was with the navy until war's end.

When Kaiser returned for the 1949 season he found Galt pretty much as he had left it the season before. It was still small-town; Alf Turley's barbershop was there, on Grand Avenue, where it had always been. Business phone numbers listed in the Terrier souvenir program had only three numbers. You could call Aitken and Son General Insurance either at the office—114—or at the house—584.

I remember Padden taking Kaiser to Toronto for a Triple-A tryout with the Leafs. They were interested in him, and actually wanted to sign him, but Kaiser's true love—hockey—meant that he couldn't seriously consider a pro ball career. Years later he would regret that decision.

"Verne Kaiser was a good ballplayer," said Sollenburger. "Hey, he could run fast, he had a great arm, and he could hit a long ball. There was only one thing about him that would have prevented him from making the majors—he would have had to learn to slide. I never saw him slide in my life. Never. He didn't go into the base sliding, and in professional ball, you've got to learn to do that." But he had so many other pluses as a ballplayer that it didn't matter much if he knew how to slide. Clark thought Kaiser could throw the ball harder than any pitcher on the team.

When Sollenburger came to Galt in early July, we had already played twenty-three games and the season was almost half over.

A few years later he took in his first hockey games ever when Kaiser was playing for Shore's Springfield team in the American Hockey League. They visited Hershey and Kaiser asked Sollenburger, who was living in nearby Chambersburg, if he'd like to meet him there after the game. "My wife and I went six or eight times to see him," Sollenburger remembered. "That's the only time I ever saw any hockey games. He was a good player, but I could never understand it."

No matter. "I thought Harry was a good guy," Kaiser said.

There was magic in the ball, and in the names that covered it.

Only the Ball Was White

Shelton told us stories of the Negro Leagues that were hard to fathom for a kid in Canada. Then we played in Kitchener and I could see a whole new world where skin colour, which meant nothing, meant everything.

THOUGH THERE EXISTS NO RECORD OF IT, BUFFALO'S JEFF Shelton was not the first black player to play in the Intercounty. That distinction belonged to either a Guelph player or a Brantford player. No one knows for certain. Several people, including Lillie and Pennell, remember a black player suiting up for the Guelph Maple Leafs in the 1930s. But Pennell also remembered Brantford having a black player in the same era. We may never know who broke Ontario's colour barrier, but it can be said with some certainty that it happened in the 1930s.

If Shelton wasn't the first black in the league, he was most certainly the first black to play for Galt. Galt, in 1949, had virtually no black families, yet the town had ties to blacks dating back to the years before the American Civil War when former slaves sought their freedom in Galt, Canada West. Indeed, many freed or escaped slaves made their way to Galt, having come into Canada via the underground railroad. Upper Canada had passed the first law in North America outlawing slavery.

Josiah Henson, commonly believed to be the model for Uncle Tom in Harriet Beecher Stowe's classic novel *Uncle Tom's Cabin*, had settled in Dresden, Ontario, halfway between Windsor and London, not far from the place where Tecumseh was killed. Other blacks followed Henson, and though bigotry was not unknown in Canada, slavery was outlawed.

In the spring of 1949 St. Thomas, which is between London and Dresden, also had a black pitcher by the name of Elmer Cook. He was, perhaps, a descendant of the colony Josiah Henson founded at Dresden.

Shelton, though he wasn't the league's first black player, still had to contend with bigotry. There were plenty of racial slurs and taunts in the summer of '49, mostly from players on other teams. That changed the following summer when those taunts came from his own teammate and fellow pitcher, Jim Bagby.

Shelton, to his credit, took it all. He'd heard the ugly voice of racism before. He knew he'd hear it again. Besides, the people of Galt were behind him. They were friendly, supportive, and made him feel at home, even though his wife, Odessa, and their young son, Jeff Junior, were back home in Buffalo. But when Bagby came in 1950, Shelton's welcome in Galt seemed over.

Bagby, whose father, Sarge, once won thirty games in the majors, was best known for the time he and fellow Cleveland Indians pitcher Al Smith, who had been traded by the New York Giants in 1937 for Padden, ended Joe DiMaggio's fifty-six-game hitting streak in 1941. Bagby had been a good major-league pitcher; he'd been in the big leagues for ten seasons and compiled a record of 97 wins against 96 losses and a lifetime 3.96 ERA. By the time he came to Galt—it was Murray who lured him here, as much for his name as for the fact that he still had a few pitches left in him—he was finished as a major-leaguer and had been for two years. It was Shelton's misfortune to return to Galt for the 1950 season and see Bagby there.

If Bagby denigrated Shelton by telling him to leave the clubhouse and change in the cow barn above the left-field hill beneath the trees, he would also curse and swear at Rosen, the Jewish playing manager that season. Like Bagby, Rosen had played in the majors, but that shared history meant nothing. As far as either of them were concerned, they were enemies.

Only a couple of years later another black player by the name of Jeep Jessop came to Galt to play for the Terriers. He used to boast, "I'ze is' the bestest hittin' pitcher in this league." Few argued. A big man, he would take all afternoon to lumber from the east end of Main Street down to the Four Corners at Main and Water. One game he hit a ball up to the cow barns atop the left-field hill, something that only Gord Bradshaw had been able to do. The ball was fair and the leftfielder chased it down. Any other player would have had an easy round-tripper, but Jessop was so slow he could manage only a triple. They called him Jeep because when he was summoned from the bullpen they would need to drive him in just so he'd get there before the game ended. But Jessop, one of the most popular Terriers at the time, was almost thwarted when he went to buy a house in town. An old city law forbade land ownership by blacks. When city fathers discovered the antiquated law on the books they quickly had it quashed.

Shelton, born in 1919 at Great Falls, South Carolina, was unusual in that he was as gifted at the plate as he was on the mound. Years later some people remembered how he could hit; others remembered his pitching. Some remembered both. Jack Scott, who was only a kid back then, remembered how he would warm up with a shot put. Someone else recalled how he hit a ball so far into centre field that it hit a cowshed at the other end of the park. No one had hit that shed since Bradshaw hit it the summer of 1930 when he hit .698.

There were many black players in the Intercounty after Shelton, including Wilmer "The Great" Fields, who was signed by Pennell to play for the Red Sox in 1951. Fields, out of Manassas, Virginia, had played for years with the Homestead Grays along with Josh Gibson, his batterymate, the greatest home-run hitter of the Negro Leagues and perhaps the greatest home-run hitter of all time.

Although my first extended exposure to racism took place that summer, I had seen racism in the deep southern U.S. the previous spring, and it had bothered me. Somehow my father had relented when I had asked him if I could accompany Gus on a scouting trip that spring. We were walking the streets of Lakeland, Florida, when I first saw coloured benches for blacks. Shortly afterward, I saw a bus filled with whites, and at the back was a Negro family. I couldn't believe it. It was 1949, after all. Hadn't the Civil War been fought nearly a hundred years earlier?

Shelton got his start in baseball at Greenville, South Carolina, playing for the Black Spinners of the Negro league in 1938–39. He stayed there three years before moving on to the semi-pro Cleveland Buckeyes. Following that, he and Odessa moved to Buffalo where he played with the Buffalo Harlem Giants, the same team that had barnstormed through Galt and southern Ontario from time to time in the 1940s. He played with the Giants from 1941 to 1943, before being called into the navy at the same time as another pitcher named Bob Feller.

Said Odessa: "He was so good they kept him stateside so he could play." It was the same for a lot of good ballplayers, though Shelton longed to go overseas with everyone else. He even pleaded with the authorities several times, to no avail. His friends were all going overseas risking life and limb, and he was stateside. It didn't sit well with him.

He played for the service team for almost two years while stationed at the Great Lakes Naval Base, before being moved to Oxnard, California, where he spent the next three years. There, not long after arriving, he was walking down Century Boulevard in Los Angeles when he saw a group of about eight navy men walking down the opposite side of the street. They recognized him first.

"Hey, Jeff!" someone shouted.

Shelton looked over with surprise. They were all friends from the Great Lakes Naval Base who had been shipped overseas and had now returned.

"What are you doing out here?" they asked. "Where did you go?"

"I haven't gone anywhere," he answered. "They've kept me here. They want me to play ball."

His friends gave him a hard time, as Shelton expected, but they could see his frustration. Still, they told him he had been lucky, even if Shelton didn't believe them.

Shortly after arriving in California, Shelton seemed to get lost in the shuffle. He was an unknown at first. Guys who weren't nearly as good were playing ball, while he was forced to sit out. "I got so mad I went to headquarters," said Shelton. He told them the team was prejudiced. Soon he got his chance. Future major-leaguer Larry Doby was in the service at Oxnard and had recognized him. That helped. So did Shelton's own efforts; he explained his situation and outlined his playing experience, mentioning that he'd played against guys like Jackie Robinson and Oscar Judd. Shelton had been a star in the Negro Leagues, and he'd been good enough at the Great Lakes Naval Base to be presented with a golden baseball. Finally the navy brass came around. "So your name is Jeff Shelton," they said. "Oh, we've got a place for you."

The first game Shelton played while stationed in California was against the Yankee farm team known as the California Seals. Someone else got the start for the navy team, which by then was, at least on paper, integrated, but after giving up eight runs in two innings, the manager, a lieutenant, put in Shelton, the only black on the team. And he pitched magnificently, allowing one hit the rest of the way. He won the game and his teammates went out to celebrate the addition of this newcomer. All the players, about twenty in total, and their manager decided on a posh restaurant in Beverly Hills. But when the lieutenant manager excused himself to use the washroom, the air suddenly turned cold. A southern player from Mississippi spoke up, looking over at Shelton. "I never ate at no table with a nigger and I ain't going to start now."

Shelton, tempted by the bait, sloughed it off with great difficulty. What a stupid idiot, he thought. But the team's catcher, a fellow Shelton could only remember as Jimmy years later, a New York native, was incensed. No sooner had the Mississippian spoken up than Jimmy had wildly jumped across the table after him. Another New Yorker and a couple of others followed suit, giving the racist player a real beating. Moments later, just after things had settled down, the lieutenant returned from the men's room. "What's rumbling out here, boys?" he asked. He had heard some commotion while in the washroom. Jimmy, the catcher who had come to Shelton's defence, explained. Pointing to the pummelled Mississippian, he said, "He says he aint eatin' at no table with no nigger." The lieutenant's face boiled red. He looked at the Mississippian eye to eye. "Look here, mister!" he barked. "You'll eat with everybody on this team. And if you can't do that I'll ship you overseas so fast your head will spin." The incident had happened on a Friday night. Monday morning the Mississippian was on a ship bound for Europe and Jeff Shelton was still playing ball.

When he was discharged from the service he rejoined the Buffalo Harlem Giants for the last part of the 1946 season. He stayed with the Giants until Gus Murray signed him for two hundred dollars a month—his friend, Connie Waite, who former Terrier George Brown believed was the smoothest guy around the bag he'd ever seen, was being paid three hundred dollars—in the spring of 1949. Shelton was thirty years old, far from washed up, but neither was he in his prime. Still, he could throw and hit and he would be a valuable addition to the Terriers. Brown could see that Shelton was one of the Terriers' aces, but perhaps even more impressive was that he could hit. "Shelton used to come down and help with the kids at the far end [of the ballpark] when they were out practising." It was a trait that endeared the good-natured Shelton to Galt fans young and old. Years later Little Satchmo, as he was affectionately called by all of us, was honoured at Dickson Park during "Jeff Shelton Night." He was showered with gifts and given a hero's welcome. It was a touching tribute for Shelton, one he never forgot. It underscored the special relationship that had existed between Galt fans and Shelton. He was so popular, as were several other players in '49, that Shelton remembered: "You couldn't just go out in public in Galt. People would mob you. It was a big thing to be a member of the Terriers back then." Shelton stood out like a sore thumb. Fans in Brantford took to Wilmer Fields a couple of years later in a similar fashion.

The right-hander had impressed Padden early. He and Waite were valuable additions to the lineup. Shelton brought up Waite from the MUNY (Municipal League) in Buffalo, aware that he had been cast out of professional ball, but also aware that he was as good a first baseman as they come. All Padden had to do was see Waite in action and he knew. There would always be a spot for a player of his calibre on the Galt Terriers. So the two commuted to games, staying with local people on a few occasions when the Terriers had several games in the span of only a few days. Shelton remembered staying with Dr. Catherwood, an avid ball fan and member of the Terrier executive. But those times when they would stay in town were infrequent. More often they'd commute. Indeed, they travelled over the Peace Bridge so frequently that even when Waite's brother-in-law wasn't on duty, they'd be waved through.

Some imports, said Murray, would put their names on a room at the Albion Hotel at the corner of Queen and Water Streets, where Padden often stopped for a drink, and this seemed to satisfy league officials. But even at that, there were limits as to how many imports a team could sign. Galt, like several other teams, often tried to sneak around the rules, if not break them completely. Laurie Brain noted in his column that the semi-annual ICBA meeting in St. Thomas early in 1950 would deal with residency rules. "It's no secret that this rule was abused more than anything else in the constitution last season," he wrote. "It will have to be clarified once and for all before several of the clubs can move to rehire many of last year's players."

Clubs that had commuting ballplayers in '49 were seeking permission to play them on the same basis for the 1950 season, but any new players would have to be bona fide residents. That made Shelton, Rosen, and Waite eligible for the 1950 season. No longer would there be any worries that someone might see them in Buffalo, or Toronto, the day following a game in Galt. "As far as Rosen is concerned," said Brain, "the former Brooklyn Dodger and New York Giant always insisted that he commuted between Galt and Toronto and not Toronto to Galt, although there were many who disputed this claim. There is a difference!"

When league president Otto Manske confronted him, Manske charged, "You're commuting from Toronto."

"No," explained Rosen, "I'm living in Galt and I commute to Toronto. I'm living here but my wife lives in Toronto." It was just a matter of how one looked at things.

Other clubs couldn't complain too strongly. They were doing the same thing. One nearby club even had a player who regularly hitched a ride home to Buffalo with Shelton and Waite. But when the league got wind that the two were regularly coming up from Buffalo, a couple of the Terrier directors offered to help. Doc Catherwood said Shelton could use his address as his residence and Shelton could stay over whenever he wanted. Another director made the same offer to Waite.

Shelton and Waite would drive up from Buffalo with a carload of American cigarettes. They would sell the much-wanted contraband to Galtonians, who were eager to buy the cheaper, and many thought, better-quality smokes. Dennis Smedley saw Waite one day at Dickson Park with cartons of Lucky Strike cigarettes. "They used to sell them for two dollars a carton," he said. "People around here really liked them." This time they apparently had one hundred cartons of cigarettes and were parked out past right field near the Agricultural Building. "Have you got any orders?" Waite asked Smedley. "If you do, meet me over there."

A few days later Smedley was in a downtown poolroom on Main Street when some RCMP officers appeared. The pool hall was a popular spot for local athletes. "All the players, hockey and baseball, would go up there, including Terry Sawchuck," Smedley said. "Sawchuck would bring his goal pads with him, set them down after a Red Wing practice, and shoot pool." He was a bit of an eccentric, even then. Girls were crazy for him, even if he was known to race cockroaches during breaks at the Galt Business School, where he was enrolled. But this day one of the RCMP officers was showing his badge around and asking questions. "We're looking for somebody selling American cigarettes," he said. Smedley left the pool hall as soon as he could. He was afraid they would talk to him and he didn't want to cover up for Waite and Shelton. When he saw Waite next he told them of the incident, and the Buffalo players stopped bringing in the illegal contraband.

Shelton always remembered that summer with fondness. But as good as those post-war baseball years were, they were bittersweet. "I could have been in there, in the majors, just like that," he said, shaking his head in regret, "if not for the service. I was supposed to go to the St. Louis Browns in '44 but got called into the navy." Jackie

Robinson—Robinson and Shelton were born in the same year—hadn't yet broken the colour barrier, and Shelton might not have been able to do it in '44 or '45, but Shelton, like countless others, knew the war years had been his prime baseball years. It was all just fate. Had he come along ten years later, or a generation later, when blacks were becoming a part of the major-league mainstream, things would have been different. Shelton had the talent; he was just born at the wrong time.

He probably endured as much abuse as any black player of his generation. Baseball, outside of the Negro Leagues, was not an easy occupation to pursue back then. Even in the Negro Leagues there were hardships. Team buses couldn't just stop at a random restaurant for a meal. Eating spots had to be carefully chosen. Wilmer Fields, who came to Brantford in '51, recalled one such experience travelling with the Homestead Grays. They were in the Deep South, and Fields, who was of a lighter complexion than most blacks, was chosen to go into a roadside eatery and order for the whole team. He had passed for a white before, something that was of benefit at just such times. But a teammate followed him in to add to his order and they were kicked out. No niggers served, said a sign.

Shelton was admired by Galt fans, but he was not universally liked by other players or fans around the league. He can still remember an ugly incident that took place one night in Galt. It was a Saturday-night game and Shelton was pitching.

"Hey, nigger!" came the taunts from the Kitchener dugout. "Hey, nigger!"

Though he'd heard such taunts before—"that stuff didn't bother me"—his Terrier teammates hadn't. Or, if they had, they didn't approve when it was their star pitcher who was the object of the abuse. The Kitchener player kept yelling at Shelton, but Shelton would just turn around, pretending to ignore it. Finally, the taunts were too much to take and we all bolted from the dugout to teach the Kitchener player some manners. What surprised Shelton was that the Kitchener bench didn't try to cover for their player. "He started running out the back and he didn't stop," said Shelton. "He never played again."

Two years later, in 1951, Pennell signed Fields, the Red Sox's first black, to a contract and promptly invested him with the nickname "the Great" to go with his name so that people would know how good he was and want to come see him. From then on Fields was known as Wilmer "the Great" Fields wherever he went. And, just as Shelton had been in Galt, Fields was a fan favourite in Brantford. Indeed, he was thought of highly around the league. No one on the Brantford team ever had a problem with Fields. Pennell liked Fields and would have Wilmer and his wife over to the house for dinner. Pennell, whose fair-mindedness was well known, wouldn't have tolerated bigotry on his club. He led by example. His players could see how he treated racial minorities with respect. In Galt there was no one to set such an example. Most of the players, at least the imports, didn't respect Murray. At times they wouldn't even let him into the locker room prior to games. But many of them, said Toronto sportswriter Milt Dunnell, didn't deserve any respect themselves.

It is not surprising that Shelton's last season in a Terrier uniform was 1950 given that Bagby was making life so difficult for him. But Fields stayed four years with the Red Sox and would always regret turning down an offer by Pennell and King to set up a sporting goods store. His home was in Manassas, Virginia, where he would return after every baseball season. This was where he would live out the rest of his life, though he felt warmed that the people of Brantford had offered him such a wonderful opportunity. He liked Canada. The fishing was great, and Brantford was where he had picked up a golf club for the first time. It was a special place where the people would invite the Fields family into their homes. "It was like a home away from home," he said. "The people accepted my family with so much enthusiasm that our stay there was the finest we ever experienced anywhere but at our home." He credited the hospitality of Pennell, King, and Art Holman with making his stay so special.

Like Padden, Fields had a remarkable background. He had begun his playing career in the Negro Leagues as a pitcher with the famous Homestead Grays in 1939, and continued with them until 1950, compiling an incredible 104 wins against twenty-one losses. With the Grays he played alongside some great black players like future Hall of Famer Josh Gibson, who was to black baseball what Babe Ruth was to the major-leagues. He also played winter ball in more than a half-dozen Latin American countries. Canada was a place he could have settled down in. But though he was treated well—he and his family were permitted to go to the movie theatre free—he would always remember an incident in Brantford that took place one day when he and a couple of other players were going to the ballpark. Driving through their neighbourhood they passed a couple of white youngsters who were out playing after supper.

"Nigger!" shouted one of the boys.

Fields stopped the car and went up and knocked on the front door of the house. The boys' mother answered the doorbell. Fields told her what had happened and she apologized and had the boys apologize. "What the boys said surprised us," said Fields. "After all, this was my family's second home—where my family almost made our permanent residence."

Pennell regarded Fields as the greatest player who ever played in the league. Fields was a quality player, but was just as good a person. One year, after getting to know the manager of the local drive-in theatre, Fields and his family would be waved in without having to pay. "My children looked forward to these outings because they were fun. Audrey would fix snacks to take along," said Fields. Fields was 9-1 that first season in Brantford and batted .381 to win the league's MVP award. He hit .379 in '53 and went 8-2 on the mound, and in '54 he hit .425 and went 6-1. Both seasons he was named league MVP. Years later Brantford held a "Wilmer Fields Night" and he returned to visit with the city that had cheered him on during four of the best seasons of his life.

Black players like Fields and Shelton added immeasurably to the league. In Stratford one night Padden wanted Shelton to start, but Shelton began poorly and then got worse. Indeed, he gave up six or seven runs in the first inning, which was uncharacteristic of him. "I didn't even wait for Tom to pull me," Shelton said. "I said: 'Take me out of here.'"

So Padden yanked him, moved him to third, and gave the third baseman the ball. "Go pitch," he said.

"I thought I was going to remain at third [that night]," said Shelton, "but then he put me back in to pitch." Stratford never got another run as we came back to win. "That's one game I'll never forget."

It was vintage Shelton. He was quiet—Waite did most of the talking for him—and talented. And Galt fans took him to their hearts that summer as he chalked up win after win. Before Perkins arrived in early July, Shelton was the uncontested ace of the Terriers' pitching staff. Warren had been impressive on the mound at times, and was hitting well, but Shelton was the top pitcher we had. When Perkins finally arrived, Shelton was still an ace. But now there were two of them.

*Looking south through
Galt along the Grand*

Young Blood

Jimmy Stewart and June Allyson starred in the MGM movie *The Stratton Story*, that summer. The movie chronicled former White Sox pitcher Monty Stratton, who tried a comeback after losing a leg. Knowing Gus, I was surprised he hadn't tried to sign Stratton. Later, I found out he had.

I T WAS LATE IN THE EVENING, AFTER AN EXTRA-INNINGS WIN OVER St. Thomas, when I felt a tug at my shirt from behind. A few people were still milling around the ballpark, but the lights were off and the only light remaining came from the naked single 60-watt bulb in the dugout, and the muted light that filtered out from the open dressing room door nearby. Mostly, it was dark.

I immediately turned, and could smell perfume. At that instant, I saw her face for the first time. She was older, I surmised, but was wearing a fairly snug pink sweater and light slacks.

"Can I have your autograph?" she asked.

"My autograph?" I said. "Are you sure you don't have me confused for someone else?"

"No," she answered quickly. "It's you I want."

"But I hardly played," I protested, before realizing that it would be a good idea to give an autograph to this very attractive woman and that I shouldn't ask so many questions.

"Where do you want it?" I asked. The perfume was drawing me closer, to smell her.

She showed me her sweater, pointing to a spot above her left breast, which was the size of a ripe grapefruit. "Here," she said demurely, and she looked into my eyes and smiled. As she did so, I couldn't help but notice her lips, accented by red lipstick, and her curves, which seemed to be located in all the right places.

"Certainly," I said. "Have you got a pen?"

She reached into her purse and produced a pen, and I duly signed her sweater, pressing ever so faintly on her breast. My heart raced.

"Are you from Galt?" I asked.

"Yes," she said.

"Hi, I'm Charlie Hodge," I said, holding out my hand to her. "What's your name?"

"I'm Janet Smythe," she said, placing her hand in mine.

It was dark after the locker room door shut, and someone had turned out the light bulb in the dugout, and now there was only the moon to light our way. "Where are you headed?" she asked. I pointed up at the western hill of the park, and, since I was on foot, I asked if she was going the same way. She said she was. "I'll walk you," I said.

Jennifer and I had officially broken up, if that is what you call it when two teenagers who had been seeing each other for too long decide to part, though our day in the meadow was fairly recent. Yet she was on my mind as I walked with Janet.

There was an edge to Janet, something about her that made her quite different from Jennifer. She was incredibly feminine, and her perfume was something I had never smelled before. It drew me to her, as did her openness and her smile. She was suggestive in her language and her appearance. She had none of the innocence that Jennifer displayed. But then, she was obviously older than Jennifer.

She reached for my hand as we walked into the darkness, up the park hill. By the time we got to the top, we were embracing wildly and kissing, and our hands were going places they shouldn't have been going for two people who had just met. My hands reached down and felt her hips and lower back, and she moaned as we kissed. I could almost taste her perfume and later, after I got home, I could still smell her on me. We walked lusting after each other over to the nearby cow barns, where we would have some cover from the moonlight, although there appeared to be no one around, and my heart was now exploding at what might happen. I could tell she was no novice at this, and I was surprised to find myself in this position, though I didn't ask any questions until later.

Soon our clothes were off. In the blackness, she took me in her mouth, the silence only being broken by the sound of her lips and tongue. She was loud, but eager. I remember thinking that we were like a couple of animals, and that it was a good feeling to be privately acting out something that was so instinctual. She introduced me to a number of new positions, and she ran her tongue and mouth all over me like a dog licking its master. I reciprocated, and I did so willingly. My enthusiasm was tempered by nothing that night.

We had a passionate evening together, and when it was over, and I was home and in bed, I began to feel guilty for what I had done, and I started thinking of Jennifer, and though we had split up, and amicably at that, I felt I had wronged her. Still, she need never know. What I hadn't counted on was Janet talking and spreading the news. It wasn't long before Jennifer heard, and showed her displeasure with me.

That came just a week or two later, when she left the ballpark with a rough player of about thirty-five from an opposing team. She called on me one night after having had several drinks with a friend, and told me, in her anguish and drunkenness, that she had slept with the older man and had lost her virginity and was beside herself that she might be pregnant. I consoled her and said I was there for her, but she had lost her innocence, as had I. In the end our actions did us no harm, and even today there are times when I am reminded of Janet by a passing woman's perfume, and I think back to that enchanting night in the cow barn, and I am glad for that memory, but at the time it felt like we had both grown up far too quickly and that our worlds were ending. The summer of '49 was a baseball summer, but it was also a coming-of-age summer.

I never saw Janet again, except for a brief glimpse of her a short time later with a toddler in tow, about a week before I left town for university.

Galt's famed Murderer's Row

Murderer's Row

Their names were on everyone's lips that summer. Creedon, Kaiser, Rosen, and Warren. For opposing teams, the names instilled fear.

SOME WEEKS AFTER LEFTY PERKINS ARRIVED, I COULD LOOK BACK at his debut in a Terrier uniform and fully realize just how much he had buoyed our team in early July. Some of our big guns, like Goody Rosen, who started slowly, began finding their groove about that time. Everything came together on Saturday, July 16, when the London Majors came to town for a night game. It was to be Perkins's home debut. More than four thousand fans were in the park, many arriving early. Padden was going to catch his friend once more. Rosen was there, as was Creedon, in right field, and Kaiser at third, Waite at first, and Warren in left field. Lillie was playing short, and Pickard was at second. Wiggie Wylie, a small but immensely talented hockey player and a good ballplayer, had been called up from the Pups and sat beside me on the bench. Everything, it seemed, was in place.

London had a good squad with Tommy White at first and Evon at short—they were considered two of the best players in the Intercounty—and they had a good supporting cast, but they could do little that night. Sometimes I think no one could have. Our power hitters—Creedon, Kaiser, Rosen, and Warren—were awesome, and they held nothing back, winning the game 21-2. We had managed twenty-two hits and saw four London pitchers that game. It was the biggest margin of victory by any team that season, and the worst beating suffered by any London team in several years. In Brantford, Pennell and the Red Sox players took notice.

Rosen had been superb. In six trips to the plate he had managed four hits, including a sixth-inning grand slam, and a triple. In all, he drove in eight runs. It was an incredible exhibition. There was little any team in the league could do when we were firing on all cylinders. Even Lillie, back in his familiar spot at second base after Adams suffered a bad gash to his hand and arm in Friday night's 6-2 loss to the Stratford Nationals, had fattened his average with three hits. Also getting three hits were Waite, Creedon, and Perkins, who earned his second win in four nights. Perkins, never appearing to extend himself, had played another strong game, scattering ten hits over nine innings with a shutout going for the first five frames while fanning six and walking three. Kaiser had warmed to this newcomer from the start; he liked the way he played. Here was a pitcher who had been around and knew the game, he thought. Kaiser himself had hit another home run with Creedon on base in the fifth. The ball had sailed over the right-field fence.

That was the night we began our run for the pennant, and there was a feeling that even though we weren't on top of the standings, we would be come August. Maybe sooner.

There was only one cause for concern. Adams was likely out for the rest of the season after badly injuring his hand the previous night, and now Warren, the early-season home-run king, was out too. He was carried off the field on a stretcher in the seventh inning after suffering what was thought a badly sprained right ankle. He had walked to first, then run to second when Lillie hit to centre field. Padden was watching from the dugout, and he cringed when he saw Warren pull up sharply, writhing in pain, after crossing second base. Warren's father, a full-blooded Indian from Oklahoma, had arrived from Tulsa on Friday, in time for the game in Stratford, only to see his son go hitless in four plate appearances. Now he watched as his son was carried off the field.

Dr. Catherwood treated him in the dressing room and later had Warren removed to the Galt hospital for X-rays and further examination. A broken ankle would finish him for the season, thought Padden. Warren was not the best player on the team, but he was not far below, and he was needed. Padden knew that a Galt team minus Warren would be a much weaker ball club. We all knew it too.

The next day we got word that Warren's injury, apart from a small break to a little bone in his foot, was just a sprain. He might miss a few weeks, but he would be back in time for the stretch drive at the end of August, which was when he would be needed most. So, after receiving the good news, Padden felt there was reason for optimism. Perkins had arrived to bolster the pitching corps. And Rosen was finally reaching his potential.

Indeed, Rosen had been on a tear. His batting average had climbed well over .300 to .313, and he was showing the fight that everyone expected from him. In the London game he even had a run-in with several London players as our side came to bat in the early innings and the London players began to ride him. Earlier, Rosen had fumbled Bechard's hit, allowing Bechard to take second instead of settling for a single. If the incident had happened to any other player, it would have been quickly forgotten, but Rosen was a former big-leaguer. In the same inning he made another mistake when he threw to the plate after catching a line drive off of Tim Burgess. He should have gone to second, which would have produced a double play. The London bench jockeys, their team losing badly, started saying things to Rosen as he came up to bat. And Rosen, always quick to anger, went over to the London dugout to tell them in no uncertain terms what he thought of them. He threatened to knock Clare Van Horne's brains out, and called the Londoners a bunch of two-bit ballplayers.

The Londoners responded by suggesting he was no better. "How much money do you make in Galt?" they asked.

"I can make more money playing ball in one year than you'll ever make," Rosen said.

"Are you waiting for another war so you can get back with Brooklyn?" one Londoner asked, in reference to the fact, so the Londoners believed, that Rosen's big years had been during the war when the major leagues were depleted of their best players. But Rosen knew he could have made it, war or no war. In fact, he had gone up in the late 1930s when the majors were still at full strength. He had been banished from the majors by Durocher; the fact that he had played so well in the majors had nothing to do with the league being watered down.

It was common knowledge that the majors were weak during the war. "There's no question the calibre of play during the war years was not what it had been," said Milt Dunnell, "and you could see that by taking one look at Pete Gray, who later came to Guelph to play. Here was a one-armed guy playing outfield for the St. Louis Browns." But

Rosen, said Dunnell, had gone up to Brooklyn in '37, before the war, and he'd hit .312. Playing the full season in '38 he hit .281. He was banished for all of the war years until 1945, when he returned from the minors and hit .325. "Besides," said Dunnell, "Goody had established good minor-league stats."

Rosen's triple and grand slam, as well as his eight runs batted in and two beautiful catches in centre field, had silenced the London bench once and for all. One young Galt boy that summer would never forget Rosen. Gord Renwick, then a junior at Galt Collegiate and an aspiring pitcher, signed up for Murray's summer baseball school, where Rosen was one of the instructors, along with Padden. The school was held at Dickson Park. One day Renwick was pitching to Rosen, and he was more than a little nervous, considering Goody had been up in the majors just a few seasons earlier. But Rosen told him to show his best stuff. "Throw it as hard as you can across the plate," Rosen told him. Young Renwick did his best, but the ball nailed Rosen in the elbow of his inside arm. Rosen headed straight for the mound and Renwick was petrified. He thought Rosen was going to give him hell. Instead Rosen said to him, "Don't ever throw at my elbow again. You can throw at any other part of me." "If you throw at my head, I can move it, or if you throw at my chest, I can turn, but the elbow is the only part that never moves." So Renwick, who years later would become vice president of the International Ice Hockey Federation, now even more nervous than he had been, gamely tried to pitch a few more to Rosen, only to discover that he could barely get it over the plate, let alone anywhere near Rosen.

"It's funny the things you remember," he said. "I don't remember much else about that camp, but I remember that. And I remember the way Rosen taught us to bunt."

The summer ball camp, to which several major-league scouts showed some interest—Padden and Murray sent letters to a number of scouts, noting it would be a good time to spot potential talent—was not to be a money maker, though it did expose Galt teenagers to some top-quality instruction.

More important, at least as far as Murray's balance sheet was concerned, were the goings-on with the Terriers. Concerned over rising costs in operating an Intercounty ball team, Murray was becoming more diligent about balls that were hit into the crowd. He considered each ball that was not returned to be stolen. A staggering number of balls were being lost each game, but Murray explained that, at two dollars a ball, it was becoming an expensive business when fans didn't co-operate by throwing the balls back. During the game one fan used his fists on Murray after Murray insisted that the man's son return a ball he had picked up. Gus, oblivious to the analogy that he would be taking candy from a baby, had rushed into the stands to retrieve it. Police quelled the disturbance and the man and his son were escorted out of the ballpark.

It was not the first time that season that Murray had been on the receiving end of someone's fists. Gus's first shiner had come from Waite. Waite had challenged Murray at Murray's paint store, something that Lillie and I would never forget. Although the incident had been hushed up, details became known to the public as the season progressed. Lillie and I had, after all, been eyewitnesses. "Gus tried to kick Waite as Waite began punching," said Lillie, who would hang around Murray's store quite a bit that summer. "I would do this or that and Gus would give me a few bucks," he said. "On the day Waite and Shelton came in—Waite would always do the talking for Shelton—they were arguing about meal money. We used to get $2.50 a game, and although we didn't ride the bus that often, when we did, we all had to go." It was just before noon. As Lillie remembered it years later, Waite was arguing for Shelton's meal money. Jeff wasn't going to argue for it or negotiate with Gus. Coloured players didn't do that, not even back then in the Intercounty. Waite first shook Murray. Then Gus tried to kick him. "Then Connie gave him a shot and he knocked Gus down. Gus tried to kick him again, and then they called the cops." But Waite was a hero in town. "Locking him up was the last thing they'd do."

In later years fans would delight in hearing the story, and about how Kaiser went after Waite. "Tex really stuck up for me," recalled Murray. Another crisis had been dealt with earlier that season after an away game in Waterloo. After getting dressed at the Galt YMCA on Queen's Square as we usually did for road games, we went up to Waterloo with Dennis Smedley in Pickard's black taxicab. Smedley would put the taxi sign in the trunk and our carload of players would hop in after turning over our watches for safekeeping. "I'd put all the watches on my arms, all the way up, and I'd put the wallets in my pockets," Smedley recounted. "Then after the game I'd give them all back."

He remembered the aftermath of one game well, as did a lot of us. Soon after the game was called in Kitchener, several of us jumped into Pickard's car with Smedley. He was still carrying all the watches and wallets, while Murray was out on the field complaining about losing the money roll. When we got back to Dickson Park and found the clubhouse door locked, we all turned to Smedley, assuming he had the key. "I haven't got it," Smedley said. "Gus must have it in Kitchener."

Finally, Creedon pulled up in his car. "I'm not waitin'," he said. "I'm goin' in to have a shower now. I'll get in. Stand back." With that he drove his fist through the oak-panelled door, unlocked it from the inside, and went in for a shower. He had bruised his knuckle badly and had to miss a couple of games, but nothing was broken. "Gus fined him fifty bucks for missing the games and breaking the door," said Smedley. So for several days Creedon was unable to play the piano at Central Presbyterian Church.

Many people never knew the other side of Creedon, the musical side. Most just knew him as a big, bruising, tobacco-chewing ballplayer. But Murray had seen his musical side. "He is a terrific piano and organ player," Murray told us one day. Murray and a few others stopped in at the Paradise Gardens just outside of Guelph one night. Gordie Tapp, who would go on to fame as a member of the popular *Hee Haw* television show, was a Guelph radio man at the time and was moonlighting as master of ceremonies at the Paradise Gardens in the evenings. This night there was a contest on and Creedon went up to perform. It took Murray and some of the others by surprise. "Creedon sang and brought the house down, he was so good," said Murray. Indeed, he won the contest. That summer he was given the key to Central and allowed to go in weekdays and play the organ. The guy who had given him the key? My father.

I remember that summer there was talk of using frozen baseballs, but as far as I can remember, it was just talk. But the next year, when Bill Hornsby was playing for the Terriers, frozen baseballs were used. "The original frozen baseball idea came from Hornsby," said Murray. "He'd learned it in the minor-leagues." Hornsby was a good utility outfielder who'd been in the service. "His dad asked me to give him the job." Though the younger Hornsby was a decent ballplayer, he was not another Rogers Hornsby, though he did help the team. "He was a favourite with the girls," recalled Murray. "I think he had a couple of girlfriends in town."

The frozen baseball trick seemed to work initially, but then it backfired when the balls were mixed up and Kaiser got one pitched to him. He hit a blooper just out toward second base. "Sure," said Murray, "he got upset and he said, 'Get rid of those.'" Kaiser remembered not being so diplomatic about it. In any case, the frozen baseball experiment at Dickson Park was over.

Murray was picking up all sorts of things. "There's no two ways about it," he said. "I learned things pretty fast that year. If I get blamed for the balls, I don't care. I was involved and Tex Kaiser knows I was involved, because I had to be involved in order to handle the balls." Early in the spring of 1994, when reports were coming in about the live balls in the big leagues—batters were hitting them further—Murray was convinced they were wound tighter. "And I'll bet you dollars to donuts that those balls are sitting on top of a stove. If the balls are hot they go further. When they're frozen, they don't."

That summer as I spoke with Murray he remembered the exact moment when Kaiser hit the frozen ball. "He had one pitched to him by mistake," he said. "You can never control the balls 100 percent of the time. We had a couple of good bat boys and they were instructed—I knew all the tricks—about scratching the balls and putting sandpaper under their belts. I can't remember Padden ever doing anything like that, but all the catcher has to do is take his fingernail when he's got the ball and put a scratch on it at a certain spot near a seam and throw it back to the pitcher. I don't believe that Padden ever did that, I really don't. If he did, I don't know anything about it. As for the frozen baseballs, I don't care if I get blamed. I was involved, but it was not my idea." The balls always had red stitching, so Murray made sure that the frozen balls were marked with a couple of black threads. "Say there were a dozen frozen balls and a dozen hot balls," he explained. "We warmed the hot balls on a little stove. My job was, when the bat boys brought the balls back, they had to hand them to me. I would put the cold balls in one place, and the hot balls in another, and when the umpire called for more balls, I would give them to the bat boys to take out. I had them in brand new boxes, and when I wasn't busy I'd put the hot balls right back into the cartons."

In those days there was a wooden box in the ground immediately behind the catcher and umpire. It was like that in all ballparks. Today the umpire has an apron to carry the balls, but back then balls went into the box. When the umpire would take out a fresh ball, one that Murray knew was frozen, he would rub it with some dirt to get its feel.

"Gee," said the umpire, "these balls are cold."

"Well, they've been sitting in the lockers for about two days and it's cool and dark in there," said Murray. He always answered quickly. His idea or not, it was vintage Murray. Intercounty teams today would never get away with anything like that, but such incidents during the summer of '49 helped make life interesting.

Take a game in Brantford as an example. It had been a particularly rough one. Bad blood existed between the two clubs at the best of times, but tempers were flaring even more than usual this night. Things were said. Fans even got into it after the game. I remember hearing Murray say to Warren, "Here, take those bats out of the bag." He made sure each of us had a bat at the end of the game. "That was a rough night," he recalled years later.

At Dickson Park, where Gus would unsuccessfully try the frozen baseball experiment the following season, Murray had to pay for police protection and security. The crowds were huge, and security was a necessity.

Also a necessity were the Gus Murray inspired promotions. One regular promotion was to give away five hundred red roses to the first five hundred women who came through the gate. Lyn Cross, the owner of Crosses Flowers, was a good friend of Murray, and Gus made a deal to buy the five hundred roses at five cents apiece. "Five cents a rose was a good deal, even back then," he said. Cross doubled the number of roses for him. "He was awfully good to me," admitted Gus. "Most people were extremely good to me." So, on those nights when we were giving away roses, almost every lady went home with a rose. On nights when there weren't five hundred ladies in the stands, Gus would gather twelve in a bunch and give them to Mrs. Padden. He was sympathetic to her plight; he couldn't forget the tea party she was unable to attend because she had no good dress to wear.

The men of Terrier Town

Newt Kenney, Connie Waite, Frank Udvari, Wes Lillie, Charlie Hodge, Cam Pickard

Saturday, June 11, 1949

The men of Terrier Town

The Hodge Boys

Through all the afternoons and evenings at the ballpark, memories of my brother Jimmy stood tall, inspiring me, comforting me, and pushing me always to greater heights.

IN OUR TOWN, MY OLDER BROTHER AND I WERE KNOWN AS THE Hodge boys. I always felt proud when I heard this, because I thought the world of Jimmy, and it was an uplifting experience to be grouped with him.

Come the war and his disappearance from our lives forever, and I never heard that term, "the Hodge boys," again. I soon longed to hear it, but really, it was him I longed for. I can't count the number of times I prayed for his return. I didn't accept his death for a long time.

When the war came to an end I was alone, an only child, left to fend for myself, to navigate the world without the benefit of my brother's experience. I felt utterly alone at times, and all too aware that I had always taken Jimmy for granted. As the years passed I tried—though not always successfully—to never take anyone for granted again. Jimmy's death changed the way I dealt with people the rest of my life, and in that sense, he lives on, as does all the promise, all the good, that he represents.

I have now spent many more years without him than with him. We lived so few years together when you look at an entire lifetime, but those years were growing-up years and were the foundation for all the living to come.

I can remember one of the first times Jimmy took me downtown to the library, and later to Reid's Candy and Nut shop. The street names were memorable even then, and though I was young, I could read. Just across the arched bridge on Main, I saw two signs at the place Jimmy called the Four Corners, where Water meets Main. Not long after, my mother got a phone call one weekend morning, from across town. I had ridden my tricycle clear across town, through the downtown and up the east hill, in one of the biggest explorations I would ever undertake. Of course, I told no one, much like I was to do when we went to Arizona when I was ten and I discreetly left my family to wander down to the bottom of the meteorite crater. That trip, down and up, had taken more than two hours, and the only reason the police weren't called in then to find this missing Canadian boy was that my sister had spotted my small white Stetson at the bottom of the crater.

But on the day I took my tricycle on an excursion across town, past the Four Corners and on to the great unknown, I learned that adventure was intoxicating. I cherish even today a picture of our father at the Four Corners on the bridge, waist-deep in water, carrying my grandmother across the bridge, from east to west, during one of our spring floods, for that bridge was part of my early exploration of the world.

Two generations earlier my grandfather, then living a few miles downriver at Glenmorris, rescued several young schoolgirls in the old stone school on the flooded river flats near the footbridge. I heard this story not from him, or my father, but from an elderly woman long after my grandfather had died. She had been the young girl he rescued, and she claimed he saved her life that day.

I never rescued anyone from the Grand except myself, when I flipped a thirty-two-foot-long single shell from the rowing club on a rainy night in late October, and so the great lineage of river rescuers ended with me.

Rosen, left, and Padden are quick to argue a call with umpire Kumornik.

Downfall

In the paper I saw a picture of Philadelphia Phillies first baseman Eddie Waitkus, sitting pajama-clad in a hospital bed holding a baseball for nurse Alice Klopfer. Waitkus, wearing a ball cap, was smiling. Nurse Klopfer, on the staff at Illinois Masonic Hospital in Chicago, was standing beside him holding a baseball bat. It had been a week since Waitkus had been shot by a girl admirer who had never met him. Nearly forty years later Robert Redford would star in *The Natural*, a movie about a young star whose career was cut short when he was shot by a female admirer. In 1949 Waitkus had been batting .306, the best he'd done since breaking into the majors in 1941 with Chicago. But after the injury he never came close to that again. He retired in 1955 having hit .291 only once since the shooting. If Murray thought crazy things were happening in Galt with such players as Waite and Rosen, things were even crazier elsewhere. A woman comes out of the blue to shoot a Phillies player? Was everybody demented?

IT WAS SOME TIME BEFORE I CAME TO REALIZE JUST HOW BAD TOM Padden was hooked on booze. Weeks earlier, when Padden had arrived drunk for a game, I had chalked it up to a one-time mistake.

I remember that game well, even today. We were all at the park early for a night game, and the crowd was beginning to arrive, though game time was more than an hour away.

Padden came walking toward the dugout from right field, and as he approached, he staggered. I was catching with Lillie when I noticed him, and as we threw the ball back and forth, I watched Padden out of the corner of my eye.

I didn't know what to make of it. I was embarrassed for him. Gus saw him and quickly went out to meet him, though Murray seemed to walk in a way that wouldn't draw attention to himself or Padden.

They were getting closer to us all the time, and they were talking, but I couldn't hear what they were saying. Soon they were within earshot, and it seemed that Gus was trying to get Tom to go home. But Padden would have nothing to do with that. I heard the Albion mentioned. It was the old hotel owned by Al Murray, the former NHLer who had coached the Galt Junior Red Wings when Gordie Howe was in town.

Gus motioned to Watty Reid, and then a couple others came over and soon Murray's station wagon was brought in and Padden was put in the back and whisked away. But not before some of the fans got a whiff of the situation. Someone yelled out, "Padden, you're just a rummy."

I took great offence to that comment, and I stared for a time at the man who said it. But I was more concerned over what was happening with Padden. Our coach, our leader, was not there to lead us. It was the only time that summer that he was not there for us, and I came to realize that even though he was a gifted manager and player, and was supportive of the younger players like myself, there was no sympathy for anyone who had a drinking problem.

Years later people would have gone out of their way to help Padden, but back then I heard from Murray that the executive had considered firing him on the spot. They gave him an ultimatum after he had dried out, and he was allowed to continue with the team, the stipulation being that he never show up for a game in that condition again.

Society, I learned much later, is not tolerant, and people did not consider alcoholism a disease back then. No one saw Padden's problem as a disease, though I somehow felt sympathy, and sorrow, over the situation. I realized that Padden was not perfect; that none of us is perfect.

But I still looked up to Padden. I would always look up to him, and respect him for what he was: a talented, and a good human being.

Billy Gibbs was one of the Brantford Aces in the summer of '49.

Billy Gibbs

He was born to pitch.

WE HAD OUR PITCHING ACES, BUT BRANTFORD HAD GIBBS and Gavey. Billy Gibbs had been recruited by the St. Louis Cardinals in 1945 at the age of eighteen. In his prime he was one of the hottest pitchers southern Ontario had produced, and he went south to pursue his pro baseball career with all the attendant publicity and fanfare that accompanies a young star. Many saw him as a lead-pipe cinch to do well with the Cardinals. But it was a different world south of the Canadian border. Though Gibbs had the size pro scouts were looking for—he was six-foot-two and 215 pounds—and the talent to match, he was just another good prospect, one of many, with the Cardinals. Still, as Red Sox president Larry Pennell said, "Gibbs was just built for pitching."

Gibbs had always wanted to make it to the majors. Baseball had been his passion, ever since he was a youngster growing up in Brantford. So he willingly played in various places within the Cardinal organization. "The best I ever made it to was B ball in Lynchburg, Virginia," he lamented.

Many people, including Gibbs, felt he wasn't given a fair chance with the Cardinals. "I had a million promises," he said. But they kept stringing him along. He always believed in himself, in his talent. Even when he finally decided to go home to Brantford in 1948, he still felt he had the talent to make it to the big time. "I was on my way to Duluth, Minnesota, and I came through this way [Brantford] and the Brantford Juniors asked me play here. I was also offered a spot with the outlawed league in Quebec."

Outlaw leagues, like the one in Quebec or Mexico, presented a problem for the major leagues. Players weren't able to get their releases from a major-league team to play there, and if they chose to play anyway, they were banned from organized ball.

Gibbs chose to stay home, which wasn't an easy decision because it meant the end of a dream. A day or two later the Duluth Dukes team bus was involved in an accident in which several players died. Gibbs counted himself lucky.

His bread-and-butter pitch was his fastball. "He could throw hard," said Lillie. "It was blistering." He could also throw a curveball at various speeds, as well as what was then called a screwball—today it's called a slider—down and away. The fastball was his pitch of choice when it was necessary for him to do the job quickly. "When I threw my fastball overhand hard enough it would kind of jump a little." That's how he got a lot of strikeouts, by getting movement on the ball.

Gibbs, like Kaiser, threw what they call a heavy ball. It hurt the catcher's hand. Other players might throw just as fast, but it would come in lightly. When Gibbs threw it the ball hit the mitt very heavy. It would hurt.

He had always loved the game. "I'd do anything to play it," was how Gibbs remembered his childhood. "We used to leap the fence at Agricultural Park when we were kids. They'd lock up the park on Sundays and we'd leap the fence and spend the day in there."

"You never saw them on their bikes without their baseball gloves," his wife, Janet, recalled. They would hitchhike, or sometimes even walk, to Burford to play softball against the farms teams. "It was a different life back then," he said. "There was no television. It was just coming in back then." To put things in perspective, golfer Arnold Palmer, destined to become one of the most recognizable television faces—and one of the first sports celebrities—was still playing varsity golf at Wake Forest. It would be another decade before he achieved television fame.

Gibbs remembered 1949 clearly because, in addition to it being his first year playing with the senior Red Sox, it was the year they made a big change at the Brantford ballpark. "That was the spring they put the lights in here." Though Galt had installed lights two years earlier, Brantford waited. Putting up lights for night games was a big expense. In some places the city would underwrite the cost; in others, the ball club and the city shared the expense. Lights meant more night games, and there were old-timers who said they were unnecessary. The Intercounty had survived since 1919 quite nicely, they maintained, without lights. Besides, people were busy weeknights.

In the end, their arguments weren't convincing enough to put off the decision any longer. Brantford had seen Galt get lights in 1947, and soon others followed suit. It was change, but it was inevitable. Those communities that failed to respond to progress would be left behind. Lights meant more weeknight games. Since most players held down full-time jobs, installing lights meant games could be scheduled for 7 P.M. or later, giving players time to go home, eat, and then travel to any of the Intercounty ballparks. Going to St. Thomas or London meant a two- or three-hour trip. Today that same trip would take about an hour, but in 1949 roads weren't what they are today.

What Brantford found was that they drew better crowds for night games. Some games they drew five thousand people or more. All of a sudden games didn't have to be scheduled just on weekends. Any night was suitable. The only problem came during night games in mid-July when the sun shone directly into the batter's eyes at home plate. "Brantford had the worst park in the league for the sun," said Lipka. It was only blinding for about fifteen minutes, after which the sun would fall behind the trees beyond centre field. Aside from that, night games promised to change the Intercounty forever, especially in terms of flexibility. Intercounty schedule makers had more freedom.

Gibbs, a fastballer, was one of two true aces on the Red Sox roster that season. The other was Hamilton native Gavey. Gavey, a left-hander, was stocky, well-built, about five-foot-eleven and 190 pounds, and threw heat. "He was wild at times with his control," recalled Gibbs, "and batters were very leery." But no one questioned his strength. When he was on he was virtually unstoppable. "Gavey could throw hard," said Pennell, "but only if he had enough rest. He could only go once a week by 1949." His arm hadn't been the same since he had hurt it playing AA for Savannah, Georgia, a couple of seasons earlier. Prior to the arm trouble, Gavey looked like he was headed to the majors. "He had all the earmarks of a major-leaguer," said Pennell.

Gavey had gone south with Gibbs in 1945. In fact, Gavey and another Hamilton native, George Fisher, who would also play for

Brantford in 1949, had met at the train station on the morning they were to leave. "There were seven or eight of us," recalled Gibbs. "I went to Winston-Salem, while Alf and George went to Allentown, Pennsylvania, to play Class B ball."

They all shared a similar experience with their forays into professional baseball in the U.S. And they were all regarded as homebrews, coming from nearby Hamilton and surrounding area. We had our big-name hired guns in Galt, players who had been shipped in for the season. Other teams had them too. London and Waterloo had talented clubs that season. But Brantford gathered for spring training in May of 1949 with local players. "And we had a good attitude on the team," said Gibbs, though he figured that wouldn't be enough to carry them to the Intercounty championship. The other teams, he knew, were just too talented. "I think Gus thought that he had the top team, which he did, in the league at that time."

Still, Brantford had players who had grown up together and had known each other for several years. In addition to Gibbs and Gavey, their roster included an excellent shortstop, Ronny Hodara, a Windsor boy who had played against Gibbs in junior in 1948 and who later went into the priesthood. "He was a great player," said Gibbs. "Tough to get out. Very quiet."

And there was ace pitcher Frank "Nig" Parker, a player destined to lead the league in ERA that summer, and Lockington in centre field, as well as third baseman Lipka, and first baseman Billy LeConte.

Gibbs always counted on Lockington in centre field, because even when an opposing player got hold of a ball, Lockington would invariably run it down and make the out. "John Lockington," said Gibbs, "was as fine a ballplayer as you'd want to see. He was probably the fastest thing on two feet."

The others were talented as well. There was pitcher Harrison Fisher, who was no relation to pitcher George Fisher, second baseman Hann, catchers Jim Borthwick and Clayton Cooper, right fielder George Carruth, and Lefty Wilson, who also saw duty at first base.

All of them, to a man, genuinely respected and liked their boss, Larry Pennell. Such was never the case with Galt skipper Murray.

Letter to Gus Murray

Across the River

The newspapers and clippings were brittle after half a century, and as we touched them the letters and words broke off and fell to the floor. The stories, like the people, were passing into history.

"THAT SON OF A BITCH IS A CROOK," SAID CREEDON MATTER-of-factly, though with a touch of irritation. It was early August and Creedon had come to understand Gus by then, having spent several months in his employ. I wasn't afraid of Creedon, though many were, but still, I kept my distance. For the most part, he left me alone.

I had mixed opinions about Creedon, who was nothing more and nothing less than a hired gun. A beer-drinking good-timer, his baseball persona was at odds with his impressive musical talents. Rarely are the two talents, which were both highly developed in his case, exhibited in the same individual.

One night after a game at Dickson Park, Creedon and a few others went to the hotel in Preston for a few drinks. It wasn't the first time, nor would it be the last. Being new to the drinking game, no one had to twist my arm, and not long after we arrived at the bar, Creedon and the other Americans began discussing one of their favourite topics—Gus.

Again Creedon used that phrase to describe Gus, but this time, when the words "son of a bitch" had gone beyond his lips and into the dank and dark air of the bar, the bartender overheard and came to our table, compelled to get in his two-cents' worth.

"Gus," he said, shaking his head. "Hmm. Do you know that son of a bitch still owes me money for some paint he double-billed me on?"

Without anyone asking, he strode over to the bar and filled a pitcher on tap and returned, placing it directly in front of me. There was a momentary pause in our discussion of Gus, and I could see the bartender's blue eyes because he was hovering over me, looming large, his aftershave reeking, and the words he uttered seemed to bolt out of his mouth and ride down to us on the silver wax of his handlebar moustache—quicksilver words—the way gravity pulls a child down a curved slide.

"You gotta hand it to him," chipped in Warren, sipping his beer slowly as he looked up to the bartender. "He probably owes us all money. Trouble is, he's got us all confused so we can't figure out what's owed and what's not. He's confounded me."

"Gus knows what he's doing," said Padden. When Padden spoke, quiet though certain in what he said, everyone listened, as if what he had to say had ordinance over all else. "I actually thought we'd be able to get the better of him, but no.... He's a shrewd son of a bitch. Shrewdest I've ever seen. And I've seen a lot of shrewd sons of bitches."

The bartender and his silver handlebar returned to his duties behind the bar, his face now hidden in the shadows but his moustache still silver in the dim light.

"You guys!" boomed Kaiser. "You come up here from down south, you Americans, figuring you could outhustle Gus." He shook his head, leaning back in his chair, and took a drink from his bottle. Kaiser never used a glass and years later, when I saw him drink from a glass, I thought it odd.

Waite said Gus owed him money, and he knew exactly how much, and I believed him. He was going to get it before the season was over, he said, even if he had to turn Gus upside down and shake it out of him.

Although I didn't offer any opinions on Gus—I felt a sense of loyalty because I worked for Gus part-time—I agreed with Kaiser. The Americans were having a tough time of it trying to take advantage of this small-town Main Street promoter. Gus had stood his ground and given the Americans a taste of their own medicine.

Wes and I left with Waite and Shelton at closing, and they dropped us off at the Four Corners on their way back to Buffalo, but not before slowing as we passed Gus's store. Waite, who was in no condition to drive, muttered something about stopping and demanding the money Gus owed him, but in the end he just slowed enough to yell some choice expletives Gus's way. A few moments later he stopped to let us out near the bridge.

"G'night, boys!" he shouted past Shelton through the open window. "Don't let mama hear you come in."

"That bastard," I said to Wes.

It was dark and silent in downtown Galt, the street lights penetrating the stillness like beacons in the night. The vacant sidewalks were quiet in the shadowed light, but the sleeping storefronts of awnings and glass were familiar.

"C'mon, Wes," I said. "Let's see if we can throw across the river." It was very late, or very early, depending on which way you saw it, and another fifteen minutes wouldn't matter one way or the other.

This was a tradition for Wes and me as it had been for Jimmy and me when we were younger. We were only a stone's throw from our dad's haberdashery, and as kids we had often accompanied our father to the store, then gone off exploring near the river. Some of my earliest memories were of the river behind the post office, and of trying to throw stones all the way across to the west bank.

We walked behind the old stone post office, the one built by the same builder who constructed the Parliament Buildings in Ottawa, and looking west across the river we could see the Galt Knitting factory, set back about ten feet from the water. The only light we saw came from lit windows in that four-storey red-brick building, the dim light reflecting out onto the black water. In the moonlight we could see the water, glass-black and quiet in that part of the channel near the Main Street bridge. To our right, beyond the arched bridge we used to climb, towered the steeple of Central Presbyterian Church, touching the steel-blue sky and heaven itself.

I reached into my pocket and pulled out a quarter and Wes did the same, and we set them down on the waist-high stone wall of the eastern riverbank. We also grabbed several small stones and fired a couple across the water to get the distance. There was first a small plop, then another, and we could see where our throws had gone in.

Wes's next throw made it all the way across, and we heard a window break, the sound fracturing the night the way a bolt of lightning cracks the sky. We ran out of the darkness between the post office and the Commerce Block, he heading east up the alley beside the police station and I going west across the bridge, past the church, the Y, and the square, and up the crescent to home. Once I got on the hill, beneath the tall trees, I felt safe under their cover, the way you feel safe under an umbrella in a storm.

It was fully a week later, and daytime before I returned to the river. There, our two quarters still waited on the stone ledge. Neither one of them made it across. The Grand claimed all the stones of my youth. Now it swallowed my coins, mere flecks in a sea.

The Galt Terriers of 1950

Hitting the Fence

It was too early to start calling Brantford a team of destiny, but that is what they were, from the moment they beat London to get into the playoffs.

ONE SATURDAY AFTERNOON IN BRANTFORD, WITH A FULL house on hand, Creedon did an interesting thing. While in the outfield, a long ball came his way. I was playing beside him in left field. All of us had been around long enough to know that any ball hitting the back fence was a ground-rule double. But on this occasion, Creedon was beat, so he kicked the ball into the fence as he pretended to pick it up. The Brantford batter only got two bases out of the deal when he should have had at least a triple.

The Brantford fans were livid, and I thought there might be some trouble, but Creedon was a big guy and things finally settled down.

I think Creedon knew every trick in the book. In his long career he came to know the game the way only a handful of men ever came to know it.

That night I went down to a dance hall we called "The Bucket of Blood," a place known for the many fights which broke out there. It sat on the corner of Ainslie and Dickson Streets. Normally the Women's Institute held dances there through the week, but there was a special Saturday-night dance this night.

The Bucket of Blood was a place good girls seldom frequented. Usually they were forbidden to go up there.

There were three of us from my high-school class, and we were hoping to have a night of fun. But this night the zoot-suiters were there, and there was trouble from the beginning. My buddies and I weren't looking for any trouble. It seemed to come looking for us.

I was out on the dance floor with a very attractive brunette from school, trying to make the most of my split with Jenny, when I thought I heard someone call my name. I ignored it, believing I was just hearing things. Then someone walked by and bumped my arm hard, and looked at me in an odd way. I let it go. The small collision had caused a pin in my watch wristband to come loose, and my watch had fallen to the floor under a table. Since I was dancing, I decided to pick it up as soon as the song was over.

When the same guy walked by me again and bumped into me once more a few moments later, I knew it was no accident. And the brunette I was dancing with knew it too. I recognized the guy—Roy—as being of my brother's age. He was wearing a typical zoot suit and had a long chain dangling from his waist. I wouldn't have been surprised if he was a member of the Beanery Gang, a group of fedora-wearing thugs with chapters in Kitchener-Waterloo, Guelph, and Toronto. They used to cause a lot of trouble at dances, and in the summers they were known to hang out at Wasaga Beach.

Roy had not gone into the service, though I never knew why. I was fuming, but he made the next move before I could even say anything.

"Jimmy'd never take that kind of crap," he said. "But I guess you ain't Jimmy now, are you?" He moved toward the table under which my watch lay, stooped down and grabbed my watch, and put it in his pocket.

The watch meant a great deal to me. Jimmy had given it to me the day he left for the war. He hadn't really given it to me, but had left it in my care, asking me to look after it while he was away.

"Why don't we step outside," I said in a cold, calm voice, beguiling a fury I could scarcely contain. He probably thought I would be a pushover because he was older, and looked tougher. He may very well have been tougher than I was. But I also knew what I was capable of when provoked, and had no fear as we walked down the stairs and outside into the night.

"I always wanted to take on your brother," he said. "He was too good. Always good at everything. I wanted to take him on, then he goes off and gets himself killed. But I guess laying a beating on his little brother is the next best thing."

My friends didn't know what was happening, and when Roy and I stepped outside, I was alone with him and three older guys. My father had taught Jimmy and I one thing when it came to fighting. He abhorred fisticuffs, and made it known very early on that we were to settle our disputes with others in more civilized ways. But he also said it was important to know how to defend yourself. If you were going to fight, then you better get the first lick in. He told us that very few men liked fighting, though they might talk the talk and look tough. That first punch, he advised, was the most important one to land.

One of the zoot-suiters jumped me as we walked out when my back was turned, and he hauled me down hard to the concrete sidewalk. I managed to get up swinging, and I was looking to land everything I could on Roy. I honestly wanted to hurt him for what he had said.

There was nothing fair about the fight and I expected no fairness. We scrapped for several minutes, and I was getting the worst of it, though I had plenty of fight in me. By then, of course, I was fighting for me and Jimmy, and I remember thinking that Jimmy was looking down at me and was at my side, and this gave me a surge, to know I was not alone and would never be alone no matter what life hurled my way. Then my two friends emerged and we more than took care of ourselves. By then there was a crowd gathered around, and a policeman on the beat came by and broke up the crowd.

My jaw felt like it had been broken, and I was sore in the gut, where I had been punched and kicked. But I had given out some good stuff in return. Nevertheless, the cop, whom I knew, took the two of us down the street to the station. My father was called.

We were at the station barely a minute when the officer, Constable McCabe, came into the small room I was sitting in and gently placed Jimmy's watch on the table in front of me. He treated it as if it were a treasure, and looked into my eyes with compassion, for he had read the inscription on the back of the watch with Jimmy's name on it. Mom and Dad had presented that watch—they purchased it at Brown's Jewellers—to Jimmy on his sixteenth birthday.

I was not worried about my father giving me any punishment, but I was worried that what I had done would disappoint him. And it did. But Constable McCabe, even before he had found the watch in Roy's pocket, had gotten wind of what instigated the brawl. He had known and loved Jimmy, and, indeed, had coached him years before.

When I saw my father at the station, he and I were alone in a room. "Are you okay?" he asked.

"I'm okay, Dad, just a little sore, but nothing that won't heal in a day or two."

"Jack tells me the other guy was defaming the name of Jimmy. Is that true?"

"Yes, he said some uncomplimentary things, and he took Jimmy's watch after it fell on the floor. Look, Dad, I'm sorry for what happened. I never went looking for this. But I couldn't let him say those things."

"I know ... You look tired, son," he said. "C'mon, let's go home."

As we got up, I glanced at Constable McCabe. "I'm sorry for any trouble I caused you tonight, sir," I said.

"Ah hell," said McCabe. "You caused me no trouble tonight, son. And it warn't your fault anyways. But from what I saw, you held your own. Can't fault a kid for standing up and defending himself. I'm just sorry I hadn't happened along sooner. Now get outta here, and don't be coming back any time soon."

We walked out to our car and got in. There was silence between us. Then he said, "I've always been proud of you, Charlie. Very proud. And that hasn't changed one bit because of what happened tonight. Sometimes there's just no way out of a situation. I'm not condoning what happened, but I believe you when you say he started it. If I was your age, and that had happened to me, I would have done the same thing. I'm just glad you're okay."

"Dad," I said. "Thanks."

"C'mon, let's get some ice on that face."

There would be other dances that summer at the YMCA's Teen Town, which hosted dances every Friday night. There was never any trouble at those dances, and usually the girls had to be escorted home by 11 P.M. The guys would often go over to Gus's for a Coke and burger afterward.

It had been much the same in Jimmy's day. The Friday-night dances. The girls we grew up with and came to admire. The ones you hated when you were very young because they were girls. The same ones you wanted to kiss when you were older, because they were girls. The town that nurtured us, fed us, and helped us grow into adulthood. The friendships. The laughter. The baseball. The times of our lives. Not all the times were good. Some were slow and painful. There had been Jimmy's death. And we lost a couple of friends to the river. But this was our town, the place we owned.

I never knew if it was different in any other town, because I never grew up anywhere else but Galt. Our town would live on in our memories as we progressed through life. No matter where we went, or who we became, we were always trying to return home.

South of Main Street

Back Door into the Playoffs

That trolley-line season in the valley of the Grand has lived on, drawn out over a lifetime, like the summer day is long and the sun-bathed western sky is far.

N EARLY A MONTH LATER, AS AUGUST WAS PLAYING OUT ITS last days, Brantford and London would engage in a one-game playoff, the winner gaining entry into the playoffs. Gibbs's belief that Galt had more talent was proven during the regular season when we won the pennant. But London, also boasting a talented squad with the likes of Tommy White, perhaps the best pitcher in the league that summer, and home-run hitter Russ Evon, had surprisingly finished tied with Brantford in the last playoff spot. Indeed, Brantford had finished the regular season ten and a half games behind the Terriers. With three games to go in the regular season, things looked grim for the Red Sox. The only way Brantford could make the playoffs was if they won their last three games and London lost their last three games.

Which is what happened. It was our team, ironically, that let Brantford get into the playoffs. We met on August 17 in Brantford, in what would prove to be a key game. Summer was closing. The cornfields between the two towns would soon be ready for harvest. For both teams it was the final regularly scheduled game of the season, and we were holding down first place. Brantford needed a win, and even then, the best they could hope for was a London loss so that the two teams would be tied. Then there would be a one-game playoff to see which team would advance to the playoffs.

That last regular-season game had been a pitchers' duel between two of the Intercounty's best southpaws. Perkins had won all five of his starts to that point. Brantford was sending Gavey to the mound. For the Red Sox, everything was on the line. A loss would end their season. It was a dogfight from the start, and both pitchers pitched brilliantly, but if anyone had the edge, it was Perkins.

It was still 1-1 when the ninth inning began. Then Carruth, Brantford's right fielder, opened with a hit down the left-field line. The ball appeared to land on the foul side of third base by at least a foot, but umpire Slim Somerville ruled it a fair ball and Carruth pulled up at second base with a double. We were all stunned. The ball was obviously foul, we thought. But argue though we did, the fact remained that Carruth was safe at second. Then Hodara beat out a picture-perfect bunt that rolled down the third base line. Carruth advanced to third, and Hodara was at first. For the first time all night, Perkins was in trouble. Hodara stole second the next play, beating the throw by catcher Johnny Clark, and Cooper hit an easy pop fly to Adams at short. It should have been a routine catch, but Adams, who sat out for nearly a month after suffering a severe hand injury in Stratford, was rusty. He dropped the ball. Lillie cringed. Now the bases were loaded and Gavey came to the plate. He promptly hit a fly to right field to score Carruth. That held up as the winning run. It was a bitter loss, because in the first inning we had threatened to take a big lead. Pickard had walked, before Waite hit a single. Then Rosen sacrificed the runners along, before Gavey hitched up his belt and struck out Creedon and Warren. Gavey was to prove as effective in nixing a Terrier threat in the fourth inning when he struck out Adams and Lillie with Warren on first.

Our run came soon after Clark walked, only to be advanced by a Perkins single. But he had been thrown out when he tried to take third after catcher Cooper let a ball sail by. Cooper had thrown to Lipka for an easy out. When Waite came to the plate he pulled Lipka in with an attempted bunt before slashing a hit through the hole at third base. Then Rosen singled to right to score Perkins.

Perkins had played a spectacular game, fanning six of the first eight batters he faced. The game was already four innings old when he gave up his first hit. In the seventh, Carruth was Perkins's seventh strikeout victim. He fanned nine in total and gave up two walks, one an intentional pass. Perkins was still being referred to as the Penn State ace. He deserved better than to lose for the first time that season in that way. Both he and Gavey had allowed just seven hits apiece.

Rosen, now hitting over .300, had played the way a former major-leaguer was expected to play in centre field. Just as Murray had anticipated, he had started the season slowly and was finishing strong, both at the plate and in the field. When Hann belted the ball deep into centre, Rosen went after it and made a nice running catch. But the feature play of the game came in the Galt seventh, with two out. Waite unleashed a long ball to deep centre, but this time it was Lockington who made a sensational over-the-shoulder catch while running at top speed and with his back to the plate. Another outfielder might have let it fall, but not Lockington. He never played baseball half-heartedly, and besides, he could run like a deer. Lockington robbed Waite, who went two-for-four at the plate, of what appeared to be a sure home run. Earlier Waite had been similarly robbed when Carruth, in the third inning, leaned over the right-field snow fence to catch his long, foul fly with one hand.

Lockington went two-for-four at the plate, in addition to playing superbly in centre field. The win had kept Brantford's playoff hopes alive. And though they didn't know it at the time, London was in the process of losing to the Maple Leafs over in Guelph. The season had progressed without deference to Brantford, but now everything seemed to be falling into place for the Red Sox. They were winning when they needed to win, and London was losing when they needed to lose. If anyone had a crystal ball, they would have started calling the Red Sox a team of destiny. But, of course, it was far too early to give them that label. They had yet to make it into the playoffs.

So London travelled to Brantford for a one-game playoff on August 22, with the winner advancing to the semi-finals against us. But no matter who got into the playoffs, they were not considered serious threats. We probably feared London more than Brantford because London, after all, had White and Evon, two players who could entirely change the face of a game. Brantford had no superstars, but they had determination and a never-say-die attitude, which sometimes counts for more.

"It was a hard-fought battle," said Gibbs. Young Rich Mirco, a six-year-old Brantford fan, remembered that game. He has had a lifetime to look back on the scrapbook he began keeping that August. For him, the game meant as much as it did to the players themselves. Everything was on the line. A loss would end the season, and Rich did not want that. Indeed, there were few things he enjoyed more than going to the ballpark, sitting on the first base line where his dad, who was on the Red Sox executive, would act as usher, and watch his Red Sox play. He hadn't missed a Brantford home game all season, and he went to Galt for those games too. But now London was in town, and the season was on the line.

They still had some natural light when the two teams took to the field that night at Agricultural Park. Rich, sitting on the first base line, was already in the stands before the teams got there. He was ready. And so were the teams. Both teams had shown up to play.

What followed was one of the closest and most exciting Intercounty games ever. Just before the game began, a *Brantford Expositor* photographer walked out onto the field at deep centre behind Red Sox centre-fielder Johnny Lockington. The three main stands were full. In fact, there were 5,185 paid fans sitting in the stands staring out at him and the Brantford players just then lining up in the field. The actual crowd was closer to 5,500. The wide-angle picture the *Expositor* photographer took couldn't even get all the fans in, the crowd was so big. Behind the photographer the crowd was equally big. Old-timers couldn't remember a crowd that had been as large. Young and old alike, they were in for a treat.

Gibbs got the start for Brantford, facing White of the Majors. For nine innings it was a classic pitchers' duel. Brantford managed one run off White, and that proved to be enough as the Red Sox, behind the pitching of Gibbs, won the game 1-0. Afterwards, there was a city-wide celebration. "They took the team around town in a fire truck," said Gibbs. Fans lined the streets, shouting and hollering like they had rarely done before. "I ducked out and went somewhere but the rest of the team went out. It was a great relief to win that game. It was a battle just to make it into the playoffs." Everyone in Brantford, it seemed, shared in the revelry. To young boys like Rich Mirco, it was as if the Red Sox, his team, had won the championship.

What no one realized that night, amidst all the hoopla, was that Brantford's season was really just beginning. There would be a lot more ball played before the autumn grew cold and the season was done.

Gibbs believed Murray thought he had the best team in the league that season. He even agreed with him on that point. "But I think Gus thought that it was a shoo-in."

That night Gibbs was given a one-hundred-dollar bonus for his mound work, which had played such an instrumental role in getting the Red Sox into the playoffs. Pennell knew nothing of the special bonus. Mike King had given it to Gibbs; he knew Gibbs was about to propose to his girlfriend, Janet Scott, a Galtonian. He would be able to put the money to good use.

Indeed, it was a welcome gift for Gibbs. He gladly took the money and the next day bought an engagement ring to give to Janet when he popped the question. She had been a classmate of ours at Galt Collegiate, and an adamant Terrier fan for years. But that summer of '49 she was one of Brantford's biggest boosters.

Tom Padden, Number 9

The Prelude

"Oh, did he rip it!" said Wes. "Goody hit this thing over the coal pile, 950 miles over the right-field wall."
As we slapped his back, he turned, spat out a stream of tobacco juice, and said, "Aw, hell, what did you expect?" No player in the history of Dickson Park had ever hit a ball into the Grand River. And though they looked for it, the ball was never found.

WHEN PEOPLE TELL YOU HOW GOOD YOU ARE, THERE IS A danger in actually believing them. My father ingrained in us a sense of Presbyterian piety, or modesty, which made it hard to ever accept a compliment fully. But it was a great gift to be taught modesty. I was eighteen that summer, and in awe of the players around me. I believed they couldn't lose, and further, that since I was a part of the team, we couldn't lose.

We should have trusted our Presbyterian instincts. It is true that no one gave Brantford much of a chance to win our semifinal series. We had won the pennant ten and a half games in front of them, while Brantford had backdoored it into the playoffs with a nail-biting 1-0 win over London. We boasted four ex-major-leaguers; Brantford had none. All the Red Sox had were a handful of players with Class B or A experience like Gibbs, Gavey, Fisher, Parker, and a few others, and, of course, the formidable talents of Lockington and Lipka. Some of us thought we might even beat Brantford in four straight games; then it would be on to play the real series for the Intercounty championship against Kitchener or Waterloo.

Laurie Brain tried to be objective, and still he came to the conclusion that Galt looked unbeatable. He was reminded of the column he had written only a year or two before when he predicted Galt would go into Guelph and earn an easy win. "The Terriers are off to Guelph this afternoon and should, without much trouble, come back with a win," he had confidently predicted. "The Guelph Maple Leafs are in the cellar of the Intercounty senior series and from impressions gleaned from writers around the circuit, are destined to stay there ... The Terriers should boost their stock considerably with wins over Guelph today and Waterloo Saturday." Of course, the Terriers had gone to Guelph and lost, and Brain's prediction found its way into the rival *Kitchener-Waterloo Record*, "illustrating the folly of predicting," as the *Record* pointed out. Tongue in cheek, the piece went on to say that "Laurie Brain now qualifies to become a member of that select group of the sports writing fraternity who called and lost. But spare those tears men; bet the Galt scribe didn't have any money riding on that prophecy."

Now Brain caught himself wanting to predict a fast series win for the powerhouse Terriers. Instead, he used caution. He would let the game be played on the field. The Galts quickly proved everybody right, taking a commanding 3-1 series lead. Things were going so well that Brain didn't have to state the obvious: that Galt would win the series easily. Brantford fans were prepared for the worst.

Though he was never a rah-rah type of reporter-cheerleader, Brain could not always resist plugging the Terriers when they were deserving. But he also carried a sharp pen and wasn't afraid to call them like he saw them. So it was not surprising when rumours began circulating that the well-liked Brain and the fiery Murray engaged in fisticuffs that season, though Murray denies it. If they had a few quarrels, they managed to patch things up. In later years Murray talked about Brain with fondness.

Brain seemed to relate well with the players. He was able to get close to them and yet still write critically about them when circumstances demanded. He was a former athlete, and his golfing prowess and baseball experience stood him in good stead with the players. He knew what he was writing about. One time when umpire Ed Fowler failed to show for a junior game, Brain was asked to fill in. The Terriers knew that though he wrote for the paper, he was almost one of them. He liked to drink and smoke, and he was fair in his treatment of players in his "Sifting the Sports" column. Players might not always like what he wrote (though usually they did), but they could rarely argue that he wasn't fair.

His son Larry remembered, as did I, how we would be invited back to the Brain house after a game. There would be a case of beer in the living room and the Brain children would enjoy rubbing elbows with the players. For years afterward Larry cherished a Terrier uniform from that '49 team. "It was too big for me, but I kept it for years." They were the heavy uniforms, wool, and itchy as hell.

Laurie had a habit of returning home late at night after games and sitting down at the typewriter he had borrowed from the *Reporter* to write up his story for the next day's paper. "He wrote his stories when he got home," explained Larry. "He always said he wanted to write it while it was still fresh in his memory. He didn't want to wait until the morning. Of course, he probably wanted to go golfing the next day."

So the Brain children would go to bed on such evenings to the sound of their father's clickety-clack on the typewriter as the letters hit the yellow foolscap on the roll. They'd yell down "We can't sleep, Dad!" but to no avail. "Get to sleep or I'll be up those steps but quick," he would answer them.

Now, as we took an early lead over the Red Sox in our playoff series, it seemed to most observers that we were unstoppable. And, indeed, we probably would have been, were it not for the machinations of several players, led by Creedon, Waite, Warren, and Rosen, who suddenly demanded more of the gate from Murray. "They wanted twenty-five percent," said Murray. "I gave them ten percent." The players had all signed contracts agreeing to ten percent, so Murray was unwilling to renegotiate now. But the crowds were huge, the players argued, and they deserved a higher percentage. Fans were coming out to see them, and only them, they said. Murray, they would tell each other in the locker room, was a crook not to give them a bigger percentage of the gate. Besides, there would be plenty of money for everyone, what with the playoffs against Waterloo on the horizon, and then the all-Ontario playoffs.

Murray wouldn't budge. He had expenses to meet, not the least of which were the salaries he had promised his big-name players, many of whom were now demanding even more. There was some resentment by the homebrews on the Galt team over the large salaries the imports were getting because more than a few local players felt they were just as good, and there was always a sense that they were being shortchanged. They could live with it to a point; but when the American imports, excluding Padden and Sollenburger, demanded more money, they had little sympathy from the rest of us.

Several Brantford players were also resentful of the large salaries being paid around the league to the likes of Rosen, Warren, and Creedon. Gibbs said many of his Brantford teammates expressed animosity toward such players. Then came the strike; a strike which precipitated a series of events that would become our undoing.

Rumours of a looming strike circulated quickly around the hill-girt town of Galt. Murray was furious. Here the Terriers had won the pennant and were in good shape to beat Brantford four games to one and advance against Kitchener in the finals, and now there was internal dissension brewing on his team. It was easily the biggest crisis of the season, and it couldn't have come at a more inopportune time. They didn't need this right now, he thought. He had paid them what he promised, and while it was true the gate receipts were higher than they'd been in years, Murray needed every cent of it to pay salaries and the rising costs levied on the Terriers for playing at Dickson Park by the Galt Parks Board. All season Murray had run himself ragged trying to dream up new promotions and ways of bringing people out to the ballpark. And now this.

In contrast, Pennell was upfront when players began asking questions. "We wanted harmony on the club," Pennell said. "That was the big thing." With it, and the right talent, he knew they could field a winner. Without it, even if they had lots of talent, they were dead. Pennell would call each of the players in to see him. "There's going to be talk about how much money some imports are getting paid," he would say to them. "Remember, not everyone's getting the same pay. I don't get the same as a lot of lawyers even though I might think I'm doing a better job than they are."

Pennell would tell them that most of the imports would have to feed and house their families in Brantford for the entire summer on their baseball income alone, while most of the Canadians had full-time jobs to support themselves. "You have to bear in mind that they've got no other jobs and they have wives and children." By being upfront and explaining the situation to the players, Pennell was able to avert problems before they started. "They seemed to accept it," he said. "I had no problems." Besides, he would point out that if people didn't come out to the ballpark, none of the players would get paid.

Back in Galt, Kaiser brought up the subject of the huge gate receipts the Terriers were enjoying that summer from the large crowds. Murray countered that the parks board was charging the team an arm and a leg to play their games and provide ground crews to keep the diamond in shape. And he said that part of the reason for the big crowds was having name imports like Padden, Creedon, Warren, and Rosen on the roster. Kaiser might be playing better than them all, but they had bankable names.

None of it made any sense to Kaiser. He was one of the best players in the league and all he wanted was to be paid accordingly. Was that so wrong? After pleading his case, and with Murray unwilling to bend, Kaiser exploded: "Stuff it, Gus! I'm not playing." But he did play. He was a hometown boy. He was a product of Terrier Town, even if it was Preston, and not Galt, where he had grown up. Preston was close enough to Galt. He had to play. He couldn't let his team down. Eventually the whole thing blew over. Kaiser was not one to hold grudges, unless it was against Eddie Shore. "Gus was a funny guy, but I loved him," said Kaiser. Years later Kaiser would still make the trip down to Galt from Kitchener, where he lived, and drop in on Gus at his store. Sometimes he'd just stick his head in the door and shout, "Hey, Gus!"

Then there was the rivalry. Perhaps the imports knew nothing of the rivalry between Galt and Brantford, or perhaps they knew and cared little about it. Murray knew it. Everyone who had grown up in Brantford or Galt knew it well. To us, there was more than a few extra dollars at stake. There was honour, something the homebrews on both teams knew well. The way some of the imports seemed to casually disregard this rivalry was just another reason the homebrews resented the imports. "We felt we could play equally well," said Gibbs. "So it caused a little hardness here and there." But over the years, the resentment faded, or at least the memory of it did, and what was left was the memory of the high calibre of ball that season. "The class of ball was very good," Gibbs said. "I'd rate the ball as A or AA ball. I had been involved in spring training, pitching for the bigger clubs, and the league itself, to me, seemed to be in that class. It was good baseball for the fans. But you've got to remember at that time TV was only just beginning and it was before other pro sports made inroads. There just weren't that many things to do in those days. Baseball was one of the sports that was exceptionally popular at that time along with hockey in winter."

Billy Gibbs knew all about the rivalry. As a boy growing up in Brantford he had played against Kaiser and Lillie and countless Galt teams. One team always had to lose but no team liked it. Gibbs didn't like losing to Galt teams, even if his wife was a Galt girl. He met Janet Scott in the summer of 1947 after she had come to Brantford with her family to see the Galt Pups play a road game. The Scotts were all avid Galt fans, and Janet was no exception. When romance bloomed between this good-looking girl from Galt and this strapping, tall young pitcher from Brantford, Janet always had a cheer for Galt, even if her fiancé was playing with Brantford. They married in the summer of '49.

Although marriage changed Janet's allegiance, she remained, partly, a Galt Terrier fan. When Brantford opened that semifinal playoff series in Galt, Janet sat with her family and cheered on both teams. Of course, she always wanted her husband to do well, and she cheered him on, but in her heart she also had a soft spot for the Terriers. In a way, their marriage was like the relationship between the two towns. They helped each other along as much as they could and they were unquestionably interdependent. Neither city wanted to lose, and Janet didn't want either team to lose. Despite all this rivalry and, for Janet, split allegiance, there was love. Galt and Brantford, like Billy and Janet, could not live without the other. In some respects, the Gibbs were reminiscent of that Depression-era fuss over Gord Bradshaw and Beaner Pickering when the two had bolted from Brantford to play for Galt. But when it came right down to it, Janet was fully behind Billy, and that meant she had to favour Brantford in the end. As for other long-time Galt and Brantford fans, there would be no holds barred in the series. There was always something fuelling the fire when it came to the intense rivalry between the two clubs.

On August 22, a Monday, we played an exhibition against the New York Komedy Kings at Dickson Park. A small crowd of 1,200 turned up and left pleased with what they had seen. We won 6-5; proceeds from the game went to minor baseball in the Intercounty. We were playing without some big guns that night. Waite, Rosen, Perkins, Shelton, and Warren were absent, but Padden gave an exhibition of his versatility when he pitched the last four innings. He gave up only one hit, but walked two, and three of the Kings' runs were charged to him after we made three errors behind him. I was charged with one of those errors.

It was a fun game, a mixture of comedy and baseball. Something light just before the playoffs, yet it gave us a chance to stay sharp. Billy Ball, the Kings' amazing one-armed outfielder, proved to be popular with the fans, and he rewarded them with two hits in four trips to the plate. Two years later, Pete Gray, the one-armed former major-leaguer, was signed by Murray to a personal services contract and played a season in Guelph.

Fans were a little disappointed when Smokey Joe Adams, the Kings' southpaw pitching ace who was billed as another Satchel Paige, couldn't play; he was being saved for another exhibition game Sunday night in Rochester. But Brother "Funny Man" Moody got the crowd laughing with his rendition of "Ain't No Pork Chops in the Sky." Moody also stole behind Preston umpire Jimmy Tait, whose sister Marion had recently been named dean of Vassar, and began mimicking his calling of balls and strikes.

Goody Rosen

The Playoffs

And so the twilight of the season came, and then it was dark grey with winter. The coming months were more bearable in Brantford. In Galt all that remained was a soothing but elusive memory of that lush green grass of summer when there had been light, and hope, and infinite promise. So it was that the seasons yelled out to us in a distant voice that was familiar, but was provident no more. Quietly, so quietly, the game had grown and it was not now the same. The century was half over and the game, which had changed, had lost its innocence. Nor would it be better. As the years came and went, the fans, the old fans, did not like what the game had become, but then, in the past, they had had it all.

TWO NIGHTS LATER THE MOMENT HAD ARRIVED. THE SEMIFInal series with Brantford was the most eagerly anticipated in Galt history. No one was disappointed in that first game, which came on a Wednesday night at Galt, with seven thousand fans on hand, as we won 4-3 behind the stellar pitching of Perkins. Two other players, Lillie and Padden, had also played outstanding games, while Gavey had pitched a superb game though taking the loss. Brain wrote that the baseball had been so thrilling it brought back memories of the Roaring Twenties when Galt captured a couple of Ontario titles. My father agreed.

That first game had indeed been a thriller. Perkins, who was the game's first star, earned the win, fanning eleven Brantford batters in what was a typical strong showing on the mound, but there was another hero for Galt, an unlikely hero, and his name was Lillie. Lillie, the game's second star, had hit twice in three trips to the plate, including a key fourth-inning double to deep left which put us back in the ball game. His stickwork had taken Brantford by surprise. In the fourth inning, when Lillie came to the plate, Red Sox manager Speed Cotter underestimated his ability to hit a long ball and called both left-fielder Mooradian and Lockington in. There was one out, with runners on first and second. Up stepped Lillie. The pitch, and crack! A long low hit to left, which carried over Mooradian's head. Lillie ran for third but was thrown out. Still, two runs had scored.

The winning rally had come in the fifth inning when Pickard led off with a single. Waite then walked and Rosen sacrificed both runners along. Then Creedon came to the plate, took the first pitch, and drove a long, high ball to deep centre that had all the earmarks of an extra base hit. But Lockington raced to the fence and made a great catch. "Damn him," Creedon said. Waite was doubled at second base but not before Pickard had tagged up and scored what proved to be the winning run.

But Brantford evened the series up Friday night with a late surge in the second game at Brantford, winning 7-6. We had shelled two Brantford hurlers to take a 5-0 lead into the fifth inning before the Red Sox made their comeback. Nearly six thousand fans had jammed into Agricultural Park to see the game, with the spillover of people lining the perimeter of the outfield fence. In the long history of Brantford baseball, there had never been a crowd to rival the one that night. Indeed, it was a new single game attendance record. The place was a zoo. More attendance records were expected to fall as the series continued.

Gavey, the burly southpaw from Hamilton, and Billy Leconte, a substitute first baseman who only got into the lineup late in the season when the starter was injured, were the heroes of that second game. Leconte had hit a high fly into short left centre to start the Red Sox rally in the fifth. It fell between Rosen, in centre, Lillie, at short, and Warren, in left field. Curiously, it appeared that Warren could have made a play, though any one of the three should have been able to get to it. But what fans didn't know was that when Lillie, the eager youngster, retreated to make the catch, Warren had called him off. Rosen had heard it. And then the ball hit the grass as Warren came in, and bounced past him. Two runs scored, Brantford's third and fourth of the inning. What had been a runaway Galt game was now a narrow 5-4 lead. Later, in the seventh, Leconte singled to Rosen to score Lockington and tie the game. A Stan Lipka blast up the middle scored Leconte for the go-ahead run.

Things began well for us—starting Red Sox right-hander George Fisher was sent to the showers. Rosen and Waite were hitting everything in sight, and Creedon too. Creedon managed four RBIs on the night. Nig Parker had come in to relieve Fisher, but he had no better luck against our bats. So, in the fifth, Gavey came in with runners on second and third and Kaiser up. But Gavey fanned Kaiser, and then forced Warren to pop to Hann to end our rally. His performance surprised everyone, though in reality he had beaten us twice during the season. Shelton, who had started out looking good, took the loss. He wasn't around at the finish, having given way to Warren in the ninth. But Warren was playing strangely. He almost allowed the Red Sox to steal a run home. The Red Sox had loaded the bases and Warren, fielding a Lockington hopper, became confused. Finally, he just nipped Carruth at the plate. Carruth was out, but it had been a made-to-order double play. A busher might have been confused, or hesitant, but not a former major-leaguer. Something was up. No one quite knew what it was, and though the average fan might not have noticed anything, Galt players, and Murray, in the stands, could sense that all was not right.

We had the tying run on third base in the ninth with only one out. Waite had begun the inning with a long blast into the right-field crowd. Rosen had done the same thing earlier and it was ruled an automatic two-base hit. Now Waite's was ruled a double. Rosen flied to right to advance Waite, but Creedon grounded out to first base and Kaiser's long hit was run down by Lockington. Anywhere else, or at any other time, Kaiser's hit would have been a double.

Brain was enjoying the series immensely. After the first game in Galt, he wrote, "Anybody who didn't get a thrill out of last night's ball game should know enough to lie down.... Brother, you're dead! It was typical playoff baseball in a way, it seems, that only Galt and Brantford teams know how to play it."

Padden was prepared to play all seven games, if the series went that long. His catcher, Clark, had broken the second finger of his left hand at the end of the season stopping an errant pitch. It had hurt, but he shook it off. He went on to catch nine innings a couple of nights later. He also injured two fingers on his throwing hand, which had to be taped up to play. So Padden, who had inserted himself into the lineup sparingly during the season—he missed almost a month due to broken ribs—would play the first three games of the series, even though his instincts told him that Clark should be in. But the Galt management had made it clear to Padden that they wanted him to play behind the plate. He had the major-league experience, not Clark. This is where Murray and the other directors disagreed. He didn't like the idea of Padden playing every game. Padden's arm was shot, after all, while Clark had a rifle. Brantford players would steal on Padden where they couldn't on Clark. Years later Murray came to believe that it was a crucial mistake to have Padden catch the first three playoff games, even though Galt won two of them. Nevertheless, Padden was named the third star of the first game. He had called a good game for Perkins. He might be old, and his arm was not what it must have been, thought Perkins, but what he lost in arm speed he gained in his ability to catch, and call, a game. Perkins thought Padden the best catcher he ever threw to and enjoyed it immensely when Padden was his batterymate. After the game Perkins would thank Padden for helping him earn his sixth win of the season. There was something special that happened when Padden caught Perkins. "Just having him catch can be the difference between a win and a loss," Perkins told me. But after three straight games, and with Clark eager to play, broken fingers or not, Padden relented. Clark was game, and Padden, perhaps more than anyone, respected that. He could remember playing with a broken finger himself fifteen years earlier with the Pirates. So Padden played Clark beginning in Game 4 and Clark, despite the broken finger, never complained.

Murray had wanted league president Manske to present the Hiram Walker Trophy to the Terriers just prior to the first game of the series at Dickson Park. The silverware was new just that season and was to be presented to the pennant winners. It was available, said Manske, but he declined the request. "No," he ruled. "It would be setting a precedent." All league-winning clubs would be seeking trophies and cups for presentation or display prior to the annual league banquet. It was usual, he noted, that such presentations be made then. So there would be no picture of the Terriers and no pennant.

We won the third game of the series that Saturday night with Warren on the mound and then won the fourth game Monday night in Brantford 5-2 to take a stranglehold on the series. We held a 3-1 lead, and had only to win one more game to advance to the Intercounty championship series. Perkins had pitched brilliantly again and earned his seventh victory. Padden had instinctively put Clark into the lineup and he wasn't disappointed. Clark had performed well behind the plate, despite injuries. He'd also managed a single. And Warren had made a couple of great catches in the outfield, as well as managing two hits; he looked like a different player.

Again Lockington had run a couple of miles, it seemed, to rob Kaiser of a home run, but Galt had won. "John was five-foot-ten when the Galt series started and only five-foot-six when it finished," said Pennell. "He'd run so much."

But something happened in the third game that would be remembered by every spectator in the stands. Rosen's grand slam, a picture-perfect blast that would take on something of mythic proportions, was the highlight of the series to that point. People weren't talking about Lockington's ability to chase down Kaiser home runs; instead, they were talking about that unbelievable grand slam by Rosen that had won the game. It was pure Hollywood.

Gibbs, who started the third game, left after three lacklustre innings in which he gave up six hits. Fisher replaced him. Rosen, batting nearly .600 in the series, came to the plate in the eighth inning, his team behind 5-3. The bases were loaded. Just minutes before, Clark had walked on a 3-2 pitch after going hitless his first three at-bats, followed by a Pickard walk. Then Fisher walked another batter. Seeing Rosen come to the plate, with his own signed bat, no less, was enough to bring Brantford coach Speed Cotter to the mound for a talk with his pitcher and catcher. They deliberated a long time. That's when Cotter motioned to his ace left-hander, Gavey, to replace Fisher. Gavey made the long walk from the left-field bullpen to the mound for his third appearance in three games. He was tired. As Pennell and King knew, Gavey was good for only about one game a week. He could pitch spectacularly well if he had a week's rest between starts, but he needed that time off. His arm was not the same arm that had taken him into the pro ranks with the Cardinal organization.

Soon Gavey had a full count against Rosen. He took a deep breath, as did the confident Rosen at the plate, and began his windup. Our baserunners had the signal to go and they were all in motion as Gavey pumped for the next pitch to Rosen. For Rosen, the wily veteran and former big-leaguer, it was the type of moment he was waiting for. He liked big games and he was confident of his ability to perform when the pressure was on. Now, with two out in the eighth and a full count, the pressure was most certainly on. In came Gavey's offering. It was the perfect pitch. A fastball, coming in right over the plate. He swung, meeting the ball squarely, and up it went high into the darkness looking like a little white pill against a blue velvet sky. It cleared the right-field fence by a mile and was still going as people lost sight of it. Bedlam broke loose. His grand slam had now given Galt a 7-5 lead. The crowd above our dugout went wild.

Earlier that evening, before the game had even begun, George Cook took up his regular spot on the hill along the third base line. He always got there early so he could get a place. But this game a friend of his, Ozzie Krull, a co-worker at Jack Patrick Motors on Water Street, asked him to sit with him in his seats in the grandstand, just above the dugout. Ozzie's wife wasn't able to attend the game due to a migraine headache. "Krull was a super car salesman," said Murray. "And he was a very loud person at the park." Everyone could hear Ozzie Krull when he spoke, which is partly why everybody in town seemed to know him. Murray used to laugh at the way he would come into his lunch counter and order a vanilla milkshake. Typically the restaurant would be filled with people and he would come up to the counter and sit down. "Give me a milkshake," he would say to the girl behind the counter. "He was a bit of a showoff," said Gus. Murray would charge an extra five cents if an egg was added to the milkshake. Eggs in 1949 were about twenty cents a dozen and if someone wanted two eggs, the extra charge would be ten cents, making a normal ten-cent milkshake twenty cents. "Ozzie would ask for two eggs, so I'd usually throw in a third egg for free," said Gus. "He'd think that was great."

Krull was a real character who never failed to leave an impression with people he met. Perhaps that's why Goody Rosen came to know him that summer. Rosen would often stop for gas at Jack Patrick Motors as he went to and from Toronto. Sometimes he'd just shoot the breeze for a few minutes. Krull, Murray said, would go into the barbershop and if there were two or three others waiting he would tell the barber, "I can't wait that long."

I remember being in Turley's barbershop one afternoon when Ozzie called. In walked the affable Krull, self-absorbed and conscious of nothing more than himself. There were three people in line before him. Alf Turley was talking with a client as he clipped his hair. Krull quickly surveyed the situation.

"Afternoon, Alf," he called out.

"Afternoon, Ozzie," replied Alf. "Be with you in a few minutes."

"I can't wait that long today," said Krull, as if he could ever wait that long.

Turley had often seen other clients let Krull go ahead of them at such times, but today no one was taking the bait.

"My time's too valuable," said Krull. "I wish I had the luxury of sitting around here and waiting." With that, he left, saying he'd try to come back later, "If time permits."

The wooden door shut hard. The spring had gone and Krull was walking down the street before Turley's words—"We'll look for you later ..."—were even out.

Turley knew Krull, the real Krull, the one who would complain about how busy he was, about how valuable his time was, and yet would stand there and talk for half an hour after having his hair cut.

Years later Krull's friend George Cook remembered Rosen's grand slam vividly. "It went out beyond the coal pile," he said. When Rosen trotted in to the dugout, Ozzie shouted out: "Way to go, Goody!"

"Aw, hell, what did you think I was going to do, Ozzie?" said Rosen, looking up into the grandstand.

Brain thought that people who saw that grand slam would talk about it for another twenty years. He was wrong. Half a century has passed and people haven't forgotten that blast. Today people can still see Rosen traipsing around the bases behind the three runners—Clark, Pickard, Creedon—he had driven in. And they could still manage to hear the roar of the crowd, seven thousand people going nuts.

When Rosen arrived at home plate it seemed like everyone was there to congratulate him. Handshakes, several pats on the back. Smiles on each of the Galt faces, disbelief on the Brantford faces. But not surprise. They were playing Galt, after all, and that meant they had to contend with our vaunted Murderer's Row. Rosen was a reality, and behind him came several others, each of whom could hit the ball out of the ballpark.

The next game of the series, the fourth, was the one people figured was pivotal, but it was the third game that everyone would remember because of Rosen's blast. Wes had left midway through the game and was headed for the showers as the Galts retired the Brantford side in the bottom half of the seventh.

"We used to be able to see through a partition from our shower area and I was in there when Rosen came up," recalled Lillie. "I was having a shower and at the same time watching Rosen at the plate. The pitch comes in and Rosen hits that thing 950 miles over the coal pile into the Grand River. I'd never seen anything like it."

Rosen crossed the plate like only a veteran could have done, as if it was an everyday occurrence. As his teammates slapped his back he turned to the bench. I saw him wink. Kumornik had watched as the ball sailed out of the ballpark, and later he heard that it landed in the Grand River.

Kumornik, who lived in the little hamlet of Bridgeport, not far from Kitchener, was accustomed to hearing a few barbs, but this night he heard more than usual. He could handle players during the game, some of whom made fun of his small-town background, but he had been a player in the Intercounty too, and most players, and fans, respected him for it. He always thought his playing background had given him an edge.

Brantford fans were yelling, "Kumornik, need my glasses," or "Kumornik, why don't you go home. Stop wasting our time." He could live with that. But now there were three hundred swearing, cursing fans circling around and he felt like a caged animal ready to be fed to the lions. The crowd was so big, and so hostile, that it didn't seem as though anybody could quell it. They were menacing. "You homer," they yelled. He literally had to run for his life.

Kumornik finally escaped to the Galt locker room, where he stripped and took a soothing shower. He was getting too old for this stuff. He received fifteen dollars that night, and he'd earned every cent.

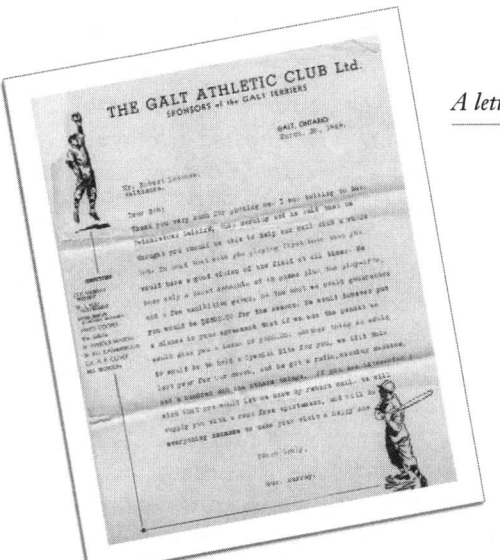

A letter from Gus Murray

The Last Game

The impossible game.

NO ONE THOUGHT THE SERIES WOULD GO TO A SEVENTH game. But Brantford, taking advantage of our internal bickering, won the next two games to tie the series 3-3, forcing a seventh and deciding game at Dickson Park. The Red Sox had surprised everyone. Down 3-1, Brantford players then witnessed our team virtually self-destruct. Now, for Brantford, it came down to one more game—winner take all.

The public first heard news of our player problems before Game Seven.

"Surely we, the fans, have a right to know what is going on," wrote one disgruntled fan in a subsequent letter to the newspaper, "or was this all a cheap publicity stunt cooked up for the occasion?" As Murray could attest, it was no scheme.

If he hadn't been so adamant he might have averted the near-strike. Lockington would always remember the fifth game because he believed it was the pivotal point in the series. "You guys beat us over the first four games, just killed us, and we came back and tied the series," he said. "The big battle in that series was down here in Brantford when Gus took his team off the field and put the juniors out."

I was one of those so-called juniors. That game, in fact, was delayed an hour because several of our players refused to play until

Murray agreed to give them a larger percentage of the gate. But to Murray's credit, he stuck to his guns. The impasse prompted a group of men from the Galt Athletic Club executive, Murray among them, to hastily call a meeting. Most of the key Terrier executive members, including Benny Bennett and Jack Moffatt, arrived at Murray's store late one afternoon. "They sat in the back in the stockroom," Murray recalled. They wanted Murray to be a little more lenient with the American imports. "We all sat back there where we kept the wallpaper and chewed the fat," said Murray. The consensus was to yield a little to the players' demands for the sake of the team. The team, they all agreed, should come first. "That swayed me," said Murray. "We made an agreement to give the players fifteen percent."

Some thought that Brantford, going into that last game, had the advantage. They had played a big game just like it, two weeks before, against a talented London squad, and they had come out on top. They were used to big games. But others thought that Galt, with all its regulars back, would show their true mettle. On paper, they argued, Brantford was no match for the Galts. When an important game like this was on the line, the Galts would probably walk away with it.

Or would we? "There were many games leading up to that game that we had to win, and we did win, just to get there," said Gibbs. "We just hung in there and did our best." Fans would line up in Brantford for a 7:30 P.M. game at 5:30 P.M. The same scenario played itself out in Galt, where fans would be lining up at suppertime to fill the park and watch our warmups.

"I still remember Bill LeConte on our bus leaving the ballpark in Galt down 3-1 saying, 'We'll be back, we'll be back,'" said Gibbs. They hadn't lost hope. If we had thought that winning the series was now only a formality, the Brantford players hadn't. They still had the desire, and the fire within, to want to win. LeConte knew it was possible.

The formidable Gibbs was to start for Brantford in the seventh game. "Whenever I pitched in the Galt ballpark," said Gibbs, "I made sure I never pitched on one side of the plate. They had such a short right-field fence. I at all times tried to keep the ball from the middle of the plate, away to the outside, or the inside to a right-handed batter because a little pop fly would go out of that ballpark quite easily down the line. You had to be very careful at Dickson Park. Very careful."

The seventh game was played on Saturday, September 4, in Galt. I never forgot that date, for it was my brother's birthday. My thoughts were of him that night, and how he would have helped us if he were in the lineup. It was a night game, and under that dark sky of late summer there came the largest crowd of the season: more than 7,600 paying fans. They knew little or nothing of the resentment felt by several of our imports, but I knew it well. It was written on their faces, and it was spoken in the locker room. Resentment lingered and it made me sick. Though our big guns were on the field, there were no reconciliations and I worried, and wondered for the first time that season, if we could win. In the press box, *Expositor* sportswriter Alan Rose was taking a licking through the early stages of the game by the other sportswriters. There was a lot of good-natured kidding, but it was Rose, in the end, who had the last laugh.

Perkins took to the mound that night against Gibbs. Our best against their best. It was a toss-up, but I knew and liked Perkins, and more importantly, I believed in him. Gibbs might be as good as any in the league, but I had seen Perkins blow balls past the best hitters in the Intercounty. He was cool under pressure, and as I looked into his eyes before the game, I could see the fire of a competitor and this had given me confidence. If ever a player wanted to win a game, it was Perkins that night. He was ready.

Gibbs, meanwhile, had already pitched a couple of games in the series and was nursing a sore arm. In fact, he'd asked not to start. So he was surprised when manager Bert "Speed" Cotter pencilled in his name on the lineup sheet just before the game. It was do-or-die for both teams. Gibbs couldn't refuse. If there was any time he needed to go with only two days' rest, it was now, he thought. It would be anything but an easy assignment. He would have to pitch to Waite, whose .380 batting average was second only to London's Joe Bechard that season. And then there was Kaiser's .360 average, and perhaps more significant, his league-leading ten home runs. Four other Terriers finished the regular season batting over .300, including Creedon at .326, Rosen at .314, Warren at .304, and Pickard at .301. It was a power lineup that was enough to give any opposing pitcher a case of the nerves, especially when they were to face them in the seventh game of a playoff series. But Gibbs, despite his youth, had already learned to deal with nerves. He accepted his nervousness completely. "If you didn't have those little stomach butterflies before you went out there, then generally you didn't last too long," said Gibbs. "It's a funny thing. You're nervous before you go out on the field, about what you're going to have to do out there. You knew it was going to be tough, but you're not nervous when you're out there." Instead, he had total concentration on his job.

He would need it. So would Perkins, as he got ready to face Brantford's top hitter, Lipka, whose .360 average tied him with Kaiser for fifth in batting. The only other Brantford player who hit over .300 that season was Lockington, whose average of .318 spoke nothing of the fact that when he got on base he was as feared a baserunner as the Intercounty had ever seen.

Gibbs had finished the regular season with a 4-2 won-lost record and an ERA of 2.73, just one percentage point better than his teammate, Gavey. Not bad, but not the best in the league. That honour had gone to his teammate, Parker, whose 8-2 record and 2.08 ERA was tops. Perkins was second in the pitching statistics, with a 7-1 record and a 2.19 ERA. On the whole, neither team had any great advantage over the other in pitching. Brantford had Parker, Gibbs, and Gavey. We could counter with Perkins, Warren, Shelton, and an aging McCrudden. Warren had finished the season 5-3 with an ERA of 3.27, marginally ahead of Shelton, but Shelton was easily the most overworked pitcher in our lineup that summer. He had pitched 117 innings; only two others in the league had thrown that much. Shelton posted a 10-4 record and a 3.29 ERA. London's White was the only other pitcher to win more games; he had thirteen, against three losses.

We played scoreless ball through four innings before Brantford got on the scoreboard first, in the fifth inning. We gave one of our gamest efforts of the season, but Gibbs proved nearly untouchable. Although he was only in his first year of senior ball, he was no stranger to big games. He had pitched Brantford to their 1-0 win over London to gain entry to the playoffs. And the season before, after returning to Brantford from his stint in the Cardinal organization, he led his hometown club to the junior title. Now he wanted nothing better than to lead the Brantford seniors to a title. He was on that night, allowing us only six hits over nine innings, and shutting the league's most potent hitter down in every inning except one. He walked two and fanned four in what was a tension-packed game unlike any other that season. But, as Brain noted, "Gibbs had to be good to snatch the verdict from dazzling Don Perkins." Perkins matched Gibbs through six innings, faltering only slightly in the seventh. It was a classic pitcher's duel. Neither team could have asked more of their pitcher. The Red Sox got four hits in that key inning; it was their winning rally. But Perkins, whom Padden left in the game, came back and finished off in fine style. He struck out six, while giving up one intentional walk and three bases on balls.

Rosen, who was batting with his own signature St. Mary's bat produced at the bat plant in nearby Hespeler, was always quick to argue what he thought was a poor call. A couple of times during the series he had taken a called third strike by Kumornik very badly. All the officials knew Rosen would become argumentative on called third strikes. Kumornik, who rarely threw players out of a game, would have to be almost physically attacked before ejecting someone. Still, Rosen tried his patience. And pushed his luck.

I remember Rosen yelled, and then Kumornik planted his feet and stared back at Rosen.

"Shut up, Rosen," he said. "If you were still any good you'd be playing in the majors."

There was silence.

The Red Sox opened the scoring in the fifth when Clayton Cooper beat out an infield hit, then went to second as Lockington walked. He scored when Hann hit a Texas Leaguer single, his first hit of the game, to left. But we took the lead in the sixth inning thanks to a miscue by Gibbs. Creedon, the big left-handed hitter, pounced on a ball that Gibbs let get away from him. "He hit the ball so hard, it took off and our left fielder, Harry Mooradian, charged," said Gibbs. "Mooradian was coming in on the ball, but it took off and went over his head. There was a little misjudgment there and that was not like Harry to do anything like that, but that's just how hard Creedon could hit a ball." Gibbs had thrown a poor pitch and Creedon had jumped on it, hitting to left field instead of pulling to right field. Then Waite got a hit, forcing out Creedon at second. Up came Kaiser. He hit a powerful triple off Gibbs to left centre that bounced up against the fence about four hundred feet from the plate, scoring Waite. Then Padden grounded to LeConte, and Kaiser, with a head-first slide, something he had only done once or twice in his life, beat the Brantford first baseman's throw home to the plate.

Gibbs, whose arm was getting tired, had a chance to atone for that pitch when he came to the plate. "I was a very slow runner," he admits. "I hit a ball that should have been a home run by all standards out past Rosen and right through to the cars and it got between him and the left fielder, and I lugged it around and they held me up at third base after I rounded it."

Playing third base was Kaiser, someone Gibbs admired and feared. "He had all sorts of talent," said Gibbs. "He played everywhere. He could run like a deer and was an excellent hitter. Could throw the ball really well. He was an all-around good athlete." His talent matched that of any player Gibbs had seen in the Cardinal organization.

Now Kaiser, standing next to the bag when Gibbs was held up at third, turned to face him. It was the eighth inning and we were up by a run.

"Well, we got you now Bill," said Kaiser.

"It's not over yet," replied Gibbs. Brantford had all the momentum; they had won the last two games.

Perkins retired the side but when we came to bat we could do nothing. At the start of the ninth inning we were leading 2-1. Now it was Brantford's turn at the plate. Hann singled off Perkins after Gibbs and Lockington singled.

That was when it all came tumbling down. On a short routine Brantford fly ball that would have been the third out and ended their side, Lillie, playing short, went back, his eye on the ball. He called for it. But behind him Warren, the veteran, was running in from left field. He called off the rookie. "I know I could have had that ball," says Lillie. "But Warren short-legged it. I'll never know why but he short-legged it." As fans saw it, Warren had hesitated on the ball, then played it safe as Gibbs raced across the plate with the tying run. Then Lipka followed with a base hit to right field, giving the Red Sox a lead they never relinquished.

Behind the plate, umpire Kumornik couldn't believe his eyes. "I could have caught that ball in my jockstrap," he would later say. "Warren was no bush leaguer, for Chrissakes. He had been up in the majors. The bloody Indian had short-legged it." Brantford had scored three runs that night, the night Warren made the most talked-about miscue in Galt history. Years later there were two plays Galt fans still talked about. One was Rosen's grand slam in Game 3; the other was Warren's missed catch in the seventh game.

Padden, standing in the dugout, was enraged. "Christ almighty!" he yelled. Murray, standing beside Padden on the bench, was equally livid. "There was no way Warren should have missed that catch," he said, echoing Padden's sentiments. Later, Waite missed a ball he should have caught. It wasn't long after the game that the rumours began. Warren, the story went, had bet a lot of money on the series, and, indeed, there was some legitimacy to the rumours. Deeply in debt back in Tulsa, he was a known gambler. Helping to throw the series to collect on the underdog Red Sox was not out of the question.

To many in the stands it appeared that Warren had simply played Hann's hit badly. But the big Oklahoman outfielder repeated his excuse: "I lost sight of it for a moment in the lights," he said later.

"Bullshit!" said Creedon eloquently.

The Last Game

On our side of the last inning, we proved ineffective at the plate. The last out of the seventh game was something Gibbs never forgot. Lipka, at third, yelled over to Gibbs on the mound, "Get the goddamned ball over the plate." He liked to give Gibbs hell and was always telling him to get it over the plate. Our second baseman, Pickard, was up to bat. Gibbs threw him a fastball. He felt good with Lipka at third. He had total confidence in him. Lipka, who was to carry on and play another eight years with the Red Sox, was "one of the best third basemen I ever played with," said Gibbs. Now he was giving Gibbs the gears, telling him the obvious: to get the ball over the damn plate.

Finally Lipka was quiet. Gibbs threw the ball. "There were two outs and the ball was hit, one bounce, to Lipka," said Gibbs. "He took the ball in his hand, one-timing it, and I'm standing there and kind of ducking because I'm in his way, and I'm saying, 'Throw the ball, throw the ball, Stan.'" For once Gibbs was wishing Lipka wouldn't take his normal hesitation before throwing to first. This was one time when he didn't want it to be close.

But from force of habit, Lipka couldn't do it. He bided his time, like he had been taught to do at spring training with the Dodgers in Vero Beach by Cookie Lavagetto, Rosen's old teammate. "I got you now," he was saying. "I got you now." Brantford fans, thought Pennell, were having coronaries just watching Lipka's delayed throw. Most third basemen had a natural inclination to just fire the ball over as soon as they got the handle, but Lavagetto taught Lipka to wait until he had his proper footing, to coordinate eye and arm, and then throw. So there was the tall Gibbs, ducking on the mound so that Lipka could make a clear throw, and Lipka, ever confident, was holding on to the ball while he was saying, "I got you now." Gibbs always remembered the way Lipka said "I got you now." The confidence that showed. And the way nothing in the world could have made Lipka throw any faster. Then he just fired it to first base. "That always stood out in my mind because you want to see that last out, and I can still remember the way he kind of held it a second or two and then whistled it over to LeConte."

That was the game. We lost 3-2. Brantford fans stampeded onto the infield. "I can remember autographing some girl's white blouse," said Gibbs. The young lady handed Gibbs a pen. "Here," she said. "Write your name on my shoulder." Janet Scott, Gibbs' fiancée, was up on the hill along the third base line watching the celebration unfold. "You should have seen the people," she said. "They came up and asked him if he'd write his name on their shirts. *Girls!* I couldn't believe it. Here I am sitting up on the hill and all these girls are trying to get him to autograph their shirts. It was very interesting." But she didn't feel threatened. "I had my hooks on him by then," she would say later. So she just stood and watched, enjoying the spectacle. She didn't want to go down onto the field. "I had to keep his swelled head down," she explained.

Others, like six-year-old Brantford fan Rich Mirco, also got autographs. Rich held out his scrapbook and asked Gibbs, the game's hero, to sign his name. The large Brantford contingent ran onto the field to share in the celebration while sombre Galt fans, and players, looked on in disbelief. Later, Gibbs and some of the other Brantford players would come to wonder how they ever beat us in that series, even if they had beaten us nine times out of fifteen meetings that year. But that night, they could find neither sympathy for the fallen Galts, nor anger. They had played a tough game. Aside from Warren's missed catch and a questionable missed catch by Waite at first, we had played errorless ball in the field, even coming up with some spectacular plays, like Rosen's unbelievable catch on Cooper's long drive to centre in the eighth.

We had played well. Even Wes—"Don't lose your glove"—Lillie had come up big in the field, playing his best defensive game of the season at shortstop, while Pickard had made a great play on Hodara after Hodara hit a hard ground ball in his direction. It bounced off his shoulder but he snagged it and threw to first in time. The game had been a classic pitchers' duel. It very well may have been the finest game ever played at Dickson Park.

The Red Sox made only two miscues, one of which—Mooradian's—played a part in our two-run rally. Apart from those errors, the Red Sox played well in the field. Lockington, in centre, had played as well, or better, than any of them. Four times he had pulled down long hit balls, three of which had come, not surprisingly, from Kaiser's bat. Some observers believed that had Lockington not been in the field that night, we would have won the game on Kaiser's long hits alone. But Lockington's speed proved Kaiser's match that night, especially since Murray had seen fit to remove a snow fence across centre field. Kaiser knew that two of those hits were good for at least double bases in Brantford's Agricultural Park.

Pennell understood Lockington's value to the team that season. "To see him run was almost worth the price of admission," he said. "Just to see him run the bases." Or make impossible catches in centre field. "I've never seen anything like it," he said of Lockington's ability to chase down long balls that series. "He went back there 450 or 500 feet to take balls off Kaiser, Warren, and Rosen. It was incredible. He was running down those long balls like they were nothing."

Years later, when reflecting on that series, Lockington would shake his head. "In '49 that was the worst team we had and we won it," he said. "It was the only time we won it. We had all the big teams in later years and we never won it." But in truth, they came up big when they had to. They had a good team. Pennell thought the Red Sox had the better pitching that series, just by a hair. "We had Gavey and Gibbs. We had a pretty solid club, but we had nowhere near the power that Galt had. They had a tremendous hitting club."

Brantford fans surged onto the field after Pickard was thrown out at first. It was late in the evening and the wind was cool. They chaired Gibbs, the winner, and carried him to the Red Sox dugout. There, all the Brantford players were surrounded by a mob of Red Sox faithful. It was an unforgettable night in the annals of Brantford sport. Our fans would have liked to forget, but their disappointment was so bitter that the game would live on for a long time. They, too, would never forget. And now, in the celebrations, it seemed as if they were in Brantford's ballpark. Galt fans had been absorbed into the night and disappeared. It was estimated that there had been nearly two thousand Brantford fans there that night. One thousand tickets were sold in Brantford for a bleacher section that held, at best, six hundred people. But the Brantford fans knew the situation. They just wanted to be there.

Souvenir hunters got every ball hit into the stands except two that night. What had looked like a sure Galt-Kitchener final just a week earlier had turned into a Brantford-Waterloo final after the Waterloo Tigers beat the Kitchener Legionnaires 5-2 before six thousand fans in the seventh game in Waterloo the same night. Kitchener, like Galt, had held a commanding 3-1 series lead before letting it slip away.

Lockington always referred to the series from then on as "The Impossible Series." That night King and Pennell wore smiles so big they hurt. All their work to get baseball back on solid ground in Brantford after the war had proven successful. They deserved the victory, and they deserved to savour it. A year earlier the Red Sox had won the senior B title. Now they were going to meet Waterloo for the A title. "It couldn't happen to two better baseball fanatics," wrote Brain.

It was reported in Tuesday night's paper—Monday had been Labour Day, and the *Reporter* had not published that day—that a lot of Galt folding money travelled to Brantford. Rumours abounded about Warren. It was becoming common knowledge that large amounts of money had been bet on the series. No one knew, however, except for Murray, just how bad Warren's financial status was. At least, no one in Canada. When the season was done the former Tulsa deputy sheriff was supposed to return to Tulsa to own up to the charges against him. Murray later told Kumornik that Warren had made a big deposit in the bank the next day.

Still, what Pennell and King would remember years later was how six players on the Galt roster hit over .300 that season. "Everybody," King would say, "except Wes Lillie. Wes couldn't hit the floor if he fell out of bed." It was a description of Lillie that King never tired of. Through the years he repeated it so often that even Brantford fans who had never seen Lillie play, knew how poor a hitter he was. And King also liked to reminisce about Lockington. "Johnny Lockington used to go out and get everything they hit," said King. "We had an all-Canadian team that year and we beat them. I think Lockington ran seven thousand miles that season." Most, no doubt, were down at Dickson Park. "He was so fast he could have played the whole outfield by himself."

Hockey would begin soon. And football, too. For Galt fans that was all they had to look forward to. Despite the success with the ball club, there was a question as to whether Galt would field a team in 1950. More importantly, there was uncertainty over whether Murray would be back to guide the team the next season owing to his much-publicized disagreement with the Galt Parks Board. There could be baseball in Galt without Murray, to be sure, but it would not be the same. And because Murray's celebrated 1949 Galt Terriers had lost, did that also mean, as some were suggesting, that his grand experiment was also therefore a failure? His critics were quick to answer yes. They need point no further than the Red Sox, a team of Telephone City homebrews. Perhaps Gus, who felt much maligned all season long, would have liked to do what a man by the name of Ray Travenner did that Saturday. Travenner, a mechanic and truck driver, taking his first ride in a powerboat, was the passenger in the Jack Shafer–owned *Such Crust II* during a heat of the Silver Cup race on the Detroit River. Travenner had taken a terrific beating in the bouncing, swerving craft. His normal job was as driver of the truck for the *Such Crust II*. So, in the rough going, he leaped from the speeding boat into the water in front of the press stand at the Detroit Yacht Club after driver Lou Fageol slowed down at the finish of the fifth lap. As he was pulled dripping from the water he said wearily: "I'm going back to truck driving."

At least Gus Murray hadn't jumped the boat while the season was still on, though God only knew how many times he'd said to himself, "I wish I'd never gotten mixed up in all this." Still, Kaiser thought most of Murray's problems were self-induced. "Gus deserved everything he got," said Kaiser. "He'd go and get big names for $550 a month and then turn around and say he was losing money and would be forced to go chase foul balls."

Umpire Johnny Kumornik is surrounded after the game by angry fans.

Old Leaves and Autumn

We went to see *In the Good Old Summertime*, starring Judy Garland and Van Johnson, one night that September. Days later my parents presented me with a new RCA Victor AM-FM Radio to take to school. I also took Lloyd Douglas's new novel, *The Big Fisherman*. Later that fall a group of freshmen, myself among them, would regularly take in the radio program *Hopalong Cassidy* at a prof's house once a week, and I would think back to the opening-day parade with Warren riding a white horse, and I would wonder whatever became of him.

THE SCENT OF OLD LEAVES BURNING IN AUTUMN WAS THERE that night. As Brantford's celebration waned, to be continued in the Telephone City, more than seven thousand fans dispersed for the last time that year, anonymous seeds in the wind. They scattered in all directions. Groundskeeper Jack Spencer hit the switch to kill the floodlights for the last time that decade. Winter would come. The season was over. During the long cold months, the lights would remain dead. The velvet green would change to white. Then spring. Baseball reborn.

For Brantford, the victory had advanced them to the championship final against Waterloo. They played superbly, upsetting the Tigers to advance to the all-Ontario finals, where they won the coveted provincial title. It was truly a dream season.

That was several weeks after Dickson Park saw its final game of the season. The last guy out of the park that night was Kumornik. He was easily the most overworked umpire in the league that season and had worked the entire Galt-Brantford series behind the plate. "No one else wanted the job," he explained. The crowds for that series were the biggest in Intercounty history, and all the umpires knew that there would be a lot of witnesses on hand if a bad call was made. And they were rabid fans. At no time during the season could Intercounty fans be described as sedate, conservative, or mild. Years later, with the advent of the Blue Jays, it became fashionable for American writers and commentators to say that Canadian fans were quiet and reserved compared to their U.S. counterparts. Canadian fans had to learn about the game to know how and when to cheer, the thesis went. There may have been some basis for this, but it was also largely a piece of fiction that Americans seemed to want to hear. Canadians were so quiet and well-behaved during games because baseball was new to them, they would say. They didn't know the game yet. Give them time. But old-timers who had played in the Intercounty in the 1920s—there were still a few of them left—and '30s and '40s would cringe when they heard that. Fans back then got into the games. They yelled at the umpires, the players, the players wives and mothers, the coaches. They started fights with players and umpires. Intercounty rivalries were some of the most poignant, and rough, of any in the country. And the baseball was good. Kumornik could attest to that.

The seasoned Kumornik was never afraid to take an assignment, nor was he hesitant to work behind the plate; it paid three dollars more than working the bases. He had been a player himself and believed that fans and players alike respected him more as an umpire because of it. But this final game between the two old rivals had been so close and exciting that it brought out the worst in fans. It was the second time in the series when he was threatened with bodily harm by spectators. Brantford fans were ready to kill him when he backed up the other umpire who called Gibbs out. And then Galt fans wanted his head. Why? Because we had lost. Warren, rightly, should have shouldered the blame. It was his missed catch that lost the game. But he had made a big stink over Kumornik's umpiring and had gone after him following the game. Kumornik and the other two umpires that night, New Hamburg principal Norm Hill and Jimmy Tait, retreated quickly to their room under the stands. "The fans blamed the loss on me," remembered Kumornik years later. At the same time as Brantford fans were flooding down from the stands and out onto the field, Galt fans, seeking someone to blame, came tearing out of the stands after the umpires. "They were shouting they were going to kill the umpires," recalled Kumornik.

Neither Kumornik nor the other two officials had anything to do with the loss, or with Warren's missed catch. "That's [the Galt-Brantford series] the only time I ever got into trouble, for cripes' sake," Kumornik said. For a while that night, things looked dicey. The law-abiding fans had all gone home. Brantford's players and fans had left, eager to get back to the Telephone City to celebrate. And the Galt management had departed in a state of disbelief. There weren't even any policemen around. No one was left to protect the umpires from the last large group of rowdy fans. None of our players, except Warren, who had good reason to lace into the officials, thereby deflecting the blame off himself, had felt any animosity toward the umpires. But the fans, riding an emotional roller coaster the whole series, were out to lynch the three. Kumornik, the best-known official in the league, would be first. As the umpire behind the plate he was to blame for the outcome of the game. It was his doing, the angry mob said. "Come on out, Kumornik, we're going to hang you."

Murray would later recall how the fans got riled up. "I remember somebody going after Kumornik and saying, 'Get his hat!'" With his hat on Kumornik stood out like a sore thumb, thought Murray. "I took his hat so he wouldn't be so conspicuous." But there were other things going on besides the fans wanting to get the umpires. Immediately after the game some of our players surrounded the Terrier executive and there was a heated discussion going on regarding payment for the final game. The players weren't leaving until they got their fifteen percent.

Meantime, the mob that wanted Kumornik's neck started throwing stones at the wooden door under the stands, which Kumornik and the other officials had bolted shut. They weren't moving. Soon the sounds of stones hitting the wooden door changed, becoming even more threatening. To the three, it now sounded as if they were throwing boulders at the door. And they kept it up for hours, a few of their number drifting away as the minutes and hours passed. Finally, at 3 A.M., the coast was clear. Kumornik unbolted the door and the three, warily, made for their cars in the dark of early morning. He was tired. He had always tried to be fair in his umpiring, taking pains never to hold something against a player or manager from one game to another. As far as he was concerned, once a game was over, it was over. The fact that some overzealous fans had wanted to lynch him was more than a little unsettling, but it came with the territory. He had just been doing his job. As he walked to his car in the still calm of a premature early-September morning, he shook his head once again, like he had shaken it several times since seeing Warren miss that catch. "I could have caught that ball with my jockstrap," he said to himself again. "How could Warren have missed that catch? It had cost Galt the game."

As Pennell and King and the rest of the Red Sox made the trip back to Brantford that night they felt on top of the world. They had just knocked off one of the best clubs that ever played in the senior Intercounty. Pennell couldn't help thinking they were a team of destiny now. Things were falling in place. They were making things fall in place. "Galt, I think, should have won it," he thought, "but you know, that's baseball." Maybe Brantford would have won it even if we hadn't had the internal problems after Game Four. Years later Pennell maintained that two things had gone against Galt. The first was the absence of an outfield fence for most of the series, and the presence of Lockington. The second thing was the internal dissension among the Galt players, when they threatened to go on strike.

A third thing, which no one could have foreseen, and for which only one man, Warren, could shoulder the blame, was the non-catch. Pennell remembered him missing the catch, but the Red Sox never believed there was any subterfuge on the part of any of the Galt players. Still, he remembered there was some discussion about that missed catch. "We were surprised," he said. "We thought he should have had that." But he believed there were many factors responsible for Brantford's win. Pennell thought that had Galt erected a snow fence for the entire series, the outcome might have been different. A couple of seasons later Brantford, like the Galts of '49, had what Pennell considered one of the best clubs ever assembled in the Intercounty and they didn't win the title either. That unpredictability was what made sports interesting.

Hours earlier, while Kumornik and the other umpires were fending off the lynch mob of fans and trying to stay alive under the stands, we had slid away into the night, quietly taking ourselves away from what should have been our victory celebration but was, instead, a day that left a bad taste in our mouths. None of us, save for Clark, Lillie, and Kaiser, were sure they would return for 1950. Galt people knew this. And they knew that even if there was a team the following spring, it would not be the same Tom Padden-led Galt Terriers.

Perkins, for all he knew, was finished. Murray had asked him if he wanted to return, and he had said yes, he would like to, but he also knew that his baseball-playing days were numbered. Padden wanted to return, but Murray was cool when Padden brought up the subject.

In the meantime, Padden would return to Manchester, but not before getting drunk once more. Drink had been the reason Murray was hesitant to renew his contract for 1950. The Galt Terriers had given Padden a chance, on Selkirk's recommendation, and he'd blown it. That winter at the baseball meetings in Baltimore Murray again saw Padden. He was broke and asked Murray if he could borrow five hundred dollars. Murray reluctantly agreed. It was the last he ever saw of the money and the second-last time he ever saw Padden.

Rosen, living in Toronto, didn't have far to go. Perhaps he would return next season; perhaps not. If the money was right he would likely come. Murray had few problems with him except for his softball moonlighting, although he had to move mountains to keep him happy. Rosen felt he owed something to Murray. Hustlin' Gus had, after all, gotten him a car. And his son a new bicycle. But there were questions, aside from who might and might not return, about whether, indeed, there would even be a team the next summer.

"Baseball in Galt next year?" asked Brain. "Time will tell."

The Pirate battery in 1935: Guy Bush and Tom Padden

The Last Game: Aftermath

He called off Lillie, and then short-legged it, missing the catch that would have ended the game. We were stunned. Padden stared out at the field, shook his head, and was speechless.

I COULDN'T LOOK AT WARREN AFTER THAT SEVENTH GAME. I WAS afraid that I would be sick. I knew where he was because I could hear his silence in a room full of silent men. Outside our small room beneath the stands there had been noise, at first, and then the solitude of night. I looked at Perkins, and I was going to say how well he had pitched, but I said nothing. In my muteness, he heard my words. He knew. I knew.

The showers were hot that night, soothing. Padden and Rosen seemed to stay in the longest. The mist grew heavy. Some of us were drowning our sorrows in the water, cleansing what had been a dirty affair, as if we could wash away the game and the series. No one spoke to Warren, nor did he speak to anyone. It was the first time all season when the air was cold.

I left the showers that night, threw on my dry clothes, combed my fingers through my hair, agreed to go to the Albion for a beer with Lillie, Perkins, and Kaiser, and stepped out to swallow the fresh air that belongs to the end of summer. I looked up at the dark sky speckled with stars, shimmering like the side of a great brown trout. The moon was its eye, staring down at us. Someone should punch that bastard Warren, I thought. But it wouldn't be me. I was no longer sick, or at least no longer felt sick at what he had done, but I was now afraid that if it was left to me to take down Warren, I would not be able to stop myself from pummelling him, and I knew he had a family and children so I kept walking. Later I would laugh at my mood that night, for I don't usually harbour such thoughts. But that night my thoughts were riveted on wanting to kill. I was bloodthirsty.

The first beers came and went, and now we drowned our sorrows with ale. I had been drunk twice before, but that night I kept up with Kaiser and Perkins, matching them pint for pint. The bar was full, and outside, Water Street seemed to bustle with people into the early morning. Ball fans were everywhere, but, mercifully, they were all Galt fans, for the Brantford fans were, at that moment, celebrating their victory by parading down Brant Avenue. Occasionally someone would approach, telling Kaiser and Perkins, and even Lillie, how well they had played and that they had nothing to be ashamed of. They meant well. But we all had something to be ashamed of, and he was our teammate. Still, the beer soothed even that. By last call we were feeling pretty good. The game was fuzzy by then, though the Warren catch, or non-catch, was overriding. Words began melting into other words, and I could hear myself slur and I knew I was drunk. I ordered a final round for us all, and there were no complaints. The sharp black-and-white edge of the night was losing its definition. My focus was leaving and it was good that it was leaving.

In the foul-smelling men's room just before we left, I stood at a urinal beside Lillie, who was also feeling good, and I said: "We can piss this season goodbye."

"Piss on the season," he replied.

"Piss on Warren, that bastard," I said.

"Piss on Warren."

"And piss on his mother and father," I replied. "No, not his father. I met his father, and he was a good man. Just piss on his mother for being a bitch who begat a bastard."

"I'll piss to that," said Lillie.

By then the beer had gone through us and we were relieved of our conversation.

Fifteen minutes later I walked stealthily through our side door at home and crept into the dark kitchen for a glass of milk. Everyone in the house was quiet. Soon I was in bed and asleep. When morning came, bright and blue, and the birds started calling, neither sleep, nor drink, nor time, nor clarity of being sober, had made the name Warren any easier to pronounce. It was a sour morning, and the hangover had nothing to do with my drinking the previous night.

I looked out my bedroom window through red eyes. My head was pounding. There were two neighbours talking near the side porch of the house next door. Behind them was a lawnmower, and the green, fresh-cut grass, which filled my lungs with a last scent of summer. That was the final day of summer in my mind and memory. And then it was autumn.

Terrier autographs

Old Man

In later years they would thirst for a season like that summer of '49. They would always be thirsting. Other seasons, they knew, may come close, in time. They may approach that season of so many summers ago, but only if a person is lucky will he live to see another season that means as much. Only then will the elemental thirst be quenched, and the glove-smell, the leather of that one true baseball summer, so long dead, will be inhaled and the mouth will be moist, growing wet for the kill.

You will know it when you taste it. Glove leather. The anticipation of a night game at dusk. The fine red dirt along third base. And the green, green grass of summer.

THE END TO SO MUCH CAME SO QUICKLY IN GALT, THE CROWD that final night the last witnesses to a season, a team, a time. The grass would grow long and untrimmed in the days ahead as summer's end became late fall too quickly. Jack Spencer's thirtieth summer of work on the grounds at Dickson Park was almost done. Autumn was calling. The Fall Fair came and went. The game was over for another year, yet no new season would ever be the same. For some, it was like the death of a child. All that untapped potential was gone too. Other children might come along, but they would be different. Now, the last game of the decade had been played. The world was changing as the small town beside the Grand River stood on the threshold of the 1950s. What would the new decade bring? Society, people, children, technology—everything was changing too quickly. The final season of the 1940s had played out. The century was now, officially, half over. Or half begun. It would never be the same down at Dickson Park, as any of the season's final witnesses would eventually come to know, if they didn't already.

Bags were packed. Futures were pondered. Tom Padden's wife and children left Galt to return to their home in Manchester, New Hampshire. Goodbyes were said. Nothing is thought of when a season is done as much as the future. What would next year bring? A word or two mentioned, as if in passing, by players about next year. "I'd like to come back next spring," a player would tell Murray. "I'll be in touch," Gus would reply. All of us felt the same. We had lost to a good club, but this knowledge did nothing to help our pain. We did not feel good. Each of us was helpless now to do what it was we had come together at the beginning of the season to do; what we had always done, or sought to do, each summer of our lives: to win. There was no satisfaction when we had not won. There might have been, if we had known and accepted that we were not the best. But none of us had accepted this. We couldn't. We didn't believe it. We had lost, and we were sickened by it. There is no room in a man's soul to harbor the knowledge that he was the best but he finished second.

As for Warren, if the man had a conscience, the viral thought that he sold out on his teammates—his brethren—would slowly eat at his soul and kill him. Or he would take the lesser evil and kill himself first. For most players there is a truth in the notion that you do not have to like your teammates—though it helps—but, by God, you lived and died with your teammates in a season and you would do anything for them, for the team, to win.

The 1949 season went the way of all seasons. It had lived; now it lay dead. And the years passed, season following season on a journey to who knows where. They tell us we should know where we come from so that we can see where we are going. Know the past, know of the past, and you will know something of the future. Perhaps. Or you will know nothing of the future.

And so, on a summer day in July as the century nears its end and a new millennium beckons, an old man—remember, he was once young—stands alone at home plate. It is barren, this ballpark. No sign of man, of bat, of glove. Hot, humid. Leaves full and green and swaying in the breeze. The maple trees still crest the left-field hill. The old man walks slowly out to the pitcher's mound. He stands on the rubber, facing home, and then turns to face the field. This is Dickson Park. It could as easily be Agricultural Park in Brantford. He breathes it in. The years have made him not ashamed to do this. A younger man would feel too self-conscious, but he is here this one day and he will not come through these parts again. It is a one-shot deal; he either breathes it in or forgets it. But he cannot forget. The half-century of seasons has not changed the place in any substantial way. His heart beats the blood of recognition. There is a thumping in his chest, a vital, healthy thumping. This was one of those moments he will look back on and remember what it was like to be truly alive. He stands and stares out to the field, then his gaze goes beyond the outfield, over the green summer grass, to the black iron train bridge that spans the Grand River in the distance. A train is rolling—steel wheel against iron track. The same noise he heard so many seasons ago. The noise of summer. The noise of one summer, 1949. The noise of the future.

Listen. He does, and he hears more than sounds. The old man turns, oblivious to a couple of young boys and their dog in left field, and he sees the grandstand. Strangely empty. The last he had seen of this grandstand it had been filled. And it had been night. That was how he remembered it. But that season was long dead, and now, as he looked, it felt right that the grandstand was empty. The people were gone, the season was gone, but the grandstand was still there, tolerating the snows of winter, and embracing the feet of summer. Sustaining the game. The noise from the train echoes off some remote part of his brain and holds him spellbound. It was just yesterday....

A dog barks. Children shouting at each other, playing with their puppy who runs tail wagging with a stick in his mouth. The words of a poem by Willa Cather come to him because of the dog, and a sudden gust of wind blowing up the dirt:

> We go big field, 'way up on hill
> Ten times high like our windmill ....
> Then all sheep come over de hills,
> Big white dust, an old dog Nils.

It was the last line, "Big white dust, an old dog Nils," that he especially liked, for he could picture a scene from his childhood of a flock of sheep coming over a hill, the white dust hovering above, and the old dog behind. Then the trance, the pleasing trance, is broken, and suddenly he is conscious of everything and everybody. For a moment time stood still, but now he becomes acutely aware of the clock ticking, the years moving toward an end. The century is closing.

He can't quite put his hand on it but that trance was deep within him and stirred his soul in a way that only a very few memories lived long ago could do. He knows the feeling was priceless, and he even tries to relax and recapture it, but it is elusive. He seized the moment, like he had seized life, and he liked it immeasurably because that was the last time he would ever know things as they were. As the park was. As the summer playing under Padden had been. As it was that very moment, when he smelled the grass, and breathed in the fresh summer air, and saw the ballpark he once knew and loved. It was a total sensory experience and had seared into his very being all at once. And the glove-smell of that summer from so long ago had returned. He knew he had remembered in a dimension that had transcended time and space. His life was nearing its end and yet just then he had felt reborn, like a kid. He sees the ballpark with more clarity than ever before. He sees it infinitely more clearly than a youngster sees it, for he sees it as it is, and as it was. A newcomer can see it only as it is and, perhaps, as it may become. There is no sentiment in seeing the ballpark the way a newcomer sees it. The old man has a soul; the kid has yet to grow one.

For a moment it had all come back to him and was more real than even the summer of '49 had been. And yes, he had actually said, in words spoken only to himself: "In the beginning there was the Heaven, and the Earth, and this park where baseball was played." The words brought him satisfaction. They weren't meant to be heard by anybody else. If the seasons in a man's life are few and could include only one such summer as 1949, he reflected, then all would be right with this world. The old man thought all these things. Perhaps ten seconds had passed. It was enough. He turned, his legs moving reluctantly, and, with a slow, satisfied gait, he left as quietly as he had come, yet solemnity now coursed through his veins. The old man had left this ballpark a lifetime ago, and now he had returned. It was Lefty Perkins.

On another day, in another year, it could have been Padden. Or Rosen. Some days it was Lillie or Lockington, or me. It was a lot of players who once passed through Galt. It will be others. Their feet have followed old footprints. And left new ones. They are fainter than before, but it is enough that they had come back and were there at all.

The people come back to Dickson Park like they do to other ballparks, other towns, yet this is no Cooperstown, no Mecca. It is Galt. The pilgrimages are real, yes, but they are of a different kind. There was no hoopla to greet Lefty Perkins this time. No parade. No people. It would do no good for the masses to come. Only a few men have come to understand Terrier Town the way it needs to be understood. They are the chosen. No, this is no Cooperstown. Perhaps it is more.

Who was this Lefty Perkins?

Just an old man who had once been young. As he turned his back and walked away from the park forever, he felt hollow, from his gut to his toes. He was a stranger now in this place he once knew so well.

"I'm just passing through," he said aloud, though in muted tone. But who could ever say more? He found that those days he had known, that time of their lives when they were young and strong, could not be faithfully relived, though for a moment he thought he had done so.

Lefty Perkins had returned to his field, like the mountain man to his hill, because he remembered he had forgotten so much.

The old wooden grandstand

Afterword

"Another game awaits. The ashwood of bats will crack. The eternal magic of a ball in your hands beckons."

JIMMY WAS THERE ONE NIGHT WHEN I WENT BACK TO THE BALL-park as an old man, though he had been dead nearly fifty years. I wanted to feel the park; I wanted to come to know its legends. I wanted to talk to Jimmy. That night I put my feet up on the bleachers, swallowed the sky and the stars, and closed my eyes. I remember thinking that in our lives we often ask for some magic, for a wish that should be granted to us solely because we feel in our minds that we deserve it. Give me 1949 again. Summer. And give me Jimmy. Make time last long so that I can remember it better, or at least remember it like it really was.

People write books about other ballparks and major-league teams, but I know of no one who has written about Dickson Park and the Galt Terriers, or Agricultural Park and the Brantford Red Sox. So I went to the ballpark last night. Or the night before. It could have been any night of any summer in the last century. Baseball games have been played there that long, and longer. The dust on the basepaths, the dirt under it, the velvet grass that grows green each season, has been there, alongside the Grand River, for vast ages. It was there when I was born. It stood its ground for all the years of my brother's life and gave him his footing in this world. It has been there all my life. It will be there long after I am gone. No one has ever really stopped to look at that earth, yet everyone has seen it. So many years have come and gone, and they have done so quietly, and loudly, and always they have passed by first one life, and then the next, so that generations have come to know that ballpark for what it is: a place of hope, of society, of grass and grandstand, of muscle and guile, and home runs and singles, of chewing tobacco and cuss words, of youth and maturity, of spit and hustle, of one man and all men, of nothing and everything.

It is sacred ground on some deep level that I know nothing about; sacred not in the way of an Indian burial ground that must be guarded and controlled, but sacred in the way of all old ballparks, sacred in the way of all old memories: to be used, and thought of, and stepped on and felt, to be smelled and inhaled, but never to be forgotten. This was Jimmy's old stomping ground.

After I quit the game there was one night, before the sun faded into the blue-grey heaven of twilight, when I remember sitting in the bleachers along the first base line. The sun was warm on our faces, and the game, which was very real, and being played, could wait while the sun of a summer's evening massaged skin and flesh. The game could be forgotten for a moment, and yet it was important that it was always there, to be seen when you wanted to look. How easily the game could be forgotten; how simply good the sun on your face made you feel. My mind wandered.

There was the grass that got greener as dusk approached, the heavens looking infinite like the depths of the ocean. The grass grew even greener—a verdant dark rich hue—when the lights went on. And I would think that people in Galt didn't know this affecting experience that I talk about until 1947 when they installed the first lights. Nor did they know the night sounds of the bridge being crossed by a south-bound train during an inning. I can still see Rosen in centre field looking west over his shoulder at the distant train pressing south across the bridge. Muted thunder, like a far-off sky speaks of lightning. When the game ends I leave the park, to come back later. I couldn't sleep and it seemed right that I go back to the ballpark in the middle of the night to smell the earth when all the world is dark.

Soon it is 4 A.M. and the night is airy and starlit and steel blue. This night there have been all the blues in the heavens: the light cold blues of a desert night, the blues of oceanic depths where life abounds but is mostly unseen. Now, looking out into the cosmic depths above, distant stars can be seen, but so much is hidden. Space, too, is an ocean. There is the silence of the city, and the nearby river, and they are two different silences. In their realms, quiescent noises are heard. They are noises that pierce the night, though you must listen closely to the dormancy of the darkness to hear them. They are the outside noises that have been heard along this river since the beginning of time. When dawn comes they will disappear. Daylight obscures like the dark of night never does.

The game was over at 11 o'clock last night. People left to go home, scattering like seeds in the wind. They listened to the news on the radio, drank a glass of milk or took a shot of something stronger, then brushed their teeth, turned out their bedroom lights, and lay down for a night of sleep before their alarms would wake them to another workday. A few people, including some of the players, were not content to go immediately home. Sleep for them would be futile after a game. At best they would lay awake and then get agitated that they could not fall asleep. So they put it off and sought solace in shared company, and beer, at the bar. There, winding down, they laughed and joked, they talked of women and baseball, and they repeated many of the same foul words that were, only hours earlier, spat out to chase the tobacco juice in the dirt of the dugout when the night was young.

The life of the day is beyond the river valley to the east. The morning dew can be smelled and the type of day it will be, inhaled, even as I sit on the bleachers near the grass. Upward, deep into the dark, now purple sky, the moon hangs in the west. It is so full and bright that it looks artificial, and the celestial glow it gives is enough to read by. There is not a cloud to obscure any of the clearness, so that the clarity I feel, the invigorating clarity of sky, and empty grandstand, and grass wet with dew, is precise and clean. I take out a book just to see if I can read by this unfathomable light of night.

The ball diamond is silent. Silk green on the ground, velvet sky above. I expected as much. The breeze soothing. Like the sun on my face before nightfall, this too is beneficent to the soul. They are both good feelings. I cannot leave this place. Not yet. After a few more lungfuls, maybe. But each breath is meant to be kept, for it slakes the soul. This was the air the first Indians who camped beside the river once breathed. And theirs was the air of the dinosaurs. Now it is the air of baseball. Breathing out dissipates the feeling and must be followed by another deep inward breath where the smell of the night becomes full and fresh again, and you remember that it was like this when you were young and you took the time to inhale life. And so too it must have been through all of time. It has taken a ballpark, and a deserted night, to give you the ancestral breath of life.

Another game awaits. The ashwood of bats will crack. The eternal magic of a ball in your hands beckons. Hearts race with anticipation. It is all so childish, yet it is the very stuff that makes life worthwhile. We need the childlike expectancy of baseball the way our ancestors needed to revel in the hunt. We do not ask questions. There will be more glory, sought after by young men who have been told, and taught, to expect nothing less. They should know this park at four in the morning. They should be made to feel its vibrations and nuances, and suck in the air of the night when the darkness owes its only light to the moon, and where the silence can be heard and seen.

The grandstand shadow is deathly still and vacant, like the empty field, and looms large on the western hill along the third base line. The grandstand is there because one January day in 1916 a thirteen-year-old by the name of Dip Nichol burned its predecessor, an all-wooden grandstand, to the ground. Serenity lives here at night, on the ball diamond. There is no story that beckons though there is summer and plenty enough to write about. In my mind there are extracts of legends that any other baseball imagination might conjure up differently from mine. It helps to look beyond the moonlit grass to first base, then up to home plate, then over to the dark pitcher's mound. Beyond everything is darkness, a domain where you and I feel uncomfortable because it speaks of the unknown and will always be unseen. Even when we journey there, other distant and dark horizons remain unreachable, and they are troubling to us so that we will, in time, explore beyond the sunset. Humans know no other quest.

There is a moonglow, a ghostly veil of light on the maples cresting the western hill, and the leaves give shade even in the night, to left field. I can write and see clearly what I write. There are only three things that need to be written: the fine dirt on the basepaths; the dark, wet grass of summer before the onset of the parching dog days; and the wide-open night sky that has been a chameleon of blues since suppertime last night.

Barely visible, but visible by night nonetheless, is the old cast-iron bridge crossing the Grand River behind the collegiate. Quiet until a train comes. Padden knew that bridge and those nights. I turn to the field where championships have been won and lost, where major-leaguers came to play out their last baseball years, where young men, some on their way up to the big leagues, stopped for a season or two

Afterword

and left their imprint on this dust that is so sacred. Remember 1930 when Bradshaw hit .698? Remember Rosen's grand slam into the river? Remember the place where poetry lived each August and was dead by October? Remember the rivalry with the Red Sox? Remember that summer of 1949? It was Gus Murray's summer. A Galt summer. It had been Pennell and King. Lockington and Gibbs, Lipka and Gavey. Padden's last true baseball summer.

Today those sounds of 1949 are but a whisper, and they are fading like all sounds have done since the beginning of time. Some day, not now, they will be completely swept off the face of the earth and they will be gone for all eternity. The Terriers played their last game in 1983 when they won their final Intercounty championship. Those sounds are still fresh. Two decades have come and gone. Soon another will pass. The summer of '49 was a long time ago. The whisper will grow softer, more vulnerable to the winds of time. There will come a day when only a story will speak of these things. When only written pages can paint a vivid picture of the way things were at the old ball yard.

It is time to go. Daybreak is near. I have come to the ballpark for some reason this morning, and I now know what it was I sought. I have found it. The heavens in all their immensity seem to grasp me, taking hold of me like the wind takes hold of a speck of dust, and I can feel the place as it relates to day and night, and I realize I have come to know Dickson Park. I have seen the summer of '49, and I am whole.

There is another game on the river flats tonight, so come old man, maiden, young man, child. Baseball and summer, breathing life and eternity, have always graced the west valley floor, where words even today speak of and through the seasons, and where the stories are written great and tall on the green summer grass, wiped clean by the morning dew to prepare for the next tale.

They are the stories of our time, and they have haunted all the seasons of my life.

Final Innings

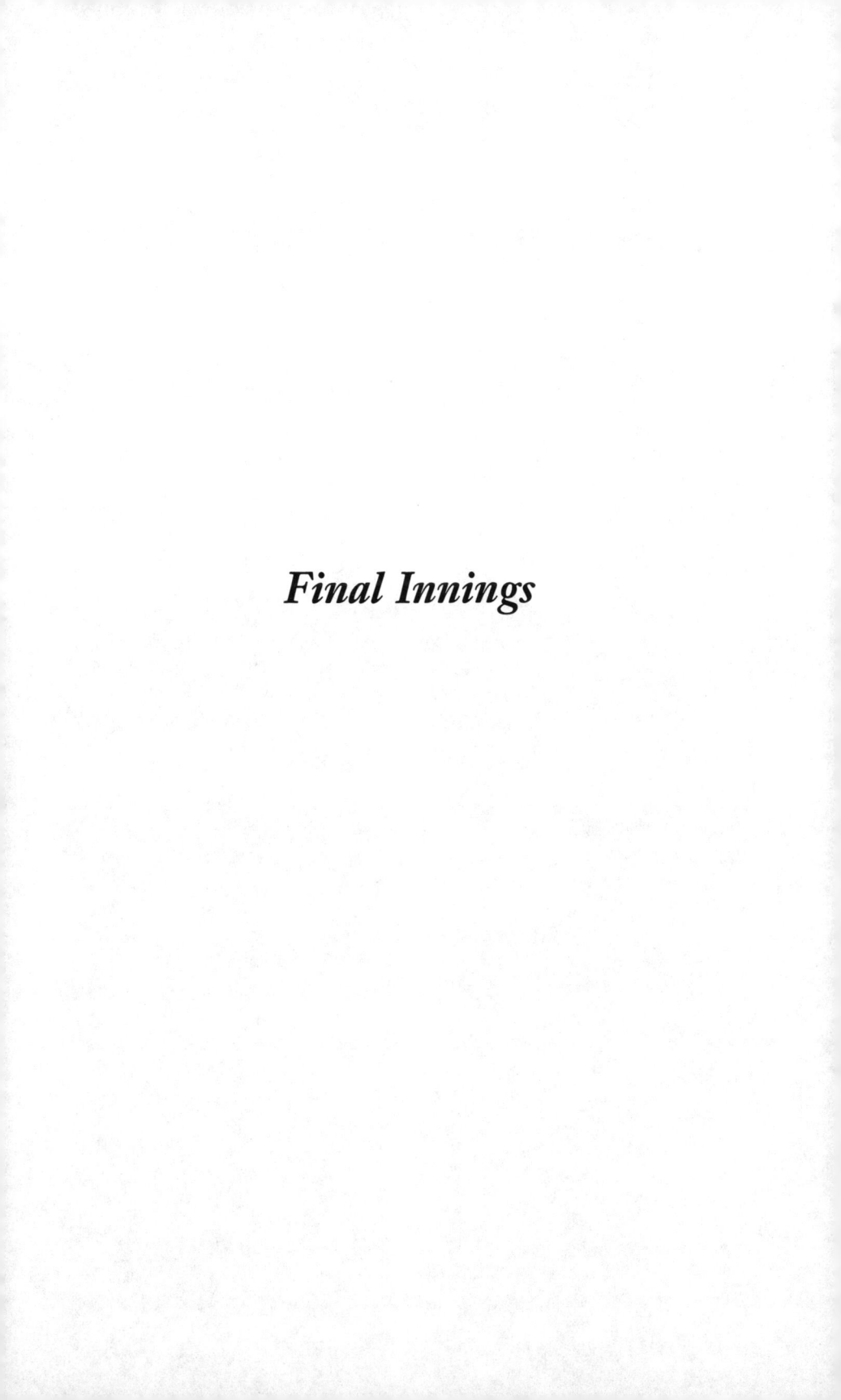

Johnny Lockington

THE CHAMPION 1949 BRANTFORD RED SOX HAD A DIFFERENT look in 1950. Some players left or retired, though the bulk of them were back. Brantford native John Lockington, the deer in centre field, played several more seasons with the Red Sox. He and his brother ran a successful sporting goods store in Brantford, and it was there that they sold tickets to the Red Sox games. "That was one of the deals that Pennell promised me if I came up from London," he recalled. "He said if you come back from the London Majors we'll give you all the business."

He never forgot that 1949 Terrier team with its Murderer's Row. "You walloped us the first three games," he said. "You guys just killed us. And then we beat you in four straight." Of course, he didn't forget the internal problems Murray had to contend with that August. "Geez, the poor guy. Y'know, the players' strike, holding him up for more money and all that. Some of the Terriers had the wool over his eyes, so he brought down a junior team and that's when we won our first game. Then it was settled, but poor Gus, he was really in a bind. We had to feel sorry for Gus. He was quite a promoter, but he had a difficult time that summer. We used to say Gus had all the tigers by the tails."

That last game, Game 7, was the most memorable of all for Lockington. "Highway 24 was bumper to bumper that night," he said.

"It was quite a victory." As the Brantford players drove into Galt that night they were given a hard time by loyal Galt fans. "They kept booing us as we drove in," he recalled. Lockington remembered the Galt players and management were involved in some sort of fracas following the game. "We changed at the Galt YMCA in those days so we were gone celebrating, but there was some commotion. They were all ex-pros and they were mad. They shouldn't have been beaten. I think they were counting their dollars before they earned them."

But no one could deny that Brantford had a good team. "We had wonderful pitching that year and we were solid down the middle," Lockington said. Later Red Sox teams looked much stronger on paper, but few were as successful as that '49 Red Sox team. "In '49 we had the weakest team we ever had and we won it. But Bill [Gibbs] was our heart and soul as far as our pitching went. And Alf Gavey, too. I think they each were jealous of the other to an extent, and they each wanted to produce the best. They had a good rivalry going and I think it helped the club."

Lockington grew up in Brantford and then went to the University of Western Ontario, having been admitted to the first physical education class Western ever had. That was in 1947. At university he ran track and played with the London Majors on the side. He was the perfect lead-off hitter, a spot he held in the batting order on every team he ever played for. Few runners had the ability to steal bases the way Lockington did. "I've still got the strawberries on my hips from sliding," he said nearly fifty years later.

In his first summer with London they went on to win the Canadian championship, a feat they repeated in 1948. They also won the world amateur title in a tournament held over seven cloudless days and nights in London. Each game they played drew a crowd of five thousand, which is how many were on hand when London beat the Fort Wayne, Indiana, Zelners, the United States representative, for the title. The next season when he went to Brantford he was again on the provincial champion team for the third consecutive year, something few, if any, have ever accomplished before.

In public school Lockington captained his baseball team at the same time that Doug Bradshaw, Gord's younger brother, pitched for the opponents. "We used to boo Bradshaw when he was pitching and one time he got flustered and threw the ball over the screen. About the eighth inning I'd be collecting the sweaters and I'd run home and he'd be chasing me." But Bradshaw, who had quite a temper, never caught him.

Lockington might very well have stayed in London were it not for Pennell. Pennell called him up one day and asked him if he'd be interested in coming back to Brantford to play for the Red Sox. Pennell had seen him play for London and knew he was a Brantford boy. He suggested the young student go into business and that they'd give his store all the business relating to the Red Sox. "My brother was at the old Imperial Bank and he was getting transferred to Montreal, so he phoned me up and said either we do it or we don't." Lockington accepted the offer, and it worked out beautifully, though he never did graduate from Western.

Pennell was helpful in getting Lockington established back in Brantford. "And he knew I wasn't costing an arm or a leg like a lot of the imports but I could play just as well or better," said Lockington. "And I knew that I would have the income coming from the store as well as from baseball, and the crowds we got that summer helped business get off the ground." Brantford Red Sox tickets were sold at Lockington's sports store. "Galt fans would come down and the tickets would be gone in an hour."

In many ways, that summer of '49 was a miracle season. In fact, Lockington always referred to that series with Galt as the "Impossible Series." Everything seemed to go Brantford's way that year after they beat London to get into the playoffs. "London had to lose their last three games and we had to win ours just to tie," Lockington recalled.

"That series with Galt was a circus," he said. "It was unbelievable to have a team like we did and win it over a team like Galt, but it just proves that if you're solid down the middle, it can happen."

Lockington attributed part of the team's success to Pennell and King. "Larry's a real super guy," he said. "He respected everybody's walk of life. He certainly didn't need the ball team any more than flying to the moon, but he was always there."

Maybe Pennell did need it. Baseball was his passion. So too was watching Lockington run. Lockington finished out his Intercounty playing career—he also managed the team—at age thirty in 1951, and devoted more time to his business and family. The store would close Wednesday afternoons in those days and he would enjoy the free time to golf. In the early 1950s the Red Sox were floundering with a 3-18 record when Lockington, by then retired from playing, got a call from team owner Harry Mooradian. "How about coming out and just playing in the home games?"

Lockington agreed, and immediately went three-for-four at the plate against London's Tommy White. Soon he was managing the team. "When I took over [as manager] we had the basis of a good team and we finished up 21-21," he said. Lockington drove his car everywhere that season taxiing players to and from games. But at season's end Mooradian left town without paying Lockington the one thousand dollars he owed him. "But I enjoyed just being with the guys," he said.

He knew when to call it quits. "That's enough," he finally said, wanting to spend more time with his brother and their growing sports store business. They eventually expanded, opening up seventeen stores nationwide. He retired from the sporting goods business in the mid-1980s.

Despite all the highs Lockington had known, the summer of '49 would always stand out. The next season, with Bagby in Galt, was another memorable year—"We used to ride Bagby from the dugout because of his lisp [he had a cleft palate]"—but it was not like the summer of '49. "We had a good ball club, but not like your Galt team. They were the best.

"You look back when you're in your seventies," said Lockington, "and you say, 'Hey, what fun we had in those years. They were the good years.' But now, of course ..." It is a common practice for old players to lament the passing of their times. The league today is not the league of their youth, nor can it ever be. They were young men then and they moved earth and heaven. "Hey," he says, as if looking for something good to say about the league as it is today. "I see they've got the wooden bats back this year." Like many minor-leagues the Intercounty had gone to aluminum bats in the last decade, even if the purists decried the move. "That clink of the metal when it hits the ball ... it's not the same, but that's an old man talking."

Lockington would go over to Agricultural Park to watch the odd game in the ensuing years. But the calibre of ball had deteriorated. Even the ballpark had changed its name and was now called Cockshutt Park. Occasionally he was asked to throw out the first ball on opening day. It was good, still, to think of those old days. "When I think of the pitchers who pitched in our league, I think, 'Wow!'" One such pitcher was Bagby. "He'd come into the ballyard and warm up and we'd all say with a lisp, 'Hney, Jim.'"

Bagby would come over to the Brantford dugout and say, "Nu said nhat?"

Lockington respected the talents of Perkins, Shelton, and Warren, but the best pitcher from Galt he ever faced was a big black import by the name of Jeep Jessop who played in '51. "He was the best pitcher they ever had. Oh he could fire the ball." That season Brantford did what Galt had done in '49. They finished the regular season ten games ahead and were beaten out in the playoffs. "It shouldn't have happened," Lockington said. But it did. Baseball, agreed Pennell, is like that.

Baseball was a breeding ground for friendships. When Lockington's first wife died in 1967, Pennell, then sitting as a Member of Parliament in Ottawa, was one of the first to call. He invited Lockington to come up for the weekend. Lockington never forgot that gesture, or the time they spent together in Ottawa those three days. "He's always been a good friend," said Lockington of Pennell.

Nearly forty years after the summer of '49 Lockington, who had remarried, was at a cocktail party when a man approached him. "Remember that catch you made in centre field?" he said. He was referring to the spectacular catch Lockington made during one of the games at Brantford against Galt. People weren't willing to forget that series, or even individual plays.

The London Tigers minor-league team of 1992 invited Lockington and other members of the 1948 world championship London team to come to a special ceremony at London's Labatt Park where the '48 world champs were to be honoured. It was a moving experience as all the players from that team received a scroll at home plate with the writeup of that game and the box score. Bill Farquharson, the former London owner and one of the big wheels on the Intercounty executive, spoke to the crowd.

The night was one of the most memorable of Lockington's ball career. And memorable too was the time he learned he had beaten out Goody Rosen for all-star centre fielder. "Rosen was a good guy," he recalled. "In '46 my uncle was in New York and we went down there that spring and saw Brooklyn play the Giants at the Polo Grounds and Goody was playing. I remember he got into a fight with Eddie Stanky sliding into second base." Just three summers later Lockington was playing on the same field as Rosen, and what's more, was judged to be better than the former major-leaguer. "That was one of my biggest thrills."

In later years Lockington would spend part of every winter in St. Petersburg, not far from where the Yankees used to stay at the Martha Hotel on First Avenue North. He couldn't help but pass by and think to himself that the hotel must hold some remarkable stories. It was the same hotel where Padden had stayed when he made his first trip south to the Yankee camp. "Elston Howard, the catcher for the Toronto Maple Leafs, could not stay there with the whites, so Col. Rupert said, 'We're gone!' and just think how many millions that cost St. Petersburg."

He would drive by the hotel, like only a true baseball fan could do, and say, "Look at that. That's where Gehrig and Ruth and DiMaggio stayed." It was the same when he travelled to Galt. He and his wife would often have dinner at a restaurant across the road from Dickson Park. "Every time I'm there I look over and see the old ball yard," he said. "Oh, the memories. I see the hill where everybody used to sit, the grandstand. They were good times." A twinkle came to his eyes when he looked over to the ballpark. "I look over there and I say, 'Oh boy! That's where it all happened.'" And he looked out to centre field, about 420 feet out from home plate, where he reigned so many seasons ago, and remembered how there was no snow fence except for one game that series against Galt, and he would think that that was a mistake. His legs allowed him to chase down many a ball that would have gone for extra bases.

His legs left him long before his heart did, thanks to a hip replacement. Still, he remained mobile enough. "The old legs got me through the wars," he said. All other things being equal, were it not for Johnny Lockington's fast legs that summer, we would have won the series, in spite of Warren.

Johnny Lockington died from a heart attack in January 1998.

Billy Gibbs

BILLY GIBBS RETIRED FROM THE BRANTFORD RED SOX IN 1952. "I was whipped," he said. "My arm was shot and we had a family we were raising, so we put baseball behind us. It wasn't a hard decision to make. Not really. It's difficult to stay in shape and keep your arm in shape as a pitcher."

He was working full-time at a car dealership and doing other things, so it was hard to concentrate on baseball. Besides, he was twenty-five years old and his dream to make it to the big time was never going to materialize. "You should be in your prime at twenty-five," he said, "but I started pretty early."

The 1949 season was one of the highlights of his career, though the season before, when the Brantford juniors had lost the Ontario finals to Windsor, was also memorable. He had come back to Brantford mid-season and played the last two months that year after leaving the Cardinal chain.

As the years passed he played a little slo-pitch, but stayed away from coaching. His son got into baseball and turned out to be a talented player, and a good pitcher, though he quit early on. "He was probably better than me," Billy said. The same thing happened with his grandson.

The Gibbs had five children and fourteen grandchildren. Family always meant a great deal to them, and leaving baseball was his way of building his family. He continued to work at the Ford dealership in Brantford until his retirement in 1993.

He rarely takes in a Brantford game now, but when he does the memories flood back. They are good memories. "We had a lot of good times," he explained. "Even on the buses we'd play bridge and really enjoy things, win or lose. That's the way it was."

When he played, his family would all show up—his father and mother, Janet and his sisters. They would follow the Red Sox around, to Stratford, St. Thomas, to Waterloo and Galt. "It's too bad," he said, "but when I got out of baseball I kind of lost interest to the point of feeling that if I'm not in it, what's the use. But I did a lot of other things."

It was inevitable that those days when he would do anything to play in a game would come to an end. They had to. He couldn't stay a kid forever.

Bill Gibbs still lives in Brantford. The other ace on the 1949 Brantford Red Sox, Alf Gavey, who made pitching look effortless, died not many years after the championship season in a mishap while working with Ontario Hydro.

The 1949 Brantford Red Sox

Stan Lipka

STAN LIPKA WAS ONE OF THE KEY PLAYERS ON THE BRANTFORD Red Sox in 1949. Pennell, in later years, would say that Lipka, who left home at fourteen to play senior ball in Niagara Falls, was the first player he would get if he were building a team. Though Lipka never made it to the majors due to the outbreak of the war, he made it to the top level of the minors and hit .325 for the Montreal Royals in 1943. It is doubtful that a better third baseman ever came out of Canada.

Lipka decided to accept Pennell's offer to come to Brantford for a couple of reasons. He was impressed by Pennell's sincerity. Here was a man of integrity, he thought. And beyond that, Pennell had offered him a good salary to play ball as well as the prospect of a decent job. Given that Lipka was married, the security available in Brantford was impossible to pass up. Besides, he could earn almost as much money playing semi-pro ball with the Red Sox as he could earn playing professional ball. No one handed Lipka a job when he came to Brantford. On his own effort he found work at 3M, only leaving when he was offered a job at the government-run liquor store (LCBO) in 1955.

The Toronto native signed his first professional contract in 1941, one season after helping the Niagara District Bright's Wine seniors win a provincial title—they beat the Intercounty's Stratford

Nationals. He spent the 1941 season playing Class C ball for Grand Rapids in Michigan, a farm team of the Brooklyn Dodgers. The pay was low, about $175 a month, but for a young Lipka, it was the beginning of a baseball career he hoped would end in the major-leagues.

He had worked himself up to the Class Triple-A Montreal Royals by 1943 and was on a tear, but he was called into the service, where he stayed for three years. In 1946, when he came out, his baseball dreams had all but died. He went south with the Dodgers that spring, and there shared the same infield as Jackie Robinson. But he was relegated to play Class B ball at Nashua, New Hampshire.

"What a team we had at Nashua," he said years later. "There was Don Newcombe, Roy Campanella, Billy Demars, Carl Furillo." The team's paymaster was Buzzie Bavasi, father of future Toronto Blue Jays executive Peter Bavasi. Nashua was virtually unbeatable that year and capped off the season by winning the pennant. At season's end Lipka was ordered to go to St. Paul. "But I didn't want to go, so I went to an outlaw league in St. Hyacinthe, Quebec." Which is where Pennell found him in 1948.

Knowing his chance of making it to the majors was gone, he had few reservations about going to Brantford, so Pennell's offer was about the best to be had. "I could make as much or more in Brantford, with the job added in, than I could anywhere else." The only thing that Lipka didn't like in the Telephone City was the way his manager at 3M would make him stay till the last second before leaving. On most days Lipka had no objection to this, but on game nights, when time was of the essence, it bothered him. Eventually Lipka worked his way up to become manager of the LCBO store.

He and his wife Madelyn embraced Brantford, settling into their new home on Dalhousie Street. Lipka, as steady a citizen as he was a player, never got into trouble and tried to be a model citizen. He retired as a player—by then he was also coaching—in 1955 after being selected to the Intercounty all-star team three times, but continued working until his retirement in 1983. When he called it quits on his playing career he was given a special "Stan Lipka Night." Pennell spoke, and Lipka was presented with gifts including lamps, tables, and chairs.

Toward the end of his playing career Lipka tried his hand at coaching minor ball, but after only a couple of months he gave up when a father of one of the boys disagreed with his methods. "I would have loved to coach young kids," he reflected years later, "because there hasn't been a coach in Canada with the experience to teach them properly." But the father, whom Lipka described as not having played sports in his life, "thought he knew more about the game than me."

Madelyn, Stan's wife of fifty-two years, died in the spring of 1995, forcing her husband to take over the daily routines, financial and otherwise, she had handled all their married life. After his wife's death he became somewhat reclusive, keeping his phone number a well-guarded secret. When the Brantford Red Sox of 1995 wanted to hold a special night to honour Lipka, Lockington, and Jimmy Wilkes, they had difficulty getting in touch with him. But in the end he came back to the ballpark. Pennell again said a few words about the former players, and their numbers—Stan was number 27—were retired. The crowd that night was only a few hundred and paled in comparison to the crowds that came to Agricultural Park that summer of 1949.

⚾ ⚾ ⚾

1995. It was early October when I drove to Brantford. Pennell had arranged for us to have lunch with Lipka. I first picked up Larry, and then we drove over to Stan's house. On the way there Larry spoke of Lipka's natural ability as a ballplayer. Few were better, he said. He spoke highly of this former star third baseman, and of Lipka's late wife, Madelyn. She was a wonderful woman, he said. Pennell first met Mrs. Lipka when he and King approached Lipka in 1948. Pennell always said that she was a credit to Stan, and that any man with a wife like that must be a good one.

Stan was waiting when we pulled up along the sidewalk. He was wearing glasses and was heavier than I'd expected, though it had been nearly forty-five years since I'd last seen him, when he was in his prime. Under a dark waist-length sport jacket was a light blue golf shirt. From the very beginning he was affable, almost quiet and reserved. Larry reintroduced us, and told Stan a little of me, then told me a little about Stan. As we drove they decided on a restaurant, with Stan saying to Larry that any place he wanted to go was good enough for him. There was a mutual respect shown by both men for each other, and I thought that this must have been how it was so many years ago when Larry was the team president and Stan was his third baseman. No wonder Brantford had been able to beat us in 1949. There were no other distractions, no internal bickering to sidetrack the Red Sox from their goal.

We entered the restaurant and Larry removed his black overcoat, hanging it up near the entrance. Then we walked to the back of the room after Larry told the waitress we'd like some place out of the way where we could talk. She took us to a back corner, though it wasn't dark owing to the wall of windows on two sides.

Stan started talking about current ballplayers, and he had plenty of ideas on what was wrong with modern athletes and how they played baseball. It was there, in the back of the restaurant in Brantford, that Stan told me he had known Jackie Robinson one spring at the Dodger camp, and about missing out on playing in the majors due to the war, and about how few Canadians have ever made it to the majors playing the infield. Most have been pitchers or outfielders, he noted. Had the war not intervened, he could have become the first.

The waitress could see the baseball I had on the table for Lipka to sign, and she asked about it. "This is Larry Pennell," I told her, pointing to my right. "He ran the Brantford Red Sox for a number of years."

"I've heard of you," she said.

Of course, it was not surprising that she had heard of Pennell. At one time he was the best-known man in Brantford. I didn't bother to elaborate on his political background or his legal career. I didn't want to embarrass him. Then I turned to my left and told her Stan Lipka was one of the best third basemen to ever come out of Canada. "We're just talking baseball, about those long ago days," I said.

She smiled with seeming interest. She was young, pleasant. "You'll be able to say," said Pennell, "that a famous book was written right over here at this table in the corner. You might even have a plaque in front of the restaurant about it one day."

Several months earlier, after Larry came to Cambridge to visit me, he had said something similar that helped motivate me. We had just parted, he about to get into his car as I was about to open my car door. It was spring and the early afternoon sun was radiant in a blue sky. I had just shown him a few pictures of my newborn grandson, and he had said, while looking at them, "That's the whole world right there." Then, as we were about to leave, he said, "I have only one concern, and that is that you finish your book and that it gets published."

Now, as we spoke with Stan, I was getting closer to achieving that goal. Indeed, Lipka would be the last major character I would interview for the book. We ate our meals that day in Brantford, and then we talked some more. Finally a couple of hours had passed and Stan said he should be getting back to his house. He had two cats to feed. Life after his wife's death, he said, was difficult, but it kept him busy. Larry told him that was good, that he needed to keep busy with daily things.

So we drove Stan back to his place and I took a picture of Stan in front of his house. I urged Larry to come out for a picture too, but he said I didn't want to get a picture of an old man. I persisted, and finally the two of them stood together. Lipka, the taller of the two, put his left arm around Pennell's shoulder, and Pennell did likewise around Lipka's back in a spirit of collegiality. Their lives had been so different, socially and intellectually, but baseball had brought them together in '49, as it was doing now.

"Brantford's been the best," said Lipka. "Just the best. They treated me so royally here, I'd put myself down as born and raised in Brantford, even though I was born in Toronto."

Stan walked through the white fence that led to his porch and disappeared behind the lonely front door to feed the cats. He was rudderless now that his wife was gone, the same way Goody Rosen had been when his wife died. Rosen had held on only a year afterwards. How long would Stan go on?

"Stan was a great player," said Justice Pennell as we pulled away.

Stan Lipka lived alone for several more years. He died on a cold wintry Monday in February 2003. There were no children. There was no funeral. All that marked his passing was a two-column story in the *Expositor*. He was eighty-three.

Tex Kaiser

TEX KAISER WAS BACK IN A GALT UNIFORM THE SUMMER OF 1950. His picture graced the cover of the Terrier program, which sold for fifteen cents. Inside, it said: "Verne (Tex) Kaiser won honours for home runs last year and is the most improved player in the league this year. Verne was recently sold to the Montreal Canadiens hockey team and is an exceptionally good hockey player. He hits a long ball and tips the scales at 180 lbs. Verne is married to a Preston girl. They are the proud parents of two children."

In the fall of 1950, after standing up for Harry Sollenburger at Sollenburger's wedding in Buffalo at the end of the season, Kaiser made the Montreal Canadiens hockey club. He was twenty-five. His linemates were Rocket Richard, whom he roomed with on road trips, and Elmer Lach. Until then Kaiser had languished in the minors, spending most of his time playing for Eddie Shore–owned clubs. Several major-league teams showed an interest in him, including the Yankees, Phillies, Dodgers, and Tigers, but Kaiser had his mind and heart set on a hockey career.

Everyone, it seemed, liked Kaiser. Everyone except for Eddie Shore, though for Kaiser, the feeling was mutual. "Nobody liked Eddie Shore," said Kaiser. "He was nuts. Just absolutely crazy." In 1943 Kaiser joined the navy and stayed until war's end. As the decade drew to a close he began playing baseball for the Terriers. Even though he was still young, years of playing in the minors for Shore's teams had taken their toll by the time he got to Montreal. Shore, said Kaiser, would have him playing forty minutes a game. "And he'd play us through injuries."

Kaiser roomed with Rocket Richard, and one night, so the story goes, he found Richard sleeping. When he tried waking him up Richard sprang from the bed and punched him hard. Kaiser never tried to wake Richard again.

One year the team he was playing for, the New York Rovers, actually outdrew the NHL's Rangers at Madison Square Garden. "We always had bad ice on Sunday afternoons because on Saturday nights there would be some event on at the Gardens and there would be no ice. By Sunday we only had a half-inch of ice and the sparks would fly."

After spending the 1950 season with the Canadiens, his big-time hockey career came to an abrupt end when Shore bought his contract from the Canadiens for $10,000. So ended his stint in the NHL. It was too bad; the Canadiens had wanted him for years and Shore wouldn't let them have him. Shore demanded so much money from Montreal that they balked. In fifty games for Montreal he scored seven goals and added five assists. "It was a good year but it was tough with a name like Kaiser and not speaking French," recalled Kaiser. "Dick Irwin was a great coach." That one season with Montreal left him with an unforgettable image of the Rocket. "He was just so intense, so strong. You can't imagine a guy of that stature and build being that strong. He just moved people. He could skate, and burst. In those days you just put the puck on his stick. And his stick was so stiff you could practically stand on it. Could he fire the puck!"

His hockey career came to a close in 1955 when Shore bought his contract once again. Kaiser was on a train bound for Chicoutimi when he learned that Shore had re-acquired his rights. "I just got off the train and goddamn quit," he said.

His baseball career ended about the same time. "My legs were bothering me, but I'd had enough anyway. I think I just got sick of playing. It was time. I had had an operation on my knee and it just wasn't fun anymore." There were few regrets, though he later wished he had given baseball more of a chance. As he got older, he came to realize that baseball would have been a better choice. But such decisions are never easy at the time. "Hockey was tough physically," he said later. "I think baseball was the easier of the two to play, but in those days I loved playing hockey."

Kaiser got a job in Kitchener and remained there until his retirement in 1989. In the spring of 1993 he underwent a knee replacement, just a year after he had undergone a hip replacement. Both were related, he believed, to his hockey days. "I don't think I'd play hurt again," he said. "Baseball was so easy and hockey was tough. In hockey you'd get bruised and hurt all the time." But in 1949 Kaiser didn't think highly of American baseball players who couldn't play hurt.

When Kaiser stopped playing baseball in the mid-1950s, young kids like Tom Conaway, later a sportswriter, and Charlie Wilson, later a high-school principal, were older, but they never forgot his Terrier days. They respected him as a hockey player, for they knew he played professionally each winter, but they remembered him as a baseball player. They remembered that summer of '49 when Kaiser was in his prime.

One young fellow who played juvenile ball in 1949, Jack Murray, would never forget an incident involving Kaiser. Brantford's junk-ball pitcher, Gavey, was on the mound and Kaiser was at the plate. Gavey's curveballs were tying up Kaiser, who liked nothing better than a fastball down the centre. "Kaiser got so mad," recalled Murray, "that on the second strike he grabbed the ball from the Brantford catcher and fired it back at Gavey. He nearly took Gavey's head off, for Chrissakes. That's how hard he could throw."

There are some things a person never forgets, and never wants to forget. The image of a big, strong, and fast Tex Kaiser in Terrier pinstripes is an enduring one. He was very likely one of the best natural ballplayers to ever play on Canadian soil.

Tex Kaiser continued to live in Kitchener, spending his winters in Florida, until later in life when he and his wife Betty moved to Penticton, British Columbia, to be near their sons.

Waterloo Tiger playing coach Don Gallinger was banned for life by NHL president Clarence Campbell.

Don Gallinger

DON GALLINGER PLAYED AND MANAGED ERNIE GOMAN'S Waterloo Tigers in 1949 before coming to Galt in a trade for Wes Lillie the following summer. He was a good player, dangerous both as a hitter and as an outfielder. Larry Pennell regarded him as one of the best players in the league, rating him just under guys like Galt's Tex Kaiser but certainly ahead of most other players.

I remembered him as a star hockey player, for my father had taken Jimmy and me to see the Bruins play the Leafs at Maple leaf Gardens several winters earlier.

Gallinger always had a dream of playing major-league ball, though there were many who believed he didn't have the talent necessary to make it to the majors. Indeed, hockey was his sport. The Port Colborne native, the youngest of six children, was the first player to jump from Junior B to the NHL when he made the Boston Bruins in 1942. He was seventeen. He stayed with the Bruins until 1948 when he left the game, involuntarily, after a betting scandal that involved placing bets on NHL games. In his seven seasons he scored sixty-five goals and had 88 assists in 222 games, and finished third in voting behind Toronto's Gaye Stewart and Montreal's Glen Harmon for Rookie of the Year honours.

Although Gus Murray was generally regarded as the most colourful character in the Intercounty in 1949, several people thought

Gallinger outdid even Gus. Goman, his boss in Waterloo, was taken aback when Gallinger told him he wanted full control in the operation of the Tigers. That was the main reason he came to Galt in 1950.

Murray liked Gallinger, and as a symbol of their faith in each other, the two never signed a contract. Gallinger said Murray's word was good enough for him, and Murray reciprocated. Indeed, that Gallinger's word could be taken at face value was something Murray always admired about the former NHLer.

Gallinger had a troubled existence after being banned for life from the NHL. NHL president Clarence Campbell suspended him on March 9, 1948, after accusing him of associating with gamblers and betting on games. Campbell wouldn't release any evidence because most of it was obtained through illegal wiretaps and telephone recordings, neither of which were admissible in court. But Scott Young of the *Globe and Mail* wrote about the case in detail in a series of 1963 articles. Gallinger admitted betting from $250 to $1,000 on games and providing information on injuries, but maintained he had never fixed a game and that, indeed, he had lost between $1,000 and $1,500 on the eight or nine games in question. Gallinger made a complete confession to Campbell twenty months after the incident, hoping to be reinstated. "I went there looking for sympathy," he said of their five-hour meeting. His livelihood was on the line. But Campbell wouldn't end his suspension until August 28, 1970, twenty-two years after the fact. By then Gallinger had no chance of resuming his career.

He continued to feel Campbell, and later others, relentlessly persecuted him. In effect, he was blackballed from organized hockey. Even his participation in Intercounty baseball was in question in 1948 when Goman, on the advice of Bobby Bauer, a former Bruin teammate of Gallingers, took a chance on him. In 1953 Gallinger was seen going into the dressing room of the Kitchener hockey seniors before a game. Kitchener had won the game, but Sarnia protested Gallinger's presence. He was outlawed from the game, so it was not surprising that the protest was upheld and the win given to Sarnia.

Life after hockey was difficult. Gallinger was bitter. Things would have been so different if he had finished out what promised to be a notable career in the NHL. Gallinger tried to stay in touch with the game, but when he began a summer hockey school he was forced to close due to his suspension.

He applied for reinstatement in 1955, some seven years after his suspension, but Campbell turned him down. So he went from one job to another before landing what would be essentially his life's work, selling made-to-measure Mansfield shirts out of Kitchener. He moved to Burlington in later years after he retired, but he lived alone. His first wife had been killed in a car accident years earlier after they split up, and his children were estranged from him. Every month or so he would drive to Galt to visit Murray either at his home or at Murray's second-floor office overlooking Main Street. They would talk of old times, but mostly it would be Gallinger doing the talking, loud and abrasive one minute, softly whispering the next, about his lawsuit against Dick Beddoes's estate. Beddoes had written in one of his books that Gallinger was dead, and in another he had copied, said Gallinger, a manuscript he and Brantford sportswriter Ted Beare had written. Beare had attempted to write a biography of Gallinger, which was never published.

The lawsuit went on for years. Major Richard Rohmer acted as his first counsel, but the two came to a parting of ways. Gallinger went through several more lawyers as he proceeded with the case, and gradually word got around that he was not a model client. Indeed, he would monopolize several hours of a lawyer's time, and the funny thing about it was the way he wouldn't let them go. People seemed powerless to leave him while he was talking. And talk he did. Few people could ever out-talk Gallinger, something that Gallinger would take great pride in.

He suffered a serious heart attack in 1980, and had a cancerous tumour removed in 1984. Just before Christmas of 1994 he had a spell and was taken to hospital. No one was sure what was wrong with him. But he bounced back and was discharged some days later.

Milt Dunnell considered him somewhat of a nut in those later years, and there were plenty of people who would agree with him. To most people a visit with Gallinger was intolerable. But Ted Beare, who collaborated with him on an unpublished manuscript, though he shared Dunnell's belief, was sympathetic. Look what he had been through, he would say. And Gus, though even he couldn't get a word in edgewise on Gallinger, respected him and considered him a friend.

The first time I met up with Gallinger after that '49 season was one summer day in the early 1990s. I happened to be in town when Gus called me and said there was somebody at his office he wanted me to see. It was Gallinger. Murray was leaving for Poland in a couple of days and wouldn't be back for six months. The Gallinger I met stood a couple inches over six feet and weighed perhaps 260 pounds. He was a big man, and his eyes bulged when he talked. Which was always. His favourite topic was himself. His arms would jerk to and fro, his voice going from one extreme to another in the same sentence. He would be talking loudly and then, without warning, begin whispering so low you would have to move closer to hear him. And he never stopped for a breath. He was like a machine gun constantly spitting out words, and it was pointless to try and interrupt. Or, rather, impossible. There was simply no opening.

"Goddammit," he said often. "Goddamn" this, and "goddamn" that. On a subsequent visit we went into a conference room at the library, and I shut the door. For the next two hours he talked to me so intensely my neck got sore. That's how little I moved. He was so animated that the library staff could hear him, and several people believed we were fighting. On later visits I learned to move, and to interrupt, but for those early meetings I was a novice.

One day he asked me to meet him for an early breakfast at the Holiday Inn, saying he felt he hadn't given me much of a chance to ask my questions in our previous meeting. That was a good time of day to meet, I thought, because we would finish early and then I would have the rest of the day free. So we met at 7 A.M. Sometime during the day my wife thought I'd gone missing. I didn't return until 5 P.M., by which time she had nearly sent out the Mounties to discover what had happened to me. In those hours he gave me his story, and detailed his lawsuit against the late Beddoes, how he believed Beddoes had used his manuscript without permission in *Pal Hal* and *Greatest Hockey Stories*. As Beare once said, a conversation with Gallinger was a one-way affair. He talked, you listened.

Gallinger had a promising future when he was banished from the NHL at age twenty-two by Campbell. Like a modern-day Pete Rose, who was suspended from baseball by commissioner Bart Giamatti, gambling did him in. Gallie, as he called himself, was in the prime of his life, too young to realize the magnitude of what he was doing, and young enough to make mistakes.

Later in life he was nobody's hero and had a life that would appeal to few. Although his selling career ended several years earlier, he was still a seller of sorts, only now he took to selling himself. The Gallinger story was not known by anybody on this earth better than it was by Gallinger himself.

The years after his brief NHL career came and went. Came too the passing of a daughter in her youth. Life might have been so different if only Campbell had reinstated him. Instead of being the self-absorbed man he became, he might have been an elder statesman of hockey. A second heart attack slowed him down for a time as the 1980s were drawing to a close. But he never slowed in telling his story, the story of his hockey life and the ugly way his playing career ended. It has remained one of the most tragic episodes in NHL history, certainly the most tragic episode in Gallinger's life.

Our meeting that summer day in Murray's office went on for a couple of hours. Gallinger talked so long that Gus had to leave for a break. I couldn't help thinking that the voice he had developed, the garrulous booming thunder which gave way to a whisper, was developed as a sales aid, a technique designed to leave a lasting impression after a presentation. There was anger in his voice and it had to do with the way Campbell treated him. The anger never left him, eating away at his life. But with only one lifetime to look back on, and no more to look forward to, it was not so difficult to understand Gallinger's hate for the long-dead Campbell.

As I drove away from one of our meetings I watched him slowly walk back to his car in the parking lot. The car was old and big, able to accommodate a man of his size. As a kid I had admired Gallinger as much for his baseball skill as his hockey skill. Now I thought of those years he spent in the NHL, and how the world seemed to hold so much promise back then. And how it all fell apart in 1948, the year he signed on to play ball with Goman's Waterloo Tigers. He was a peripheral figure in the summer of '49 as far as the Terriers were concerned, but he was one of the best-known players in the league. Six-year-old Rich Mirco of Brantford, who took in every Red Sox game, thought the world of Gallinger. He knew, though he couldn't elaborate on it at the time, that the Intercounty of '49 would have been a far less interesting place were it not for Gallinger. He was part of that magic season, part of the mix that saw Murray and Pennell and all the others transform the Intercounty into a league that had few rivals anywhere in North America.

Don Gallinger died in the winter of 2000. Reports of his death were spread through the CP wire service and were carried by almost every newspaper in Canada.

Ernie Goman

BACK IN THE LATE 1940S AND EARLY '50S ERNIE GOMAN, WHO operated the Waterloo Tigers—some say he was the second best promoter in the league behind Galt's Gus Murray—was concerned with the way the league was headed. Others shared his concern. The big worry around the Intercounty in 1949 was whether the eight senior teams would be able to meet the swollen salary demands of American imports. "This could be the season that is entered into the record books as the year of the big bust," wrote one reporter. "Competition may be the best ever, but there is more than a little anxiety around the league due to the high salaries."

Goman always worked hard on behalf of his Tigers. "We had to do a lot of work," he said. "We were one of the smallest centres in the league." Yet they were consistently a contending team, much to the surprise of Pennell, who used to say to Goman, "I don't know how you do it."

Goman could sympathize with Murray in Galt. "You'd hear reports of problems he was having with certain players," Goman said, "but every player you dealt with was tough to deal with on a financial basis."

Goman was no slouch when it came to contract negotiations. One of his players, Ike Koslowski, once told *Kitchener-Waterloo Record* reporter, Lloyd Johnson, that Goman was tougher than Toronto

Maple Leaf boss Connie Smythe, author of the famous saying, "If you can't beat 'em in the alley, you can't beat 'em on the ice." Tough though Goman was, Koslowski respected him. Later the reporter told Goman, "You've got a great press agent there." Koslowski, who'd grown up in the tough east end of Toronto, didn't have any direction when he first came to play for the Tigers. City parks employees once found Koslowski, who was himself working for the parks department, lying asleep under a tree. Goman told him he was going to release him if he didn't straighten up. He had lost three straight jobs, and Goman wasn't amused. Goman said he would try to help him as much as he could, but he had to take responsibility for himself. Koslowski told Johnson, "If it hadn't been for Ernie I'd have wound up a bum."

Another player Goman advised was Cy Bricker, a descendant of one of the first Mennonite families to emigrate from Pennsylvania to Waterloo County. "I made him manager of the parks concessions and I got him signed on as a greenhorn with the city assessment department," recalled Goman. Later Bricker became commissioner of assessments. He never forgot the help Goman had given him starting out.

Goman, who worked for Equitable Life Insurance Company his entire adult life, was busy in the winters with hockey. For years he was president of the Kitchener Dutchmen hockey team, winners of the bronze medal at Cortina, Italy, in 1956, and four years later winners of the silver at Squaw Valley, California, in the 1960 Olympics. During the 1956 Olympics Goman was presented with an Olympic medal for his outstanding contribution to hockey in Canada.

Balancing his sporting interests with his business life and family—he had four children—was never easy. There were always players to sign, problems to solve. "Many times you had to burn the midnight oil," he said. "My wife often kids me about when we were first married and we rented a cottage up in the Port Elgin area for two or three weeks. The only time I'd be there was on weekends, and even then, not on Saturdays when we played." On the day we talked, though retired and over eighty, he still held his licence to sell insurance. He was then the oldest agent with Equitable Life, though he admitted he was not active.

Goman, who was born in Denbigh, near Renfrew, Ontario, in 1914, had a lifelong involvement in the Waterloo community. At various times he served as president of the Tigers, Dutchmen hockey team, the Lions Club, the Waterloo County Underwriters Association, was the original general manager of the Bauer Foundation, a trust fund that assists students, president of the Granite Club (curling and badminton) and the K-W Athletic Association.

His father came to Canada from Germany in 1912 as a missionary and retired to Waterloo, taking over at the Waterloo Seminary for a term while another professor was away on sabbatical. Ernie got his start in the Intercounty with the Waterloo executive in 1935, but when Dutch Erison, a Galt product, enlisted in 1939, Goman took over. "I got a couple of wins in me so I wound up taking over the junior club." Then there were years of involvement in minor hockey when he served as president of the K-W Boys Hockey Association and had as his secretary Beland Honderich, then of the *K-W Record* and destined to become owner of the *Toronto Star*.

Goman, an inductee in the Waterloo County Hall of Fame, was a longstanding member of the Ontario Minor Hockey Association and was later awarded the gold stick award. He added curling to his activities in middle age, and had some success, prompting someone to ask him if he was ever sorry he didn't take up the sport earlier. "Well," he said, "you can't do everything in life. I enjoyed the baseball, I enjoyed the hockey, and the curling."

It was a beautiful afternoon in late February of 1995 when I visited him at his Waterloo home, and he didn't look the way I remembered him. He was not well, though he was kind enough to have me over. "I've got heart problems," he told me. He had had a pacemaker installed seven years earlier and had developed Parkinson's in the last couple of years. "I was in hospital recently for ten days," he said. "I haven't been well." He had deteriorated greatly from the days when he was a big, robust, athletic, and busy man about Waterloo.

Only a few years earlier he had still been playing tennis on a regular basis. Now he walked slowly. Every step was an effort. It was even difficult to speak. He answered the door slowly. His walking was laboured; he looked very thin and brittle and his skin had blotches of purple. I shook his hand gently.

It was 1:30 P.M. We talked for an hour. He smiled often, and there was a spark to his voice and his eyes at certain times, but he looked as if he was in pain. As if every breath was work. He sat in front of the TV most of the day. At 3 o'clock he had a doctor's appointment. "There's not much they can do for me," he said with sadness. But he was not lamenting, even though he had every right to be.

Soon it was time to go. He had struggled long enough in the presence of a virtual stranger. And I was a stranger, for he could not remember me, nor would I have expected him to remember me.

In truth, I would have loved to stay and talk away the afternoon, to listen to the Waterloo Tiger story. When I left he said, "It was a pleasure to see you again after all these years. I'm sorry I'm not very well." I was sorry too.

The last time I talked to him on the telephone I immediately called his old friend from Brantford, Larry Pennell, and told him Goman said hello. Pennell picked up the phone and called Goman. They hadn't seen each other in years, but they had a shared history back in the glory days of the Intercounty. Both men were glad to talk to each other.

I couldn't help thinking how Goman was trapped inside a failing body, and how he had no way of fleeing his own skin. There was no escape. Such a fate awaits many of us. Tennis, curling—everything was behind him now. And what was there to look forward to? Nothing, except death, and the times when he could look back on the life he had lived. It did give him pleasure to talk that one afternoon about those long-ago days.

He was not the man I expected to meet. He was more. It was with regret that I left him that day, but I knew I had to. I didn't know if I would ever see him again. Still, I had gained insight, or gotten a sense of the man he was, and for that, I was grateful. He exuded class. He had every reason to complain, but he did not. He talked, and smiled from time to time, and his eyes lit up more than once. It was no wonder the Waterloo Tigers, or the Kitchener Dutchmen hockey team, for that matter, were so successful. They both had Ernie Goman in common. He was one of the vital forces shaping the Intercounty during the league's halcyon years.

As I left his house I hoped he knew how much I valued our afternoon together. I had this terrible feeling that it would be our one and only face-to-face meeting. It was almost spring, a time of new life, but Ernie Goman was dying.

Not long afterward I happened to be driving down Union Street in Waterloo and I passed Ernie Goman's house. I glanced over, and saw a "Sold" sign on the front lawn. I wanted to believe that I had mixed up Goman's house with the one beside it, that Goman's house was not for sale.

Ernie Goman died in 1997.

Frank Udvari

It was summer when I walked into Frank Udvari's Kitchener office and he was on the phone. He motioned me to come in. We hadn't seen each other in almost fifty years. Around the walls were hung various pictures and memorabilia showing vignettes of his long and successful career as an NHL referee. Not far from his desk was a picture of the late Toronto Maple Leafs coach Punch Imlach and a five dollar cheque Imlach paid him after losing a bet on a goal Udvari once called. Imlach told Udvari he'd pay him five dollars if the puck had crossed the goal line. Pictures proved it had.

Soon Udvari, the businessman, was off the phone. We went outside into the heat and sun that was the summer of 1995, and we walked the short distance to his car. He turned on the air conditioning and we drove off to lunch outdoors under the shade of a cluster of tall trees at the Westmount Golf and Country Club. There was a pleasant breeze, and a number of people greeted Frank as we walked in.

Udvari played a minor role with the Galt Terriers of 1949. One sportswriter wrote that "Husky Frank Udvari is no fancy Dan around the first base station, but if willingness to learn means anything, the former Kitchener player will prove his worth to the Terriers. You can't laugh off a .417 batting average, even for twelve official trips, and Udvari hasn't had any boots in twenty-seven fielding chances."

He was one of the young local players—the others were Lillie and myself—who seemed to get better because of the quality of people around him. Padden spent a good deal of time with us, and it paid off. For all the knocks against Lillie's hitting, he had blossomed into a consistent .286 hitter in 1949, one of the best averages he'd ever had in his brief career, while Udvari was playing better than almost anybody had predicted. Words like eager, conscientious, and determined were used to describe him. The team was so talented that Udvari saw little action that summer, though he remembered it well. As we talked about those old days the conversation invariably turned to Lillie. Udvari leaned back in his chair and smiled. We had already ordered lunch. Then he said: "What you have to remember about Lillie is that he couldn't hit."

Udvari always blamed Bobby "Shaky" Schnurr, the playing manager of the 1948 Kitchener Legionnaires, for selling him to Gus. "Shaky, you traded me to Galt in '49 for a jockstrap and a bat."

In reality, Gus Murray persuaded him to come to Galt, and as many people know, Murray was nothing if not persuasive. So Udvari came, though he didn't fraternize much with the other players that summer in Galt. He was a Kitchener boy. In fact, few players hung around together that season. The imports were on the road a lot, while there were only a few homebrews, including Lillie and myself, who were too young to even technically have a drink. The only thing the entire team did together happened between the white lines on the ball diamond, and occasionally we travelled together to an away game, though as often as not many drove in their own cars. Perhaps Udvari's best friend on the Galts that season was catcher Johnny Clark. "He was a great guy," Udvari recalled. It had been years since the two had seen each other. Clark, who remained active until a massive heart attack in the fall of 1995, is a few years older than Udvari. Both men have bad knees, and Udvari, like Kaiser, has had a knee replacement. A year after surgery, he had completely recovered so that on this day he walked briskly.

"That was a good year," he said of that summer of '49, having had no cause to regret coming to Galt. He was interested to hear that Jeff Shelton was still alive and well and living in Buffalo. "He had good stuff," he said. "And he could hit." So too could Creedon, he said. "He could hit that ball like it was a bullet." But as good as they were as hitters, Udvari believed London's Evon was the best hitter in the league. "He was the best hitter I ever saw in the Intercounty."

Following that season in Galt, Udvari went on to become one of the most successful Terrier alumni ever. After signing on as an NHL referee in 1951, he carved out a distinguished career, retiring in 1966. At that time he was named the first supervisor of NHL officials. In 1973 he was elected to the Hockey Hall of Fame in Toronto. "That was the highlight of my career as a referee," he said. Three others were inducted into the hall that day, including former Montreal Canadien great Doug Harvey. Harvey was the only no-show for the ceremony at the hall's Canadian National Exhibition site. The ceremony was notable for one other thing—women were permitted to attend the ceremony for the first time ever.

Udvari's last game as a referee, prior to his election to the Hockey Hall of Fame, was a controversial playoff game between Detroit and Montreal. Detroit had won the first two games in Montreal. Roger Crozier had left the Detroit goal after suffering an injury earlier in the series. It was an emotional series pitting Rocket Richard against Gordie Howe. Udvari wasn't the most popular man in Montreal because earlier in the season, in a game between Montreal and Chicago, he had ejected Bernie "Boom Boom" Geoffrion after Geoffrion pushed him into the boards. Geoffrion was later fined $250. So during Udvari's last game before retiring, at least half a dozen times the crowd, which at 13,920 was the smallest of the season, tossed paper onto the ice in displeasure at Udvari's calls, and there were short delays while the paper was cleared away. A Montreal writer wrote that Udvari was the man fans "would most like to try out our brass knuckles on." Udvari had also worked the Boston Garden game when Rocket Richard went berserk in what came to be referred to as "Rocket's" Boston Stick Party. NHL president Clarence Campbell, after hearing evidence from Udvari and others, suspended Richard for the balance of the season for his attack on Hal Laycoe of the Bruins and linesman Cliff Thompson.

Now it was a playoff game between Detroit and Montreal, being played at the Montreal Forum. The Pocket Rocket, Henri Richard, was skating near the Detroit goal when he was upended by Bill Gadsby. The puck was centred and hit Richard in the shoulder and bounced into the net for a goal. Montreal won the game, and Udvari took a lot of heat. "I had to allow it," Udvari said of the goal, but Detroit's Gadsby immediately skated over.

"Frank," he said, "is it a goal?"

"He never saw it," said Udvari of Richard. "It wasn't done deliberately. I have to allow it."

After the game, Red Wings owner Bruce Norris bumped into Udvari. He was beside himself that the series was over and that he wouldn't have any more home games. Home games were a great boon because of the potential to earn big profits through concession sales. "Frank, you just cost me a half-million dollars," he said.

That should have been Udvari's last game in the stripes. But circumstance would alter destiny, for on December 30, 1979, Udvari would be called on one more time to take to the ice as an NHL official. That night Udvari, dressed conservatively in a grey pinstriped suit, took his place in the Nassau Coliseum press box for a game between the host New York Islanders and the Atlanta Flames. He was there to observe the night's assigned officials, referee Dave Newell and linesmen Claude Bechard and Leon Stickle.

But late in the opening period Newell took a puck to the head and fell to the ice, blood flowing from his head. It didn't look good. Minutes passed, and finally Newell was able to get to his feet and leave the ice. There was 1:32 remaining to be played in the period, which was simply added to the second period. Newell, nursing a suspected broken jaw, was sent to the hospital for X-rays. His departure presented a problem for there were no backups in the building. So the fifty-five-year-old Udvari, half in jest, said to the Islander trainer, "You got size eight-and-a-half skates?" Soon the trainer appeared with a pair of Bryan Trottier's skates. They were a perfect fit. Although it had been thirteen years since the NHL's supervisor of officials had worked a game, he took to the ice because he didn't want the game to be delayed a couple of hours.

What was amazing was not that Udvari stepped onto the ice after a so long an absence, though that, in itself, was a considerable feat. The impressive thing was how well Udvari refereed. Slow and tremulous at first, he returned to mid-season form by the end of the second period. He almost looked like he hadn't lost a step. His whistle was quick and decisive when he called his first penalty on Atlanta's Greg Fox for cross-checking Bob Nystrom. There was no doubt who was in charge. Two minutes later he disallowed a Trottier goal, saying Trottier's deflection occurred with his stick above shoulder height. Again he was firm. No one argued, except for Trottier, and even then it was more in jest than anything.

"That's a hell of a thing to do when I lend you my skates," said Trottier, whose Islanders nevertheless went on to earn a sloppy 4-2 win that night on Long Island. Udvari had officiated a good game. So good, in fact, that no one seemed to notice him, something which is regarded as the ultimate sign of a well-officiated game. When the game ended Udvari felt a strange sense of exhilaration. "I feel great," he said. "I play a lot of squash and this is like having a workout for forty-five to fifty minutes on a squash court. I enjoyed it. I thought it was great to get back out there."

He'd had little hesitation in donning Newell's jersey again. (He also wore his gray suit pants). "I thought that if I did the best I could, the players would co-operate with me—and they did." He had left the ice in 1966, and in the intervening thirteen years the game had grown considerably faster, while he had grown slower. "When you first get out there, things go pretty fast," he said. And he noticed too the size of the players. They were much bigger than what he remembered. "At least they look bigger. Maybe I just shrunk a little."

It was a historic night, for it was the first time someone had participated in an NHL game after election to the Hockey Hall of Fame. Gordie Howe became the second. Someone had to ask the question that night on Long Island: "Will you do another one?"

"No way," he shouted. "This is the last one."

Udvari still lives in Waterloo, where he runs a successful construction company. He also sits on the Hockey Hall of Fame selection committee.

Lefty Perkins
(Harry Sollenburger)

LEFTY PERKINS PICKED UP A COPY OF *USA TODAY* FROM THE newstand in Fayetteville, Pennsylvania, in the spring of 1994 and noticed that Goody Rosen, his old teammate from the Terriers, had died. It brought back a flood of memories of the two seasons Perkins had played with Rosen at Galt.

Perkins had distinguished himself during the last half of the 1949 season and helped the Terriers win the pennant before going home to Chambersburg, Pennsylvania, for the winter months. He thought he had one more season of ball in him and was looking forward to returning to Galt. He knew it would likely be his last season. But when he arrived in the spring of 1950 he was hit with a ten-game suspension by the league for using the fictitious name of Perkins. While the local media and fans tried to refer to him by his real name, Harry Sollenburger, even after half a century had elapsed he was still known as Lefty Perkins.

No matter, the suspension was a costly penalty. It was nearly a fifth of the season, and worse, he couldn't practise with the team under conditions of the suspension. So he sat out, and waited. Then, in late June, he made his debut. Things in Terrier Town had changed.

Padden was no longer there, and the dugout was not as friendly, even if his good buddy, Tex Kaiser, was still around. Something was missing, and there existed a friction that originated with American import pitcher Jim Bagby. Team morale sagged.

Sollenburger chalked up an impressive win that first game back, but because he had not prepared properly through spring training, his arm was not ready to go all out. Not surprisingly, he seriously injured his throwing arm. It was never the same again, though he did finish out the season.

One game stands out in his memory that summer of 1950. Galt was playing in Brantford. There had been a meeting of the Intercounty executive the night before in Galt, but Gus never mentioned anything about the meeting. In any event, Sollenburger was on the mound for Galt. He had a habit of putting his fingers to his mouth before every pitch, something he had done for years. But this night, only minutes after the game began, the first base umpire came over to Sollenburger and said something. Sollenburger heard him speak, but he was unable to make out what he had said. So he just continued pitching. A couple of pitches later, after he had again put his fingers to his mouth without wiping them off, the umpire simply walked over to the mound and ejected him from the game. Sollenburger couldn't believe it. As Sollenburger made for the dugout he saw Rosen cutting into Murray. "Gus was charging around the dugout with Rosen on him," he recalled.

Murray, it seemed, had forgotten to mention to Rosen and the players that at the meeting the previous night the issue of pitchers touching their mouths was brought up and it was decided that any pitcher who continued the practice would be immediately tossed from the game. It was a new ruling, one that Sollenburger, just back from a suspension, had no way of knowing. That about summed up his season after he injured his arm.

He kept throwing, giving all he had, but it was over. He knew he couldn't pitch. At least, not the way he wanted to. "I was there the whole year but I wasn't beginning to be the same pitcher," he said. It was a difficult decision to quit ball, but it was the right one. And he'd been thinking about it for a couple of seasons before he was forced to face the facts. He was too old, and his arm was shot. Perhaps if his arm had been strong he could have lasted another year or two. But he was through. The following spring he would go through a strange experience, for that was the first spring since the time he was a youngster when he didn't pick up his glove and spend most of his time at the ballpark.

Sollenburger was born on Christmas Day, 1920, and from the time he was a youngster baseball was all he thought about. Baseball had been his life. When he came to Galt in 1949 he'd already been to Canada thanks to baseball. He'd gone to Montreal and Toronto when he played Class AAA for Baltimore of the International League, but like so many other ballplayers, his war service had robbed him of some of his best playing days. Had the war not come along he might have made it to the majors. "I'd have been younger and that would have given me more of a shot, anyway."

In the years following that 1949 season Sollenburger thought often of the team they had back in Galt, and of his old teammates. He had good memories of those days. There was that one game in London when Padden said he wanted to catch Perkins. That game was one of the highlights of Sollenburger's career. Sollenburger never regretted playing in Canada, though he often wished they had taken a team picture. After so many years, it was difficult to remember what his teammates looked like.

Sollenburger believed Padden was one of the greatest managers he'd ever come across. "There isn't any doubt in my mind that, as a manager, he would have made it back to the majors except for one thing. Alcohol." He liked Padden, respected him. But he knew, perhaps better than most, that alcohol was his downfall. Padden was a good man, but like other good men, the bottle was a destructive force as he tried to carve out a managerial career. "That was a shame," he said, "because he was really knowledgeable about baseball. He had all the tools. I talked to different guys when I was with the Manchester Yankees, some of whom had been up to Newark and elsewhere, and they told me, 'This guy knows his baseball.'"

As for Murray, Sollenburger never forgot the little Galt Terrier president. "Everybody remembers him," he said nearly fifty years later. He was just as jittery as heck. What a character! A nervous wreck. Oh my golly, he was just a little nervous wreck. But he was a great promoter and they said he was a shrewd businessman. He was unquestionably why most of the imports came to Galt in '49. He and Tom Padden."

Sollenburger always believed Galt had the better team in '49, even though Brantford beat us in the playoffs. "They had a good team, but we had the best team," he said. "We had some good ballplayers." The strike was not something he was a party to. "I remember some of the players came up to me in the morning. I was in bed and I forget what the heck they said they were going to do. They wanted me to go along but I said I'm not going along. Forget it."

In the winter of 1951 Murray sent Sollenburger a letter asking him back for the 1951 season. But he knew how badly his arm had been the summer before; it had been a terrible year. Every start was misery. "I didn't enjoy that," he said. "Every time I threw I was awful." Still, he gave Murray's request some thought. "Finally I just decided it'd be ridiculous because I tried to throw at home and couldn't. That ended me."

Harry Sollenburger and his wife still live in Fayetteville, Pennsylvania, not far from his boyhood home in Chambersburg.

Umpire Johnny Kumornik, rear, explains a call to players.

Johnny Kumornik

MANY YEARS PASSED BEFORE I SAW JOHNNY KUMORNIK again. I arranged to meet him at the Waterloo Legion when I was back in Galt in the early 1990s.

We talked for a few hours that night.

"Christ, that team of yours," he said. "That was the best one I ever saw in the Intercounty, bar none."

Other things stood out in his mind, including the fire some kids set in the in-ground wooden ball box behind home plate, and he could remember the frozen ball episode with Gus. But the thing he remembered best was Warren's missed catch. To his last day he would remember that.

"Warren should have had that ball," he said. "I could have caught that ball in my jockstrap."

Kumornik, who would one day become the owner of both the Waterloo Tigers and the Kitchener Panthers, could sympathize with Gus. Running an Intercounty team was not a profit-making venture; indeed, he knew he'd be lucky to simply break even. Now, seeing him again after so many years, he related the story that Goman, considered one of the best operators in the league, eventually lost ownership of the Waterloo team due to mismanagement. "He was in the insurance business," said Kumornik, "and he would bring guys in there [to play] and then stick 'em for insurance. He was tricky." So, by the mid-1950s, when Goman lost the club, it was Kumornik who took over. "I got that one for nothing," he said. "And then the next year Gallie [Gallinger] went under in Kitchener. So I went up to the Legion when they were auctioning off the ball club and Tim Turow was sitting beside me at the time."

"Why don't you put in a bid for it," said Turow.

"Okay," said Kumornik with little hesitation. He stuck up one finger to signal he was offering one dollar for the club. Turow laughed. "What the hell," he said. "You'll never get the goddamned club for a dollar." But Kumornik, much to his surprise, got it. No one else had even bothered to bid. He already owned the Waterloo Tigers and was now the owner of the rival Kitchener Panthers.

What's more, he now owned a player, Joe Yosurak, whom Goman had brought up from Pennsylvania to play for Waterloo but whom Kumornik, upon taking over the Tigers, had cut. Frank Udvari, who had played for Galt in 1949, was, by the mid-'50s, before Kumornik became the Kitchener owner, Gallinger's business manager with the Panthers. He showed up at Kumornik's restaurant one day near the end of the season, just after Yosurak had been cut.

"I hear you've cut Yosurak," he said.

"That's right," said Kumornik.

"What do you want for him?" asked Udvari.

"A hundred bucks," answered Kumornik.

"I'll give you ten."

"Okay," said Kumornik, "I'll take 'er."

So when he bought the Panthers the next year at auction, he reacquired the services of Yosurak, a player he didn't want, for a dollar, and he had become the owner of a club nobody else wanted. He always figured he had actually been given nine dollars to buy the club since Yosurak's sale the previous year had netted him ten dollars. Such were the circumstances of the Intercounty in the early 1950s. Kumornik had been around long enough to know that, in most cases, owning an Intercounty club was a money-losing proposition. Owners relied on local businesses to come through and bail them out, hoping that their losses wouldn't be too great. And they all knew—Kumornik, Murray, Pennell, and Goman—that it was vital to hold the concession rights, just as it was vital to draw out lots of fans.

A few seasons later, in 1953, the Waterloo Tigers won the Intercounty pennant, but, despite drawing good crowds, they were in the hole when the playoffs began. "Before we started the playoffs," said Kumornik, "I was three thousand bucks in the hole. When we finished the seven-game series with Listowel, Chrissakes, I wound up with eight dollars and five cents to the good." Had the season not gone on as long as it did, he would have lost his shirt.

When I think back on the summer of '49, Kumornik is always there. Circumstance meant that he worked many of our games that season, and he was the head umpire for our playoff series.

Johnny Kumornik died in the fall of 1998.

The Lowry Street gang. Wes Lillie is second from right.

Wes Lillie

W ES LILLIE CONTINUED TO PLAY IN THE INTERCOUNTY for several years after that 1949 season. He was always regarded as a strong fielder and a weak hitter, and he never shook that perception. After being traded to the Waterloo Tigers early in the 1950 season, Lillie played a key role in helping Waterloo win an all-Ontario title.

On September 25, 1950, it was "no-hit" Lillie who got the key hit to win a marathon twenty-one-inning game against Brantford in the third game of the senior Intercounty finals. The win gave Waterloo a 3-1 stranglehold on the series. Neither an Alberta-born fog, an eclipse of the moon, or a screening of *Frankenstein* at the Waterloo Theatre could cheat the Tigers, or Lillie, out of their share of the limelight that night. The game, played at Waterloo Park, lasted five hours—an all-time Intercounty endurance record. When it ended, on what was described as Lillie's Texas Leaguer, Waterloo had scored a 7-6 win. It was an impressive victory. The Tigers erased a five-run deficit and then struggled through eleven innings with a makeshift lineup after three players were expelled from the game. The contest was won and lost by both sides at least half a dozen times, but the spotlight fell, for most of the game, on the relief hurling duel between Brantford's Alf Gavey and Waterloo's Al Dumouchelle.

Kumornik worked behind the plate that night. It was the longest game he had ever been involved in. What most people didn't know, however, was that he had umpired a seventeen-inning game in Kitchener that afternoon. Either one of those games would have been exhausting, but working both—thirty-eight innings in twelve hours—must have been a record in itself.

Pitcher Joe Yosurak had started the game for Waterloo while Bob Whitcher had gotten the nod for the Red Sox. Yosurak was an interesting player. He first came up to Canada from the Pennsylvania coal mines to play for the Tigers. He'd played pro ball with Whitey Ford, among others. Upon arriving in the Kitchener-Waterloo area he happened to stop at Johnny Kumornik's restaurant in downtown Kitchener en route to Waterloo. That's where Kumornik first met him. Kumornik quickly realized that Yosurak had a penchant for swearing. "He really used a lot of vulgar words," Kumornik said. "Every other word was 'fuck this' or 'fuck that.'"

Lillie was there when an ordained minister, who was also a good ballplayer, tried out for the Waterloo team. As might be expected, it didn't take long for Yosurak's foul mouth to irritate the minister. So the minister went up to Yosurak and politely asked him to stop swearing. It was a reasonable request. There was no need for that kind of language.

"What the fuck do you mean?" Yosurak shot back. The minister, who didn't make the team, kept his mouth shut after that. He could see there was no hope. Yosurak stayed on in the Kitchener area and married a local woman, eventually taking a job with the City of Waterloo's cemetery department. He lived out the rest of his life in Waterloo.

In the twenty-one-inning marathon in late September of 1950, Yosurak started on the mound for the Tigers. Before two innings were up, the Red Sox held a 5-0 lead. In the third inning some pajama-clad freshmen from Waterloo College, the forerunner of Wilfrid Laurier University, paraded in front of the home-plate bleachers. It was just one more unforgettable moment in the historic game. Five hours and 103 put-outs later the Red Sox players solemnly walked off the field, each of them cursing Lillie and Dumouchelle. Dumouchelle had relieved Yosurak in the eleventh after Yosurak had given up six runs on twelve hits, and was credited with the win after going ten and two-thirds innings in relief. He played superbly, holding Brantford to two hits and striking out eleven while walking three. But it was Lillie who was the hero of the day.

It had been a game no one would soon forget. As the game progressed the air grew cool and it became quite foggy. It was late

September. In the dugouts were small heaters that the players could use to warm their hands and feet before going out into the field. At one point, midway through the game, Goman took his car into the outfield with men inside swinging the doors in an attempt to blow the fog away.

Gavey, Brantford's ace, relieved Whitcher in the eleventh inning and fanned eleven while walking two. Between Gavey and Dumouchelle, the game was a thriller of epic proportions. But the fan turnout that cool September night was only moderate. Lillie had gotten his game-winning hit when Dumouchelle drew a walk and Bob Fisher moved him to third with a two-base hit. Then up walked Lillie, who even then was highly regarded for his fielding but was virtually dismissed as a hitter. Though Gavey was a pitcher feared by most players in the league, Lillie had been almost relieved to see him. He'd always had luck hitting Gavey. Lillie remembered something that Padden had told him the year before. "One of the things Tom Padden always tried to tell me was to try to hit it back down the middle," he said. So he walked up to the plate in the twenty-first inning for his tenth at-bat. He had already managed two hits. Everyone in the ballpark knew that the game had to end soon. But few figured it would be Lillie who would win it.

Lillie wasn't one of them. As he walked to the batter's box he took a deep, almost solemn breath. Pennell said something to Mike King about how Lillie had been up so many times that he had to get another hit. He, too, had a notion that Lillie, who everyone dismissed as a poor hitter, could get the game-winner. He didn't feel good about the way Lillie walked to the plate, though it was only a sense Pennell had, nothing more. Often Pennell and King would act a little superstitious during games, trying to stand in the same location where they had stood when a previous batter had struck out, for instance. When Lillie came up for the tenth time that night, they remembered where they had been standing during his last at-bat, and they stood there again. But now Lillie worried Pennell. How many times had Lillie been up? Was it seven, eight, ten? And he'd already had a couple of hits. Pennell figured that if you gave anybody enough chances they're bound to come through. The law of averages would work in Lillie's favour. Pennell turned to King and told him he had a bad feeling; that Lillie was going to get the winning hit.

"He's gonna kill us," Pennell said under his breath. "He's been up six or seven times already. He's gonna get a hit." That would be typical of Wes, Pennell now thought. With Dumouchelle on third and

Fisher on first, Lillie knew he could win the game. Then he heard somebody say something. He turned and saw Brantford playing manager Bob Whitcher speaking to him. Whitcher was trying to throw him off.

"It'd be just like a little bastard like you to win this," Whitcher said.

"Fuck you!" replied the indignant Lillie. Whitcher's words meant nothing to Lillie, though he could not let them go unchallenged. He was purely focused on the game, and on what he needed to do. There were runners at first and third and no outs. Lillie wasn't looking to belt any home runs. He remembered Padden's advice to hit it back up the middle. If anything, Whitcher's comment seemed to give Lillie more incentive than he already had. Whitcher was right, Lillie thought. It is going to take some little bastard like me to win this game. Never for a moment did he think he was not going to get that hit. "So I got on the ball and I didn't hit it hard. Hell, I never hit it hard." The ball lined out over Pedro Juarez's head at short.

"Geez," said Pennell with a sour expression on his face. "To get killed like that, by a little bleeder that just fell in there." Later Pennell would say to Lillie: "You struck out six times that night, and then in the twenty-first inning you get a little blooper out there with two out and two on." Pennell also joked to Lillie that he would never forgive him. Said Lillie: "Everybody always said it was a Texas Leaguer, but I always said it was a line drive." That was typical for Lillie. Even when he got a winning hit in twenty-one innings to end the longest-played game on the books, he got little respect. Sure, his name made all the headlines the next day—at least, in papers that came out in the afternoon—but it was as if he had lucked out on the hit, blooping a Texas Leaguer to score the runner rather than hitting a line drive up the middle. In truth, Pennell said Lillie never got as much credit for his late-game heroics as he deserved because all the deadlines had long since passed when the game continued past midnight. Radio stations broadcast Lillie's feat, but many newspapers couldn't report fully on the historic game and Lillie's big hit until the following day, and by then it was old news.

The fact is that throughout Lillie's Intercounty career, he got plenty of key hits. He was never a batting champion, or a home-run king, but he could be counted on in the clutch.

There had been two thousand paying customers when the game began at 8 P.M. Monday, but by game's end, at 12:57 A.M. Tuesday, the newspaper estimated only two hundred remained. Many of them, said Kumornik, had driven over because the lights were on so late at

Waterloo Park. "People were curious," he said. "They wanted to see what was going on that late." Indeed, Kumornik's account differs from the official reports of the game. "That was the only game where there were more people at the end than at the beginning because people had to see why the lights were on so late," he said.

Long after he hung up his glove, Lillie was still trying to battle the lifelong knock that he couldn't hit. Perhaps it was only natural that Lillie, having started in the senior Intercounty with a powerhouse Galt team that boasted the famed Murderer's Row of Creedon, Kaiser, Rosen, and Warren, would get little respect as a hitter. But it was always an unfair rap.

One early winter day some forty-five years after that summer of '49, Lillie, who lived in nearby Kitchener, returned to town with his two scrapbooks in tow. They were freshly uncovered from his basement.

"I want to show you something," he said, opening one of the books with their browned and brittle newspaper clippings that chronicle his baseball years. "You've got to see this," he said, pointing to a box score, "because this louses me off."

He was pointing now at a headline that said "Lillie the Hero." It was the headline that appeared the day after his twenty-one-inning hit won Game Three of the Intercounty final series in 1950 against Brantford. "You tell Eddie," he said. Eddie was Ed Heather, owner of a sports awards store and long-time Galt sportsman. Heather—his stepson Rob Ducey switched from softball to hardball as a teenager and eventually broke into the majors with the Toronto Blue Jays—was only a youngster back then but eventually became a trainer with the Terriers and the Galt Hornets hockey team. He never fails to mention Lillie's lack of hitting prowess when talk swings around to those Intercounty years. But Heather also said that Lillie could get key hits when they were needed.

So Lillie continues. "And I'll show you something else. Errors: None. You tell Heather that's enough of that crap." To be fair, the myth that Lillie couldn't hit didn't originate with Heather. Heather jokes about Lillie's hitting, but stands up for his clutch hitting. Others haven't been so charitable.

"That's 1945," Lillie says, pointing to another clipping from his scrapbooks. "Nineteen forty-five," he repeats slowly, as if even he can't believe how long ago that was. He was sixteen that season. He turns the pages, and suddenly it is 1949. August 1949. The dream summer, one that he probably wouldn't believe himself if it hadn't happened. He looks immediately to the box score, then points. "I got a base hit. Show Heather that." Then he turns to another clipping. July 1949. "Base hit. Show Heather!" Another clipping. More evidence in Lillie's defence. He is building a case. "Look," he says, "I had two hits there. Jeez, Eddie!"

On other pages can be found news of the trade that sent Lillie to Waterloo for Gallinger, and the trade that brought him back to Galt. Each page holds special meaning for Lillie, for on these pages are his personal history. So many baseball memories. Good memories. Good days. Good summers. "See that?" he asks. "What's that say?" It says he had two hits in three at-bats. There are numerous other clippings that attest to his hitting ability. In other games he went three-for-five at the plate, and one-for-three, or two-for-five. "Show Heather that." The box scores show that Lillie had hits in most games.

Lillie ended his Intercounty playing days in the late 1950s, finishing up where he had begun, with the Terriers. Not too many years later he became involved with the Galt Terriers senior hockey club in an executive capacity, and over the next decade or two he helped mould the team into one of Canada's finest. The team changed its name to the Hornets in the early 1960s and won several Allan Cups, emblematic of senior hockey supremacy in Canada. Lillie also did some radio work as a commentator for Junior A games in Kitchener and was a key member of the baseball Terrier executive as they won two more Intercounty titles in the late 1970s and early 1980s.

Near the end of his playing career, he took delight in a special night for groundskeeper Jack Spencer, who was retiring. It was August 13, 1958, almost a decade following that summer of '49, and Lillie, who had been traded back to Galt from Waterloo by then, helped present Spencer with an easy chair. It was officially called "Jack Spencer Night" and Spencer was surrounded by gifts at home plate. The ceremony preceded Galt's final regular-season game, which they went on to win 5-3 over the St. Thomas Elgins. Spencer had been in charge of the ballpark for almost forty years and said he was hoping to take a trip to England as soon as it was possible.

Terrier captain Wray Upper, who had played in the San Francisco Giants organization and was regarded as the best third baseman in the league, and Lillie, by then the oldest member of the team, gave Spencer the easy chair on behalf of the Terriers. Two youngsters, still dressed in their ball uniforms after an early evening minor game, gave Spencer a humidor of cigars. When it was all over, Spencer, wearing a suit and tie, retrieved his rake and went back to work one final time, like he had done hundreds of times over the years.

Jack Spencer Night signalled the end of another era in the life of Galt baseball. Lillie could appreciate the night because he knew his playing days would soon be over. But this was Spencer's night. Lillie's would be later. That night, Lillie paused to think about how Dickson Park would never be the same without Spencer, because he carried the continuity of the seasons with him. He had seen the Intercounty from it's earliest days, and he knew the Terriers and what they had been and would become. Now he was leaving as an old man, and the seasons of the Terriers would never be the same. No one could say they would be better. No one was willing to say they would be worse. But everyone knew, even if they weren't saying, that baseball at Dickson Park was going to be different, and when the new era began the following spring, it would be a modern era, with little connection to the old days when the game of baseball, and the century, were both young.

Fans knew that Lillie's days as a ballplayer were numbered by then. In 1949 he had been young; now he was older, wiser, slower. He had known Spencer when he was a kid, when he would sneak by him into the grounds. Spencer had been as much a part of the ballpark as the green grass. It would be strange, he thought, not seeing him out there. His thoughts drifted back to 1949 when Padden had taken him aside and shown him some pointers.

Just days before Jack Spencer Night, Lillie had figured prominently in a 7-6 Terrier win over Brantford. "Lillie was the key to the offense," said the newspaper. "It's a strange position for Wes who has never been known as a strong stick man. But of late, his base hits have been more frequent and more timely. His improved plate efficiency has coincided with his move to second base. At the keystone Lillie has been solid and a steady performer through the stretch run. In the last three Terrier wins, Wes has poked five base hits."

Not surprisingly, much of the 1949 season was in his scrapbooks. On one page Galt's Murderer's Row of Creedon, Kaiser, Rosen, and Warren are posed kneeling with bats in hand, looking like they mean business. "We had some characters on that team," he recalled. "Creedon was one mean son of a bitch," says Lillie. "Christ, he could hit. He tattooed that right-field wall all season. Another time he had Gus against the wall one night." Lillie, who was going out back of the ballpark to get his bicycle for the ride home, saw the whole thing. There was Creedon holding Gus up in the air and threatening him, saying he was going to inhale him and then spit him out.

It would have been impossible for 1949 not to have left its mark on Lillie. He was only twenty that summer, a perfect time for him to live, and learn from Padden and Rosen and the rest. By the time his playing days were over he realized just how special those days were, and how extraordinary that summer of 1949 was. "That was the end of an era," he laments. "Those days are gone forever. We won't see them again." If only they could be recaptured ... but they never will. And at the centre of it all was Murray. No one was more extraordinary than Hustlin' Gus. "You have to understand," Lillie would say, "Gus was a character. I swear to Christ he could come in now and start a league all by himself. And he'd make it interesting." The often frazzled Galt president and promoter was a busy man that year, running from one thing to the next. "If Gus was selling wallpaper at the store, he was running," says Lillie. "Gus was a character." A character who loved baseball.

As did Lillie. Baseball had always been his first love, from the long ago days when he was a youngster growing up with the Lowry Street gang. But unlike many gifted young ballplayers, Lillie, who continues to work for a large insurance company, never aspired to play in the major leagues.

"No," he says candidly. "I never thought I could make it to the majors."

"Why not?"

"Because I didn't think I could hit." He pauses for a moment. "Don't tell Heather that."

"Well, what about the myth. How did something like that ever get started?"

"What," asks Lillie, "the myth that I couldn't hit?"

"Yes."

"Because there's a lot of truth to it."

Tulsa Tommy Warren

TOMMY WARREN DIDN'T STAY LONG IN GALT AFTER THE season ended. The day after our final loss, Warren deposited a large sum of money at the Imperial Bank. Bill Gregg, the bank manager, alerted Murray to Warren's situation. When Warren asked Gus to sign his release papers in preparation for his return to Oklahoma, Murray refused. There was no way Warren should have had that kind of money. Besides, he had heard stories about that missed catch in the seventh game. So Warren had someone else sign the release papers to take the money back across the border, and then he was gone. He had not asked Murray about the prospect of playing for the Terriers in 1950. After he failed to show in Tulsa, where trouble was waiting for him, the authorities began a search. His whereabouts were unaccounted for.

When he had arrived in Galt, no one knew that less than a month before he left Tulsa that spring, Warren had been in serious trouble with the law. In early March he had been arrested by his former boss, Tulsa sheriff George Blaine, and charged on a felony count of obtaining money under false pretenses. The arrest had drawn a good deal of publicity because Warren, a hometown star—he had graduated from Tulsa Central High School and then enlisted in the navy the day the United States entered World War II—and deputy sheriff, no less, was well-known around town. Kids looked up to him. People respected him solely because of his baseball ability. Many liked to rub shoulders with him, if only to say they knew the former major-leaguer. Baseball, Warren knew, could carry a man a long way in life. For one thing, being a star player meant there were certain advantages that came to him. Doors were opened, whereas without baseball, he knew they would have been shut solid.

On March 24, not long after Warren was first arrested, two new charges were laid for alleged fake car deals. The trial was set to take place in district court in April, which would give Warren time, he thought, to head off to Galt for the home opener. But State crown attorney Elmer Adams had what he believed to be a strong case. Adams's plan to set all three cases against Warren on the next district court jury docket was announced shortly after Warren pleaded innocent to the two new embezzlement charges in common pleas court. Two Tulsa residents had lost thousands to Warren's schemes. Lee R. Eller was reportedly swindled out of $13,800, while Warren W. Fulton lost $2,200 in another shady deal. The two new charges followed demands by four used-car dealers and a tavern operator that additional charges be filed against Warren covering part of the $20,000 they reportedly lost to him. Warren was accused of promising his victims new cars that were never delivered.

But Warren, who had been released on $1,500 bond paid by professional bondsman C.B. McAllister on the first charge, pleaded innocent before common pleas judge H.E. Chambers. McAllister now put up two new thousand-dollar bonds for the popular pitcher. Preliminary hearings were scheduled for the following Monday, but Warren waived his right to the hearings on all three charges and Adams was ready to prosecute the best of the three cases first for the opening trial. It was customary for prosecutors, when a defendant was slated for more than one trial on a docket, to try one and strike the others for trial on a later docket. One charge alleged that Warren, acting as agent for Elder on February 4, "unlawfully, willfully, wrongfully, fraudulently and feloniously" appropriated $6,600 entrusted to him by Elder. Elder told Adams that he lost a total of $13,800 to Warren in two car deals and sought to file two charges, but Adams decided to file one charge for Elder and one for Fulton. Fulton claimed that Warren bilked him out of $2,200 which he entrusted to the former deputy sheriff. But there were other victims in the car-deal racket who were indicating that they, too, might file charges later.

When Warren was first charged in February, the thirty-year-old Tulsa native was the acting deputy sheriff in Tulsa. Gilbert Asher, a reporter for the *Tulsa World* newspaper, wrote that Warren had bilked his friends in order to help with his gambling losses, then estimated to exceed $70,000.

The headlines came soon afterward. Tulsa's Deputy Sheriff Warren, one story said, had been charged with obtaining money under false pretenses. Warren had been released from the Tulsa Oilers baseball club the previous year when his betting activities were discovered by the team's management. On December 11, 1948, he had bilked his boss, Tulsa's sheriff, of more than two thousand dollars. He promised new cars from Detroit at wholesale prices. People turned their money over to the popular pitching star, but no cars turned up. He had gambled away roughly $70,000, the report said, including nearly $40,000 of other people's money. But his wife stood by him. "Tommy is a grand fellow," she said. "He just got entrapped by those gamblers. Why, he wouldn't have had this happen for a million dollars. It isn't that it hurts Tommy so much, or me, but it is what it does to David and the hundreds of boys who depended upon Tommy." Indeed, Warren had been revered by Tulsa youth for several years.

Gradually details came to light. Warren had left home and his job to go off to gamble. "He was like a crazy man," Mrs. Warren said. "He has suffered a thousand deaths since he got into trouble, which started right after the ball season ended. He had a good deal arranged in Texas but had to borrow money to swing it. Then the deal fell through and Tommy started gambling. Why, those gamblers hounded Tommy to death, telling him they had good tips and sure things and he was so gullible he would go right ahead."

But Warren was not eager to face the music. He had left town suddenly the previous Saturday night after losing seven thousand dollars in bets on basketball games and a prize fight. The sheriff's office was awaiting his voluntary return, but while Warren was on the loose, county authorities were wading through a maze of reports relating to Warren's misdeeds. Friends, associates, and acquaintances fell victim to his story that he could buy new automobiles at wholesale prices at factories in Detroit. According to a list left with Warren's wife, six people gave him a total of $24,760 for new cars he never delivered.

The money was lost by Warren during a wild, seven-month gambling spree that saw him at dice tables and betting establishments in the Tulsa area and throughout the Southwest. Blaine knew he gambled, but until then had no idea he had a problem. Two days later Warren returned, but he denied any wrongdoing. Blaine wasn't amused. He claimed he had given Warren $2,135 as payment in advance for a new car at factory list price. Blaine handed Warren the money on December 11. Christmas came and went, and still no car. Blaine waited patiently as Warren offered excuse after excuse. The final straw came in mid-February when Warren racked up enormous gambling debts and fled the city. He later admitted to collecting $38,755 in cash from Tulsans, all of whom thought they were buying new cars at bargain prices. Meantime, Warren was sinking deeper into debt. He probably realized long before his debts totalled $70,000 that all was hopeless. But he kept trying to recoup his losses, and sank deeper and deeper in the hole.

A day before Warren appeared in court to post a bond of $1,500, he was still attempting to obtain cash payments from Tulsans he named as gamblers in a statement given to the county attorney. He still believed he could make partial restitution to at least ten people he had bilked. He admitted to having lost more than $50,000 to local gamblers in just a three-week period. He claimed to have lost another $16,000 earlier at Oakhurst-area clubs. At that time, only the sheriff had filed a complaint. Warren was hoping to get a quick seven thousand dollar infusion of cash to satisfy his boss and Eller and Fulton.

There was also a report that a Tulsa man, hearing of Warren's troubles with the law, had offered Warren a new Pontiac automobile, "which Warren could turn over to the sheriff." Sheriff Blaine refused to name the make of automobile he expected to buy from Warren. He also refused to reveal the number of raids made on Tulsa-area establishments suspected of harbouring gambling activities in the previous four months. Blaine was also unwilling to answer several questions from *Tulsa World* reporters concerning his deputy.

Clearly, Tulsans were interested in Warren's activities, just as people who are accustomed to reading glowing reports of an athlete—only to find that he was not who he appeared—are eager to do. Warren had been accustomed to positive press in the past, but when the news reports of his gambling activities and the subsequent criminal charges hit the papers in early 1949, everything seemed bad. It was quite a change. Just two years earlier, in the summer of 1947, Warren and long-time *Tulsa World Tribune* sports editor Jack Charvat conducted the state's first junior baseball school under sponsorship of the *Tribune*. It was only a one-week school but was so successful, drawing more than 1,200 youngsters, that it had to be extended to three weeks.

People in Tulsa had followed his career the same way people in Manchester, New Hampshire had followed Tom Padden's. Warren had joined the Brooklyn Dodgers in 1944 after his war service, when Rosen was with the Dodgers—Murray once had a picture of the two in their Dodger uniforms—but he was no longer the same Tommy Warren. He had been severely wounded during troop landings at Casablanca in North Africa and spent eleven months recovering in the hospital. Still, in his first major-league start with the Dodgers he beat the St. Louis Cardinals 10-4. He played ball for the next couple of years, travelling to several different countries to do so. He had plenty of accomplishments in an eighteen-year professional career, including the 1945 season when he helped the Montreal Royals to an International League championship. He was a fearsome hitter, batting .330 in fifty-eight games. And, in 1946, he posted a 20-6 record for the Oklahoma City Oilers.

When Warren, who by then had a year-old son, David, pleaded innocent to the 1949 charges, it did him little good. He was convicted on all three counts and faced at least a three-year prison sentence. But he appealed the jury verdict and, having already been in contact with Murray, was permitted by the court to go to Canada to play ball that summer. He came north with some big debts haunting him and no realistic way of ever being able to make good on them. And back home, he was being pressured by Tulsa gamblers to pay up or suffer the consequences. He may have been a popular figure in Tulsa in the past, but money was money, and a debt was a serious matter.

That October he failed to show up, as promised, in a Tulsa court as Lee Eller was awarded a $13,800 judgment by district court judge John Ladner in a civil suit designed to recoup his lost money. Meantime, the criminal charge Warren had appealed was still to be heard. Finally, in late fall, Warren's conviction and three-year sentence were overturned by the appellate court.

It only took a couple of years before Warren was in trouble with the law again. In the meantime, he had served as playing manager for teams in Seminole and Miami, Oklahoma, which wasn't unusual since he had managed teams in Corpus Christi and Borger, Texas, prior to arriving in Galt. And before 1949 he would also work as Blaine's deputy sheriff in the off-seasons.

The following June he was convicted of bilking a Tulsa used-car dealer of $6,600 and sentenced to three years in state prison despite several pleas by Warren supporters for parole. Again Warren sought to appeal, and after serving notice of his appeal, was given ninety days to lodge it. County attorney Lewis J. Bicking had pushed for the three-year prison terms and, although Judge Taylor acknowledged receiving some strong pressure and several letters recommending probation for Warren, he thought a jail term was in order.

"Much as I would like to give probation to Mr. Warren, I do not feel it would be consistent with the administration of criminal justice if I did so," he said. "We should bear in mind that there is a difference between a public officer who commits a crime and an ordinary citizen who violates the law. In deciding such cases," he said, "we must attempt to deter other public officials from violating the law."

Taylor didn't like what he saw as the breakdown of moral fibre in the community in recent years, especially "in government employees, some of whom feel they can get away with anything."

Ironically, the judge hinted that had Warren entered a guilty plea he might have stood a better chance for probation. Warren's lawyer, John Ward Jr., had previously indicated he would plead Warren guilty to the charge, but when Warren appeared before the judge he had pled not guilty. Again the bondsman McAllister put up a three-thousand-dollar bond for Warren, who was at the time playing manager for the Miami, Oklahoma, baseball team in the KOM Class D league.

This time his conviction was upheld and Warren went to prison. But he was back out of jail the following spring, and he expressed an interest in returning to Canada. He got in touch with the Guelph Maple Leafs, writing a letter to Guelph secretary Jim Kendrick. In Galt, Murray had already gone on record as saying Warren would not be back. Wrote one sportswriter: "The two didn't see eye to eye in '49, and their relations were so strained that Gus, in some unaccountable manner, came in contact with Tommy's bony knuckles." Indeed, Murray wore a king-sized mouse for a week after the encounter, but he always explained it away by saying it was caused by a foul tip.

Guelph never did respond to Warren's letter. He was too expensive for their tastes, and besides, they'd heard about the things he had done in Galt.

By 1967 Warren was the owner and operator of the Woodlawn Lounge at 3525 East 51st Street. That June a story appeared in the *World Tribune* about Warren, "the one-time Brooklyn Dodger and Tulsa Oiler pitching star who stays close to the game by working with youngsters." He had only one losing season in eighteen years of professional ball, the story said. "The righthander spends a good deal of his spare time now working with handicapped youngsters and young aspiring baseball players."

Warren explained how he got his start with minor ballplayers: "The late Bill Skelly of Skelly Oil Co. got me interested in the little ones in 1947 when he asked me to visit the Tulsa Children's Home, and I have tried to work with them ever since." Warren said young boys could retain correct instructions in the fundamentals better than older ones. "That's why I like to work with them," he said. "If you get them started right at an early age, they have a much better chance of succeeding in baseball. I try to stress that all-around ability and determination can mean success on the diamond as well as size or strength."

Through his entire pro career, Warren had never been replaced by a pinch-hitter or a pinch-runner. He had been in the big leagues, and youngsters looked up to him. That May his only son, David, completed his first year at Southwestern College in Winfield, Kansas.

To outward appearances it seemed that Warren had turned things around. Then, in early November of 1967, Warren was arrested for buying merchandise with a bogus cheque.

December came and went and Warren checked into the Ramada Inn in Tulsa on January 1, 1968. The next day he picked up a loaded 16-gauge shotgun and fired it into his chest. He died instantly. He was fifty. A short note was all he left behind, saying he intended taking his life. His son, his father, Fay W. Warren, and a brother, Lawrence R., both of 2109 West Easton Street, survived him.

News of his death never made it back to Galt.

Johnny Clark

Gus Murray always said Johnny Clark was one of the nicest guys on the 1949 Galt Terriers. "He was a real gentleman," said Murray. Clark, one of the few homebrews on the team, didn't like the way some of the imports wanted to go out on strike during the playoffs against Brantford. "Not everybody was in favour of the strike," he said, "but you had to go along with it." The Terriers were never the same after that. "It took a little bit of the fight out of the team." Still, he respected the Brantford Red Sox and their two aces, Gibbs and Gavey. "At any given time either one of them could put you down," he said. "And Gibbs—oh, could he throw that ball. He could throw it like it was a golf ball." But Clark also respected his own teammates and knew, from being a catcher, how good Perkins and Shelton were. "If Perkins was on you couldn't hit the guy," he remembered.

Like a lot of players, Clark had been through the war. In 1943 he enlisted at Hamilton and became an engine room artificer. From there he was shipped overseas early in 1944. It was while he was on the troop ship *Andes* that he saw a familiar face. It belonged to Ebbie Edminson from Brantford, someone Clark had played against in the junior Intercounty. Edminson was a great hockey player and a good second baseman. They talked a lot on their way across the Atlantic, and they even discussed the possibility that they might never return. Later, after the war ended and Clark was back in Canada he learned that Edminson had been killed overseas.

Clark was stationed at a naval base in Scotland, before being moved onto the British battleship *Nelson*, where he stayed through the D-Day battle. He was a couple of miles from shore that June day bombarding the German fortifications. "We'd take turns, all the ships, going in circles. It was really something. There were planes flying around all the time, PT boats going around the ships, smoke screens. You often wonder how you got through it." They almost didn't. The *Nelson* hit a mine and was damaged, but Clark survived. Afterwards he went to Southampton, where the *Nelson* linked up with a convoy going to Philadelphia to undergo repairs. They made it across the Atlantic just after Christmas, and he stayed at the naval barracks before returning to Canada on New Year's Day, 1945.

But just before that, he had signed on to go to the south Pacific for the battle against Japan. "Then, a day or so before we were going to leave, we were all drafted off." The atomic age had begun. "Boy, were we mad."

Returning to Halifax, he was drafted onto a Tribal-class destroyer, the *Sioux*, and ended up in the Mediterranean. "Then we got flashed a message and we had to turn around." They returned across the Atlantic, going through the Panama Canal to Vancouver, with stops in San Pedro and Hollywood, where they got shore leave for three days. Returning east across Canada by train, he was stationed in Hamilton before getting his release from the navy late in 1945. He was married the next year and two years later got a job at Butler Metal, where he remained until his retirement in 1987.

Clark played Intercounty ball for a few more seasons after the summer of 1949, and then played with the Preston Intermediates for a couple years. He had figured Padden would be returning to coach in 1950, and, like a lot of local people, was surprised when he didn't. But no matter. Clark had a job to do. "All we did was play ball," he said. "I was just glad to have the chance to play."

He would run into Gus, and Lillie, and Kaiser from time to time. "I used to kid Wes," he laughed. "Gus is still jumpy and I used to say, 'Hey, Wes, you're getting to be just like Gus.'" It was all in good fun. Kaiser would rib them too. They had a lot of baseball years together. Clark recalls someone once saying to Wes: "Hey, Wes, are you related to Gus? Are you his son?"

It was typical of Clark that what he remembered most about the 1949 Terriers was not a specific game or play, though there were many that warranted attention, but rather the men he played with and against. The scores are all forgotten now. Or, at least, most of them are. The years have done that. But Clark would never forget the guys who made up the Terriers that summer. And they never forgot him.

Johnny Clark was active into the autumn of 1995. He was curling one morning—something he dearly loved—when he had to sit down. He mentioned he felt light-headed. It wasn't like him to complain, or sit out. His friends noticed his colour go white, and that he was perspiring. They suggested calling an ambulance, but Clark would have none of that. He would be all right, he said. All he needed to do was rest, perhaps go home. It was his good fortune that his friends didn't listen to him. The ambulance got there just in time. A minute or two later and he would have died. He suffered a major heart attack that morning, and they lost him several times both on the way to the hospital and while there. But almost miraculously he pulled through. Johnny Clark was never one to quit. The doctors said if he had arrived at the hospital any later, he wouldn't have made it. He had never really been sick in his life, nor had he suffered any medical condition more severe than a bad knee, something catchers often contend with in their later years. Now he was forced to slow down. It wasn't easy. Indeed, he hated the restrictions on his life after the heart attack. Still, he felt lucky to be alive.

That winter his curling buddies continued on, going to the rink once a week for their fellowship. They missed their friend dearly. It was a pleasure to hang out with Clark again, if only briefly, all these years later, and to share a few laughs. He was one of the guys. He'd always been one of the guys, and everybody loved him for it.

Jeff Shelton

JEFF SHELTON RETURNED TO THE TERRIERS FOR THE 1950 SEASON and had another good summer on the mound, though it was not a pleasant one. His Terrier teammate Jim Bagby, who'd had a lengthy career in the majors, was on him constantly. Bagby hated blacks and was always telling Shelton he'd better go change in the cattle barns with the rest of the livestock. Shelton expected such talk from opposing players, but when it came from his own teammate, Galt became a less friendly place to play. Not surprisingly, he went to Kitchener in 1951, even though Bagby didn't return, and then, in 1952, he returned to the U.S. to play with the Cleveland Buckeyes.

By then his baseball career was winding down. He played his last season in 1955 at home in Buffalo, in the Municipal (MUNY) League, where he could be close to his wife and son. Some of his friends in Buffalo had talked him into playing one final season with them. Then, in one game, he hit two home runs, a triple, and a double. "This is it," he told his teammates. "No more baseball for me." That was the end. His teammates laughed when he said that, not knowing he was serious. But he was. He knew it was right to end it there. So Jeff Shelton went out on top. That last game would always be one of his fondest baseball memories.

Years later he returned to Galt's Dickson Park for "Jeff Shelton Night." The popular pitcher, Galt's Little Satchmo, as his teammates and the media called him in '49, was showered with gifts. It was a moving moment for the Buffalo pitcher as Galt fans, who never forgot him, had a proper goodbye.

He went on to win an American Grand National age-group skeet shooting championship and had a wall full of shooting trophies to prove the extraordinary nature of his hand-eye coordination. He lived the rest of his life with his wife, Odessa, in Buffalo. A son, Jeff Jr., also lives there.

⚾ ⚾ ⚾

EARLY AUTUMN, 1994. There were seemingly hundreds of Sheltons in the Buffalo phone book, and for a moment I wondered if I had gone crazy thinking I would be able to locate the Jeff Shelton who had once been my teammate. So many years had come and gone.

It was early Friday night on Labour Day weekend. I was in Buffalo for a five-kilometre race called the Bullfeathers Run, which was to begin in about half an hour. I asked the waitress in the Bullfeathers bar for a phone directory, and then spent the next few minutes scanning the Sheltons in the book. I also tried to look up Connie Waitkoviak, but Buffalo is a city with a large Polish population, and I wasn't even sure if Waitkoviak was the proper spelling. There were several variations, and I tried a few, but the prospect of finding the former first baseman looked almost impossible. Besides, I reasoned, if I could locate Jeff Shelton, perhaps he would know Waite's whereabouts.

Trying to dismiss the very real possibility that Jeff Shelton might be dead, I had written about thirty-five Shelton phone numbers down in a small book, and among them were several J. Sheltons, any one of which might have been the one I was seeking. So I picked up the pay phone, dropped in a quarter, and began. The first one I called lived on Sherman Street. A woman answered.

"Is this the Shelton residence where Jeff Shelton, who used to play baseball for the Galt Terriers, now lives?"

"Yes it is," she said in barely concealed amazement. It was Odessa, his wife, and I had struck paydirt. No one had mentioned the Galt Terriers for years, perhaps decades. We spoke for a minute, and then she said Jeff was there, so she put him on. He invited my wife and I and our grown daughter and her husband back to his place after we had run the race. Clearly he was interested in seeing an old teammate. He had fond memories of those Terrier days. So he gave us directions, and said if we had a problem, to call.

My daughter Hazel decided not to run the race. She was newly pregnant, and she wasn't feeling well. Besides, she was carrying a precious cargo. Only that afternoon had she been able to confirm the pregnancy, and when her husband had arrived home she had a couple of wineglasses, filled with milk, ready so they could celebrate. We were taking a week's vacation beginning that afternoon, and from Buffalo we were heading off to the beautiful Finger Lakes area at Watkins Glen, then proceeding on through Corning and Elmira—Mark Twain country—and finally on to Glimmerglass State Park on Lake Otsego, outside of Cooperstown. We were on top of the world that day. That was the night Jeff Shelton had us over, and though it took some time to find his street in the dark—we had been thrown off when we saw a Herman Street—we finally found it.

It was in a downtown neighbourhood, but the Shelton home was like an oasis in a wasteland. It was in fine condition and it stood out among the others. Although it took us a good half-hour longer to find his house than it should have, Jeff was waiting on the front porch for us. He welcomed us in with a smile and a friendly face, even though we hadn't seen each other in years. There was still a warmth in this man, like there had been a half-century earlier, and I knew I would not regret having sought him out. Indeed, the day was as fine as they come after learning a grandchild was on the way. The warm hospitality of the Sheltons was a fitting way to end a wonderful day. We all felt fortunate for having found them.

We spoke about those seasons in Galt, about his ball career prior to, and following, those Terrier Town days. About his other great love, besides Odessa, of skeet shooting. Although he was a first-rate pitcher, the trophies and medals he had hanging in the house were for shooting. He had no idea where his old friend Connie Waite was. He had gone around to see him a few years back, and found no trace. He had either died or left town. Even Shelton didn't know the correct spelling of his name. Finally, it was time to go. It was getting late and we had a long drive ahead.

The next summer we again stopped off in Buffalo to see the Sheltons. This time it was during the day. We were off to Cleveland to visit relatives and take in a game at the newly built Jacob Field, but I had a baseball that had been signed by everybody on that '49 team except Shelton, Perkins, and Waite. I wanted Jeff's signature on that ball. It belonged there.

Again they invited us into their home. Our grandson Erik had been born just two months earlier and they were delighted to see pictures of him. Shelton took one look and said, "A baseball player."

Shelton was a baseball player. Just how good we'll never really know, for he never got a chance to play in the majors. The late Jackie

Robinson, who was born in the same year as Shelton, broke the colour barrier. But for Shelton, it was too late. Like so many other young players, he was in his prime when the war came. Had he gone to the St. Louis Browns, as he had agreed to do before going into the navy, he very well might have worked his way up to the big leagues. Instead he was destined to spend the war playing for a highly successful navy team comprising black players based in Illinois. Although he never made it to the majors, he did break a colour barrier of sorts. After being transferred from the Great Lakes Naval Centre to Oxnard, California, he became the first black to play on the navy team on the west coast.

But that was a long time ago. Now it was the summer of his twilight years. Again we talked about those old times, and again there was warmth and fellowship in our meeting. I handed him the ball I wanted him to sign. He reached out and tenderly held it in his right hand. For an instant he held the pristine baseball, now full of signatures, before signing it. You could tell he still had a reverence for the ball, and a wider reverence for the game itself. A pure, simple respect. It was there in the way he held that ball. The years had not changed this.

He signed the ball and then handed the pen back to me, but kept the ball, holding it carefully, the way I would hold Erik in those first few weeks after he was born. He held it so that it became more than a baseball in his hand. No longer was it an inanimate object. It breathed life through the white leather of its hide. It seemed to come alive in his palm as he placed his fingers in the fastball position, then moved them as if to throw a curveball.

He was lost in the ball, his mind having gone back to who knows what game fifty years ago. I was surprised by the way he gingerly handled the ball. I hadn't expected that. I had expected him to take the ball casually and sign his name and then hand it back to me. Not this. But it was beautiful to watch. Never had I seen a ball that way before, though I have loved playing ball and throwing balls of all shapes since I was young. For a few moments, Shelton was oblivious to the rest of us in the room. It seemed as if he hadn't seen or held a baseball for a very long time. He caressed it with his throwing hand, slowly, deliberately, passionately. He smelled the ball, and savoured the smell.

There was a smile that came over his face. An unadulterated grin, the way a child might show pleasure, a true smile that was both genuine and satisfying. The kind of smile that is a wonder to see, but the kind that the majority of adults manage to suppress over most of a lifetime. But Shelton was seventy-six, and so it was a joy to see the ball and what it had done to him. He knew this ball, or one just like it, and he knew how to throw it with the best of them. That is why the smile. And with it he knew the barnstorming days before the war. And the years in Galt; the friends, the summers.

A man lives all his life to be able to have this kind of knowledge. A man, any man, would do well if, in that lifetime, he knew the sensation, the texture, the seams of a baseball, as Jeff Shelton had come to know them.

Now he comes out of his trance and is back, suddenly, in the room where everyone else is. His eyes are at peace. He lifts and turns his head, looks over at his wife of nearly fifty years, and embraces her with his eyes and his dark face. The smile which left him when the trance was broken returns, and is wide on his face. It too is childlike in a way that we would all recognize, for we have seen it if not in ourselves, then in a playmate when we were young. Odessa knows that smile, where it came from, what it means.

"It has gone quickly," she remarks of their years together. "Too fast. It doesn't seem like that many years have come and gone. But they've been good."

"Yes," says Shelton in a reflective, contented way. "We've had good years together. Fifty-three years. It's been fifty-three good years," he adds, looking Odessa's way, though lost in thought. "Do you think others can make it that long in this day and age?" the man who played against Satchel Paige asks us.

He hands back the baseball, and now I hold it with a reverence I had not shown it before. The way he held it, the way he had been unashamed to hold it, taught me to savour this ball, and others like it. He didn't know it, but that is what he gave me that day.

A year later there was a Terrier reunion, and players came from all over to meet fellow alumni, and reminisce about days gone by. Jeff Shelton never showed, and later that day I got a call from Odessa, saying that they had planned on coming to the reunion but Jeff had to be admitted to the hospital that day. It was a bitter disappointment for them.

"Jeff was a good pitcher," said Kaiser, ehcoing Lillie. "I used to holler at him from the outfield to throw strikes, and he always did."

Clark remembered Shelton's control. "He could really throw that ball in there," said Clark. "He was a good-natured guy and everybody liked him."

"Jeff was one of my favourite players," said Murray.

The next several months were painful ones for Shelton, and he deteriorated slowly. In the summer of 1998, Jeff, who was in extreme pain and failing quickly, was admitted to a Buffalo hospice. He died there, at 5:30 A.M. on Saturday, June 13.

Connie Waite, second on left

Connie Waite

ONNIE WAITKOVIAK, ALIAS CONNIE WAITE, CONTINUED TO live in Buffalo following that summer of '49. After their playing days ended, he and Shelton saw little of each other. It was generally agreed that Waite was one of the best ballplayers to ever grace the field at Dickson Park.

I remember much about Waite, and I could tell you more than I have written, like the time he and Shelton, who used to breeze through border customs because his brother-in-law was an officer, had a trunk full of ladies' nylon stockings to take back to Buffalo after unloading a trunk full of American cigarettes, which were in demand back in those days.

There was the time Waite punched Gus, and the ensuing chase by Kaiser, who I'm sure would have dealt with him severely if he had caught him. And there was Waite's play on the ball diamond. He was as smooth a first baseman as I had ever seen, and why he wasn't in the majors I'll never know.

Waite returned to Buffalo after the summer of '49, and kept in touch with Shelton for a few years, then disappeared. He was never seen, or heard from, again.

Laurie Brain

Laurie Brain and his brother Horace—Horrie, or Goose Brain—came to Galt from Toronto in the late 1920s to play baseball. Horrie, tall and thin, played on some provincial champion intermediate teams from Preston in the late 1920s and then played with the Terriers. Laurie, shorter than his brother, and stockier, didn't have as much success on the ball diamond and turned to sports reporting. He got his first break in the business when he was hired as a cub reporter by the *Galt Evening Reporter*, working out of the small Hespeler office.

Lawrence Richard Brain was born Halloween day, 1910, in Plymouth, England, and came to Canada as an infant. Growing up in Toronto, he got a taste for hockey and baseball and even developed a liking for golf and curling. He won the Ontario Sportswriters and Sportscasters Association (OSWSA) Bonspiel in Niagara Falls in 1961, beating *Globe* sports editor Jim Vipond's rink in the final. He served as president of OSWSA in 1956. He would also claim several golf titles through the years.

When he first came to Galt he worked at several jobs before landing at the *Reporter*. After toiling at Scroggins Shoe, where he played on the company ball and hockey teams, he worked for Bell Telephone, then was a lineman for the hydro company. When the war came in 1939 he tried to join the army but was rejected because he had four young children at home. Finally the air force accepted him and he was sent to Lachine, Quebec. He was discharged in 1944 and began as a cub reporter with the Galt newspaper shortly afterward, covering Hespeler news and sports, as well as the courts and the Horticultural Society. Eventually he worked his way up to the sports department. He was there, at the main office of the paper, when the *Reporter* moved from Water Street to Ainslie Street.

The years came and went, about ten of them all told, with Laurie covering the Galt sports scene. He and wife Rose had four children in the decade of the 1930s—Barb was born in '33, Lorraine in '35, Larry in '37 and Ron in '39. Eventually he became the sports editor. He continued there for several more years after that summer of '49. Considered a good writer, and a good man, his passion was the horses. "That was his true love," said son Larry, who was a twelve-year-old in 1949. But he also held an affection for baseball. His favourite assignments were in the spring and the fall of the year when he would cover the Kentucky Derby and the World Series.

In 1949 Larry would accompany his father to the press box behind home plate at Dickson Park to play records between innings and during breaks. Occasionally Earl Werstine, a veteran columnist for the *Reporter* and a member of the city's parks board, would be there with them. Larry remembers going down from their Glenmorris Street house to the ballpark on the river flats with the entire family on many occasions. Mrs. Brain and the children would be in the stands, while Laurie would be in the press box.

In 1955 Brain went to the *Windsor Star*, where he stayed until 1956, before accepting an offer from the Toronto *Globe and Mail*, Canada's most prestigious daily. The day before he was to leave for Windsor, he and King, both avid horse racing fans, decided to have one final day at the races together. They wanted Pennell to join them. But Pennell, who was in the midst of a court case in Cayuga, declined. He wasn't a horse racing aficionado. Still, King and Brain persisted. They would watch Pennell in action at the courthouse in the morning, they told him, and then they could all go to the racetrack at Fort Erie in the afternoon and proceed on to Buffalo for dinner. Maybe take in a ball game there.

"Court opened at 9 A.M.," Pennell recalled. "I had this case and I had to be there." So Brain and King went to Cayuga in the morning and saw a master at work. Pennell was so good that one time an American visitor, whose avocation, while travelling the continent on business, was to observe courtroom lawyers, approached him afterwards. "I've seen a lot of top lawyers in the big cities. I've been to New York, Chicago, Los Angeles, watching the best lawyers in the land, and you rank up there with the best." On the day that Brain and King went to Cayuga, Pennell won the case. They spent the afternoon at the Fort Erie racetrack. Pennell was out of his element. The three of them went down to the paddocks—Brain and King were veterans of the racing game—and looked over the horses. They all studied the racing program, though Pennell did it blindly, finally deciding on a horse called "My Mother." The name sounded good to him because, as he would explain years later, he loved his mother. "It was a 10-1 longshot and it won. It was my lucky day."

He continued in his naïveté all afternoon, and when they left the racetrack for Buffalo, he had one hundred dollars more than when he arrived. But Brain and King looked gloomy. They didn't say anything was wrong, but their demeanours had changed.

Pennell bought dinner that evening in Buffalo, and afterwards, when Brain got up to go to the washroom, he asked King why Brain seemed so morose. "Laurie has got a problem," King said. "Tomorrow morning the movers are coming to take their things to Windsor. He's got to pay them two hundred dollars. But he just went through the moving money at the track. He can't go home to Rose without that money. It's all gone. Could you help him out?"

Pennell, who only went to the races three times in his life, had eighty dollars remaining from his winnings. He agreed to give Brain the eighty dollars, and would write a cheque for $120. He had always liked Brain. "He had written a couple of nice stories about how well organized we were in Brantford," Pennell said. "He was a good writer and a good man." Pennell didn't hesitate to loan him the money. Nor was he overly concerned when Brain never paid it back. Brain had always been good to him. In a way, it was almost worth it. So the next day the movers came to Laurie Brain's home in Galt and moved all their furnishings to Windsor.

One day not long afterward Mrs. Pennell was doing the family bookkeeping. She noticed that Larry had written a cheque for $120, and asked him about it, but he pled ignorance. "It must have been for some law books or something like that," he said. Of course, he never told her about the eighty dollars he'd also loaned Brain.

Brain didn't want to leave Galt, where he had deep roots. But to move up he had to. Besides, the sporting life by the mid-1950s was not what it had been. But perhaps the biggest factor was money. The

Reporter didn't pay well. He asked for a raise, but they gave him an ultimatum, telling him if he wanted more money he would have to get it elsewhere. So Brain wrote letters to all the major papers in the province, and Windsor picked him up as an assistant sports editor. By then Larry was old enough to stay behind, though he'd go down to visit and they'd take in the Detroit games.

That summer in Windsor was a hot one and a melancholic Rose, already gloomy over having to leave Galt, was feeling the heat. "I'll bring you a fan," said Laurie one afternoon as he said goodbye to Rose before heading off to a Detroit game. Larry was with him. He was driving a '53 Ford, and on the return trip to Windsor he hid the fan under the hood to pass through customs. Life was different in Windsor than it had been in Galt. In Galt he had spent much of his time curling in the winters, and playing golf in the summers. "I curled in my first bonspiel at Guelph as lead on Jack Patrick's Galt rink in 1948," Brain recalled. Patrick had won the British Consols playoff the year before and gone on to the Brier in Calgary. "I curled quite regularly while at Galt, but didn't get much ice time at Windsor, and I've been less than a once-a-week curler here for the past couple of years."

Neither Laurie or Rose liked Windsor and eleven months later he accepted an offer from the *Globe and Mail* in Toronto. In contrast to Windsor, he loved Toronto. Racing was his primary interest, though he also wrote about boxing and other subjects. Winters he and Rose would spend in Florida, usually close to Hialeah and the Gulfstream tracks. Like most racetrackers, he enjoyed the excitement of stakes events.

The Brain name became known in Intercounty baseball circles years later when Bob Brain, Goose's son and Laurie's nephew, cracked the Terrier lineup. He had been a young kid back in '49, but was old enough to remember all the players. He remembered how Creedon used to hitch at home plate before hitting the ball, and how Waite liked to hit to right centre field. And how Rosen used to blast home runs over the right-field fence. He could even remember the money dispute between the players and Gus, and seemed to recall one or two players dragging Gus down the aisle of the grandstand after one game. But one thing he remembered clearly was the missed catch by Warren, though with the passage of the years he thought it was another player of a later era who missed it. But it had been Warren. Young Bobby Brain, Laurie's nephew, was there at Dickson Park on that last night game of the decade. The catch should have been routine, but Warren missed it. "I was just crushed," he said, nearly fifty years later. All the young Galt kids were crushed.

When Bob finally made it to the Terriers as a player, Lillie was still playing. Wes, he said, was one of the most superstitious players on the team, though the players of that age were all superstitious. When the Terriers would travel to places like London or St. Thomas, or Stratford, and Wes would see white horses in the fields, he would keep track of how many he saw. I once asked him why he was counting the horses, and he told me a white horse meant a hit. Other guys would wear the same socks, their lucky socks, until they almost rotted off their feet. So it had been with Bradshaw a generation earlier when he would wear the same unwashed uniform for weeks on end that summer he hit .698.

Like a legion of players before and afterwards, Bob Brain would try chewing tobacco. It was a rite of passage for a young ballplayer. So too was being sick from chewing the stuff. One time, while staying with his Uncle Laurie and Aunt Rose in Scarborough, a suburb of Toronto, after Laurie had left Galt, Bob recalled how his Aunt Rose liked to have a snort of beer in the morning. One day, after obtaining a quart of beer from Quebec, he put it on the table for her. "I was her favourite nephew after that," he said.

Laurie Brain spent the rest of his newspaper days at the *Globe and Mail*, covering the Hamilton Tiger Cats of the Canadian Football League for a time, and writing a horse racing column. Milt Dunnell of the *Toronto Star* knew Brain in those days. "He was an enthusiastic guy," said Dunnell. "He was very knowledgeable about horse racing." So was Dunnell, who always liked covering the races more than anything else. "I got a kick out of it," Dunnell said. "The characters, the colour, the excitement." Like Brain, he counted the Kentucky Derby as his favourite assignment. It was there, in Louisville each May, that he would spend some time with Brain.

One year, Dunnell remembered how Brain won some money in the week leading up to the Derby. "He liked to bet, and he'd had a pretty good week." So on Saturday for the big race he wagered all the money he'd won through the week on a horse he liked. "But he went overboard in the Derby," said Dunnell. "All his profits were lost."

Another year Brain had bet, and lost, all his expense money in the week leading up to Derby Saturday and had to borrow some money from Dunnell to finish out the week.

It was typical of Brain to bet on the horses he was covering. But there was a lesson in that. "If you're covering the races the last thing you can do is bet," said Dunnell. "Some reporters fall into a trap trying to beat the horses. But you can't do it." Brain might have known this, but he took great pleasure in playing the horses. If he never learned the lesson it was perhaps because he never wanted to learn it. He got so much pleasure out of being around the racetrack and betting on the horses. Like Dunnell, he soaked up the excitement, the colour, the characters of the racing world. In many ways it had been the same with the Galt Terriers those summers in Galt, and especially that one summer when Padden came to work for Murray.

Larry remembers how he first learned of his dad's final illness. It was June 21, 1969. Though ill and weak, his father was getting ready to go to one of his favourite races, the Queen's Plate. He had exerted a great deal of effort just to get dressed in his tuxedo the day of the Plate. But there was nothing left, even though he desperately wanted to go to the track. He knew it would be his last Queen's Plate and for that reason alone it was a special one.

But before he got to the front door he stopped and turned to Rose. "I can't make it," he said as he collapsed. Rose called the *Globe and Mail* to let them know, then she called her children, including Larry in Galt. Brain picked his last winner from home that day, Jumpin' Joseph.

In the summer of 1968 Brain had given his readers a $203 daily double at Woodbine when Sam's Wish ($56.20) won the first race and Rody Octo ($9.80) the second. But it was in 1959 that Brain had his hottest streak as the *Globe's* handicapper. He picked eleven winners in thirteen consecutive races over two days. The other two were beaten by a head and neck.

He wasn't averse to following his own advice, as his friends well remember. He compared making a wager to a person working in a candy store. "You have to reach for the goodies sometimes," he reasoned. That was the Laurie Brain that Milt Dunnell knew. He was one of the best-liked sportswriters of his day. And he loved his work. "I can't believe they would pay me to do this," he would say.

"Dad always wanted someone in the family to make it big in sports," recalled Larry. Ron made it in hockey as far as Junior A, but it was Brain's grandson, Greg Stefan, a goaltender with the NHL's Detroit Red Wings, who made it to the big time. Greg is the son of Brain's firstborn, Barb, who married in the early 1950s and moved to Brantford. Stefan and another Brantford native by the name of Wayne Gretzky grew up together. Laurie died before ever seeing him play in the NHL, but he would have been proud.

In the days leading up to his death, the family was close at hand. "We all went down to Toronto to see him," Larry remembers. "That was the first we knew he was even ill." He died a few weeks later at East General Hospital. In the *Globe and Mail* that August his obituary noted how he always enjoyed bucking the odds. "But Saturday he lost his greatest gamble to cancer."

Laurie Brain, the newspaper voice of Terrier Town that summer of '49, died in August of 1969. He was fifty-nine. Brain's son Ron still lives in Cambridge, though Larry died in the autumn of 1996, ironically, at age fifty-nine.

If you visit Laurie's gravestone in Galt's Mountview Cemetery, you will see an engraving of a horse above Brain's name. And if you look at it long enough you will see Whirlaway, or Al Sash, his two favourite thoroughbreds. You know he would have loved a horse by the name of Secretariat who came along just a few years after his death, if only he had lived long enough to see him.

Connie Creedon

CONNIE CREEDON HAD LIVED WITH THE MORTON FAMILY ON Stanley Street that spring and summer of 1949. One day young Herb Morton came home and sat down to eat supper, but Creedon wasn't there.

"Where's Connie?" asked Herb.

His father looked up at him and said, "Don't ever ask about him again. He's not welcome in this house any more." Herb, then a teenager, didn't ask any questions, though he was able to put two and two together and figure out that it was Creedon's penchant for keeping company with young boys that got him into trouble.

Creedon had wowed the fans at Dickson Park all summer long, but by the end of the season Murray was glad to get rid of him. By then it was Murray's belief that Creedon was a pedophile. The big barrel-chested ballplayer who always had a wad of chewing tobacco in his jaw, it seemed, liked young boys. Indeed, Murray could remember the way he left town. The police had ordered him to leave after an incident with a youngster. They didn't press charges on the condition that he leave town immediately. A generation later it wouldn't have mattered that he was one of the most popular Terriers; he would have been hauled immediately off to jail. But in 1949 such incidents were generally kept quiet. So Creedon, outwardly a man's man, the guy who had wrestled on a card in Hespeler and wound up winning instead of losing like he was scripted to do, left town in disgrace.

Nothing was heard of him for years. Cornelius Stephen Creedon, who was born to John Creedon and Ella Crosley in Danvers, Massachusetts, on July 21, 1915, changed his name to Lee Burton shortly after leaving Galt—he had been in trouble with the law before—and he quit ball soon afterward, deciding instead to become a full-time musician, something he had done part-time for several years. I remembered the way he would play the piano at the Y. Other times he would venture into Central Presbyterian Church, where he had an agreement with the organist, and play the big Cassavante pipe organ.

On February 1, 1972, his wife, Joanne, wrote a letter to a Mr. Simenic, a baseball researcher, in answer to Simenic's letter asking for information about her late husband.

> I have filled out the questionnaire as best I could, but there are several things I just don't know or can't remember. Lee was very proud of having played in the majors, but he didn't keep records or anything to which I could refer. It seems to me that he had mentioned also playing with Atlanta in a southern league, but I have no idea when that would have been. I have left blank the dates of his pro ball. Perhaps there are record books somewhere and you could fill in this information.
>
> If it isn't too much trouble, could you tell me how I could get Lee's records. I know our son would really enjoy knowing about his dad's career as he is quite a sports fan. Lee would have been thrilled to know that his name is somewhere in the Hall of Fame and I am very proud of it.
>
> Yours Truly,
> Mrs. Lee Burton

As for the name change, even his wife didn't know what prompted him to change it. In another letter Joanne Burton explained:

> Dear Mr. Kachline,
>
> I'm afraid I can't give you a very sensible reason why Lee changed his name. I know that he never liked the name Cornelius, and I would guess that "Connie" sounded too sissy to suit him.
>
> He changed his name when he began working steadily as a professional musician. I'm sure he felt that "Lee Burton" would be simpler and easier for people to remember.
>
> Sorry I can't be of more help.
>
> Yours Truly,
> Joanne Burton

Maybe Lee Burton was simpler and easier to remember. But his real name, Connie Creedon, had a ring to it, one that Galt fans who saw him play that summer of '49 never forgot. Brantford sportswriter Ted Beare was still, forty-six years after the fact, talking about the shot Creedon put over the left-field fence at Agricultural Park that summer. It was the longest ball ever hit in Brantford.

Creedon had used Cornelius—Connie—for all his thirty-four years when he arrived in Galt that spring. He had played in the majors with that name. It seems unlikely that he would just arbitrarily change it in his late thirties, unless he was trying to escape his past. Joanne claimed she had no idea why he changed his name. Perhaps. Or perhaps she knew what had happened in Galt, and elsewhere, and she was protecting him.

In the next two decades after leaving Galt, Creedon made his living as a self-employed professional musician. Life had not been easy, but somehow, he managed to keep his marriage to Joanne Daigle together, pay the bills, and raise a son. By 1969 they had called 607B East 1st Street in Orange County home for less than two years, though they had been in California for half a decade.

Creedon collapsed at home on the evening of November 30, 1969, and was pronounced dead on arrival at Santa Anna Community Hospital in Santa Anna, California. He was buried at the Good Shepherd Cemetery at Huntington Beach.

Galt's famed Murderer's Row had lost a second man. Warren had preceded Creedon by a year.

Goody Rosen

WHEN ROSEN RETURNED THE NEXT SEASON AS THE PLAYING manager of the Terriers he was dismayed to see a new teammate by the name of Jim Bagby, the onetime Cleveland Indian reliever who helped end Joe DiMaggio's fifty-six-game hitting streak in 1941. The six-foot-two Bagby was an avowed racist from Georgia. The two didn't get along, but it wasn't any fault of Rosen. The only people Bagby hated more than Jews were blacks. He was openly contemptuous of Rosen. Oftentimes when Rosen, as manager, was explaining some point in the dressing room, Bagby would snort derisively and attempt to ridicule him. Shelton, too, was the object of Bagby's contempt.

But Rosen wasn't the diplomat that Shelton was. It wasn't in his nature. He had performed in '49—people were still talking about his eighth inning grand slam which won a playoff game against Brantford the previous season—and Murray wanted him back. He was a name player who could perform, even if his best years were behind him. "He was a good solid ballplayer," said Murray. "A good contact hitter."

"I could always hit," he said. "I could have been a [major-league] manager too." Murray didn't doubt it. And besides, his name drew out fans. "He was tops," Murray would say years later. "He had the smarts."

But 1950 turned out to be a bad year for everybody on the Galt team, including Shelton and Rosen. There was a lot of dissension that year. "Things never got off to a good start," said Murray. Although Murray had signed someone else to manage the team early on, Rosen was eventually given the job.

Galt didn't win any pennant that summer. It was Rosen's last year in the Intercounty. After his retirement he worked for Biltrite Industries in Toronto for more than three decades, played a lot of golf, and generally enjoyed life as one of Canada's elder statesmen in baseball. He became known for his left-handed golf swing. "Honest," he once told Dunnell, "with the ability I had, there's no tellin' how good I might have been if I hadn't run into a wall in St. Louis [his second season]. Shoulder never was right after that." His career had spanned several decades. He had played for the Dodgers the year before Jackie Robinson came up. One of his friends on the team that year, outfielder Dixie Walker, passed around a petition saying they didn't want to play with a black. "You've got to understand," said Rosen many years later, "those were different times and Dixie was from the south. He was wrong but he was a friend of mine."

Rosen's best year was 1945, when he finished second in the NL with a .325 average, including 197 hits, 126 runs, 75 RBIs, and 12 homers. He was the last Canadian to hit .300 or over for a full season in the majors until Melville, Saskatchewan's Terry Puhl hit .301 in sixty games with the Houston Astros in 1977.

He was always sorry he didn't win the NL batting title in '45. "Shoulda won the battin' championship that year the way I was hittin' into September," he said. "Tommy Holmes [Boston Braves] and I were neck and neck most of the season. But I'm playin' centre field between Dixie Walker and Augie Galan. Neither of them had any speed. They wore me out."

In later years I remembered with clarity our day fishing on Mill Creek, and how we had talked and whiled away most of that hot summer day under the cool shade of those trees along the bank. He told me a lot that day about his background, about how he had played sandlot ball with the Toronto Lizzies before getting his first pro contract with the Toronto Maple Leafs. The year he joined Brooklyn, Babe Ruth was a first-base coach with the club. Ruth smoked cigars, like Rosen, and he would hide them, with Rosen's tacit permission, in Goody's suit jacket because he never liked to carry them around. Whenever he needed a cigar he would come over to Rosen.

I was fascinated by his history. Most of the names he spoke of, like his nemesis Leo Durocher, were household names in our home. That he could speak of such people on a first-name basis helped bring the world to Galt. Jimmy would have enjoyed all those stories that summer, if only he had lived.

Rosen, like many Jewish players, faced an uphill battle early in his career. As a struggling minor-leaguer during the Depression era, he caught freight trains from one town to another in Arkansas, dodging railway police as he looked for teams that would accept a Jewish player. As a junior in Toronto with the Elizabeth Playground side he had attended a tryout camp staged by the Rochester minor-league team. Later, invited back to Rochester to play in an exhibition game, he managed two hits against the New York Giants. Encouraged, he went to spring training with the Louisville Colonels of the American Association in 1933 after a stint playing semi-pro ball. In Louisville manager Burleigh Grimes signed him, despite his small size, which had been the stumbling block with Rochester. It was Grimes who, after being hired by the Dodgers in 1937, persuaded New York to give him a shot. The Dodgers bought Rosen from the Colonels for the then astronomical sum of $125,000, and later, after he'd been up in the majors, sent him to their Triple-A farm club, the Montreal Royals, in 1940; he spent the war years in the International League at Syracuse. He was not to see Brooklyn's Ebbet's Field again until 1944, when general manager Branch Rickey invited him back up.

Part of Rosen's early trouble was that he didn't look like a major-leaguer. As we sat and ate lunch that summer day long ago, I sized him up. He still didn't look like a major-leaguer. When he arrived at Louisville he was initially told to go home and not waste their time. But it wasn't in Rosen's nature to pack and go home. Instead, he showed the pluck that eventually took him to the majors. Born in 1912 in Toronto, Rosen always had tremendous self-confidence. That day we went fishing I remember how he washed down his sandwich with a pop, and I figured he was born with confidence. He wasn't afraid to voice his convictions. His stubbornness cost him four years in the majors when Brooklyn manager Leo Durocher and general manager Larry MacPhail failed to appreciate his candor.

At Louisville in 1933, Rosen, only twenty, hit .301. Later, in the majors, he often hovered around or above the .300 mark. Although he had only six years service in the majors, Rosen figured that if it hadn't been for injuries, he could have put up some decent numbers over a career. "I ran into a wall in St. Louis in my second year [1938]," he explained. "I had a lot of different injuries that hurt my career, but I played with most of 'em." But his outspoken nature, his unwillingness to swallow his pride and bow to Durocher, hurt his career inestimably. Still, I respected him for the way he stood up to Durocher.

His wife died in 1993 and it was obvious that after her death, he was rudderless. Her death had taken a lot out of him. His mind started wandering and his health began to fail. Up to the end, he spoke of his distate for Durocher, and he told anyone who would listen about how his big-league days closed out.

People in Galt would have found it ironic, perhaps, that a collision with an outfield wall ended his major-league career in 1946. That wall was at Forbes Field in Pittsburgh, the same ballpark that Tom Padden had played in for most of his major-league career.

Rosen died on April 6, 1994, at the age of eighty-two, a dozen years after being enshrined in the Canadian Baseball Hall of Fame. News of his death was carried in newspapers across North America.

Bert McCrudden

Pitcher Bert McCrudden, a Galt native, played his last full season of baseball in the summer of 1949. He returned at the beginning of the 1950 season but only for the pre-season. He'd had enough. It was a gruelling schedule for those players, like McCrudden, who had to work full-time during the day and then go play baseball at night. Keeping it up for a forty-two-game season over the course of the summer was not an easy thing to do. In McCrudden's case, he would always race home from his job at McDougall's, where former Terrier great Speedy Oliver was the general manager, grab a quick sandwich and a glass of milk, and then ride his bike over to the ballpark. He had worked full-time and supported his mother after his dad—a rabid ball fan—died of pneumonia in 1940 when Bert was only sixteen.

Even though McCrudden officially retired from the Terriers, he continued in sports by coaching minor teams in the city. He had always loved sports. His older sister enjoyed telling the story that when he was just three, little Bert would beg to stay outside and play hockey all day long, even on the coldest days of the winter, and the only way they could coax him inside to eat supper was to tell him there was Jello waiting for him.

Years after that 1949 season someone wrote a piece in the local paper about how McCrudden pitched the first-ever night game for the Terriers at Dickson Park. But McCrudden knew better. "It wasn't me," he said. "It was Chuck Mercer."

In 1967, Confederation year, the year of Expo in Montreal, McCrudden coached a minor Galt ball team that went to Michigan to play in a tournament. He knew his rulebook inside out, and at one point he disputed a call and was required to put up twenty dollars with his protest. The Americans were certain that the Canadian was wrong, but his protest was eventually upheld. The Canadian, it turned out, did know a thing or two about America's national pastime.

He retired from work in the late 1980s and was, in the late 1990s, the only surviving member of the 1949 Galt Terriers who continued to live in Galt.

Bert McCrudden died on a Saturday night in July 1998, at Cambridge Memorial Hospital.

Tom Padden

THE WINTER OF 1949–50 DIDN'T HOLD MUCH PROMISE FOR Tom Padden. There would be high-school and college basketball games to referee back home in Manchester, New Hampshire, perhaps a little work through connections he had made during his major-league days. Little else. He wanted to return to Galt to manage the Terriers the next summer, and, as far as anyone could tell, that was likely to happen. Murray was pleased with the way he had handled things in '49 with the club winning the pennant, even if they lost to Brantford in the semifinals. But that was Warren and Creedon's fault as much as it was anybody's.

Murray had few reservations about Padden returning. The only concern he had was about his drinking. Twice in '49 his drinking had given Murray and the Terriers problems: first, when Padden and several players stopped off at the tavern in Blair in their uniforms. That hadn't gone over well with the Terrier directors. Then, of course, there was the night Padden showed up plastered for the game at Dickson Park and had to be whisked away by Murray before anyone saw him. He had been given a stern warning and there had been no further incidents.

What Murray liked about Padden was his obvious knowledge of the game and his soft-spoken manner. He could be reasonably certain that with Padden at the helm in '50, the Terriers would field another contender. When Padden left Galt after the devastating semifinal loss to Brantford, he honestly believed he was going to return in '50. He and Murray had discussed the matter, and Murray had said he wanted him back. But something was to happen in the off-season that changed Murray's mind.

The baseball meetings were in Baltimore that winter. Murray was planning to attend, as was Padden. Even Sollenburger, who was beginning to think of entering the coaching ranks, had been coaxed along by Padden. Padden was hoping to get a job with a major-league organization, perhaps land a position as manager of a minor-league team. He'd told Sollenburger to come along. Padden would take him into a few meetings and introduce him to friends on various major-league teams. When Murray arrived in Baltimore he brought with him a good deal of cash. He, too, was hoping to benefit from the meetings, both personally, and for his Terriers. At the very least he would get a few leads on players. Murray lined up a meeting with Billy Rogell of the Detroit Tigers. Rogell, a Springfield, Illinois, native, had played in the majors for fourteen seasons, mostly with Detroit. After his playing days were done he stayed on with the Tigers as a coach. When Murray mentioned Padden's name, Rogell told him, "You are welcome to come, but not Padden too." Padden might be a knowledgeable baseball man, but word had gotten around about his drinking. No one wanted any part of it.

"Before Baltimore I was seriously considering bringing him back to Galt," said Murray. But Padden, struggling to make ends meet that winter, had asked Murray for a five-hundred-dollar loan. Murray had reluctantly given it to him. Then Padden told Sollenburger about a meeting he had set up with a major-league team to discus the possibility of them both being hired as coaches. "Tom was going to help me get my foot in the door," said Sollenburger. But by the time Sollenburger arrived, Padden was dead drunk. Any hope either of them had of getting a good job had vanished. "He really disgraced himself and me down there," said Murray. And worse, he had drunk himself out of a job that summer in Galt. There was no way Murray could consider him for the Terrier post the following summer.

That winter back in Manchester Padden wrote Murray a couple of letters, pleading for another chance. But Murray's mind was set. He was already seeking another manager, and on the list was a former major-leaguer named Wes Ferrell. So Padden spent the summer of 1950 at home in Manchester pondering his future. And Murray never saw his five hundred dollars again, though he kept the scrapbook Padden had given him as collateral.

Not much was ever heard in Galt about Padden again. With the excitement of the new season he was almost forgotten, though it was assumed he had moved on, and up, in his managerial career. Few people knew the truth. Murray didn't make it well known what had happened in Baltimore. He told only close friends and those on the Terrier executive. That was it. It was a bitter disappointment for Padden not to return to Galt. Even his wife was dismayed at not being able to return. "I liked Galt very much," she reflected years later. "The neighbours we had were very nice to us and showed us around. We did different things, went out to eat and things like that, and we went to games when they played. It was a nice town, a nice country."

Though he was a relatively young man—in his early forties—Padden's last true season in baseball was the summer he spent in Galt. His children grew up in Manchester, where their father was somewhat of a local hero. He was the guy who had been up with the Yankees and Pirates, the guy who once threw a half-dollar across the Merrimack, that river of industry and romance that all of New Hampshire knows. Indeed, most of New Hampshire knew of Padden, too. He was regarded as one of the greatest major-league players to ever come out of the state. Kids would still ask for his autograph, even though it had been years since he retired from the majors. "He gave away little baseball bats and pins with his name on them," said Theresa. "Friends who had children were always after him for these things."

In later years he worked as a steward at the Daniel F. O'Connell Club in Manchester and refereed college and high-school basketball games at night. At one time he was part owner of a nightclub, but eventually sold out. And, in addition to working as baseball coach at St. Joseph's High School, his alma mater, he also worked for a close friend who owned a company in Manchester. Winters he liked to travel.

The end came rather suddenly. The tall, trim Padden went to work one morning, but not long after he arrived he got a terrible pain in his stomach. Later Theresa would say she believed it stemmed from an incident years earlier when he had been in the big leagues. "He got hit badly in the stomach," she said, "and he was operated on at that time, so maybe it came back."

Padden doubled up in pain. His friend, the business owner, quickly drove him to the hospital. The pain got progressively worse and it was clear he was suffering great agonies. "His pancreas had burst," said Theresa, "and poison coursed through his system."

Doctors did everything they could to save him, but he died the next day. He was sixty-four.

That was June 11, 1973. All of Manchester mourned. Friends poured into St. Anne's Church for the funeral. All the seats were taken. Of his three children, only Robert was then living in Manchester. Janice was out in Venice, California, while Tom Jr. was living in New Orleans. They all heard his former Holy Cross batterymate, Ray Dobens, praise the hometown boy who had made good so many years earlier. "He was one of the smartest baseball men I ever knew," said Dobens, echoing the description that had gone around the Intercounty. Dobens, like Padden, made it to the majors, eventually pitching for the Boston Red Sox. "Tommy and I went down together from Manchester [to Holy Cross] in the fall of 1925 and we played one year together as an all-New Hampshire battery. Tommy was an excellent defensive catcher and a very smart baseball man, and a pretty good hitter as well. In short, he was a hell of a catcher. Tommy made a lot of friends along the way and we're all going to miss him."

A teammate of Padden's at St. Joe's, Walter J. Tafe Sr., also praised Padden. Tafe, then assistant principal at Memorial High School, said Padden was a special man. "A more dedicated team player than Tommy, I have never played with. He was always willing and ready to encourage those not blessed with the natural ability that he possessed."

Tafe's friendship with Padden had gone back years. "We were teammates on what we called the Old St. Joe's team, and our coach was Barney McLaughlin," he said. "Tommy made the team as a freshman and it was easy to see that he was headed for stardom." Tafe was truly saddened by his death. "This is a great loss for his family and for me," he said at the time. "My heart goes out to Tommy, his wife, and family. I am deeply grieved."

So was Nick Gabardina, who, at the time of Padden's death, was the coach at Memorial High School. He had played under Padden on the 1947 Sweeney Post team that finished second in the nation at the American Legion finals in Hollywood, California. Said Gabardina: "He was probably one of the sharpest baseball minds I've ever run across. He was definitely able to communicate with his players and the people around him. He insisted that his players do things properly in practice because he believed if you did them right in practice, you'd perform the same way in a game. He was rightly respected by all people as a coach and as a human being. I'll miss him."

The accolades didn't stop there. John Clark of Mont Vernon, former state and international president of the International

Association of Approved Basketball Officials, of which Padden was a member, said Padden had been one of the best basketball officials he'd seen. "Tommy was a great friend and officiating partner of the late Johnny Burke and the two of them made up what I consider to have been the best officiating pair of their time. We all remember Tommy in the big leagues and what he contributed to baseball. All Manchester was proud of him for his achievements. He was a personal friend of mine and I always considered him a fair-minded official who called them as he saw them. He was a good person to have as a friend."

Artie Gore, who played against Padden in the Old New England League and then umpired when Padden played for Newark in the International League, said Padden was a great catcher and "a grand person. I always had the highest respect for him. He had the biggest pair of legs of any catcher I ever saw, and by the way things are going now, he'd have been a star of the highest magnitude if he'd played the game today."

Everyone in Manchester, it seemed, knew of Padden's tenure in the major leagues. Even later in life, his name would appear in the local paper from time to time. But few knew exactly how good Padden was. They didn't know, for instance, that Waite Hoyt would always ask for Padden when he was scheduled to pitch. The same with several other pitchers. And most people in Manchester, or Galt, for that matter, didn't know of Padden's problem with the bottle. If Theresa knew it was a problem, she never admitted it. "Sure, he drank a bit," she recalled. "All the players did. They'd go out and have steaks and a couple of beers." For several years after Galt he would dutifully send in his résumé to various teams, but he never got any offers. "He should have been a major-league manager," said Theresa, "because, I tell you, he knew his baseball. And as a catcher, he knew every trick of the trade. He always knew when the pitcher didn't have it."

Even when he was in his prime as a player, Pittsburgh coach Pie Traynor would use him as he would another coach. "Some people say he really managed the Pirates instead of Traynor," Theresa said. "Pie Traynor relied on his judgment about pitching and catching."

He was a likable person. Even Murray would have to admit that much. Who knows. If he had gotten help for his drinking, things might have turned out so differently. When Padden was playing in Pittsburgh, he was a fan favourite. "He had a heart of gold," said Theresa. "He was too good for his own good sometimes. He'd do a lot of favours for friends."

Today in Manchester a field is named after him. It was the same field where he learned to play ball. There is also a plaque in his memory up near the front door at Gill Stadium on the corner of Valley and Maple Streets. He played there too. And he's a member of the New Hampshire Hall of Fame.

The man who knew his baseball, old number 31 for the Pirates, was dead just twenty-four years after leaving Galt. He was sixty-four when he died. The last time he had seen Terrier Town was the summer of 1950 when he had returned to Galt hoping Murray would hire him to manage the Terriers. He didn't have the money he owed Murray, but he said he could deduct it from his pay. Murray just wanted to cut his losses. If he hadn't seen him so plastered at the baseball meetings in Baltimore, he might have taken him up on his offer. There were a lot of ifs. So Padden was back on the train to Manchester after only two days.

Today the Merrimack continues to flow through Manchester, past the fields and houses and the factories where a town still lives and grows. It speaks of much, but it does not tell of the day in 1930 when a man threw a silver dollar clear across its waters.

Larry Pennell stands beside his friend Syl Apps's grave in Galt.

Larry Pennell

LARRY PENNELL ALWAYS CONDUCTED HIMSELF WITH A QUIET dignity, whether it was operating the Brantford Red Sox, running his law practice, or performing his duties as a federal Member of Parliament. He had definite views, and he would articulate these—they were usually proven to be right—but if others vehemently disagreed, Pennell wouldn't argue. Rather, he'd state his case with persistence and conviction. If, in the end, they were still at loggerheads, he'd walk away. It was part of a lifelong philosophy handed down from his father. "I've always believed in it," he said.

When he was appointed to the Supreme Court of Ontario in 1968, he changed little. "That philosophy fit with my life as a lawyer and a judge," he said. Most of all, he would treat others with respect and dignity. Sometimes the other party was argumentative, or perhaps belittling, but Pennell would never fall to that level. "I just don't believe in it," he said. "Others can abuse me all they like but I won't do it. I never saw my father get in an argument in his life." His father was his role model. That's not to say he hasn't gotten mad, or made others angry, but he would refrain from quarrelling. "If you can't reason with someone you're not going to change his mind." He discovered early that if he treated people with respect, no matter how much abuse they heaped on him, they would eventually realize that they were letting anger get to them and they would apologize. By treating others with respect, they would come to respect him. Then a worthwhile discussion might ensue.

It was a philosophy he used in Ottawa with great success. Rather than argue, he would reason. "I've reasoned with people, not always successfully," he admitted. As part of Lester Pearson's cabinet in the early 1960s he was both respected and well-liked, and, as Peter C. Newman described in his 1968 political classic, *The Distemper of Our Times*, he was part of the new, progressive guard of the Liberal Party.

Pennell continued his activity in Intercounty baseball for several more years after that 1949 season, and was also active on the Brantford hockey scene during the winters. He entered federal politics in 1962— "Some people convinced me to run federally and, through no fault of my own, I was elected"—and went to Ottawa, taking a drastic pay cut. His legal practice earned him $26,000 per year in 1962; as a Member of Parliament he had to live on $10,000. "It was hard going," he recalled many years later. "I had a family at home and I had to keep an apartment in Ottawa." But he had no complaints, nor would he do anything differently if he had to do it over.

Weekends he would return to Brantford by train, then make the trip back to Ottawa Sunday evening. He was re-elected twice more—in '63 and '65—and served for eighteen months as both solicitor general and, when Justice Minister Lucien Cardin became ill, as attorney general.

As solicitor general, Pennell was the first such minister in Canada to be given full ministerial status. Prior to his arrival, there had been solicitor generals without a full portfolio. But for Pennell, the role was in keeping with the hallmark of his life, which was the law. "The law," he said, "was the voyage of my life." Indeed, he had represented more than six hundred clients for free during his practice. His father had often repeated an old Welsh saying, "There comes a time for you to make your soul," and Larry took the words to heart. The law always gave a purpose to his life, and he forever believed that everybody ought to have representation of a lawyer in court. "Your freedom, your rights, are worth no more than your lawyer can win for you," he reasoned. "Otherwise, all the rights and freedoms are just words written on paper."

He was destined for a life in law at an early age. At fourteen, he accompanied his father when his dad had been called for jury duty. "I knew then that I wanted to be a lawyer," he recalled. Years later he was to article for the same lawyer he saw in action that day when his father was called for the jury.

In the House of Commons Pennell would give closely reasoned, sometimes legalistic views. In many respects, he was similar in temperament to Pearson. During moments of crisis, the optimistic Pearson would ride in, "the shining man of reason" as Newman described him after a heated debate between Cardin and the leader of the opposition, former Prime Minister John Diefenbaker. Wrote Newman: "Just as disaster seemed imminent, in rode the shining man of reason, smiling his boyish smile, under-reacting to the torrent of events threatening to engulf his government." Pearson would offer what seemed like the perfect diplomatic compromise. That too had been part of Pennell's nature from the time he had been very young. When former Finance Minister Walter Gordon, the leader of the Liberal Party's nationalistic left wing, let it be known he was about to resign, Pennell and a group of Gordon supporters—Gordon had often encouraged young members like Pennell when Pennell was first elected—organized a Gordon-must-stay dinner. Emotions were high, and Pennell, along with thirteen others, including Pearson, Keith Davey, Dr. Harry Harley, and John Munro, spoke passionately, appealing to Gordon to stay on. Several Quebec members of the cabinet also encouraged Gordon to remain, including Pierre Trudeau and Jean Marchand.

In April 1967, when Lucien Cardin's successor was named in the justice ministry, most political observers were surprised that it was not Pennell. Pennell was the obvious choice. Sincere, reasoned, intelligent, a successfully adroit lawyer, respected, he had proven himself as solicitor general. But Pierre Elliott Trudeau and Lester Pearson were developing a close relationship. Trudeau's father loved sports—he had once been part-owner of the Montreal Royals baseball team—as did Trudeau and Pearson. Pearson had been educated at Oxford, Trudeau at the London School of Economics. There were many long discussions between the two in Pearson's study at 24 Sussex Drive. Trudeau would outline his views of federalism and show Pearson a fresh insight into Quebec society. "Pearson, in turn, gave Trudeau a crash course in the politics of statesmanship," wrote Newman. No one knew, at the time, that Pearson had passed over Pennell in favour of the man who would go on to become one of Canada's longest-serving, and most popular, prime ministers.

Pennell first met Trudeau following the 1965 federal election. All the Liberals converged on Parliament Hill to meet, and Pennell greeted the newcomer cordially. "He was more or less on his own," said Pennell, who had no idea who the rookie was. A group of

Pennell's colleagues were gathered about, talking, and when they were done, they decided to all go to lunch. Pennell looked back to the newcomer from Mount Royal. "He looked a little lonely," said Pennell. "So I asked him if he'd like to come to lunch with us." He did.

The only time Pennell gave Trudeau advice was an occasion when, with great respect, "I suggested that he might be a little more tactful." Trudeau smiled at that.

For a time, Pennell and Trudeau sat beside each other in the House of Commons. There was a bill on capital punishment that was going through its second reading in the House. Conservative member Davey Fulton, the justice critic, rose and asked to make an amendment.

"I was on my feet and Pierre was beside me," said Pennell, who turned to Trudeau, the minister of justice, and asked, "What do you think?"

"Tell him to go to hell," replied Trudeau. His answer was never recorded in Hansard.

"Did you get the answer?" Pennell said to Fulton.

Pennell was convinced that Trudeau intentionally made his remarks audible to Fulton, but not to the speaker. All Pennell could say to Fulton was, "I'll give it some consideration."

When Trudeau won the Liberal leadership in 1968, he asked Pennell to stay on as minister of finance, but Pennell had always dreamed of becoming a judge.

"Trudeau was often quoting Plato or an author," noted Pennell, "so I had a trademark reply to him when he asked me to stay on." Said Pennell: "Like Hannibal, I've crossed the Rubicon and there's no turning back, Pierre."

"Fair enough," Trudeau replied.

Following his departure from federal politics, Pennell was appointed to the Supreme Court of Ontario in 1968, a position he would hold for eighteen years. He also served for the maximum two terms, from 1970 to 1976, as chancellor of McMaster University, his alma mater in Hamilton.

But he never forgot his hometown. He remained active in the Brantford community, serving as president of the Optimist Club of Brantford, chairman of the Brantford Suburban Planning Board and chairman of Brantford Parks and Recreation. He also found time to help coach a peewee hockey team that his son played on and he took two teams to provincial championships. It was a busy life. When people asked him how he managed to find the time to do it all he would reply, "It's easy. You just work eighteen hours a day and sleep six and it's no problem at all."

Not surprisingly, he was a much sought-after speaker. Indeed, the last time he and Waterloo Tiger president Ernie Goman met, years after their affiliation with the Intercounty, was when Goman asked him to speak at a joint Lions Club and Rotary Club meeting in Waterloo. Pennell flew in and Goman drove him the forty-five miles home at the end of the evening. But as Pennell's political career gave way to one on the Supreme Court of Ontario, many of the old Intercounty friendships grew distant. They all had their own lives to live. They were all busy. They continued to have respect for each other, and for those days when they had the Intercounty Baseball Association in common. It was like an old boys club. They might not see each other, but they more or less kept track of where everybody was. They valued their membership in that club of so many years before. It had been a special time. Pennell always had a great ability to recall past events, an ability his legal colleagues could see when he would remember the gist of a legal argument in a book he had read, often even recalling the page number. So he remembered the baseball years better than most.

"The years rolled by so fast I didn't know they were going," Pennell said when he turned eighty. Baseball had been a big part of an extremely active life. "The only thing I didn't do was make a lot of money," he said. "I could never make money but I was always busy." And through it all his wife supported him fully. "She was a gold brick," he would say. She had always told him to pursue his dreams.

After his days on the Supreme Court of Ontario he served as vice-chairman of the Ontario Mental Health Review Board, and continued to practise law in Brantford. Finally, in 1993, he had to slow down due to illness. "I've had a rough spell lately," he said back then, in a way that showed he was still a fighter. Eight decades of living had not diminished his will to live. For some people, eight decades would be enough. But not for Pennell, the man who had always gotten an energy, an intrinsic joy from each day, from people. He did not have the temperament of a complainer. Doctors had found fluid on his lungs and he had a lengthy stay at the hospital. There they found a cancerous lesion around his eyes which was removed. Still later they believed he might be suffering from leukemia. "I've had a few problems but I'm cheerful about life. I don't think I'll make it for the doubleheader but I'll be able to finish nine innings."

He never tired of talking baseball, or of those seasons near mid-century when the Intercounty reached its zenith. Indeed, he found it almost medicinal to talk of those days. He loved baseball. "I think it's a great game. I attended most of the games of the Brantford Red Sox unless I had a case," he said. When Brantford installed lights in the summer of '49, it meant Pennell wouldn't have to miss as many games. He'd get his work done in the day and be free to go to the game at night. It was a godsend. "It was like the difference—forgive me—between day and night," he would say. "Baseball is a game where you never know if you're going to win or not. You may have the best club but somehow fate could be against you." He was talking about the Galts of 1949, and about the Red Sox of 1950. "Sometimes we won when we shouldn't have won, but it all levels out, I guess."

What intrigued Pennell about baseball was the way each player on the team had an important individual role to play in the team's success. "The great thing is that although it is a team sport, everyone is an individual. You get a hit, or an out. You're on your own out there all the time, and yet you have to be part of the team to succeed." But it was more than that. "It's played at the right time of the year and under the lights," he said. Something was special about the fact that baseball heralded in the promise and expectancy of spring and closed out summer when the cool winds of autumn were blowing. And there was always that magic of playing under the lights. "There was great camaraderie. It was just wonderful. So many fine memories."

On a beautiful spring day in March of 1995 Pennell drove eighteen miles upriver to Galt. He had just passed his driver's test a few days earlier—being over eighty, he was subject to the Ontario law that requires drivers over age eighty to be tested annually—and he was feeling good. It was a challenge to pass that test. He didn't look at it as a slight against his age. Rather, he would say he felt privileged. He had to wait eighty years before he could take that test. So now it was spring, he was mobile once more, and he hadn't felt better in months. Passing his driver's test as spring wetted the land was somehow invigorating. This was baseball weather.

He was smiling when I met him. We had talked several times, sometimes for an hour at a time, but we had never met. He wore a navy blue suit, the suit of a judge or a cabinet minister, and tie, and his white hair looked almost fashionably long for a man of eighty. Perhaps what made it look long—it wasn't—was that he still had a good head of hair. He looked distinguished, and he looked healthy. That smile betrayed his inner delight at life.

We talked for a time and looked at pictures of his African softball championship team from the war, at his scrapbook, at other pictures.

There were pictures of he and Lester Pearson in there, as well as some of the notable cases he presided over, or in which he acted as defence counsel. There was also a picture of the team he and Mike King organized in Brantford immediately after the war. Some of the old baseball clippings and pictures were kept by his late sister, who, he noted, was "the greatest ball fan in the world." He could still hear her calling balls and strikes.

Soon it was time for lunch. We drove to downtown Hespeler, which wasn't far, and stopped at Ernie's restaurant on the corner of Queen Street and Guelph Avenue. We got a nice table out on the balcony, which was open, looking out toward the Speed River. The spring air was fresh and the sun was shining. It was warm. There was so much to talk about. He remembered that one day—May 24—in 1946 when the Brantford Nine-and-a-Halfs were beaten in Brantford by Galt, and then came to Hespeler for an afternoon game. He looked over his right shoulder and pointed down the road. It was Guelph Avenue. "Hespeler played in a park just over there," he said. Brantford got their first post-war win that spring day—which was much like this one—forty-nine years ago. I knew that Jimmy, had he survived the war, would have been there that day.

Finally, we had talked enough for one day. Through it all I could sense his passion for baseball, but I came to recognize that it was not solely a passion for baseball. He had a passion for life. For people. Several times he remarked how good his life had been; how many fine people he'd had the opportunity to meet and come to know.

Our conversation was uplifting. Pennell's passion for living was infectious. "When I was christened," he said, "my name was registered as Lawrence T. Pennell. My middle name was "T." Just the letter. That was it. Why my parents did it I don't really know. There were six in my family and all had middle names. I was the youngest." Now, at eighty, he was thinking of changing that middle initial to a name. "I want to change it to Thankful," he said. "I'm just so thankful; thanking life, my parents, and everybody. I haven't actually done it, but I intend to. It was a great handicap to me just to have the letter 'T' because on all legal documents, when I'd notarize it, it would say, 'Write your name in full' and it would always come back. It was taking so much time that we finally had to have a form printed saying 'Please note that T is the name.'" It was unusual, he admitted, for his parents to have given him the initial and not a middle name. "But they must have had some premonition that I would fill it out as I wanted it." Indeed, as he started thinking about it, he could recall his parents saying precisely that. "Few children can make out their own name," they told him. "You can insert what you like."

"Someday," his mother had said, "you'll know what the T stands for. It will come to you." It was a small thing, he thought, but it was a pleasurable thing to him. "We all live for the day, I guess," he reflected. "We don't think of the future, and then, of the past." But Larry Thankful Pennell was thinking of both. "There's an old saying," he noted, "that if you can get five senior citizens together they can remember everything."

Memory tells him the baseball had been good. The weather had been good. There had been the pleasure of seeing Lockington run down long balls in centre field, and of running the bases like a deer. And the pleasure of beating the Galts of '49. Of knowing Pearson. Of having lived some great days and nights; having met some wonderful people over the years. Then there were the near-dozen murder cases he worked on. There was Lillie's famous hit in the twenty-first inning of a playoff game that gave Waterloo a win over Brantford in '50. There had been the pleasure, and dread, of seeing Rosen, Warren, Kaiser, Creedon, Shelton, Perkins, and Waite that one season. The thrill of watching Gibbs pitch Brantford to a win in the seventh game, and of waiting for Lipka to fire the ball from third to first. And the enjoyment of getting to know Wilmer Fields.

In the early autumn of 1995 I drove to Brantford, picked up Pennell at his ranch-style home, and continued on to pick up Lipka. We lunched not far from Lipka's house, sitting in the back corner of a quiet restaurant so we could talk baseball.

"How are you?" I asked Larry as we drove back to his house. He had mentioned he had to go down to the cancer clinic in Toronto in a day or two.

"Oh, pretty good," he said. There was a pause. "Some days not so well. Some days I feel like I could pitch a doubleheader and others I feel like I can only pitch relief for a couple innings."

One of the things that keeps him young in spirit is his schedule. People still call him asking him to speak to various groups. And a law firm in Brantford has been asking his help of late. He obliges. He loves a good legal problem.

We continue on to his house on this cold fall day. It is October and the sky is grey. Winter can't be far off. The days had come and gone since that early spring day in Hespeler. Another baseball season had come and gone. Larry shared a story with me about a trip he and his wife took the previous spring. They were in Harrisburg,

Pennsylvania, eating at a restaurant, when a tall, good-looking fellow, about Pennell's age, entered. The other man was eating with his wife at another table. After seeing the man, Larry looked at his wife and told her he would bet money that the other man was a lawyer. "He just looked like a lawyer," he said. "I don't know why." To settle his curiosity he got up and approached the fellow. Yes, as a matter of fact, he was a lawyer. Pennell told him he just looked like a lawyer, he had the same air about him as a former colleague of Pennell's, John Robinette, one of Canada's most renowned lawyers. "You have that same presence," Pennell told him, "that way of carrying yourself, of commanding respect."

"Where are you from?" the man asked.

"Ontario," said Pennell.

"Ontario?" the man replied. "I went to Osgoode Hall Law School."

"I went there too," Pennell said. They talked some more, shaking their heads at the coincidence. It's a small world, they both thought. What possessed Pennell to approach the man in the first place even Pennell can't say. He just had a feeling. But he has always enjoyed the communion of his fellow humans.

He has held a personal philosophy about life, about happiness, that makes him reach out to others. "Happiness is in the daily routine of your life," he said. "That's where you find most of your happiness. We're all going to get hurt in life. You can't help it if you're a participant in life. But happiness is not in material things, or in acquiring things. It's not in your office, or in how much money you have. It's in our everyday lives and how we get along with other people. By that standpoint, I've had a happy life."

He was hesitant to continue. "Here I go moralizing," he observed, "but I'm not really. I'm just a country boy and it's my general-store philosophy that I have. You can't develop as a human being without going out and mixing with other people. It's in the mixing with other people you develop yourself." Socializing, he always believed, is the best way of growing spiritually. "It's that interrelationship, that intercourse, that develops character and personality."

Even at eighty Justice Pennell's nature compelled him to reach out to another, to satiate his curiosity, and to reaffirm his affiliation with mankind. As he and the other man spoke they realized they had both been walking the halls of Osgoode Hall at about the same time. Though Pennell was four years older, it was probable that they were there at the same time for at least one year. After the American graduated his parents encouraged him to return to Virginia, and so ended his stint in Canada. Then the stranger's wife spoke to Pennell.

"You have the nicest titles in Canada," she said, noting how distinguished the title Queen's Counsel, or Q.C., was after a lawyer's name.

"I'm a Queen's Counsel," said Pennell. "If your husband had stayed there he would have been one too."

"He should have stayed there, but then I wouldn't have met him," she said.

The inner voice that told Pennell to go up to the other man was the same inner voice that spoke to Pennell at home in the streets, arenas, and ballyards of Brantford. It was why he was probably the best-known man in the city in the 1950s and '60s. Now he goes out and no one recognizes him, though it doesn't disturb him. "I don't mind in the least," he said. "Young people are coming up, new people, with their own interests, friends and heroes. They have to have their chance. All the old-timers are forgotten, but it's the same with every generation." As we spoke, Lipka, who but for the war would likely have worn a Brooklyn Dodger uniform, sat alone at home, his wife having died just months before. The thousands who had once cheered for him, and spoken his name with reverence solely because of the things he could do on the ball diamond, were long gone.

In September of 1996, Pennell once again drove down to see me. We would have lunch, and chat about sports and life. We talked little of baseball that day. As we ate, a well-dressed middle-aged man walked by. He did a double take as he passed our table, having obviously recognized Pennell. "Excuse me," he said, "but aren't you Justice Pennell?

"Why, yes I am," answered Pennell.

The man introduced himself, and Pennell recognized him. He was a fellow lawyer in town on business. They spoke for a few minutes. Pennell rose to talk, his face showing the great delight he felt at having been recognized. The other man had an obvious regard for Pennell. "They still talk about that judgment you wrote," he told Pennell. The other man even asked Pennell to venture over to his nearby table to meet a colleague. The colleague also knew of Pennell. They spoke of mutual friends.

Pennell always took great care and pride in writing his decisions. One such decision even made it onto the CTV national news. The case involved a man and woman who were never married but who obviously loved one another very much. When the man died the woman was made the beneficiary of his will, even though the man had only one witness sign the will. The will was contested by the man's children. But to Pennell, it was obvious the man wanted his long-time friend to be the rightful beneficiary. The side representing the children, who were grown, contended she was only a woman with whom he'd had an affair. Justice Pennell ruled in the woman's favour, calling it "an affair of the heart." Pennell happened to be in St. Catharines the next evening and turned on the television to hear the case mentioned on the news.

Now, while at lunch with Pennell, I couldn't help but notice how much respect the two men had for him. When Pennell returned to our table he wore a great smile and his spirit had been lifted tremendously. He thoroughly enjoyed the collegiality of life. And every time I talked with him or saw him, my spirit grew, seemingly from within, and it would become infectious throughout the day. I cherished those times spent with Larry Pennell. They were like a tonic to the soul.

Pennell had begun to write about the pluses and minuses of his life, the inspiring things and the times that proved less positive. As we departed one day he told me not to get discouraged about the book I was writing. "I have only one wish and that is that your book gets written," he said. I told him how much I had enjoyed the afternoon with him. Then he added, "This is definitely going to go in the plus side."

I have thought often about the time when Pennell was first elected to Parliament and was called over to 24 Sussex Drive by Prime Minister Pearson. On the back lawn overlooking the Ottawa River, Pearson outlined his plans for Pennell's progression, from parliamentary secretary to cabinet minister.

"What do you think about all that?" Pearson asked.

"Well, Mr. Prime Minister," Pennell replied with some humility, "I have to tell you that I feel very inadequate."

"Good," said the Nobel laureate Pearson. "If that's all you feel then you'll be prime minister one day."

Had circumstance worked a little differently, he very well might have become Canada's prime minister. As it was, Trudeau tried to entice him to stay on in federal politics, offering him the finance portfolio, but Pennell declined.

Later, when Trudeau was championing the Charter of Rights and Freedoms, Pennell told him he had overlooked one important thing.

"Pierre, you should have included the right to solitude."

Trudeau grinned. "Well, Larry, we are doing our best, but it's not always possible to think of everything."

For Pennell, politics, like the law, sport, and his long marriage, made life worth living.

"Baseball and hockey are the two greatest games in the world," he said one spring day many years ago. We had gotten up from the table that day after a long lunch and he looked satisfied, contented, like Mother Earth looked on that remarkably fresh spring-like day. "I couldn't have had it any better," he said. He was talking about baseball, about politics, about his marriage, about his legal career, about anything and everything he has been a part of. "It was wonderful," said one of Canada's most eloquent and sincere elder statesmen. The Intercounty never had a better ambassador. Nor did the law have a more eloquent master, someone whose joy in life, and people, touched deeply all he came into contact with.

Larry Pennell continues to live in Brantford.

Watty Reid and Gus Murray

Gus Murray

Gus Murray had great reservations about returning to run the Terriers in 1950. The 1949 season had been a trying one. He had been run ragged by several of his high-priced imports, including Goody Rosen, who demanded both a car for himself and a new bicycle for his son. Two players, Creedon and Waite, had physically assaulted him. The near-strike during a pivotal point in the playoffs, led by Creedon and Warren, had virtually negated all his hard work in building a contender and bringing fans out to the ballpark. In truth, he had done wonders; the season just past was likely the most exciting Terrier season ever, and there had been plenty of exciting seasons over the years. Still, it had taken its toll. "A guy has to be awfully thick-skinned to put up with all that stuff," reflected Murray years later. "Some of these guys had major-league experience. I didn't. It was my first year in senior ball."

Several decades later a local sportswriter, highlighting the city's sports history, barely touched on Murray's 1949 team. He wrote at length about the championship teams of the 1920s and '30s, but there was only one line about the '49 Terriers. With a team of imports—he erroneously reported they had just two homebrews when in fact, they had six or seven—they lost out to Brantford in the playoffs, he wrote. When people looked at Intercounty titles, it was easy to dismiss the

'49 Terriers. They won the pennant, but lost out in the playoffs, whereas a number of previous Galt teams had won the Intercounty title and then gone on to win the all-Ontario crown. If the writer was an out-of-towner or someone who hadn't known the summer of '49 firsthand—and he didn't—it would be easy to dismiss them and concentrate, instead, on the championship seasons.

Murray was so dejected over the hassles he had with his players and with the Galt Parks Board that he intimated he might not be back for the 1950 season. At the heart of his argument with the parks board was money from the concession. "We are investing heavily in baseball talent to provide the citizens of Galt with the best baseball this coming season," he said, "and we feel that we should have the concessions at Dickson Park for senior baseball games." If the Terriers could count on that money it would help them finance the team, Murray told city council.

But the Galt Parks Board had turned down the Terriers' request. The park concessions had been granted to someone else in 1948 with a two-year renewal option. It would be unfair, council argued, for them to cancel that contract midway through the term. Besides, Mayor Mel Moffatt, who had thrown out the first ball the previous spring, noted that if the agreement was broken the city would have a lawsuit on its hands. "The agreement was made at a time when it was difficult to get anyone to take the park concession," he said. Furthermore, Mr. Dedman had quit his job in order to take over the concessions.

But Murray, whose Terriers had paid the parks board $10,000 for groundskeeping and maintenance—he'd paid a further $21,000 in salaries—was upset that his team could not profit from the concession like other teams around the league. The club finished the year with a surplus of only two thousand dollars, even though Murray had done wonders to draw fans. He had good reason to expect his club to reap the rewards, but, in fairness to the parks board, no one had figured on a Gus Murray coming along.

That spring someone wrote a letter to the editor about Gus. They were highly critical of his constant whining over how the parks board was being uncooperative with the Galt Athletic Club. Clearly, some people had heard enough. But a Murray supporter countered:

> Dear Gus,
>
> What a man you are. How you have stood above the abuse and criticisms heaped unjustly on your head since the beginning of the ball season without blowing your top is beyond me....You contacted Mickey Owen, and how the average person laughed at your audacity. Some,

probably Mr. Fan himself, claimed it was just for publicity. However, Mr. Brain, the sportswriter, can confirm that it was true and can also confirm how close Mr. Owen was to coming to Galt. Then on your own you contacted the head of the New York Yankees and so impressed him that George Selkirk was sent to Galt to look the situation over. All of us were dumbfounded to learn that Galt could interest such leaders in baseball. No one can claim that that was just a figment of your imagination because Selkirk was here and his picture was in the paper and the result was that Tom Padden came to Galt as playing manager.

Then you promised Galt fans a winning team and a heavy hitting team. Again you were laughed at. You also said you would have crowds in excess of 5,000 at the games and this caused a bigger laugh. Well Gus, in both of the above respects, with all the abuse you have taken, it must be some consolation to take the last laugh there.

Yes Mr. Ball Fan, Gus Murray spent many a sleepless night along the way doing just that. But he did it ... and if there is one person in Galt who should be awarded a medal for doing the most for Galt in 1949, it should be you.

It was ironic that in the years when the Terriers had their biggest gate receipts—1949 and 1950—they had no control over their concessions. Years earlier, when they did have the concessions, attendance was poor and the parks board could barely give the job away. And, in 1951, when tenders for the concession at Dickson Park were up for grabs again, attendance had dropped off. But by then, Murray was gone.

In January of 1950, just months before spring training was to begin, Laurie Brain interviewed Murray once more, asking about his plans for the upcoming season. Murray said he would go to the United States. No one seemed to know just where the Terriers stood; nor did anyone know where Murray stood with the Terriers. "Latest word from the energetic little man who lifted baseball in Galt out of the doldrums and placed it on a plane unreached by anyone else in this city in more than twenty years," wrote Brain, "is that he is thinking of shoving off for the Excited States. Rumors to that effect have been circulating throughout the Little Manchester city for some weeks, but yesterday was the first time that Gus could be pinned down to a concrete statement."

Said Murray: "I intend to go to New York next month and later to other points in the United States. My trip will concern baseball. I have had several offers in the United States, some of them varied, but one very interesting proposition has been made to me. It is quite possible that I may take a position as assistant business manager with one of the clubs, with some say in the club's affairs." Selkirk, who two seasons later would manage the Yankees' Kansas City farm team where a young prospect named Mickey Mantle was playing, had made him an offer to go to Binghampton. One destination, after New York, was Sarasota, Florida, but Galt's "Bill Veeck" would not confirm his plans. As for the Terriers, he said that a meeting of the Galt Athletic Club directors, to be held that night, might clarify things locally.

It was inconceivable that Galt would not field a Terrier team for the 1950 season, especially since the Terriers had always been one of the strongest organizations in the Intercounty. And they were coming off a banner year, albeit a disappointing one in the end. Murray said the directors had just received copies of the financial status of the club from their auditors. He wouldn't rule out a return in some capacity to help prepare a team later in the spring, but everyone knew that his dispute with the Galt Parks Board was a stumbling block. He had made it clear that he was far from happy over what he thought were excessive fees the Terriers had to pay for park rental in 1949. "I'm not pulling any punches," he said. "I feel that I was unfairly dealt with by both the parks board and city council. I was given to understand that under no circumstances would the park rental exceed six thousand dollars. That was the figure on which we based the season's operations." Instead, once the rental was added to the fees for ticket takers and sellers, police, park improvements made at the club's expense including the erection of bleachers and lockers, the club paid out more than $19,000. "Very few Triple-A ball clubs pay half that amount of money," Murray argued.

In November, just before he left to attend the winter baseball meetings in Baltimore, he contacted the parks board for a final answer, one way or the other, on the operation of the park and concession for the 1950 season. No action was taken. Said an angry Murray: "I, myself, will never attend another parks board meeting." Murray admitted that Rosen was interested in running the ball club, "But if I can't come to reasonable terms with the parks board, I know that Rosen won't have any success."

Murray had the franchise with a three-year option and, if need be, he would not field a team for a year. Under Intercounty rules, a team could drop out for a year and then return. "Of course," said Murray, "I'm not saying that's what's going to happen." In the meantime, he was speaking to boys at baseball banquets and elsewhere. He was far from through with baseball. In November of '49, only two months after the season ended, he travelled to Baltimore to the winter baseball meetings.

Only days before Murray's expected departure for Florida, *Guelph Mercury* sports editor Rex MacLeod wrote, "If you know Gus he should return with more than a tan." He continued: "Over in Galt last night Gus Murray cleared the decks for another big year in the Intercounty. He has been keeping the Galt baseball public guessing for the past few weeks but last night he finally made a decision." Indeed, Murray had sent out a dispatch just that morning revealing that he had leased the franchise for another three years. "Gus Murray," said the short statement, "will field a strong team." MacLeod didn't doubt that. "Like many others," he wrote, "we chuckled last year when Gus decided to organize a team, but before the schedule was finished he had us pop-eyed in disbelief. Gus learned a great deal from last season's operations and he might do even better this year. For his sake we hope he learned the secret of preserving harmony on his club. Disunity cost him a provincial title last season."

In Florida that spring Murray put out a few feelers with some players, including Bagby and Bill Hornsby, the son of Rogers Hornsby. Rosen was returning to play for Galt, and so was Kaiser. Perkins too. With Lillie back, and Shelton promising to return, the team looked fairly strong. It was while he was in Florida that spring that Murray spoke with Wes Ferrell. Ferrell, a Greensboro, North Carolina, product, was a big-name player. He had broken into the majors in 1927 with Cleveland of the American Association, and had finished up with the Boston Braves of the National League in 1941, posting a lifetime .280 batting average over fifteen major-league seasons. His best year was 1935 when he hit .347. Murray was persuasive: Come to Galt, he would tell prospective players and managers. You'll be well looked after. What's more, he used his friendship with George Selkirk to good advantage, making sure people knew that Selkirk was ready to help the team.

If people back in Galt had been surprised when Selkirk showed up the previous winter, they were just as surprised to hear that Murray was negotiating with someone of Ferrell's stature. And perhaps most surprising of all was that Ferrell just might come. Years later, his brother, Rick Ferrell, was inducted into the Hall of Fame at Cooperstown, having caught more games than any other American Leaguer (1806) until Carlton Fisk came along. A great defensive catcher, he also hit over .300 four times in his eighteen-year career. In

1933 Connie Mack showed just how much respect he had for Ferrell when he had him catch all nine innings of the first all-star game. The Ferrell name carried a lot of weight in baseball circles.

When Murray returned from Florida he thought he had an agreement with Ferrell. Then, on March 22, a special-delivery air mail-letter arrived from Sarasota. It was addressed to Mr. Gus Murray, Gault, [sic] Ontario, Canada.

> Dear Gus:
>
> I've decided that I won't be able to play for the salary that you offered me. I expected at least a B contract, which ranges from four to six thousand dollars. Since your league has a salary limit, I know that you can't pay that much. I hope that I haven't bungled things up for you — I enjoyed seeing you and here's hoping you have lots of luck in the coming season.
>
> Sincerely,
> Wes Ferrell

Murray lost no time in responding. On March 23 he wrote:

> Dear Wes: Your special delivery letter of March 21 has just been handed to me, and to put it mildly, I am very disappointed. My primary objective for my trip to Florida was to get a good manager and after I contacted you, I thought everything was OK. So then I started for home. Vic Barnhart really wanted the job here and he waited until Monday of this week and now he has signed with the Guelph Maple Leafs. If this will make it any easier for you, I will run the team until you get here around the 6th of May. We would still give you the same salary as agreed upon and which I will put in writing at the bottom of this page. After I got back from Florida I contacted Mr. Charlton about the house for you. I really hope you will reconsider our proposition and I will certainly do everything I can to make your visit to Galt for your wife and family a very happy one.
>
> Yours truly,
> Gus Murray
>
> Season Salary $3,000
> Rent Free house $450
> Finish first bonus $100

But Ferrell declined the offer, leaving Murray to find someone on short notice. And, despite all the quality players who signed on in 1950, the Terriers struggled. Gone was the magic of the season before. Crowds were smaller, though still large compared to the preceding few years. The next season, 1951, Murray abandoned the Terriers, though unofficially he still had a hand in the club's operations behind the scenes. He signed on to help Guelph, a team and town that sorely needed his promotional wizardry. There, he signed Pete Gray, the one-armed player who had been a novelty for a year in the majors during the war, to a personal services contract, and he also signed Pat Seery, the only player to that point—other than Babe Ruth—to hit four home runs in a single major-league game, to the same kind of deal. He would take them with him wherever he went. Murray promised big crowds and exciting baseball. Eventually he pulled out of Guelph after running into some of the same types of problems he had faced in Galt. "I never got along with the top man in Guelph, Kendrick," he said. As the years passed he distanced himself more and more from having an active hand in baseball. He remained a fan though, and as the years came and went, he could remember with fondness that summer of '49.

Several years passed before Murray severed all ties with the Intercounty. When he did, the league was poorer for it. He had given baseball in southern Ontario a breath of life. "Gus always seemed to work on the edge of legality," someone later said. "We used the phrase that 'he was a crook' loosely, but he wasn't a crook in the literal sense. What he was was an entrepreneur. He was doing things that conservative Galtonians couldn't believe, and it was always at someone else's expense. But he was an extraordinary promoter."

Shelton, like some of the other imports that summer, believed Murray was raking in the dough with the huge crowds that were the norm all season. Said Creedon, "To hell with glory, we want the dough." But it wasn't that easy. The expenses Murray faced were very real. Shelton's image of him as a crook was just that—an image. Another long-time Galtonian figured Murray had a penchant for doing things that were unethical, though he stopped short of saying Murray was crooked. But had Murray been doing what he did that summer in a major-league city, he would have been called a genius. Still, Murray's work didn't go entirely unnoticed.

None other than the esteemed Pennell proposed that the Intercounty Baseball Association give a yearly award to people like Murray for the work he did in '49. It would be an annual award to the man making the most outstanding contribution to Intercounty ball. Pennell said the award could be granted to the man for his services and interest in any division of the association. "For instance, Ernie Goman of Waterloo has done much to further ball in that city and has always lived up to the rules. And Gus Murray has done wonders in Galt."

The years came and went. Murray concentrated on his business interests, though he always had one eye on the baseball scene. By the time he sold his paint and decorating business he had acquired a fair amount of wealth. His wife, Grace, died in the 1980s, but he still put in an afternoon of work each day above his old business after it moved from Water to Main Street. By 1994, he was frail and even though he had lost sight in one eye, his mind was sharp. One day he thought he'd get to the bottom of a mystery that had plagued him for some time. By the mid-1990s the pennant the Terriers won in '49 had been missing for forty years. As a child, his son, Keith, had boasted about it when he was down at Alf Turley's barbershop. So Keith took the pennant down one day to show it off and the barber asked if he could display it on his wall. A couple of decades came and went, and the barber who had worked there at the time finally retired due to ill health. The pennant, presumably, went with him. Somehow Murray never took the time to call up the old proprietor to ask for the return of the pennant.

Until the summer of 1994. It took some time for Murray to think of the old barber's name, but finally it came to him. He walked unsteadily to his phone in the upstairs office he still frequented on Main Street.

"Norm Nicholson?" he asked. Standing, he lost his balance for a moment, almost falling over, then recovered.

"Yes," came the reply.

"Are you the famous piano player?" He waited for an answer, and then said, "I'm starting up an orchestra." Murray, who many people around town believed was losing his marbles, still had a sense of humour. "I need a piano player. I've got Red Pratt lined up and I need you."

But Nicholson, even more brittle than Murray, couldn't appreciate the humour. Finally Murray asked him if he remembered the pennant he had once hung up in his barbershop. Nicholson could only vaguely recall it. "Do you still have it?" Murray asked.

Nicholson hadn't seen it in years. "Well, ask your wife if you still have it," Gus said. But his wife was dead. "Oh, I see," said Gus. And that was it. All hope for the pennant, one of the most storied pennants in Intercounty history, and won by perhaps the greatest semi-pro team to ever play in Canada, was lost forever. Nicholson died a few weeks later.

One cold winter day in February 1993, Murray was sitting on his couch at home, enjoying a few hours of idle chat with his old friend, Watty Reid. They couldn't help but talk of that season. Soon the talk moved on to the kittens Murray kept at his downtown store. "You always had kittens in the store," Reid said. "Those kittens made more money than the wallpaper did," Murray explained. Even off the field he was the consummate promoter, with an uncanny knack for knowing what would work and what wouldn't. When customers came into the store, their kids would always be drawn over to the kittens. That way their parents could spend more time looking at wallpaper and paint. But the store, and the cats, had been gone for years. "So you're out of the cat breeding business now, are you, Gus?" joked Reid. But until a few years previous, Murray had still been breeding cats. He sold one young couple a purebred and told them, "That cat is going to pay your daughter's way through college." That never happened. Instead, the young couple ended up spending thousands on the cat in medical expenses.

Gus had his detractors, but he also had some vocal supporters. League president Otto Manske, like Pennell, had gone on record as saying the Intercounty should give him an award for the great work he had done in Galt, while *Guelph Mercury* sportswriter Rex MacLeod, writing in 1949, after Galt was put out by the Red Sox, said: "At season's end the Intercounty should give the diminutive Galt maestro a vote of thanks for his contribution to the league. There isn't any doubt that Murray's high-priced help has pulled in several thousand additional spectators around the circuit. Win or lose, the Terriers are the most colourful band in the loop, but none of them can outshine their leader."

Murray believed in baseball all the rest of his life; believed it was a worthwhile, even desirable pastime for youngsters to pursue. He never failed to give a receptive youngster a few tips on how to throw a fastball. Once, in 1993 when talking to a friend whose young son was not intending to sign up for ball, Murray figured he could help the boy. "I'll talk with him," said Murray. "He's got to play ball." He and the young teenager were three generations apart and had never met, but Murray figured he could convince him to play if he had a talk with him.

⚾ ⚾ ⚾

APRIL 20, 1994. The birds were singing the song of the season. An aging Gus Murray sat in his spacious office on the second floor of an old stone building on Main Street. Below was his old paint and decorating store. When he sold the business below he kept his second-floor office. How many more spring days like this would he be able to look out his office window and see a summer of baseball looming, bright and fresh, on the horizon, I wondered. I knew that this might be the last afternoon we would ever spend together, talking of that long-ago summer and those players who last picked up a baseball forty years ago. I would pick up a clipping, and he was there to interpret, to explain, to expand, and tell me what wasn't written in the column.

The windows were long and faced out onto Main Street, to the old stone buildings across the street. Looking out you could see the Four Corners, which is and was the heart of downtown Galt. And coming in through those large windows, all of spring—its brightness, its blue sky, its freshness after a cold, dreary winter—poured in. Soon a new baseball season would arrive. Already the major-league teams were playing. The light from outside on this afternoon was ample, and the office lights were left off. It was better that way, more serene, contemplative. Like it must have been in the spring of '49, or, indeed, in a spring late in the last century when two other people stood or sat up in this very building (which was even then old) and perhaps talked of a baseball team from the 1870s. Gus Murray had lived through eight decades of springs like this and you wonder how many more he had in him. He was looking pale. The frailty of his gait, the way he had difficulty balancing when standing or walking. His inability to see clearly. Said Gallinger: "He's not of this world for long." Yet Murray's mind was sharp and he could still smile.

"That was a long time ago," he says of 1949. There are some details he has forgotten. Not many, but some. So we talk in the natural and warm light of what seems like the first day of spring, and we talk for hours. He pulls out old newspaper clippings from that season. The paper is brittle—pieces break off as we handle them and scatter on the carpeted floor—and they have browned in the fifty years since they were new. As the old newspapers disintegrate in pieces onto the floor, I see words and letters broken from their paragraphs. History is leaving us. Nothing lasts forever. Some people assume the written word, unlike the writer, is eternal, but the words and letters of just half a century ago were disappearing before our eyes.

Two large windows overlooking Main Street dominated the room, and underneath, on the sidewalks, people were basking in the radiant warmth of the spring sun which was lighting their faces. It was a good day. You wanted the crystalline day to flourish and last forever. To

Murray it was reminiscent of one spring day long ago. "On April 19, 1949, we had an exhibition game with Toronto," he reminded me. When Gallinger would make one of his frequent visits the two would talk baseball and hockey and anything else that mattered to them. It was the same when Watty Reid came over. Or Lillie. There was a bond between each of us that had its origins in 1949 and the years immediately afterward. We all described Murray as "a character," and none of us was wrong for saying it.

Murray was blind in one eye and as I looked at him, and listened, I could see only one eye light up. The other looked dead. He talked like he always talked, in a high machine-gun staccato. He was always high-strung, which was neither good nor bad, but was just the way he was. "Did I ever tell you ... ?" he asked countless times throughout the afternoon, about this and that. "Did you know ... ?" His back was ailing him of late, and he was becoming very unsteady when he walked. When someone came up the stairs and into his second-floor office, he could not recognize them with his eyes. He saw the form, but it was only when they talked that he knew them.

It had been a year since I knew, in my heart, that I had to write about that erstwhile Galt Terrier baseball season. The story was one that needed to be told. It would be criminal, knowing what I knew, if it was never written about the way it should be written, from beginning to end. That afternoon he introduced me to a woman who was doing some bookkeeping for him. "This is Charlie Hodge, one of the best ballplayers I ever knew," he said. "He's also one of the leading professors in Alberta. He used to play for me." I thanked him for the compliment.

Murray was retired and maintained his office only as a symbol, and to oversee his investments. There was a bed, sink, and counter in an adjoining room, and once when I sat with him he had to lie down while he spoke. It was more a meeting place than an office. It was a good place, a place to go and remember all the yesterdays; to contemplate the tomorrows. Old clippings and pictures were there. A television. And those large windows that let in the vast light of day were there, too.

There was so much that happened that last not-so-sleepy post-war season before the decade ended; so much that happened along the banks of the Grand, at the river flats where the ball yard is, when the crowds came out to watch the Terriers. People were hoping for an enduring peace as the year 1949 unfolded. Mankind could not stand another global war. So the world prayed, fearful of the utter destruction another war would bring. They were ready to gather by the thousands at a baseball game, to follow their team through a season, to cheer and gossip, to share in something special, even magical. They may not have been quite ready for Gus, but most embraced all he did. I now looked back at Gus, through the filter of fifty years, and realized how instrumental he was to the community in the 1940s and '50s.

Even in his later years he was at the centre of controversy. When he was forced to move his store—there had been a bad flood of the Grand in 1974 and the conservation authority bought up all the Water Street buildings they could—he bought a building on Main Street near the Four Corners. A long-time tenant of that building, Law Photography, was ordered to vacate, much to their chagrin. But Murray countered that there was nothing he could do. He needed a place too, and he owned the building. It was too bad, he said, but someone had to go.

One day Gus, emerging from the long staircase that descends from his office to Main Street, stepped into a hole on the bricked sidewalk. He took the city to court. If anything, he was still feisty. About this time a customer of his got a bill for work Murray Swain Decorating had done on one of his rental properties years before. But the customer had paid the bill years earlier. "I know what he's doing up there," said the customer. "He's earning a lot of money doing that." He shook his head. "I was armed," he said. "I had the receipt and the endorsed cheque." But what made him angry was that other people might not be so well armed. "People get an old bill that Gus says hadn't been paid and they get nervous. Many people will just pay it without realizing it had already been paid." Or, if they couldn't find a receipt, even though they were sure they paid it, they'd pay it again just to be done with it. The customer, who was in the medical profession and rents property out, would have liked nothing better than to go to court with Murray. But the time and expense were just not worth it. He never paid the second bill. "Even if I didn't have the endorsed cheque I don't think I would have paid it," he said.

It was not the first time Murray had been accused of underhanded techniques. Years before, when he bought property on south Water Street, he raised the rent and evicted people. Some people who had lived there for years had to leave. One died of a heart attack, his death being attributed to the distress caused by the move. But Murray dismisses it by saying the man must have had an undetected weakness.

Rosen died that spring when I was meeting with Gus and I knew that many other teammates would be gone soon too—some already were—and once that happened, their story, the real story, would never be told properly. Murray gave Galt and the rest of the Intercounty a taste of big-league baseball, though on a smaller scale. Yes, it was there in Galt that summer, in Dickson Park, on the streets alongside the Grand River, within sight and sound of an entire town. Indeed, the very air that season carried a scent that blew only once, but for a summer, there wasn't a person in town who wasn't caught up in the aroma. The afternoon wore on in Murray's hideaway. Soon it was six o'clock. We descended the long staircase to Main Street, and Gus met a middle-aged woman and her red-headed young daughter, whom he recognized. They chatted for a few minutes as the sun was dying into dusk. It was warm; there was promise of green buds blooming, and of a leafy summer. She remembered the cats he always used to have in the store. Gus told the daughter she had beautiful hair. He still knew how to ingratiate himself to people. The years had done nothing to that intuitive sense.

We slowly walked down a narrow alley between the old stone block he owns and the one adjoining it, and continued out back to the parking lot. Gus shuffled along. As we drove up the Main Street hill and emerged from the downtown valley he suggested I get some cards printed up for the dashboard, telling people to buckle up or walk.

"You would have had every right to tell me to get out and walk if I had refused to put on my seat-belt," he said.

He would never tell me his real age, nor would he tell anyone, but he was old enough for me to know I had no such right to ask.

"Age doesn't bother me now," he told me, "even if they say I'm ninety. I was young when I got mixed up with the Galt Terriers in '49." A couple of years later, in the summer of 1997, I learned from his son that he was eighty-six. An hour before that revelation I had been talking to Gus and the conversation went something like this: "Hi, Gus, how are you?" I asked. "Not bad for an old man," he said. "An old man?" I asked, seeing an opening. "How old are you Gus?" There was a pause. "Well," he struggled, "well, I'm seventy-seven you know."

Now, as I drove him home on that spring evening, he said I might be able to get an insurance company, maybe the Gore Mutual, to pay for the seat-belt cards. He laughed when he heard himself say that. "Oh, what am I doing," he said shaking his head, talking aloud and more to himself than to me. "I'm too old to be thinking up new schemes."

Two winters later Gus was still getting around, but he was frailer. He'd had several bad accidents. Each winter was fraught with danger, as it is for so many elderly people. His eyesight deteriorating, he was unable to see the ice, and invariably he would suffer a couple of falls in the snowy months. We still kept in touch though our long afternoon sessions were over. But half a continent separated us. More often, he would call me on the telephone to comment on an article I had written or to tell me something he'd remembered about that summer of '49. He had been overly generous with his time the last several years. Were it not for him, the story of that Terrier Town summer could never have been written. That he was still living and had so much time to give I count as a great blessing, for the story began with him and would end with him.

Early in the winter of 1996, when I was back in Galt visiting some relatives, I dropped by the YMCA, just a stone's throw from Murray's office on Main Street, and an acquaintance, unaware that I had played on that team—he'd heard I was writing a book—offered me a tip.

"Have you ever talked to Gus Murray?" he asked. "He'd be able to tell you a thing or two."

"Yes," I said. "Yes, I have."

⚾ ⚾ ⚾

Postscript:
It was inevitable, of course, but Gus Murray finally suffered a fall he could not recover from. It was in the early winter of 1997, and he was hospitalized for some weeks. Eventually it was decided by doctors and his family that he would be better off in a nursing home. For a time it almost seemed like he enjoyed the social aspect of the home; he was even heard to comment that he could build a better nursing home. That was Gus to the end. At eighty-eight, he was still scheming, still wheeling and dealing. A dreamer never stops dreaming.

One of my last visits with him came that summer. As I was readying to depart, he motioned to come close. He wanted to whisper something in my ear. "I don't know if you've noticed, but some of the people in here ..." He paused, smiling. "Some of the people in here are not what you would call normal."

As I walked away I waved goodbye to Gus and his friends lining the hall. "Oh, I won't be here too much longer," he said. "I'll bolt one of these days, and I'll take John here with me."

In the summer of 1999 Gus was unsettled. He called me and I told him I was coming back to Galt for a week. When I dropped in to see him he looked better than I remembered, and he asked me to sign him out, which I did, thinking he wanted some fresh air. But as soon as we got outside he started for my car, asking me to take him downtown. He was bolting, and I was the unwitting accomplice. Just then a nurse came outside, and said there was a call for me. She said she'd supervise Gus while I took the call. Moments later Gus sprinted away, running down a country road where the speed limit is posted at eighty kilometres per hour. They had to commandeer a car to retrieve him.

There would be one final meeting between Gus and Larry. Both were in their late eighties. It was a good visit, and many old memories were shared and discussed. The pride Gus felt for his Terrier team was evident. Larry made reference to the missed catch by Warren, something that Larry tended to discount, and Gus was clearly agitated at the suggestion that it was intentional. "He protested against the suggestion," said Larry. "I could see it in his eyes and in his very being. I was moved by our visit and I could see that here was a man in his later years who was rejecting that notion very strongly."

His mind soon wandered, and though his body remained bound to the old age home for some years, his soul had long departed for the green, green grass of summer.

Charlie Hodge

And me? A week after the season ended I took my dog out for what would be our last walk together. The leaves grew old and fell early that autumn in Waterloo County, and as we walked along the riverbank, where the great Mohawk river was flowing into eternity, I stopped at the side of the old chestnut tree like I had done hundreds of times before, to contemplate my scant eighteen years. I still collect chestnuts, as if trying to hoard memories of the world as it coursed through Galt, though a lifetime has passed since I used them in play.

My dog had been failing for weeks. Just four months earlier, at the start of the season, we had run together. Now she was struggling even to walk slowly, and though there was a wag in her tail when I called her name, it too was slower. She was Jimmy's dog, a remnant of summer days spent along that ancient river, when Jimmy would take me fishing behind Scroggin's Shoe Factory, or out back of the old stone mill near the dam. She smelled of the river and reminded me of the clouds. She was always jumping in to fetch a stick Jimmy had thrown. But those days were done by 1949, and she was my dog now. When I looked at her I could see and hear Jimmy's distant voice. Despite my longing for Jimmy and the emptiness I felt at his absence, there was continuity in her presence, warmth in her coat, and friendship in her eyes. Her journey from Jimmy into my hands was really a rite of passage for me, and I cherished her for that. But now the soothing warmth of her breath on my arm as she slept beside me was coming to an end, even as the excitement of beginning life's great journey and going out into the world was before me. I knew she wasn't right. The wind was wrong. Her tail no longer flowed. I was at her side two days later when she died.

I mourned her death more than I had the loss of the season. She was my link to Jimmy, and her time with me was too short. I had learned that nothing lasts forever and that even love is quiescent when the calm of life stills the lonely night.

I had already begun my freshman year at university, and though I had experienced a great deal that season, I had a lifetime to go before I felt some sense of certainty about life and death, and one summer long ago.

In my youth I had placed too much importance on a catch that never was. Years would pass before I could be truly objective about that last game, and that season. Gibbs had been outstanding, after all, and a very talented Red Sox team had outplayed us. They deserved to win. So the years tempered my view of the whole thing, and I no longer blamed Warren. All I had was suspicion, and aside from circumstantial evidence, nothing else. There were lessons I learned in the summer of '49, though it sometimes took me many years to know them the way they needed to be known. The circumstances surrounding Warren fueled our suspicions, but these were suspicions from the vanquished, not the victors. Today I feel no malice toward Warren, just charity. I am reminded of a judgment that Justice Pennell once wrote, a passage that seemed entirely appropriate to my later views on Warren. "Suspicion once raised," wrote Pennell, "is easily entertained."

My brother Jimmy had left me with a signed baseball on the day he went off to war, and the ball gave me inspiration countless times over the years. It carried his signature, and a message: "Can't wait to play on the Terriers with you."

My ties with Galt soon abated as life events took me far afield. I would return home to southern Ontario to visit my parents from time to time, though once they were gone, I seldom got back. But I never forgot that town in Waterloo County, the town I grew up in, and with. Long years afterward I became a professor, and raised my own children, and they came to know and love Terrier Town through the stories I told.

In baseball I found life, full and rich and unreserved in its splendour. Dickson Park spoke to me in a language that was as pure as art. Altogether beautiful was its power and its glory. The park had its red dirt, and each grain held a word. The words flowed into stories. Some of the stories became legends.